Points of Who

Suzanne Walsh

Contact:

Suzanne Walsh
zannewalsh@gmail.com
zannewalsh.ca

ISBN 978-0-9802111-5-3

Cover art by Suzanne Walsh

Greater Reality Publications

Contents

Thanks

To all those who helped me workshop the beginnings at the QWF & writers groups and Erika White.

Thanks to Heather Mallette for reading an early draft. Denise Devine and Brough Perkins for your encouragement. And Penny Grigg who gave me the great gift of always laughing at my stories.

To Craig Hogan who appears generously at the right time full of light and know-how. To Sandra Stepehenson for giving her gifts so graciously. And to Pat Machin for her time teacheresque attention to detail, and being an original role model.

To Carole-Anne for playing the part of the 'average person' with above average enthusiasm. And Matthew and Peter for support from afar.

Amanda, for being an inspiration, and Sawyer for keeping me honest.

Noel the 'bestest' husband, who left me to it, just the right amount. You are so very appreciated.

With love and gratitude,
Suzanne

Preface

perspective

noun

1 *her perspective on things had changed*: outlook, view, viewpoint, point of view, POV, standpoint, position, stand, stance, angle, slant, attitude, frame of mind, frame of reference, approach, way of looking, interpretation.

2 *a perspective of the whole valley*: view, vista, panorama, prospect, bird's-eye view, outlook, aspect.

Shadows are aspects of the self, eclipsing the outlook. If you are to be my mirror, what then of my own shadow will I be facing? After all, it's only a shadow; obstructed light. What of our own light shall we be shading?

Suzanne Walsh

For all the queens in shadowy exile, happy, homecoming.

1

Just my Imagination

Elsie

I used to have an imagination. A more fanciful kind of imagining of a more fanciful kind of life. That was before I became a single mother and traded it in for prayer and pragmatism. Now I imagine not braving the cold, walking across the parking lot towards the bus, now in this moment, I imagine a ride home. I see a familiar face. Dan waves me over. Seems I've gotten lucky; the bus ride home will be cut in half. Wishful thinking may be just a fortune hunting cousin of true imagination, but hey, a gift horse and prayer. There is someone already in the front passenger seat so I climb into the back seat. I can see him through the rear view mirror.

"This is Al." says Dan flatly. I look into those pale green eyes and it feels like infinity. Time is all wobbly, and it's as though I've touched something so essential, it's unreal. I guess that's what they mean when they say a guy is dreamy. Could this really be happening to me? He just turned around to say hello. Dan, the driver, isn't a close enough friend of mine for his peripheral warning glances and head shaking 'no' to have any impact. I am hooked into this gaze, this contact, and know without doubt that we'll meet again. Forever may be peeked at in a moment, but as the car stops I'm lurched back into running time and say 'good-bye and thanks for the lift' as though this is any other day.

I frequent this cozy, kid-friendly café; they always make a fuss over Zoë. So, I get some adult company and we get out of the house. Since Zoë's father Sam died, I guess I've been looking for some community, I feel good here. They specialize in Jamaican fare, and have great dumpling soup that Zoë and I both love. She calls it "dumpsy oop" and now, so do I. The upstairs server Katie whisks Zoë off to the upstairs section, to *help* her, as is their habit as soon as Zoë is finished her soup. I don't expect to see the guy from the car again quite so soon. Synchronicity, serendipity, fate? He's playing his guitar at a table in the back corner. There are little earth-tone teapots and large glass bottles of dried herbs for tisanes lining the shelves above the table. It's clearly a staff table. Every so often, the downstairs waitress reaches behind him to get some lemon verbena or chamomile and a teapot. He stops playing and looks over. He doesn't seem to mind being interrupted; neither does he seem to think he might be in the way. He keeps looking at me and I will him toward me, giving permission with a glance. The door behind me opens and the cold winter air rushes in. I'm momentarily distracted; the chimes on the door signal a wake-up, and I become aware my attraction is girlish, young, and worse yet, obvious. The door closes, no one I know, and I'm warm once again. I think he's living poetry. His long, wavy, almost-blond locks fall forward as he looks at the hand that chooses the chords. He murmurs the words, every syllable as gentle as dandelion tufts, freshly blown, floating. Although the language of romance is new to my ears, I'm certain this is it. I'm a bit nervous that I've misunderstood this silent conversation and quell my desire to burst the bubble with words. The just-arrived customerette orders her coffee and saunters past me, directly to his table; they kiss each cheek in greeting. He puts down his guitar. His attention is gone.

Zoë returns with the friendly young waitress and we prepare to leave. "Thanks a lot Katie, " I say.

"Oh, no problem, she's adorable." I smile proudly down at Zoë, "Got your mitts, sweetie?" I'm still eyeing the corner table out of one eye, hoping he's not taken. They speak in muted tones. I hope he's here the next time I come; I make a mental note of the day and time, pay for Zoë's soup and my coffee. The door chimes fade and the bracing cold bites us back to practicality.

It's three weeks later. I'm on my way back from a late afternoon class and finally I have a chance to stop in at Café Calliloo again. There he is, sitting at the same table. I nod hello.

"Hey, you were the girl in Dan's car," he grins. "Elsie, right? Come and have a seat." I'm unable to move without disturbing the whole encounter. When I catch his eyes, it's overwhelming; the strings being plucked feel rooted in my chest. Somehow, if I start to look away, I'm pulled back.

Thank God he begins to speak, "Do you know what's going on here?" Before I have a chance to answer, he says, "Of course you do, I saw it in you in the car." I nod helplessly in complete agreement. "Don't worry," he teases. "I remember you from the other day, here, as well." It's as though he's reading my mind.

"I was just going to ask you about that." I look down, feeling sheepish, as though I've been caught in the act.

"Listen, I'm done here. You seem like the kind of girl who'd appreciate an evening walk to the island." This is more a statement than an invitation.

"How do you get there? On the ice?" I ask but before he can answer, I remember I've got to go, so I say, "Did you mean now?"

"When else is there?" His eyes are trained on mine, but there's no question in them.

"Let me just make a call." I use the payphone in the entranceway to call Mia and ask how the kids are getting along and if she can watch Zoë for a little while longer. I turn my back to him, the Mum slash friend voice, my own, a jarringly recognizable tone illuminates the fog I've rolled into, "It's the guy from the car, Mia."

"No problem, they're watching that French kids' show *Passe Partout*. Have fun. Be careful on the ice. He seems like a bit of a slippery character to me," she snickers.

"You are forever clever. See ya later, and thanks, eh? Hey Mia, how do you know him?"

"I don't, not really, I just saw him at the Calliloo the other day. I just assumed it was that guy from your description. He's one of those 'looks like Jesus,' long-haired guys you're so enamored with." I'm not sure what she means by that, so I shoot back, "Yeah, well, at least I don't go for Cro-Magnon man," in reference to her latest muscle-bound specimen.

"See ya later, slick." And with that she hangs up.

We are walking to the island out on the river; the sounds of town fade with every exhale of visible breath. Now, the crunch of our boots on the dry snow-layered ice is the only sound, except I can practically hear my own uneasiness. I guess he does. I'm nervous about the safety of ice, and whether to trust his confident stride.

"Elsie, I do this all the time. You didn't strike me as the timid kind."

I don't say a word, as I mull over whether I would define myself as timid or not, and how being careful in the dark on ice might make one so. He's big and very comfortable in his body, comfortable in the middle of the river. He catches me again just staring.

"You're not with Zoë's father anymore?"

"No, he died." I know this is sharper to hear than it is to say. What kind of sentence can tell the whole story, Sam's life, a short one, story over, narrative complete? Al doesn't give me that 'pity the widow' look and for this I am grateful. Instead he nods.

"That explains your old eyes in such a young face." He smiles.

I was hoping for wisdom not projected grief, as my signature expression, but I nod. "Maybe, who knows?" We are about three quarters the way across, might as well keep going. I quicken the pace a little, "We weren't really together, Sam and I, we were more like friends; we experimented with more, y'know, to see if it was there but in the end it just wasn't like that. And Zoë, well she was a gift, kind of crazy but it just felt absolutely right to have her even though I knew we wouldn't be together. She got her hair from him; midnight colored and bouncy curls," I pause and wonder how he'll hear my next sentence. "I knew she would." I'd sometimes feel like I'd gotten them for her.

"Did you know he was going to die?" He reaches down and takes my mittened hand in his bare one; we both look straight ahead towards the island.

"No, it was an accident," cold air visibly billows around my explanation. "He fell asleep at the wheel, he wasn't even drunk. He was just nineteen years old. Makes you wonder, why couldn't he just stay awake? Well it made me wonder that anyway. He was a good guy." He wasn't my guy, is what I think, but I don't want to sound too callous. I've had some time to absorb this. So I leave it at that.

"I knew there was something different about you. You've lived through something. Something very real and it shows. We can take this as slow as you like Elsie. We can "experiment," he raises his eyebrows, "to see if there's more."

He slowly takes my mittens off, and cups my hands in his before placing them inside his coat around his body. "This is what's important, being together, the stars, the quiet. I brought you here to show you where I like to come. Some nights I just walk and walk. I wanted you to see it through my eyes, y'know."

I feel privileged. There's an intimate focus to the air. When he touches me, I feel like the chosen one. Sam was a boy, it's like we were two kids. Al is a man, an enticing mystery to me, I get the feeling he knows something I don't know, maybe it's my heart.

After that night, he sends me wistful little poems about sailing away together. He leaves a drawing on my kitchen table, it's two suns rising together, side by side. Their reflection on the water extends to a point, and so they form a heart. It was quickly scrawled in pen on loose-leaf paper. I decide that he must be very creative to whip up something so sweet. I've never really been the mushy type. Now I savor every morsel like sweet fluffy meringue with the after taste of profound truth. We're spending so much time together that he practically moves in immediately. I can't find the part of my voice that knows this is all too fast. He has no home; he'd been staying upstairs at the cafe on one of the owner's couch, so I figure he's okay because they seem to like him.I wondered why I'd never noticed him before, but he's been away and works in the kitchen since he's been back. I don't think he was someone I could overlook.

I'm enjoying this quiet, awestruck side of my character; it's odd, though, because I'm usually so talkative. But with him I aim to please, I am softened. He can touch spirit, finally a guy that embodies what I've been looking for. We speak often about the relationship, it's as though the relationship itself is larger than the two of us, and it has a life of its own.

"Let's just be for each other," he coos one blissful morning.

"What do you mean? Like, not see anyone else?" I move away imperceptibly; I thought that in a love like this, fidelity was implied.

"Isn't that what you really want?" He strokes my hair and draws me away from my questions with every move.

"Sure, I guess," best not to quibble about the details.

"We could get married, right here in the backyard, by the water." His pool green eyes are envisioning the scene and I follow him there.

My heart is racing and the vision of vows keeps coming in and out of focus. I'm grappling with the confusion and trying not to spoil the moment. Marriage hadn't been on my list of the necessary. Proposals, on the other hand, are quite disarming. Zoë runs in and jumps on the floor level futon, Al tickles her affectionately. She rolls onto the floor and does one of her dances in front of the mirror. "Look at my dance," she squeals, her coiled hair bouncing like springs. "It's great, Zoë!" says Al.

I offer, "I'd like to set helium balloons free at the shore--no, that wouldn't be good for the environment, too bad..."

"I was thinking a big corn roast..." He lets his suggestion float. "You know, a corn boil?"

"Yeah, that sounds like fun," I grin 'cause the idea is nice, although it's probably closer to a grimace 'cause my stomach is in knots of disbelief. This is all so fast, am I being swept off my feet? The idea takes me back to community corn boils at the local pool, sunburns and general carefree running around. "We'd have to wait 'til corn season," I say and leave it at that. I wonder why in the event of a proposal I'm imagining myself as a ten year old. Zoë's making faces in the mirror.

2

Stray Cat Strut

A couple of blurry-edged love struck months pass. The river's thaw takes with it our walk to the island, now a memory. Echo, my cat, dies, run over by a car. We bury him in the back garden, down by the lake. Al wraps him in a paper grocery bag beforehand and thank goodness, because I don't want to see Echo dead and mangled. We have a little service for Echo and Zoë and I shed a few tears. Zoë watches me; she isn't overly grief-struck at only just over two years old. Al talks about him feeding the earth now, and we plant some flowers. Al seems to punctuate emotion. By his sheer presence I let myself feel.

The strange thing is, I saw Echo in the driveway earlier the day he died, and I knew he would die. I don't understand why I didn't put him in the house; I just looked at him, knew it was his last day, thought he looked happy basking in the sun, and walked away. I don't know how to feel about that, so I don't mention it. I didn't want to interfere with fate, somehow.

Al comes home later on in that same week and announces there's going to be a huge, out-of-town party at a friend's farm. He has offered to bring the stage, and he told his friend that he and I could probably put together a food kiosk. Al and I are officially a couple now, and he has managed to convince me that we should provide food for a hundred people. When I'd agreed I thought that we were going to do it together, but he got too busy. I'm not exactly sure what he is busy with but I don't want to pester. I really want him to think I'm the kind of girl who can do these things, and so I do. I figure out how to order foodstuffs in bulk and roughly how to make massive amounts. I'll sell the food cheaply but still may manage to make a little profit, at least get my money back. Mia has pitched in, so after some initial resentment, it's turning out to be fun. It's difficult to stay upset when everything seems to turn out, plus I never would've discovered that I could do this. I'm almost grateful Al didn't help.

So, here I am at the biggest party ever. I got a ride up a bit early to set up. I'm running this tofu burger stand; I also made chili and have pancakes ready to go for breakfast. We've set up a table in the old, somewhat dilapidated circa eighteen hundred farmhouse; it's only ever used for short visits or parties like this. Some people are pitching tents. We are serving through an open window from the kitchen.

Al says it's important to keep the people fed. I'm actually having a grand old time. Mia is yelling, "Step right up, fresh meat, boys!" and wiggling her body in all sorts of enticing ways while wielding the spatula like a whip of some kind. Shock value is her middle name, and I can't help but get a small thrill from her antics, although they're not my style. She is comfortable with overt sexual behaviour from her job as a dancer. She has done it on and off over the years. She hates the term stripper. She's a dancer. Al once referred to her as a healthy mare. When he said it, it sounded like a compliment. I could see what he meant; when she turned around and glanced back as she walked away, (as she often did for effect) somehow her hips still swayed in the picture. I asked him what kind of animal he thought I was like. He pulled himself back from his equine reverie to tell me that I was like a squirrel. I tried not to be jealous, just because a squirrel did not strike me as a love of your life type of animal. He also called her a black widow one time because she had all my attention. Now black widows are venomous it's true and I wouldn't want to be an enemy of Mia's. She has what could be perceived as a dangerous streak. I see it more as a mixture of defense and daring. The black widow also has a red hourglass shape on its abdomen; the stamp of an hourglass figure, the effects of which are not to be underestimated in a young woman. I think Mia is the most enthralling friend I've ever had, almost anything she does is okay with me because well, she's Mia. I say *almost* because she leaves her son Keifer, with her parents a lot and part of me thinks she is shirking her responsibilities. But when she explains how overwhelmed she gets, how it's very difficult for her and frankly makes her suicidal after a while, well then I have to admit that being a mum must be easier for me, and somehow I don't understand her plight. She usually goes on a holiday at those times anyway so I don't see her much. I don't think Mia is very appreciative of the help she gets from her parents, but it's difficult to be critical of someone who presents going on a vacation as the only alternative to suicide. I mean it really makes me feel like I have no compassion, if I dare to think that her answer to being overwhelmed is tad extreme. Actually Mia hates the word vacation. She travels. Personally, I think it's vacating here for there. And here I am again, trying to accept and kind of failing. Who am I to judge someone else's suicidal tendencies? She says she is very sensitive. I often don't get how some people are supposed to be more sensitive than others. The very sensitive usually need special treatment, so they seem more aware of their own needs, that's for sure. You can't miss what you are not worried about missing I guess. Anyway, I just love her and those observations don't seem to kill love. Can you have love without total acceptance?

Speaking of missing, Al is nowhere to be seen. He's supposed to be bringing the stage and is about five hours late, which, I begin to notice, isn't unusual for him. Every so often, I'm asked where he is, but I don't know what the holdup is, so their eyes roll and the party continues with a makeshift stage. The eye rolling disturbs me. I don't like to be accountable for someone else's eye roll causing behavior.

The people are all milling around; the farm is filled with music, kids running around, dogs running after them. Zoë and Kiefer, and several other little ones, run up, red cheeked and puffing with excitement, although they haven't gone far. They get refueled and race off after each other. People are staking out their rooms by leaving sleeping bags and blankets strewn on the floor.

Dan has been hanging around the food or possibly Mia. He tells me that it might not be wise to get too serious with Al, as he's a womanizer. I really don't get it, 'cause this guy has been pledging his undying love and asking me to marry him. That isn't what womanizers do, is it? As far as I know, a womanizer would use a girl and then dump her. I wonder what Dan's motives are, isn't it possible that Al has just fallen for me as I have for him? I have another concern. Last week, when Al got frustrated when his truck wouldn't run, he started beating it with his fists. It's an old maroon milk delivery truck abandoned by its purpose. It just took the beating for the most part; the sliding driver's side door slammed shut, as he got out, and then bounced back, wide open and slowly came to rest halfway. The old solid metal panels barely cringed, in recognition of the flailing arms of an infant tantrum. I don't know if it was the size of the truck or the ridiculousness of punching the body, but Al didn't seem dangerous, just seriously aggravated as he ran out of momentum. I sat frozen, noticing the amplified quiet of the backcountry road and trying to remember my last tantrum, trying to imagine myself hitting metal as a release, to no avail. This was between him and his truck. I was relieved Zoë was at play-care. When I mention the tantrum to his all-knowing friend, he, on this subject, shrugs. There is still the question of the broken window in my living room, which occurred mysteriously when Al's duffle bag hit the window. I wasn't home at the time and that's the story I got. Now, I'm not just some idiot, I don't want to be involved with someone who is potentially violent. So, we're going to have to address this.

There's the not so small matter of my having become pregnant to address as well. This is an added complication what with the other issues yet to be worked out. I'm thinking that with Zoë already two and a half years old, this will be our last opportunity to have a sibling for her, one that she could grow up with, someone to share Christmas and Easter, someone close enough in age to really share with. The way I see it once I'm out of baby land completely I probably won't want to go back. It is awfully soon, and it's true that after already having one child you'd think I would have figured out how these things happen. In a moment that is somehow not connected with any thought to consequence, that's how. I decide the violent behavior is first on the list.

Al has finally shown up, something about trying to make some extra money giving someone and a fridge a ride, just a little out of the way. I'll talk to him tomorrow after the party has settled down.

The food stand is closing for today at any rate. I am tidying, and washing up in the old porcelain sink, (I leave the frying pan to soak) and making sure the eggs and pancake mixture are ready for the morning. I'm proud of myself for pulling it off and confident the morning pancakes will be a hit. I head off to do some dancing with Zoë. She loves it when I whirl her around, a leg wrapped around either side of my hips and her chubby little arms around my neck, both our heads thrown back in a giggle. The wispy light of the late afternoon sun dances with us as the band is playing Talking Heads, Naïve Melody. I am simply having too much fun to deal with serious matters now.

The morning sun is a little overbearing, bouncing harshly off the long, dry, dew- stiffened grass, instead of soaking in and sun softening the grass, as you'd expect. Some dehydrated partiers are waking and some are yet to rest. Many arrive bleary-eyed looking for coffee. I only have pancakes, which they accept. (How could I forget coffee?). After a successful morning, Zoë and Keifer taking orders, Mia and I clean up. I ask her if she can keep an eye on Zoë so I can go find Al and address a few things. I find him by the creek that runs through the property. He is still damp from a morning dip and the wave in his hair is just beginning to return. He lights a cigarette. "Hey, you goin' for a swim?" He offers me the smoke, taking the first haul. I wonder why he didn't come and find me to go with him or offer to help with the breakfast, but I have specific things on my mind and I don't want to create confusion. I will have to curb the smoking, I think guiltily and shift my focus back to Al, anyway, we are not each other's shadow after all. The broken window, turns out to be a misunderstanding; he explains to me that he moved something and his bag accidentally flung toward the window. And no, he doesn't beat up his truck on a regular basis; he was just embarrassed that it broke down in front of me. It also turns out that I am sooo special that I can see past these small transgressions in the name of true love and loyalty. I'm not like those other girls who don't understand, I'm made of tougher, realer stuff than that. Love really is worth going the extra mile. I've just got to have a little faith. I get frustrated sometimes, too. Nobody's perfect. We seem to have made up, and so hold hands walking back across what was once the farmer's field.

There are big trampled patches where tents or large groups had congregated last night. I feel a little uneven myself. Maybe it's hormones or maybe it's me not really believing I'm as understanding as I'm trying to be.

3

Ways to Leave Your Lover

I'm not as glib about being pregnant, as it might seem. I'm just letting it sink in. I've been on my own with Zoë and I have no desire to try it with two. He said he wanted kids and this is surely a child of love even if it's a little soon. I expect him to be taken aback and then excited. I imagine he'll hug me or at the very least tell me everything will be okay, but he doesn't. In fact he doesn't say anything. He just stands there and then fianlly says, he's gotta go to work. He doesn't even kiss me good-bye. Maybe I should've waited until evening, maybe in the morning, even if it is sunny, it's too soon in the day for important information. I don't know what to do; I'll give him time to digest. He was the one who was moving things along so quickly, all the romantic talks about marriage and family being so very important. He said he wants to do it right, not like his family, no divorce. I realize it's soon, that we haven't been together that long, but here we are. There's nothing lonelier than true love in a holding pattern, someone else at the helm.

I haven't let Al *officially* move in, meaning use my address, because I don't want to have to quit school or trust him to pay for us, or have to leave Zoë in daycare. He does live with me though, and basically has since we met. His lack of response to the pregnancy has me rethinking the whole thing. Thank goodness I'm on welfare, with that and a few clown shows (for kids' birthday parties) on the side, I can afford my little house and part time university. I've got time to be a good mum and go to school. I figured that the government was at least reliable. Therefore, as a citizen and mother of a future citizen it's a good investment. I choose reliable poverty and time over prestige and money. (Although, the latter aren't exactly readily available.) Why should other people's kids get a mom who is home and has time to give them personal attention? Geez, they'll give foster parents money. Two kids on my own, though, that's too much. With the first one you don't know exactly what you're in for, but two, I don't know if I want to do that. It's still early. I have a choice.

I joke at the wrong time. He's shocked at my outspokenness, says he didn't think I was that kind of girl. Which kind? The kind that speaks? I guess he means he'd love me more if I were quieter, more reflective, like I seemed at the beginning. I have no idea how to read the situation. I can't help being opinionated, although I prefer to call it speaking with conviction. Anytime he says he'll pick me up somewhere I'm expected to wait for hours because someone else really needy needs his help. He says by way of consolation, "Don't worry; I'll always get there, eventually." He says this in a dreamy way, as though I'm some damsel locked in a tower and every time he shows up, it's heroic. Since we are a team, I too should sport the heroic proclivity and want to wait. The heroic tone wears thin pretty quickly; since I'm amusing a two-year-old while I wait. I tell myself that I'm a special damsel who doesn't really require rescuing, and so his turning up at all is quite a bonus. A few hours of my time is nothing in the grand scheme of things. I am sooo independent that I can understand this; in fact, I've become such an integral part of Al's life, I don't really need any attention at all. Zoë and I have become last because we've become family. This is because the *idea* of the family unit seems to be more important than we are. I'm not like those weak women who demand attention and reassurance; I'm easygoing, I can adapt, I will not deign to have expectations of another; I don't want to be a bitch. You get more flies with honey my mother always said. Well, I'm beginning to choke on the honey and it's becoming clear that I'm the only one eating it. Why do I want flies I wonder?

I'm just about to end the whole relationship, pregnancy included. I told him yesterday that by the time he got with the program the kid would be eighteen; so much for not being a bitch. He comes home late in the evening, Zoë's already tucked in. It's dusk and a little drizzly out. What with the hormones and this increasingly dramatic mess, I'm a little drizzly on the inside as well. Al must sense I'm at the end of my patience because before I can tell him anything, he insists we go to the river's edge at the bottom of the garden. I stubbornly refuse to partake.

"We can talk here." I fold my arms.

"Trust me, Elsie, it's important." He says pleadingly as he grabs me by the arm and insists with his physicality that I go with him to the shore. He starts to pull.

"Fine, fine, let go, I'll go." I heave a big sigh and shake my arm loose. He lets go and the tug turns into a gentle escort down the garden path. Once at the river, he turns to me and without saying a word, he takes off his shoes and gallantly throws them in the water. There is hopping involved and some balance required. "You see what I'm willing to do for us, those were my best shoes. I just want you to understand I'm not going anywhere. I love you, and Zoë, and I want you to have the baby." He starts to cry, and I suppress my laughter at what feels at once romantic and ridiculous. I'm still a little miffed about him grabbing my arm, designing the scene. I feel like an anti-romantic for wondering how he's going to replace those shoes.

Even in my semi-cynical state I cave, acquiesce; tears are shed all round. I think I may have just embraced the perfection of the dusk-lit play, movie-like, black and white, rainy shiny, celluloid, reflecting some strange memory of childhood when the lovers hit each other and then kiss passionately. Oh, this would be a life of passion, I had certainly asked for that. Hurray, and a family we will be. It surprises me to note how much disappointment and despair are required.

The more hormonal I get, the more I realize my "partner" is the kind of man who goes to the corner store for bread and doesn't come back for hours. The first time he said he'd be home at dusk, Judy the baby sitter was visiting and gave me an incredulous glare as he strode out the door.

"How," she said, " do you get dinner ready for dusk?"

"That's the beauty of rice." I answered wondering if I should be more bothered. Of course we weren't just eating rice, we had vegetables as well, and some cheese. Dusk came; I gave Zoë her bath and got her ready for bed. When he still wasn't back I was slightly worried but distracted myself with bedtime stories, keeping one ear open for the sound of the car, starting at every distant engine rumble more irritated with every false start. I wondered as the sky gradually lost its colours if dusk actually had a formal end.

Finally, feeling forgotten, I fell asleep, in Zoë's room. When I awoke, groggy a couple of hours later and he still wasn't back, I began to panic, I wanted to call someone to find out if something had happened. The only person I could think of at that time of night was Mia, and she wouldn't know. My sister would think this was typical of our hippie-like lifestyle. (Her words not mine). The last thing I needed was to sound like a hysterical housewife. I am not his mother. I wouldn't want to feel I *had* to call home if I'd got caught up somewhere. I'd just replaced the receiver to nowhere when I heard the front door open. The words "why didn't you call," were there, offering their use to me, but somehow I couldn't bring myself to sound like a parent. I didn't realize it was a one time offer, and now months later his vague explanations about stopping off for pie, meeting people who need to talk, or just being 'out', seem all that's available.

I don't really know what this says about a person, except that they're called to a greater duty awfully frequently. He's the kind of man who stays up late into the night and drinks a lot of coffee. He has an inordinate amount of stories wherein he's been misunderstood. His favorite line in a song is, "Don't confront me with my failures..." I'm beginning to see why. The café is calling. Why hasn't he turned up for his shift? He always says he replaced himself and the other guy misunderstood. They're very patient because he's a creative cook, and actually brought the famous dumpling recipes, he learned from a Jamaican buddy. But he thinks he should be part owner in the restaurant co-op and they're ripping off his talent. He always has a reason; his truck broke down and he had to cross a three lane highway, and he got his pants caught on the fence in the middle and they were so badly torn that he had to go shopping. He couldn't possibly show up with torn pants. He simply had to sit in the café for hours because it will drive the owner insane to watch Al sit there. He thinks this will provoke better working conditions, possibly even a partnership. He was on his way, but there was this seagull with a fishhook in its mouth and he had to stop and save the seagull. He was an hour late for a gig with his band to save that bird. Even his screw-ups are like poetry. I feel that it's my job to be as understanding as I can, as frustrating as that can be; it does seem his life is tricky; those seagulls just don't cross my path. One guy is threatening to break Al's legs, I'm not clear on why, something about a misplaced amplifier but we're certain he's just bluffing. Sometimes, Al says he has to be somewhere and then he just sits and plays guitar. The kids, Zoë and friends, love to sing and dance with him, and in those moments I too slip momentarily into a place where whatever there was to do couldn't possibly be more important than a song. He made up a special song for me.

Elsie, Elsie Shaw

Sometimes, *des fois,* Elle-see, Elle-saw

Like a teeter totter,

By the water,

Sometimes she's up (descending picking notes) *des fois,*

she's down.

Her self she hides inside, a clown

Her smile can please, for miles around

But she sees,

Y'know, y'know, y'know, she sees, *tu sais,*

She saw,

Me.

At the end it slows down and he almost whispers the last two lines, whilst picking gently.

When I'm around Al it's as though there's a hole in time. Time keeps moving and we can't get out of the hole to catch it. It's a warm mid summer Sunday. The grasshoppers and cicadas are the buzzing concert to my frustration, as we can't seem to get to Ottawa to visit my older sister Elaine. Elaine generally thinks I'm a bohemian mess so I'd like to at least be able to get there to prove my reliability. One can most certainly adhere to a different value system and still be reliable. She believes that it is important to follow society's proper order of events. She dated her husband Steve for the appropriate three years. They saved money for their wedding, planned a cement walkway into their future with a picket fence for adornment. Six years in; so far so good. I think she has the next sixty years mapped out in a china pattern.

We made it to the driveway a couple of times and then Al disappeared back into the house, then he got a call he had to go pick up a guitar so that took up a couple of hours. I just kept telling myself to go with the flow. I did notice that I seemed to be in someone else's river that was moving at a trickle. I had hoped to tell Elaine about the new baby and introduce Al. I guess I'll have to do it over the phone.

"Where are you guys?" She says as she picks up the phone, "You were supposed to be here hours ago."

"I know, I know," I stutter, "It's just that things kept coming up all day, and we just couldn't seem to get out of here."

I hear a short snort of disapproval.

"So I guess you're not coming?" She asks tersely.

"Not today," I say, and then quickly as though the faster I change the subject the less noticeable it might be. "I've got some news for you though, do you want to hear it?"

"Sure," she breathes a fake reluctance. "What's the news?"

"Well, Zoë's to have a little brother or sister!"

"Wow, that's incredible," I can practically hear her mind reeling. "That's very soon Elsie. Will you be getting married? How is he with my Zoë? I mean what about school? I don't suppose you planned this, or, did you?"

"Don't worry about all that stuff, life takes care of itself, you'll see. I fell in love, Lainey, remember love." I want to reassure her, and I had in fact called her delighted when I'd first met Al.

"Don't let him move in," she'd advised conservatively. I'm not ready just yet to complain about how disappointed and humiliated I feel about not getting there to see her, so I make light of it.

"Listen it'll be perfect for Zoë, not too many years between the kids, and Al is great with Zoë, he built her a sandbox." I'm well aware that this tactic will send her to her own thoughts of her only son Aaron already four. Steve isn't sure he wants more kids and this is a bone of contention between them as Elaine had planned on two. I feel slightly guilty.

"Anyway we'll talk more, soon okay?"

"Okay then, give Zoë a big hug from her Auntie Lainey."

"I will, one for Aaron too, see ya." I hang up.

Al has decided that welfare breaks up families. What! He actually believes that if women have a way to survive with their youngsters, they're more likely to leave the fathers. So, he thinks I should get off it. This is very scary, as I feel like I'm being asked to trust him, a noble gesture on his part, to want to look after us. I wish it were doable, maybe if we could visit my sister or get anywhere without time getting away from us, that might give me some incentive. I think I have some difficulty in trusting people after Sam dying. Maybe I should try harder, take a risk. He insists I really don't need to go to University. I totally disagree. He insists that I disagree because I don't know what's going on; furthermore I'm against family. Against it or not, this baby is on its way, and what I really don't understand is how to rely on someone who's making less sense by the day. I do agree, though, that university is an institution and therefore potentially untrustworthy and potentially elitist. I don't want to be institutionalized. At any rate, this is theoretical at the moment, as I'm finding this live human on the iffy side of trust. But, I commiserate with him that a professor once flunked Al's paper because it was too long and on the so-called wrong topic does prove how limited the thinking in these places can be. He says he didn't use their *jargon.* I'll just finish the semester before the baby's born. He seems to agree. And I am doing what I want anyway. Even if he sneers at me whist he mutters some nonsense about feminists. I mean as far as I know welfare to ensure independence from a man was not Gloria Steinem's idea of feminism. Even though we might agree on elitism in academics, I don't feel like much like the poster child for female success right now. Maybe the pregnancy has got me down.

The intimacy seems to have returned. When Al takes his bath in the too short claw-foot tub, he calls me in to keep him company. I perch on the toilet balancing my toes on the edge of the tub. The heat from the hot water keeps the small bathroom cozy and our conversation follows suit.

"Lets pick a nice soft colour for the kid's room." he says scooping up his hair to lather.

"Yeah we should get it organized so Zoë can get used to the idea of sharing. Maybe periwinkle," I muse.

"Hey did I tell you I found an old piano? It's broken but I think I can fix it up. Can you get me the saucepan to rinse?"

I return with the pan, the one we always use in the bath, "Wow, I've always wanted to have a piano, the kids could learn." I watch his tilted head peacefully as the suds flow off his hair. This is domestic bliss, steamy and peaceful.

We've renewed our commitment to each other and the kids; I've begun to relax into the routine and breathe a little easier. The eggshells I was walking on seem to have been ground to a barely recognizable dust.

This new day is red and lingering green, early fall when the air is energized and has a taste of cool. I run out to the truck as Al is leaving this morning. When I was little, I used to run out to my Dad's car to give him a kiss good-bye, so it's a natural thing for me to do. "What are you playing at?" he sneers, backing away, getting in the truck and closing door.

"Playing? I just came to kiss you. Is there a problem?" I stand stock still.

"Don't think I don't know this little game, trying to make things look all normal and suburban. It's all about you, isn't it, and when you think it's a good time. Well, this scenario is silly Elsie; it's not real. It's contrived." He is in the driver's seat, leaning on his elbow out the window.

I'm completely taken off guard and the lump in my throat is only being held in check by my burgeoning rage. I take a second to decide which response will take precedence and decide vulnerability is the most honest. We can't have a decent relationship if we aren't honest. And so I let the tears fall, the hurt kind that fall slowly without a lot of sobbing.

"This is exactly what I'm talking about, Elsie; look at you, none of this is real." And with that, he pulls out of the driveway, leaving me the much too large question of discerning what's real. I thought it was a simple gesture to kiss someone goodbye, I hadn't before contemplated it being contrived. Now, I recognize that I chose the tears to some extent, maybe that's contrived. How do you know if something is real? Does being conscious make it unreal? I seem to be in trouble all the time, I hug at the wrong time, and I don't hug at the right time. I'm rethinking the whole thing. Again.

I'm being accused of not being supportive enough; this has arisen when I don't seem able to understand why he isn't able to be where he's expected. I'm told that I don't understand anything; I'm blind to what's really going on. At this point, asking for an explanation is tantamount to admitting I don't in fact understand what's going on. I think to myself, well, you never really wanted to be a wife, so you don't have the right skills. I actually begin to bake peach pies, his favorite. I try to pay more attention, in an effort to find out what this being supportive is all about. It seems I just can't stop my opinions, though, and really don't make too much of an effort. I'm getting bigger and bolder and lonelier. He's rarely home, but I don't believe in dictating someone else's lifestyle, because frankly I don't want anyone dictating mine, so I surround myself with friends.

We have no television, we have books and music and lots and lots of tea. Often, there are up to six people as I read the Narnia Chronicles aloud to my daughter. Lukas is one of the neighborhood kids who comes over and drinks tea and hangs out. He loves to read, and I let him help me with some of my English Lit papers. Lukas and I talk about names for the baby and take Zoë in the garden to make leaf piles to jump in. When the first snows come, we make a snowman. When he arrives, it's often thirty seconds after I was wondering if he'd visit today or not. He's great company and his girlfriend Judy is a willing babysitter who doesn't require payment the day of. Since Mia quit stripping and moved downtown, she's not available as often to watch Zoë when I go to class, so Judy is a great help.

.

4
Having My Baby

It's January. I'm in labor and in the cab with Al on the way to the hospital; I'm at least six centimeters dilated. I had a doctor's appointment and she sent me directly to the hospital. The truck is broken. Judith is taking care of Zoë, she will keep her til Al gets back. The labor started almost immediately after she told me there was no more room in the womb, and that baby needed to be born. "What've you got in there, a whole band?" She'd said cheerily. I thought it was odd, when we both knew there was only one baby. Feeling like a walking winter whale precluded my questioning her humor as well as her orders. So here we are on our way. Al wants to stop the cab and buy me a ring.

"This is not the time." I manage through gritted teeth. Al shifts in his seat but doesn't say anything.

My beautiful son is born, and we're all in love and isn't he the cat's meow and aren't I the earth mother. I am ecstatic if not a little tired and still in pain. Apparently the contractions now have to go in reverse, who knew? Al turns up at all hours in his Cowachin sweater and paint-covered Billy boots. He prowls around the ward after visiting hours trying to sneak into the nursery and generally gets kicked out. He can't seem to manage visiting hours. We agree that he should be allowed to see his baby anytime. Granted they are pretty lax during the day but Al tends to favor late night visits. We had discussed painting the baby's room prior to my having gone to the hospital. I'm nervous. Why is he painting now? He often very lovingly decides to do major tasks, like paint, on the day of an event. He's so sweet to want to make everything nice for the baby. Oh, well, no matter. I woke with a flutter of anticipation. I whisper to my newborn love, telling him that we are going home from the hospital today."Now tell me sweet smelling boy," I coo, "what's your name?" The ringing bedside phone interrupts our potential exchange.

"Hi, it's me. I was up all night, but I finished. The room looks great," says Al.

"When are you coming? I can leave anytime now, I told you they said the maximum stay was seven days but I can leave after five. Where's Zoë, is she still with Mia?" Zoë was to stay with Mia for the weekend; today is Monday so I'd have thought she'd be back with Al by now. Mia was going to bring them all to pick me up. With the truck finished, he needs a lift. Might as well make it a party.

"Zoë's fine, she's having a great time playing with Kiefer, Mia says she can stay another day. I don't think it's a good idea for you to come home today 'cause the paint's not dry and it might not be good for the baby."

"Well, we can just close the door to the baby's room then. He'll stay with us anyhow, at first."

"I know, that's why I painted our room instead." He says cheerfully.

"Oh." I'm trying to stay calm; this probably isn't a big deal. "So, you painted our room the blue I got for the kid's room?"

"It's for his first room; it looks great, you just have to wait an extra day until it dries, just a day."

"I've been here a week, I want to go home." I whine.

"Enjoy the time. I'll see you tomorrow. Don't whine, it's just a day, you two can rest."

"But Mia said she'd drive us home today." I'm still whining although I'm making some effort to sound factual. The truck is finished so he needs a lift.

"I know, I told you, I already took care of that with Mia. she doesn't have class until Wednesday and she's going to pick me up at the bus tomorrow."

"Oh, okay, I guess I'll see you tomorrow."

So, as it turns out I'm not going home. I'm so sad, but hey, it's just one more day, it isn't all that bad, and at least they serve me my meals in here. In slightly different circumstances would I take a cab? Women have been known to continue to work in the fields I've heard tell. I meander down the hall and visit the recovering junkie who is pregnant, and fancy myself in a pretty good place in this life. The next day, Mia peeks around the corner of the hospital room. Zoë runs in and climbs on the bed. She looks gargantuan in comparison to the new baby. "Sweet pea, you're such a big girl! And you're a big boy!" I add, realizing Kiefer is here also, barely visible at the foot of the bed. "Where's Al?" I gleam.

"Ahh," she stutters, "I don't know, I couldn't find him."

It seems he missed his ride. I'm over the top of disappointment and beyond furious. I kick the garbage can down the hall of the maternity wing, cursing with postpartum nicotine withdrawal rage. I'm embarrassed, calm down and search myself for some semblance of sane-making reason. Like a smoker looking for a light.

"Thanks Mia, for being someone I can rely on." I say and begin to count my blessings, the only way out of my rage.

We pack up; hey, at least I have a ride home, I'm not on methadone and I have my perfect son. We're driving along, the world looking new, because with us is a new being, just arrived. Daddy's absence is very loudly not the topic of discussion… when…. "Whoa! Stop the car!"

There he is, on the side of the road thirty miles from home and about fifteen from the hospital. We pick him up; he missed his ride, that's all, it could happen to anyone. There is some confusion about the time and place they'd agreed to meet. I can't figure out who misunderstood whom. At the end though here they both are. He was trying to get there…I'm feeling weepy... It's January, it's gray and somewhere in the back of my brain, I believe it's not too much to ask that he would be able to come and get me. The confusion is blurred by feelings of relief that he is here; I must be tired from having the baby.

Life with the new baby is lovely, the house is less full of visitors, and we seem more of a family, although I'm alone an awful lot. I miss Lukas' company; he's only dropped by once in the two months I've been home. I'm not sure why he is keeping his distance, possibly he's giving the new family some alone time or maybe he doesn't like my new no smoking in the house rule. The little one still has no name, as we can't agree on one. Al suggests "shoes" in reference to the gallant gesture when he threw his shoes into the river. No way.

Spring is hinting at itself, a February thaw, simultaneous relief and frustration. I've read about guys getting jealous of babies, but Al is jealous of me. He tells me I nurse the baby too much, that I'm babying the baby. I know what I'm doing in this arena. I'm annoyed at the insinuation that I don't, but I think I'll double-check with some other moms in order to be certain. This is tricky; I don't want to make him sound like a nut bar just because he's got maternal leanings. Mia, whom I trust, didn't have to deal with the baby's father at all. Kiefer's dad seemed to be of the mindset that you could say you love a stripper, sleep with one, but then be invisible if the situation leaked into your life. It broke Mia's heart. I don't think she thought of herself as just a stripper. She thought of herself as his girlfriend who happened to be a well-paid dancer. She stayed on as a stripper after Kiefer was born. Luckily for her, her figure was in agreement with her decision. She believed that it was a morally superior choice to welfare, to be able to pay one's own way. Her parents offered to help, but it was on their terms, Mia said. I think that stigma is stigma, but hey to each their own. When I thought I might give it a try she told me in no uncertain terms that it wasn't the right place for me. It's kind of heroically tragic when someone so vehemently tries to protect you from becoming like them. I never could figure out how she could do it. She said you sort of separate from yourself and focus on the dancing. I wonder what makes her able to separate like that, I try but I can't imagine it. She gets a different voice when she talks about it so I don't push.

Anyway, Mia didn't breast feed and I imagine that although she'd back me on anything, she probably wouldn't get why it was so important to me. And Sam, well, we were both so young that he deferred to me as the expert in all baby matters. This deference he had to my instincts seems like a compliment now. Then, I saw it as a lack of interest. I suppose it could've been a bit of both given our age at the time.

I decide to call one of the playgroup mums for support. This is about as objective as calling the pro breastfeeding LaLeche

League. Once when I was breastfeeding Zoë, I got the pump stuck on my breast and I remember screaming, "Get this thing off of me! Help!" Sam was laughing and laughing at me and then finally explaining something about vacuum principles, as he unstuck me. Remembering that easy friendship really highlights the present uneasy tension. This isn't quite the romance and mystery I'd so recently thought it was going to be. And it's certainly not friendship. I decide Al's not home often enough to warrant the effort of expressing my milk; it would probably go bad in the fridge anyway.

5
Going Pains

April is the cruelest month breeding
Lilacs out of the dead land, mixing
Memory and desire, stirring
Dull roots with spring rain.

－ T.S Elliot.

The little guy is almost three months old and still has no name. Everyone has a different name for him, Shoes, Francis, but mostly we just call him Little Guy. Spring is still attempting to make good on its promise, it takes several tries in this climate. As though spring itself sticks a toe in the cold water and pulls back for another go. This is when I get the call that my father has had a heart attack. Al is great; it seems this is a duty he can be there for. We still don't have a car; so getting to the hospital is difficult. I try to arrange to borrow my dad's or get a ride with his girlfireind Denise. She doesn't call back. We bum rides or take a series of buses. Al comes to the hospital with me very other day and takes care of the baby while I visit my dad. Al says Denise wants my Dad and his car for herself. He says she wants to pretend we don't exist. Al puts his entire life on hold to support me. When I finally run into her at the hospital, she says Dad's car is being fixed and doesn't seem to want to pick us up en route. I don't understand why she is so cold. Al says this is blatant conspiracy to keep us away. I mean, how is it possible for my dad's car to be broken for two weeks? Perhaps I'm beginning to understand what's really going on, in a vague sort of not-quite-getting-it kind of way. I'm confused. Even if she doesn't seem to like me surely that would be overruled by these circumstances. Al points out the malicious nature of this woman. I don't trust people who are so sure of their position. Both Al and this woman are falling into this category; I figure they cause wars. It seems the flaw in my reasoning is always looking to give people the benefit of the doubt. Since I have so much doubt, there's a lot of benefit to give.

Finally, Dad is given the okay to go home. I visit him at the hospital the day before his release; he looks like a shy and vulnerable little boy sitting on the edge of the bed in his burgundy polo P.J.s. I wonder how naked he must feel without his shield of drink. The next day, I call him at home; Denise says he's too weak for visitors just yet. He shouldn't be getting weaker, is what I think, but I respect her wishes. Heart attacks are new for me.

Things return to the way they were. The kids are good, we have play care co- op still continuing for Zoë, the baby is well and the long awaited warmth is still awaited. Al is working steady and generally, I feel things are finally stable. I'm a little nervous to disagree with him. I get the feeling I still don't quite behave properly in some way. I like my friends too much, and I refuse to dislike certain people whom he thinks aren't trustworthy. He has a tendency to get in my face, so to speak. I certainly wasn't trained to deal with this. I talk to my Dad on the phone after his week of rest. It seems Denise is out. He says he's frightened of his medication. This isn't the time to delve into questions concerning my life. My dad has never expressed an emotion let alone fear. I think he might die. I chastise myself for what seems like dramatics in my head. I feel terribly guilty for imagining how to deal with his death. For heaven's sake, I tell myself, how dare you make this about you, when he would be the one actually dying?

My Dad dies at eleven a.m. the following day. He was rushed from his home in the middle of the night with another heart attack. I don't find out 'til six o'clock, this next evening. His girlfriend didn't want to wake us up. How thoughtful.

It's so much easier to bury your cat in the back yard and take solace that flowers will bloom there; I notice it comes in waves, actual physical waves of grief that roll over me racking me with anguish and then rolling away. I suppose it's not surprising that it's physical. I read somewhere that elephants act grief-stricken. So it must be part of having a body, and then when someone isn't in a body we are one body short in the physical fabric of life, or something. Plus we miss them and there is sadness in their story being over or at least out of their hands. I'm short tempered with Zoë and feel so guilty, but no one gets this. It seems like everyone expects me to be normal in a week, either that, or he or she're afraid of me. It's as though I've touched a scary monster and it might be contagious. I can hear them not mentioning "it". When Sam died it was awful and out of order, but somehow this is a direct line to my own mortality. There must be some kind of genetic inevitability inherent in my father's death. I have nothing to wear to the funeral, which is all organized by Denise, without us, his grown children. I borrow a dress from Elaine. She looks very well put together as always. The dress I get is brown and taupe plaid and a terrible fit as she's a good three inches taller than me. It's the sex symbol and her compadre *potato woman*. I'm fairly convinced that funerals are formal just to create a wardrobe distraction from the grief. I'm generally miserable. It's only Elaine and me as far as family goes; a few years after the divorce, Mum transferred to Toronto with her company. We only saw Dad on and off once we got older. Where is Al? Who knows? Gone somewhere in the car that was my father's which we have now managed to borrow. By this time, I've organized a back-up lift to the funeral. Dad was a popular guy; the small country church spills over with people. I keep seeing his face slide off the faces of the men in the crowd. My sister and I push our way through a throng of people who whisper, "Gee, I didn't know he had kids."

We whisper to each other, "most of the time neither did he." And burst into giggles, as if this is the funniest thing we've ever said. We both know that it is not funny that we saw him seldom since we were eleven or twelve. The giggles turn to tears and back again. Behind our expressions, we're both confused and grateful for the emotional release. Holding each other for strength, we take our places at the front for the first and last time. Somewhere between birth and death, I've learned to work with the unreliable. There must always be a back-up babysitter, a back-up food source, a back-up ride, and back-up support. Plan B. Thanks Dad, for the initial lessons. He wasn't entirely absent afterall. It becomes a glorious event when the person I'm supposed to rely on actually comes through. In a way, then the mundane can be a source of happiness and I'm forever grateful to have back up. Happiness and gratitude are mine. Even if they're the inside pockets to my invisible cloak of disappointment, they're the insulation of hope.

The spaces between the waves of grief are gradually getting longer and longer and I'm feeling somewhat more like myself although I know I will never be as I was before. It's rainy. There's no icy chill to the rain as it washes away the lingering piles of mud fringed crystallized snow. Through the kitchen window, the cleansing rain reassures the expectation of spring; it should be called the season of mud, possibility and patience. It's so slow. And then voila, one certain day, faith is restored through a window or found in a patch of grass, or smelled in newly revealed earth. And then things seem quite doable. Life goes on, and the baby gets a name. Well, actually, I can't take it anymore and there is threat of a fine if we don't register the baby. So I just go ahead and name him Jye, and James after my father. J.J..

Sprouting sunshine and forget- me-nots energize me as I hook up the washing machine to the kitchen sink to do a load of laundry. The kitchen is more like a nook and there is only room for the appliances and me. J.J. is quiet in his little chair in the living room and Zoë is cooing over him pretending to read one of her books to him. So I jostle around the machine that has taken my place in the middle. I empty Al's jean pockets: matches, a quarter and a piece of carefully folded loose-leaf paper. Hmm, I think I'll just take a little peek. It might be important, a new recipe or an address or something. This is both confusing and frightening; it takes my breath away. This can't possibly be…a suicide note? Well, it is, and gee, I thought things were going so well. Did my grief totally eclipse what has been going on?

Hey, I'm not even mentioned in this note. Does that mean he is angry with me? He is leaving all his money to his mother (Which is wise because she hasn't given it to him yet). He says the world is an awful place and he wants to go to a better one. Now I get a bit frantic; he wants to take our six month old with him to this better place. I stand there, the sun washing over the blue ink, the chug of the wash the continuing soundtrack as I read and reread in utter disbelief. I decide I'd better show this to someone, so I phone Mia. "Mia, hi, can you come over right away? I need you to read this note I found in Al's pocket." My voice is an echo of business like importance; a tone I know conveys a controlled freak out.

Mia doesn't miss a beat. "I'll be right there, just gotta get gas. You okay?"

"Ya, ya, I'm alright, I'll explain when you get here; you've got to read it for yourself." I sit and I read again and again, hoping some other method of interpretation will surface. Maybe if I read it backward, it'll turn into a love note. Maybe I'll find a clue as to what the actual problem is. The complete absence of a mention of me stings; it seems a deliberate low rating in terms of existence. I am supposed to be the beloved and mother of the intended victim. An oversight?

Mia bursts through the door with her rescue face on, and directs Kiefer to go play with Zoë in the bedroom. She motions for me to hand it over and I do.

I know there is more. I can't take it anymore. This place, this world of human doings and beings is distorted unreal and people are asleep to it all.
I believe in more and I want to go a better more beautiful peaceful place.
Jye and I will be happy there and he won't be forced to endure the messy insanity of the destruction of this earth or the selfish maniacal people who conspire to keep us down.
I leave all the money to my mother and tell her thanks but I don't need it where we are going.

"I think it's a suicide note, Else." She looks up, as confused as I feel. "I can't find any other way to read it unless the better place he intends to go is Mexico."

She smirks.

"Then, why would he leave his money pointedly to his mother?" I can't resist adding, "except she still has it?"

"It doesn't feel like travel plans." Mia purses her lips and tilts her head, signaling her verdict is in agreement with mine.

"Mia, I hope this doesn't seem too egotistical or narcissistic on my part, but do you think it's strange that I'm not even mentioned? I mean, it's not like I am dying to be in that letter, but it sort of seems like I should be, at least mentioned, if you know what I mean?"

"Well, you might be dying if you were in the letter." Mia does a little head toss, amused at her joke.

"Ha, ha, be serious. I can't make sense of this and I'm not sure what to do. I just can't get my head around it."

"I know, sorry, it's just too bizarre."

"Did you get that he plans to 'take' Jye with him- so, he wants to kill Jye as well as himself?" I mutter still grappling with the implications.

"Yes, Elsie, that's what it seems to say. What are you going to do? Has he been strange or depressed lately?"

"No, that's the thing, I thought things were actually going really well. How could I be so far off the mark? Have you noticed anything?"

"Nothing out of his usual dreamy nature, but I don't see him that often."

"Maybe he's done this before. Oh God, Mia, maybe we should call his mother! She would know if he's got some kind of problem." I suggest, relieved to have a plan of action. I find the number, and phone her long distance. I explain the situation and my obvious concern. I don't receive quite the response I'd expected. I hang up.

"Well?" says Mia.

"It seems I've overreacted."

"What? How? Did she say if he's done this before?"

"She suggested that I somehow get him to take vitamin B."

Mia puts one hand on her hip and spits out her particular brand of snarkiness, reserved for idiots. "Really? Did she suggest that Jye take some vitamin B as well, just as a preventative measure?"

"No, oddly, that didn't come up." We stand there in mutual disbelief.

I decide to confront him with the note when he gets home. Al comes in just after supper. I've just finished tucking the kids in and making a cup of tea. It's been a long day and the dishes can certainly wait. I'm nervous about how to approach this. I want to get to the truth without causing him to withdraw.

"Would you like some tea?"

He nods.

"Al, I found this note in your pocket today…" I hold onto the piece of loose-leaf paper firmly. Tangible, awful, potential proof.

"You were going through my pockets?" He appears confused.

"I was going to wash them—your jeans, I mean. Did you write this?" I ask to be fair, like a lawyer gathering steam.

"What?" He doesn't seem at all concerned. Does a person just forget about a suicide note?

"It says you want to kill not only yourself, but Jye, too. I'm really worried, what's going on with you?" I make a real effort at covering fear with deep concern.

"Haven't you ever had a bad day? No, not you, eh? You don't have bad days, do you?" He's sneering.

"Of course I do, but not bad enough to fantasize about killing my kids! What's this all about, and what's the deal with bequeathing money to your Mom?" I am quickly losing my composure and he is disconcertedly nonchalant. "I'm worried about you, Al. Don't you even think this is just a little weird?"

"It was just a bad day. I was just killing time and imagining a better place, that's all. I just wrote it to get it out of my system." He is so calm and not even trying to explain the note. "Elsie, it's nothing, just scribbling on a piece of paper. You had to be there, it was a mood." He is audibly still.

"Is it me? I noticed I'm not in the note. I thought things were going pretty well." I'm treading water, waiting for the dunk. Silence. "Your mom suggests vitamin B." I crawl back to shore.

"You called my mother? Are you nuts? You really jump the gun at any opportunity, don't you? She probably thinks you're crazy. You should really try to relax. You've got too much time on your hands and you use it to get all worked up."

"She actually didn't seem that upset. What's with the vitamin B? I thought this was serious. I just wanted to know if this was something that had come up before."

"What do you mean, 'this'? It's nothing; it couldn't have come up before. Anyway, my mother thinks vitamin B cures everything. It's good for stress. You thought…well, you just weren't there…" he trails off and then says decisively, "Can I have that piece of paper, now that you've taken it out of my pocket and read it? It is mine, after all."

"I told you I was doing laundry. I can't believe you're upset about me finding the paper or calling your mother. Put yourself in my shoes for one second. I just want to make sure no one is going to get hurt, and especially not my baby." I want reassurance, and I think I should hang onto the note. I notice I said *my* baby.

"Elsie, don't worry, you are all worked up for nothing. Sometimes, I think you like it. It's just rambling, it was a bad day; it was last week for God's sake. Nothing's going to happen. Just give it back. The last thing I need is for you to show it to someone and for it to be taken out of context." Al stretches out his hand in perfect expectation. "Look, you know I love J.J. as much as you do. Mothers aren't the only ones who love their kids. We're a family. I just get down sometimes, something you don't understand. It's over, it's fine, and I was just venting, really."

Taken out of context, what context: the context of the living? I reluctantly hand him back all of it; the paper, the testimony to a bad day, and the "possible" suicide note, on the grounds that it does in fact belong to him.

6

Summertime

I have to say that after this, I'm beginning to feel distant. What with being the mother of two, some semblance of reason and self- preservation prevails. Al has a boat and he has a dream that one day we'll all live on this boat and travel. This fits quite nicely with my love of this non-conformist adventurer, and we enjoy many hours making vague plans about a different lifestyle. After several people ask me if I have in fact ever seen the boat, I venture to ask of its whereabouts. I'm surprised to discover how much relieved I am to hear the boat does exist, and even more relieved to discover that it's nicely far away, out west. Al produces a small old style photo of a barely visible rotted-out hull. The photo is about two inches by two inches and framed in a white border. He talks frequently and longingly about getting back to this boat. He teaches the song, "Sail Away" to Zoë as he plays it on the guitar. Moments like these make it seem temporarily inconsequential that he's going to be late for work, as she dances freely around the room, her momentum telling us life is a celebration.

Al doesn't seem bothered by the state of his boat and oddly, I don't want to spoil his dream, as I'm now aware there's little danger that we shall all die at sea. At least, not in the near future.

He's found an ad in the paper and he's going to enter a contest to be a dental patient. If he has enough plaque he could win a trip, to be the bring along patient for the dentist's exams. Am I supposed to hope for my guy to have an excessive amount of plaque? Is it a noticeable thing? 'Hey honey I'm sure you'll win' just doesn't seem fitting so I don't say anything. Are we reduced to hoping for plaque?

Al has now found a new boat; no one will help him bring it home. "No one has any vision," says Al. So, he leaves early in the morning to bring it home himself. He manages to roll the twenty-foot boat onto a borrowed trailer attached to my Dad's Skylark. Come evening, he's painstakingly using logs to roll and settle his new treasure into a corner of the garden. I watch from the screened in back porch as he studies the scenario, gently pushing his hair behind his ears in peaceful absorption. I feel the purity in his waste of time. One has to admire that sort of tenacity. I'm not entirely convinced he won't just prove everybody wrong and fix that rotting remainder of a vessel right up. I'm distanced enough to feel like a witness. It fits somehow; the vulnerable craft just waits in the garden for someone to believe in it. It's far from functional. Surely, it will pass for a jungle gym. The broken piano he carried in on his own a while back is now passing for furniture. If you reach inside the workings of the piano, you can pluck the strings. There's something resonant of faith here, it's a shame the keys don't work. He sure isn't a quitter.

I've gotten off welfare, proof positive that I believe in us against the world and family values. I figure it's worth a try to have some expectation, to trust; at this point, I'm just trying to find any which way to make this a workable situation. There's some difficulty around money as we hardly have any. Al's shifts are part-time. I'm doing clown shows for kids' birthday parties to get some cash. Al doesn't show up on time with the car. The show must go on, business is business and I find myself crumbling under the frustration with Al and the pressures of two little ones. I book fewer shows. Just as well, because I'm not feeling very entertaining, even behind the safety of the whiteface.

The stove breaks in midsummer. I know a cheap one will come along soon, but in the meantime, I'm making campfires in the backyard. This is like camping. I've moved the couch outside, too. The neighborhood kids—well, I call them kids, even though most of them are only a couple of years younger than me--they come over, and it's a lot like I imagine a commune would be. Sitting around the fire, friends from the Calliloo, guitars, collecting wood with a babe in arms, I feel like a pioneer. I'm actually quite

impressed with my ability to roll with the punches. I hope Al
notices my resilient nature, but he seems to be eating at the café.

Life goes on. It's mostly me and the kids and whoever
drops by. Al misses most of the fun, but is home every night and
he lollygags with the paper every morning. Since he takes the car
most days, I walk to the grocery store with the kids and tell myself
I'll "borrow" the cart to get the bags home. Occasionally if there
are more kids or a friend for company we'll pile several kids in and
take the cart for a neighborhood tour of singing, the rough sound of
the hard rubber cart wheels on cement keeping time for us. Zoë's
favourite is a Dr. Seuss version of Hard Times that I made up for
school on one of these walks.

A Bounderby Ball, all hot air and clowny,
Rides his hobbyhorse high, round his smoke filled towny.
He bounces and bobbles and bosses about,
Capitalist, ruthless, without much a doubt.
'Til, it's his mother, who lets all his air out.
(At this point we act like a balloon blowing out its air. then,)
There is factory man, named Gradgrinder, you see,
In his fine system, there is really no glee.
And his very own children will pay a great fee.
(We look very sad for the poor children. Then,)
The children got ground up in facts and notation,
All in the guise of a fine education.
He would grind his child's mind, from beginning to start,
'Til all folly and fancy is gone from their heart.
(And really the only lines the kids remember, so they wait in
anticipation and then belt them out:)
A hole would be left like a crack or a crevice,
And holes left in persons can be… quite a menace!
But even though grinders can grind things to dust,
The fairies find children and find them they must.
They sing; the fact of the fact is some facts must be wrong,
So this is the end of our silly song.

Truth be told, I know I'm stealing the cart, and I don't feel badly
about it. I inherit the car and two thousand dollars, which saves the
day. I guess I knew I'd get something. I just couldn't fly without
any net at all. So much for trust.

7

The Theme from the Andy Griffith Show

I've decided to take a course in meditation and positive visualization, controlling my own mind. I'm determined to create a positive future. There's this cute little blond waitress at the Calliloo,whenever I ask her how she is, she answers, "Better and better." She's the one who told me about the course. I don't want to sound quite that contrived, although "Fine and you?" really isn't much better at including the other person. I'll use a little of what's left of my inheritance, before it's all gone, to pay for the course. I believe in change from the inside out. Mind you, I was meditating a lot when I fell for Al. I hope that's not indicative of anything. We get a stove, twenty-five bucks. I've got money left to invest in my future insides. I tell Al about my plans to take the course. It's just before supper. Zoë's in the sand box outside, and J.J. is crawling around the living room, playing in a giant cardboard box that I found by the side of the road.

"Are you nuts Elsie?" is his initial response. "You know those courses are nothing but brainwashing. They're a waste of time and money."

I don't quite believe that he could even think that an all out dismissal of the idea is in any way a convincing argument and so I press on.

"Listen Al, maybe you don't even know what the course is about, it's all about being positive and creating a life you want. How can that be anything but good?"

"You're going to go around like an automaton, saying you're well even if you're not.Is that what you want, to sound like that ditz at the restaurant? Who by the way is probably a lesbian. That's insanity." Al shifts his weight and his posture turns more to intimidation, as is his usual stance when I disagree. I'm glad I'm on the other side of the room, as he doesn't seem as big at a distance. I vaguely note that, unfortunately, he is by the door so my escape route is blocked. I find myself staying on the other side of the room. This is not quite the intimate chat about a plan that I imagine is possible.

"I think the idea is to create well-ness. I know for a fact she is not a lesbian as if that has anything to do with anything." I say this with a bit of a sneer, my disappointment in the exchange leaking into my tone. Some might call this provocative. I add, "Well, I'm not asking your permission. I am merely telling you my plans. Anyway we wash every other part, what's wrong with a little brainwash?" I'm trying to lighten the mood, so I add, "I don't want to fight."

Al smiles at my humor, but only with his mouth, his stance doesn't really change. "I just don't think you should waste money on that." I let him have the last word, because I know I'm signing up for the course anyway. When I don't argue he softens, so I say, "Are you hungry? I made my pizzas." I think my pizzas are cool because I slice zucchini to replace pepperoni and use pita bread instead of dough for the crust. The schedule of the course is two weekends. Judy has already agreed to baby sit, so this shouldn't interfere with him at all. Mia is taking the course with me. Her parents are paying.They are very supportive of self improvement. I like that about them.

The seminar is at the Meridian downtown, so I take the train in and meet Mia there. After we pay, we are ushered towards the entrance to the big conference room. A husband and wife team, Sally and Peter run the seminar. Sally and Peter took the course themselves and moved up the ranks to provide this service. They are proof positive that it works. They are dressed very conservatively, him in a suit, and her in a deep red skirt, matching jacket, nylons and black pumps. She has a hair do, the kind that requires a blow dryer and possibly dye. At the door they ask everyone their name as we come in. They shake hands with a hundred and fifty people, their smiles never flinching for a second.

Once we are all seated in the hall, Peter points towards each person individually, and one after another he says their name. He has used the methods of the course to remember a hundred and fifty names. We all clap, very impressive, although I remain unconvinced that remembering names is going to change my life at this point. I already remember the names of important people in my life. They say it makes people feel important if you remember their name. That might be true, but during his demonstration I feel more like a prop than a person. Plus I'm really unnerved by anyone who repeats my name when they are speaking to me as though they are studying for a test. We are all sitting in rows of hotel chairs and I have chosen an aisle seat near the middle. Mia is beside me. Sally and Peter promise us all that in the past they wouldn't have been able to get up in front of people and do this. Sally describes being able to diagnose problems with her washing machine by using visualization and just knowing the answer. She adds, "Isn't that right Peter?"

"It sure is," Peter assures us. "And that's with no technical training! Just practice!" They pace the stage in a lively fashion explaining that we can find lost items and Peter confesses that he used to often lose things. He says, " I was a real loser, ha-ha, I used to lose things all the time, as Sally can tell you." Sally nods like a loving but slightly disappointed mother. Despite their cheesy sales pitch, their high energy and positive attitude is likable. We are promised that there is no limit to what we can create for ourselves and that we too can have a marvelous life like theirs if we follow the program. The workbook can under no conditions be shared with anyone who hasn't taken the course. It could be dangerous without proper instructions. We don't get the workbook yet. I'm dying to find out what secret code is in that workbook. I try not to think that it is just a ploy to make sure everyone pays. After lunch we are walked through an introduction into getting ourselves into alpha state, the state used for visualization. They use a metronome to help us achieve it. We are asked to play in our imaginations with the numbers as we count backwards. Imagination seems to be a big key. It's fun to imagine all the things you can do with the number three in your mind.

When I arrive home I find Judith and a young guy in the living room playing with the kids. "Simon is just having the best time!" Judith gestures to him on the floor, Zoë and J.J. are both in the big cardboard box taking turns popping up and scaring Simon who flies backward in feigned fright. He waves to me on the way down. I laugh.

"Are you and Simon staying for supper, Jude?"

She follows me the five steps into the kitchen, "Sure."

"So, is he . . .?" I ask wondering if Lukas has competition.

"Simon? No, he's just a new friend from school. He was actually Lukas' friend first. He wanted to come hang out. I hope that's okay. They're having a ball with him. I started the spaghetti sauce because I wasn't sure exactly when you'd be back." Judith stirs the pot. "So how was it?"

I wonder where Al is but I don't say anything. This is pleasant enough I think. "Yeah actually it was interesting; it was just an introduction today really. I'm looking forward to tomorrow to really get into it, y'know. Are you still able to come tomorrow?"

"Yup, no problem." Judith sips at the sauce with the tip of her tongue on the wooden spoon. " Its yummy. That tumeric is really the trick isn't it?"

"Mhmm, and the touch of cinnamon for sure." I reach for the spoon realizing I'm famished. Shortly after the kids have been put to bed, Al comes in. Judith and Simon are still hanging out. Al decides to make his case against the course again. It sounds more like a case against me, as he doesn't know much about the course. He puts forth that I am a brainless follower of the café ditz. He looks to Judith and Simon for support. I suppose he takes their silence as agreement. Sweet blond Simon with his silver ring on his thumb, innocently playing with kids. What an awful introduction to my family. Embarrassment turns out to provoke bravado in me. I hear myself exclaim,

"Why don't you talk about something you have a clue about? I think your negative attitude toward the world could use some brainwashing!" I've popped out of the kitchen and taken the stance and tone of a kid who is yelling *Oh yeah, I know you are but what am I?* My feeling of trepidation slinks in afterwards and there is nothing I can do as I watch him grab a shoe from the doorway and launch it. The shoe comes hurtling across the room. It's a running shoe, one of mine. I don't try to catch it, but I do try to move. I realize my mistake as it hits me in the head. I turn to Jude and Simon, "He hit me with a shoe. He launched it at me! You saw that didn't you?" Neither one says a word. It's like they are frozen or something.

Then Judith says, "Maybe we should go." Simon looks at her with a subtle nod and they prepare to leave, getting their jackets on.

"But he threw a shoe at me . . ." I am shocked at the intentional aggression.

Al goes and sits on the couch in a relaxed way. "I didn't throw it at you. I threw it in your general direction." He seems confident that the witnesses will back him.

The *witnesses* are running for the hills. I can't believe they are leaving me here. Simon plummets in my estimation of a man. For some reason I think that if a male were to tell Al he's acting like a fool, he might listen. They make a quick exit, leaving me to deal with the situation. Well, in all fairness I guess Simon is just a kid, and a guest at that.

Al eats. We spend the rest of the evening in a tense discussion about the course taking up too much of my time and being a waste of money. He doesn't want to come home to a babysitter. I am careful not to posture and to *try* to see his point of view. I don't mention the shoe. I am not very convincing because I would have to agree not to go to the course for Al to think I've actually understood him. I want to go to bed as I've got an early train to catch, but he wants to keep talking, and I comply.

When we arrive at the conference hall door they are handing out little cards to everyone. Mia's says YOUR LIFE IS YOUR MIRROR. When I read it I say to her, "It's like everyone just reflects different parts of you."

Her message seems like less work than mine. She sneers at me; "Maybe your life, I think I reflect onto others, so they can see their puny selves in my wondrous light!" Laughing she adds, "Let me see yours."

I look at her aghast as I often do, which is why she thinks I'm a bit of a suck, and hand her mine. Mine reads; YOU CONTROL YOUR REACTIONS.

I think I understand the larger truth of this statement, but I don't understand how to control not getting hit by the flying shoe-other than ducking, that is. For that matter, my immediate reaction is to fall asleep for the better part of the morning as an uncontrollable response to having been kept up all night. I keep nodding off during the sitting alpha exercises. We do what is referred to as a body-scan this is where we lie prone and check our internal organs in our mind's eye. I'm not that familiar with the placement of my internal organs. I see a bunch of little elves running around inside me playing and kind of jeering me for having no idea where to direct them. The imagination part of the program seems to have spilled over into this exercise and I notice myself slipping into a pleasant slumber. I wake up to the sound of the announcement for lunch break. I groggily muse that perhaps Al is getting his way; as I have now paid for a morning's sleep. Oh well, I guess a Mum who doesn't get much time off has to go to some lengths to get a nap. Mia does well on the body scan; she seems to have a knack for it. She consoles me by referring to my elves as "healer elves," which I accept without argument.

The course does help me, though. As I become more aware of my thinking, I see how my point of view is always slipping away as I try to be fair and see someone else's side. Maybe understanding is the consolation prize. The second weekend focuses on more detailed positive thinking and accessing one's inner imp. Mine showed up early. Putting an imaginary black X through any negative thoughts is one of the exercises. That's being a little disparaging towards the negative, but I don't mention this. On the second day we are encouraged to ask for spirit guides to come into our minds, one male and one female. Different people will get different results we are told. I get Richie Cunningham and Glenda the good witch of the North, who floats gently into my psyche in a bubble, saying, "There's no place like home."

When people are asked to share I don't say a word because I'm ashamed and amused by my fictitious visitors, they aren't exactly characters on the edge. I'm somewhat relieved to hear someone else confess to getting obi-one-Kenobi. Mia's experience is so profound she is weeping. This provokes Sally to give her some special attention. She takes her aside. I feel so superficial, so un-moved, so damn Richie Cunningham; and yet admittedly safe with him; potentially well adjusted.

By the end of the course I can describe the family members of absolute strangers, an aspect of the clairvoyant part of the program. I'm uncertain how knowing someone's grandfather had a strong attachment to his leather belt plays into a better future for me. I will however try to meditate on positive outcomes. We all cheer each other at the end of the course. Everyone goes up on stage individually and gets positive energy from a hundred and fifty people. It's supposed to feel great, and I tell Mia that it did. But all I notice is that there are not a hundred and fifty people coming to my house to tell Al to stop throwing things at me.

Now, I don't imagine for a second that the shoe thing is going to go unaddressed. I'm just going to pick the right time, maybe tomorrow. Often just before I go to sleep, I see emergency vehicles. They usually aren't moving, and there are ambulances, fire trucks as well as police cars, in a line. This is a new dream because they are moving. I dream that the police are pouring down the driveway and storming into the house. I wake relieved to feel the warm sun on my face and recognize I must be a little stressed out. I'm stretching in the morning light, the yellow flowers on the sheets are joyous and the sheets themselves seem especially crisp like late summer, and smell of the window heated sun. They help me to recover from my dream.

We are all having breakfast and I say, "Hey, Al, it was so strange, I just dreamt the police were here." Before he even has a chance to answer, I do a couple of double takes as my dream reenacts itself in the driveway. I guess the clairvoyant part of the course must've worked. There is no knock on the door, but suddenly the small living room is full with five green uniformed Quebec Provincial Police. They're looking around the tiny room, speaking to each other in French and the short balding one is asking for some money. I herd the kids into their bedroom and stay in the doorway to keep them in. The policeman is aggressively close to Al speaking in broken English, "You hoe lot huv money, heh, for some tickettes." Since when do the police collect at the door, and without knocking at that? They have no respect for my little crappy house. The fact that the previous tenants were druggies coupled with Al's long hair may be a contributing factor.

"You pay da munay or you come wid us."

Al is going crazy, running in and out of the bedroom, dumping drawers and yelling, "You can't do this in front of my family! I paid those damn tickets! I have receipts!" He takes one top drawer from the bureau and pours the contents onto the living room floor. "Jesus, fucking Christ! I have receipts!"

This doesn't make any sense to me. Four of the cops are just standing there looking uncomfortable. The one who spoke has now lowered his tone to one of calming the situation. "Okay, okay, you look for dem."

Al is very convincing in his certainty that he has paid, but he doesn't ask to see the paper work. He doesn't find the receipts, but the police finally leave. I certainly see first-hand how the world is a different place for Al, and more and more for me by association. This does begin to explain why he's so mistrusting. This clearly isn't the time to bring up the shoe incident. Frankly, I'm a little confused as to the purpose of the preview dream. Perhaps the police thought we were the previous tenants of questionable repute.

8

Snowbird

The nip in the air and the dry leaf smell signals it's time to get ready to cocoon. I always feel a sense of abandonment as the geese squawk their departure plans for the south, bragging about their easy escape from the cold. Viewing them in their organized "V" is like seeing off a friend at the airport and wishing them a safe flight in good faith that they'll come back. I'm always a bit astounded that anyone can get that together.

There seems to be a problem with the plumbing. The bath won't drain completely, so I have to bail. At first, we suspect a frozen pipe; the temperature did dip pretty low during the night, but it's unlikely. We try hot water and borrow a blow dryer. We even try evil chemicals, but nothing seems to work. The landlord is unconcerned, we can move if we don't like it, or fix it ourselves. Al seems to think this sort of activity, bailing, is good for my soul. I think I'd rather follow my friends to a posh suburban house for a while. My soul was sufficiently replenished by the earlier lack of a stove. I love my little house, the waterfront, the canoe, but the plumbing must be repaired. I'm lonely and fed up and bailing the bathtub just isn't doing it for me. In fact, the only bailing I intend to do is to bail out.

Al doesn't seem like the issue now. Impressing him with my pioneer spirit is not on my list today. He can come or not come, I am not living like this. So the kids and I pack up and move in from the outskirts. Mia's parents have gone away for the winter and left Mia and Keifer the house. The five bedrooms fill up quickly as Lukas and Judy follow soon after and Simon pops in

and stays frequently. Well Judy on her own as they have split up.
and Simon pops in and stays frequently. Lukas comes ostensibly
because it's closer to school and he is, after all, friends with Mia as
well as Simon. Others drop by at will. So we're back in commune
mode. Lukas and Judy are going to CEGEP, which is college in
Quebec. Mia is doing a couple of nights a week bartending, for
some unspoken reason she has decided to quit stripping. I think it's
part of the strings attached to staying in her parents house. Anyway
she is taking some dance classes during the day, and I watch
Keifer. We are all rather enjoying the luxurious surroundings,
cable TV and VCR. I rent the "Never Ending Story" for Zoë and
Keifer, and they learn "The Song That Never Ends," which they
sing at the top of their lungs for what seems like an eternity.
There's a nice stereo and even a piano that works. It turns out Judy
is a pretty good pianist. Learning a few "Raffi" tunes for kids is
easily doable for her and she has quite a lovely voice. I notice that
the close bond I shared with Lukas is being extended to Mia, who
is lavishly accepting of any and all attention available. Flaunting it.
Mia is, as always, flamboyant. She still has her stripper costumes
and enjoys parading around in the likes of a long pink boa, just for
doing her stretches.

    "To liven things up," she says coyly. Sometimes I almost
envy her exhibitionist nature, and I do love her sarcastic wit. But I
sense something a little self destructive about her, an edge, which I
continue to defend to others as though it's my own.

    "Oh, Lukas, you can take me to class in my parents' car,
just pick me up after," she offers casually. Her offer only extends
to Lukas, so he's having a bit of fun. Judy is starting to fume, but
she's keeping her jealously neatly hidden from Mia with whom
she's becoming fast friends. I suppose there are certain perks to the
house owner, and the cute younger guy. Lukas winks at me as he
walks through the living room heading into full flirt mode with
Mia in the kitchen. Mia glances back over her shoulder as she goes
upstairs, her shapely hips like a ringing bell. It's difficult to know
who's playing with whom. I prefer my spot, safely trusted on the
sideline, collusion of friendship on all fronts. I watch like an old
woman as they spruce themselves up for a night on the town. Judy
and Mia bonding over the layers and layers of scarves that have
just come into fashion,they are maidens, I'm a mother and for the

time being Mia's babysitter.I don't know how she got to stay in maiden mode. By being single I suppose. I'm not sure if it's them who won't let me play 'girl,' or just the nature of things. I have a boyfriend.

Al is getting frustrated with me. He comes over on and off, usually to sleep, and to his credit, gives me some cash so I can pitch in for groceries. He thinks I deliberately sabotaged the plumbing so I could go live with my friends. I don't think I did that. That would be a bit extreme, but things are confusing and I do wonder if it is my fault. Maybe I cleaned out something with dirt in it, and the dirt went down the drain. Maybe I unconsciously clogged my own drain. I'm getting a little worried, so I call the local hospital. I ask the lady on the other end of the line if it's possible I'm causing all his aggression. When I say he's frustrated, I mean he leans in close and hisses his accusations, insisting I'm deluded. When I tell the woman from the hospital, she says I'm probably a provoker and I should watch myself. She doesn't give me a follow-up number or anything—I guess she doesn't like provokers. That isn't very helpful and I think she's an idiot. But still, could this be my fault? At least if it is, then I can fix it.

Al and I are starting get along pretty well when I'm not waiting for him or relying on him for anything. He says we are going home soon. We snuggle when he comes in at night and I share the day-to-day mellow dramas of our roommates with him. "Mia is a spoiled brat," he remarks, "and anyway Judith is still in love with Lukas, he's just making her realize it that's all. I hope Mia realizes that she is going out and leaving you with Keifer almost every night, I hope she appreciates it." I'm enjoying Al's defense of me. His recognition. I try to ignore it when he goes too far like insinuating that Mia has now turned into a lesbian and is just toying with Lukas out of some sadistic tendency. I laugh it off. Plus I feel disloyal then, because Mia is generous to let us stay. So I try to stick with that.

The landlord finally fixes the plumbing. He wants his next month's rent. These little cheap houses rented on a verbal agreement don't come with a speedy warranty. Our little family is going home. I've had about enough of group living; fighting over the last fish stick and watching the other girls get decked out is getting tiresome. I am conflicted though, there is safety in numbers, and luxury is comfortable. But I do know this can't go on. Mia is sharing what does not really belong to her after all. I feel badly around the mess kids can cause, and that I am responsible for more of it than any of the others. It might be different with a bunch of Mums and kids. I have some guilt around that, but it was Mia's call to have us all.

Once home I enjoy the peace and quiet frozen in time; Christmas, birthdays, Zoë is four, J.J. is one, and I'm twenty-two and waiting for the February thaw. Everyone's still at Mia's and they don't get out here that often. I feel left out. Zoë misses Keifer. I chose this life, I repeat to myself when I feel too isolated. I don't know how those older women do it alone in their houses, without having people in and out spontaneously. I enjoy my children, but winter is long and without the visitors, I'm starting to notice again that Al isn't home much. I don't feel loved or cared for. I'm starting to see that maybe those "weak insecure" women who demand a certain kind of behavior perhaps know something I don't know. Maybe it's possible for love and expectation to co-exist; maybe I won't be killing love if I ask for something for myself.

Does this mean I don't love Al anymore? Did I? Love just doesn't go away. Can it be killed? Somehow I thought the goal was unconditional love. Is there some point of convenience when conditions pop in? Maybe being born on the tail end of the baby boomers has had an affect; we teethed on peace and free love that doesn't work so well in practice. He scares me and I don't trust him. That doesn't sound like love. I really thought that it wouldn't be necessary to have rules. I thought love was the rule. I get that you're supposed to love yourself but I don't get how that will change someone else's expression.

This is not the reality I believe in; I believe there is something more.

When I try to talk to Al about it, he responds in ways I don't understand. It hurts my brain to listen to him. I feel like I'm grinding gears in my head. He's talking in first gear, ever so slowly, and I'm grinding down from fourth. I'm really trying to be a good listener, but when he pauses, it seems like he's absent forever and I feel as though my brain will explode. I wonder if the pauses are designed to draw in my attention, as I scoot to the edge of my chair willing his words out. On top of this, he uses metaphors that are so difficult. How is our relationship like an egg that has to be protected? And where am I in the egg? I'm thinking I'm the runny white undercooked part, and that's why these thoughts just won't congeal. He talks so softly. He sings so sweetly, it makes me cry. I know I shouldn't criticize him. Damn why am I so critical? Am I really as critical as he says I am? Why don't I know what the blues are? No one likes to be confronted with his or her failures. I just can't help myself. His plans are riddled with holes, pipedreams. 'The boat,' I screamed the other day, 'is nothing but a rotted-out hull.' No wonder he doesn't like me, I'm a dream wrecker, but I just want to make real plans. I don't believe that other people are so responsible for my experience. Maybe I am a conformist after all; I do want to be able to live in the world and be on time, sometimes, or at least create a world where there is some time for me. I refuse to be encased egg mucous.

***

That's it! I've had enough. I seem to have thawed with the river and this year, there's spring flooding. Something has to give. Maybe I'm not so nice; maybe I'm not as strong as I thought I could be; maybe I'm selfish, and not meant to be in a relationship with anyone. That's just who I'll have to be then. I'm so sorry, my babies, but our so-called nuclear family is on the verge of destruction. Damn, and I wanted it so badly. The flooding abates, and I see that it's possible to mistake flotsam for artifacts and drama for truth. It's a choice.

I'm supposed to pick him up at two in the morning at work, providing someone is over who can stay with the kids, otherwise he'll find a way home. This is another example of the kind of organizing that I can't quite comprehend. I got to keep the car today so I didn't question. I ask Lukas, who by now is back in my neck of the woods, to stay with the kids.

"I don't want to be the babysitter. That's Judy's job." Lukas doesn't look pleased when I practically beg him to stay. "It's awfully late, Elsie. Why is he still at the restaurant, long after they've closed?"

"He offered to help clean the vents, which of course he's doing by himself." I shrug. "Lukas, what do you think of Al?"

"Don't give me that look. I don't want to be in the middle of this. I won't talk about Al specifically. What I will say is I wonder how a man has a family and then doesn't really seem to pay them much attention. Let's face it, Elsie, I spend more time with you than he does."

"I know he's busy, but we might say the same for Judy, little miss scholar at the moment. It's not that so much, but you've seen him with me. How he talks to me, so intently, so abstractly. I feel a bit like an idea, an idea that keeps bursting out of its box and has to be stuffed back in."

Dark shoulder length curls flounce as Lukas throws back his head smiling, "I can't imagine you in a box to start with, except maybe a Jack in the box, with your different colored shoes for each foot! I don't quite know what you mean. Everybody wants to be loved, Elsie, and you do seem a little tense when he's home." Lukas shrugs his unique blend of knowing and innocence. "What do I know? I'm just a kid."

I punch him gently in the arm.

"Well, answer me this, kiddo, do you think I'm mean to demand he be here when he says he will, or to want some time off or to need to have fun, like I do with you? I asked him about his relationship with his mother, and he just about went through the roof. I always push it. Lukas, I feel like I can't believe in him much longer. I don't even know where he is most of the time. Is that normal? I need to find out why this doesn't seem right. I need to talk to him. Can you please stay? It won't be too long, I promise." I give him my cutest pleading look.

"Okay, but you owe me. And Else, I don't think you're mean, but I think sometimes people just don't know how to give each other what they need. I don't know if they can learn that."

He's being careful; ever since the baby, it's hard to get a real opinion out of anyone, I need a loud, clear one. I'm still thinking about that and I wonder if Lukas thinks it's me who can't give. I head for the door. The mere thought rankles; I turn. "Y'know, I never wanted to have to tell anyone how to act. I thought their actions would show me how they felt. But then he says he loves us and there are just things I don't understand. I'm willing to admit I could be missing information. He told me once he's given his life to me. I don't want his life, for crying out loud, just a decent relationship! Would you give someone your life?"

I am working myself up as I go back for the keys and pause again. Lukas looks a little bewildered as I carry on without waiting for a response. "You're damn right there are things I don't get! Gave me his life, oh yeah, where is it exactly? Better move over, Lukas, you might be sitting on it! One more thing, have you noticed his luck?" I stand by the door waiting for his answer.

"I will concede that he seems to have the worst luck of anyone I've met, like when the house fell on his head when he was helping those friends renovate…Too bizarre…Who has a house fall on them?"

"Well, to be fair, it was only the porch roof. Nonetheless I guess he's special. Thanks for staying; I won't be too too long."

About that porch roof, well I only found out when I tried to ruffle his hair and he cringed severely and pulled away. I was upset and rejected and about to make it a big deal when he confessed to having had ten stitches to his head two days before. He didn't want me to think he was accident-prone. Sweet, he was trying to protect me from knowing him. Later on, the next week in an unusually tender moment he cajoled me into removing the stitches. I protested and suggested he return to the clinic. I was ashamed at my own revulsion; he was putting his broken head in my hands and I wasn't sure I could manage. But he insisted in a purring voice that lulled me into a nobler being for a moment. I removed all ten of them. The generosity of his confidence made me into that quiet girl again, momentarily.

But now, I don't care anymore. I drive to the restaurant. There's no one else there, just him. "This isn't working out." I say. "I was hoping we could talk." The next thing I know he's pushing me up against a stack of beer cases that lean against the wall near the walk-in fridge. They're wobbling behind me; I can hear the clink of glass on glass and he's in my face looking very ugly, snarling. He starts to punch me, the punches are carefully directed at my arms and thighs. They're only charlie-horse hard, but his muscular six foot two frame barely restrained makes it scary. He yells in a strained whisper, "If you ever take my son away from me, I'll kill you."

"No, I would never do that," I protest. "Calm down, I love you." I keep my voice as even as I can. I sense he's walking a fine line of self control teetering on madness. Anything but a smooth tone could push him over the edge. I've now become a full-fledged liar. I'm concerned only with protecting my teeth. I'd like to have another relationship one day and I think there's no way I'm going to let him make me toothless. That's what I'm thinking all the while I croon, "I love you," to soothe, to calm.

He keeps punching. "You need to understand."

As the words seethe through his lips, he looks at once terrifying, determined, desperate and exhausted. I have no idea how long this goes on, the threatening jingle of the bottles behind me, the soundtrack of the fear that things could go from bad to worse. And then, suddenly, he stops. It seems he was just trying to scare me. He's certainly succeeded. I make my way slowly to the door saying,

"I'm just going to go to the dep and buy a drink and come right back."

He sees right through me. The strange thing with him is it's as though, if you think it, he accuses you of it. He grabs me again and reiterates his threat. I didn't want to take his son away. Even immersed in fear and outrage, I know I wouldn't let anyone take my kids away from me. For a moment, I almost feel sorry for him. I continue to reassure him, thinking, 'You're bananas if you think I'm staying with you after this. In fact, I'm fairly convinced you want me to leave.' I slowly get nearer and nearer the door and then, saying ever so sweetly,

"It's okay you've misunderstood, I just came to talk, I'll get us a drink,"

I run like hell. It's weird, though, because he knew I was thinking of leaving him, even though I really didn't want to. I didn't fully know it myself and I hadn't planned it. Maybe it's just because that's what he says women do. They leave, with the kids. So now I'm taking the rap for his version of the whole gender.

9

Gone Daddy Gone

We're going for a drive. Last night still sears the air. I guess I was too stunned to organize myself to leave at two in the morning, reeling in shock. I don't know how he found his way home; he must've taken a cab, I suppose. I'm exhausted and spend the day with the kids, breakfast, playing outside, lunch, and a walk. We avoid confrontation and communication. He plays guitar in an effort to soothe the household wound. I work at not being lulled into forgetting, concentrate on a plan. Why do we have this, what would be a lovely day now, only after? It's cruel. Is this the honeymoon phase in a cycle of abuse? Am I in a cycle of abuse? He seems so peaceful and suggests we get some baguettes and cheese and take a drive to Windmill Point. It's evening and the kids fall asleep in the back of the car after a picnic dinner. He won't drive home; apparently, this drive won't be over until everything is resolved to his satisfaction. He insists it can work. I soften; it's that tenacious nature again. I'm tired of crying. I'm tired of thinking that my dream of our family isn't happening. I'm tired of being afraid the kids are going to be fucked up by all this lunacy. I tell him as much.

When I realize he's not hearing me, and won't head home, something inside me snaps and I begin to blubber. "I'm so disappointed. Do you think I haven't been believing…in us?"

"Elsie, we can choose to stick this out. All your fears, your worries about the kids. They don't necessarily need to happen." His pale green eyes show nothing but compassion, and I'm aware my emotional breakdown consoles him in some way. He continues. "Don't worry about yesterday. I was just trying to wake you up. Y'know, I would never really hurt you." This is somewhat romantic, the intensity, the importance. I see a glimmer of love through the veil of emotional exhaustion; he's wearing me down. Drama for truth. I just want to go home. Then, it dawns on me it doesn't matter what I want until he gets what he wants.

"You could've acted like you loved me… hitting me isn't love…"

He interrupts. "I knew I should've gotten you a stove…"

I don't understand how a stove, a mere material object, has even made its way into this discussion. This causes me to pause.

"I don't care about the stove, but yeah, sure, a stove would've been good. Why did you turn one down? Don't answer, I don't want to know. I'm not talking about that…do you think I wasn't humiliated all those times you made me wait? Even my father's funeral…then bringing J.J. home. I've used all my reserves… Now my arms and legs are aching…"

He interrupts again. "I was there; I got there for the wake." I let it slip by. "C'mon, Else, you're stronger than that."

"Al, once you've seen the love in someone's heart, you just don't turn away, it's sacred and yet we're not bringing out the best in each other… I feel like a failure." I stop to lick away the saliva I feel stretching between my lips and wipe my nose on my sleeve. He reaches out and I crumble into his arms. "You shouldn't screw around with the sacred," is my last blubbery statement. I give in, and we go home to the exhausted sweetness that follows trauma. I'm such a liar, but hey, this is survival. The next day, I'm sweet as peach pie. I leave for the women's shelter as soon as he's gone. Consequently, I will have to leave the car, for now. Judy borrows her parent's station wagon to give me a lift. "Whatever you need to do," is all she says. Al isn't one of her favourite people.

10

Gimme Shelter

The shelter is absolutely wonderful. It's a split-level bungalow in the middle of the suburbs. They have everything. They have a playroom and bedrooms set up to accommodate the mother and kids in one room. All I have to do is make a grocery list and we get food. We all cook. Last night I made a veggie stir-fry with melted cheese and everyone seemed to like it. They even have a VCR. At last, I can relax a little. I enjoy talking with the social worker, Marilyn. She's an easy laugh and open minded, a bit on the straight side but not as old and stressed as the other women. When she arrived on the day the kids and I decided to plant a garden she just started to laugh and said I was way too cheerful. "This is fun," I said threatening to wipe my dirt covered hands on her. I tried to explain how just groceries could be a source of strain, something I never would've learned if I'd taken the safe road like her. "Ah the safe road." She nods and goes back inside chuckling.

I talk to him briefly on the phone. I plan my new life. I'm thinking Victoria, British Columbia; they have a university there, and I'll get loans. It's very far away, perfect for a new beginning. Things are looking up. I've broken out of something toxic. I talk to Mia on the phone; he's over at her house. She doesn't seem to think he's so bad, she tells me how much he loves me. Doesn't she believe me? I know he's sleeping with her in the name of comfort or conquest or chemistry. A lot of hard C names I think, but I don't say anything, and the thought slips out of my mind, as do most intuitive flashes.

We are sitting in the kitchen, in the evening; the kids are in bed and the other women are off somewhere else. There is only the small tiffany lamp over the kitchen table emitting a warm yellow light. We are having tea; it's cozy and safe. "So, Marilyn, why would you want to work in a place like this?" I ask.

"Well, I finished my degree in social work and this seemed like a good place to start, they needed people and I needed a job. Life takes us where we should be, if we let it."

"I believe in fate too. Do you think we are all the same story, all the women who end up here?" I hate being viewed that way, and I want to make sure she sees me. Not teenage pregnancy, single parent, widow without marrying, abuse victim, welfare mother, what the hell might as well throw in Anglo Quebecer, since she is Marilyn Lecroix after all, she would notice I am English.

"To tell you the truth, there are a lot of similarities, but you seem to be working on a new life. This isn't a place where I'd say that 'people end up.' It's more of a transition place." Marilyn explains.

"Oh, that's good news, cause I'd hate to think I'd *ended up* already! I've recently thought of writing a book about being a statistical disgrace, what d'you think? You know because I have already hit so many marks. Too bad they don't give out stars for being a stigma achiever," I say.

She looks puzzled, so I explain, "You know what I mean; teenage welfare mum, abuse victim blah blah," I sigh. "You know, the status quo."

"Some book, you could call it Status-Woe, considering your present circumstance." She looks quite pleased with herself and we start to giggle uncontrollably, one of those good ones when as soon as you think you've regained control the other person gets going again.

"Yeah, or status, whoa! " I say, as though it's a directive. Status has now become personified and into a horse like creature.

"Run status run!" Status is now at the track in my mind's eye.

"Status, wins by a nose!" She makes a snobby nose in the air gesture.

I now know we are becoming friends. Finally catching her breath she asks, "What's your story with the garden anyway?"

She smirks as she has told me earlier she's not the digging type.

"You'll see, people will tend it, I'll have contributed something, that's all. Something alive, something hopeful and new. I know that it sounds silly, but this place has been good to me. It's a heck of a lot better than having to stay at some couple's house and have their lousy relationship make you feel extra lonely." I'm not sure she knows what that feels like and she only nods. "Did you decide you don't want a guy in your life after you started here?" I feel impish, baiting her.

"I didn't say I didn't want a guy in my life." She tries to look nonplussed.

"If you do have a guy, which I think you've just told me you do. Either that or you want one. I bet you'd make him jump through some hoops, to make sure he was, let's say, philosophically compatible."

"Well, that's true to a certain extent. Jeffrey and I have a lot of long talks about how we want to live," Marilyn confesses.

"Sounds passionate." I grin, "Jeffrey, is it? And when do you find time to see him, working the afternoon/evening shift?" I probe.

She tugs at her blue denim shirtsleeve, confiding. "That does cause some problems. He thinks I'm hiding in my work, actually. But I do my best work here in the evening. When the bustle of the day is over, like now," she adds.

"Well I'm glad you're here, and I'm happy to be of service." I bow my head, "but I've got to say no amount of talking can show what a relationship will be until you're in the thick of it. I'm not sure how you can get in the thick of things if you're not there."

Marilyn takes a sip of her tea. I forge ahead on side with 'team Marilyn,' "This issue wouldn't even come up if you were a guy, so maybe you're not hiding at all. You'd think you'd pick a more cheerful spot if you were."

"You'd think." She muses, "and you are bang on, it wouldn't have come up if I were a guy," she says resolutely.

I want to know more about how it works for everyone else. Or how it doesn't work for that matter. Marilyn seems like *a someone* to ask, "Do you think you're in love? 'Cause I still believe in that, even after my colossal mistake, but it's less an idea than I thought and more of a behavior. If you're in love then there's hope. Al does have some lovely traits."

I shake myself back to where I am. "Maybe Jeffrey can work nights too," I offer.

She shakes her head, "No, that won't work," she pauses, reconsidering. "I shouldn't be so negative. It is worth looking into that's for sure." Marilyn drifts and it's clear to me she is with Jeffrey. I notice she didn't answer my question about being in love.

"Well, I'm not going back to Al anyway," I announce, "Just so you know, I've got a plan. I have no intention of ending up here when my kids are teenagers, like that lady who came in yesterday. Has she been here before?" I ask. The woman was glaringly middle class and worried about going to her cottage or country home as she put it. She had two sullen looking teenage boys with her. I found it hard to relate.

"No, this is her first time." Marilyn smiles her soft smile prodding me on for her amusement.

"That other one," I whisper, while I exaggerate looking around and lean in."She's been to every shelter on the island! It's like a mini holiday every month; I mean this has got to be better than an apartment in the Pointe!"

She sits up, in what seems like feigning disapproval of my comments so I add, "Okay, well with five kids and one with cerebral palsy, I guess she can use a break. Does her husband beat her on top of all that?" *Beat* sounds so extreme to my ears. I don't feel I was beaten.

"I guess it's fair to say the situation becomes overwhelming." Marilyn sounds professional; she isn't going to give up the goods on the other lady.

"Well, as I said, my mind's made up. I was confused by the romantic love at first sight thing. When I think back now it sounds more like a car wreck. God, I even remember Dan; he was the other guy in the car when I met Al, he was yelling '*nooah!*' with his eyes, hoping to stop the inevitable attraction. I suppose I should've paid attention, but then there is J.J.." I smile.

I still remember that meeting, it's so clear and yet in soft focus, blurry edged, unavoidable really. If I was in a novel I would probably just have taken to my bed by now, and then after a suitable period of time Al could return very contrite and live up to my expectations, and his intentions would've been true all along except he had to deliver rice to starving people, and I hadn't understood because it was a secret operation, and once I did actually understand, all would be forgiven and my blind faith rewarded. I'm afraid I just don't have the patience. I put out my smoke.

"Best to look forward. And J.J. is the best forward to look," says Marilyn. "Tired?"

"Yeah, you?" I take the last sip of tea, and get up to put the cups in the dishwasher.

"Yeah, I'm done for tonight. I'll see you tomorrow," she says getting up.

I head out of the kitchen. "See ya." I wave.

"I'll expect a copy of that book one day," she calls after me. "Status-Woe," she mutters and I hear her smiling to herself.

I call Lukas from the shelter. Everyone is awkward with me again, like I've touched another scary monster. It makes them uncomfortable, and me, alone.

"Elsie, yeah, it's a bit strange. I'm not used to talking to you on the phone. I'm having some trouble with, well you know, where you are." His voice is so soft, I'm acutely aware that he is living at home. I feel ancient and embarrassed.

"Look it's not like I'm in jail or everybody here is black and blue or something. I had to make a statement. Would I be less *hit* if I went to stay with a friend? I guess so, 'cause now it's a big deal. Mia is acting very distanced. I need some time to organize getting away."

"A women's shelter, it sounds so serious. How many people are there?"

"There's four others right now. There's room for about eight, but I don't really talk to them much except at supper. Oh God Lukas, there's one and she just goes from shelter to shelter, she's been in them all. She has five kids! And one with cerebral palsy. Some people have a lot to contend with. She's quite friendly, though, and smokes, so we chat. But she never leaves her husband. What kind of life is that?"

"Can you go out?"

"Yeah, it's not bad. I just have to be back by eleven."

"Do you want to grab a coffee?"

"You know what? Let's just meet me at the park tomorrow." I give him directions to the nearby park and we agree to meet the following day. I have to call back though, and cancel because I discover I am listed for household chores and then he can't meet until the end of the week because he has exams. So I'm disappointed that it won't be 'til the end of the week. I'm really looking forward to seeing Lukas.

Mia comes to visit midweek. She doesn't bring Keifer, and it's as though she thinks we're in a school principal's office, she's so tense. I make us some tea and show her the perks,

"Look Mia, a dishwasher. Who would've known?" I'm trying to be an imitation casual hostess showing my new home.

"Yeah, and all you have to do is run for your life to get it." she whispers to me as we head for the TV room.

"I'm hardly running for my life," I say.Can you run for your life in small sprints?

"Listen Elsie, I need to know, exactly how hard would you say he hit you, I mean was he trying to kill you?" She is totally serious.

"Let's see, after careful deliberation I'd say he punched me in the good kind of way! What're you saying?"

"Just show me, "she braces herself "c'mon, hit me."

"Mia, I'm not hitting you, relax. I'm not here because my bones are broken or anything, but my arms and legs were sore for a few days. Is that hard enough or do you think I'm overreacting? It was scary!"

"He's a mess, Elsie." She sounds sympathetic. It's making me queasy. I was so sure of myself.

"Really? How so?" I'm not sure if I'm hoping for remorse or revenge.

"He's just kind of lost. He misses you guys." She pauses and lowers her voice. "I got him to show me how hard he hit you." She offers.

I bite, "well, was it hard enough?"

"Hard to tell." She says.

Juliette, the two year old with cerebral palsy lies on her back in the middle of the kitchen floor. She is unable to hold herself upright; her soft ginger curls splay to the sides. I wonder how the world seems to her as we step over her with the occasional "Bonjour Juliette." She can't tell us. Her brothers run in and out, accustomed to jumping over her, until we shoo the other kids from the kitchen as we prepare an afternoon snack for everyone. Zoë takes J.J. with her. Sylvie seems to understand her daughter's attempts to communicate; she gets her bottle and holds it to the pretty little elfin face. We continue to chat, Sylvie at floor level, business as usual. We are discussing the merits of hot-dogs vs. tofu dogs and whether the untrained child can tell the difference.

Sylvie says, "I tink doze 'ot dogs could be ca-lle not-dogs tu sais." Laughing we all turn to look. Gesturing while speaking, Sylvie has let go of the bottle. Silent awe fills the room as we all take in the scene. Juliette is holding the bottle, all by herself. The joy wells up in me from a place I didn't know was there. A place reserved for the special ones, like Juliette. I swallow hard and look from Marilyn to Sylvie and back to Juliette, she is smiling, bottle in hand. We are all crying. Finally Sylvie breaks the spell by trying to take the bottle, Juliette isn't giving it up, and we are all laughing again. A moment that recognizes itself, and in doing so makes us recognize each other.

I meet Lukas in the park so as not to give away the location of the house. He's a guy and even though I trust him it doesn't seem right. Marilyn has agreed to keep an eye on the kids. I thought of bringing them but I feel like just talking and not playing. It's one of those bite-size parks plunked in the middle of the suburbs. The kind you can ride your bike to when you're really little. The kind, later, you go to in the dark to get felt up and smoke hash until the police chase you away from clinging to your childhood. Green space. We stand there awkwardly, until I say, "Hey, it's just me." He smiles but he still looks sheepish. Now, the park is like one penny in a wishing well, it makes the well look emptier. I perch myself on the lone picnic table and light a smoke as Lukas takes one too. I notice his teenage habit of over dressing in the hot weather, long pants, black biker boots and a long sleeved jersey.

"Elsie, I went by your house to get my book." He is still strangely hesitant.

"Yeah, so, did you find it?"

"Al was there, the door was like right off its hinges. He said when he found out that you'd gone, he'd lost it."

"How badly did he trash the place?" I sneer.

"Oh, no, it wasn't like that. It was only the door." He looks so uncomfortable, I'm getting nervous. He shuffles his feet and then continues, "He asked me to stay, and he just sat there crying. He was begging for my help. I was worried about what he might do, so I just sat there, smoking cigarette after cigarette while he broke down."

"Oh please… doesn't he have his own friends?" I begin rolling my eyes, "Your help for what exactly?"

"He asked me to help him get his family back, Elsie. I didn't know what to say, a grown man crying like that. He said that you'll listen to me, you trust me."

"And, what do you have to say to me?"

"Maybe you should talk to him."

"Is that a question or a suggestion?"

This is exhausting. I was so excited about starting over. This is going to be difficult. Why aren't I the one coming unhinged?

"It's okay Lukas, I'll talk to him. I have to talk to him eventually, but my mind is made up, it's over. Does he even understand why I left?"

"All he said was how badly he wants his family back. You know, he can't live without you, stuff like that. Elsie, one more thing," he pauses shifting his weight, "he's waiting for us now, in the parking lot on the corner." He pulls away raising his shoulders and sucking in his breath. Walking to the parking lot I wonder if I've been tricked or has Lukas been duped? "You know I didn't mean right now," I say, too worn down to put up a fuss.

"Yeah, I know," he half smiles. I just can't help liking that kid, in spite of myself. Also in spite of myself, I want to see Al.

On the way Lukas explains that Al has won a contest to go to California to be a patient for a dentist who is taking his American exams. I'd forgotten all about the ad he'd answered. It seems he has the right amount of plaque on his teeth. The prize is four days in California and getting his teeth done. He just needs to cut his hair. He wants us all to go. So Lukas thought I should hear him out. I can see the metallic blue Skylark reflecting in the sun, Al sitting patiently at the wheel. I stop in my tracks.

"He has to understand, he's not allowed to hit me. Can you go tell him that?" I plop myself down and sit cross legged on the corner of someone's very predictable home, picking absently at the curbside dandelions. Lukas turns from the driver's window and heads back towards me. "So?" I ask, "Did you tell him?"

"He says he totally understands, and he's sorry." He gives me a bedraggled look designed to release him as errand boy.

"Forget it," I say, "you got yourself into this. Tell him if we go with him on this trip I will need to have my own money, in case I have to escape, if he goes weird." Lukas turns on his heel, and I watch him, torn between the call of the west coast, reuniting my family or going it alone. Maybe my coming to the shelter was the wake-up call Al needed. Maybe somebody else acknowledging that you can't hit women has enlightened him.

This is a perverse version of grade five, when first crushes are negotiated through a friend. I call Lukas back, "One more thing and this is important. Tell him he would have to agree to get counseling when we get back to Canada. And don't say the weird part okay?" he nods setting off again. Lukas is trudging, surely wishing he was somewhere else, I continue to pick. This isn't all bad. He walks up lighting a smoke, his head to the side, hand cupped over the flame.

"He says, yes, yes, whatever you want. I'm done, go talk to him yourself, Elsie."

"Y'know, Lukas he was right, he knew I'd talk to you and that you would get me to talk to him. I feel kind of strange, like you're feeding me to the lions." I stare at him, trying to assess his loyalties. I shake it off. "Okay, I'll talk to him." I stand tall, I hand Lukas a dandelion. Dandelions aren't for the 'she loves me, she loves me not' game anyway.

I talk to Al through the car window, keeping a little distant. He seems sincere and agrees that I can have my own money; his mother had finally sent his share of a house they'd sold. (We don't iron out the details). I've always wanted to go to California, and this might be my only chance and the kids would have such fun on the beach. Maybe it could work. Maybe he's learned. He is so calm and I notice the peaceful and sexy undercurrent to his energy, something I'd intended to forget. I insist we plan to get counseling as soon as we get back to Canada.

He agrees. "This is what you wanted, Elsie, to travel with the kids. Just give it a chance, you and the sun, the sand, me. We'll play it by ear. Life is long and I'm still here."

I'm not sure what the last bit means, I think it's a commitment of some kind. But it could be a song lyric. It feels nice to be wanted and although I still feel a tinge of fear, I can't totally deny the magnetic pull I'm feeling. I tell him I have to think about it, but I'll have to think quickly as the departure date is in less than a week. Maybe we can take the kids to Disneyland. We don't kiss good-bye, I just walk away and Lukas looks helpless as he gets in the passengers seat. I hear a hopeful "Elsie, I do love you," And then in a slightly more desperate tone, "and I want our family back together." I don't turn, and I let these comments bounce off my back pretending they won't influence my decision. I walk in the opposite direction toward the *depanneur*, I don't want to give up the location of the house and I might as well get the kids a Popsicle. Depanneur comes from the word *panne,* which means breakdown. It's literally a store that could be handy in a breakdown situation, and here I am. He says he still loves me. He said it in the voice that wasn't too pleading and there was no trace of aggression. It is possible that I really don't belong here; I sure don't want to belong here. It is within the realm of possibility that the situation of our relationship could be healed, if both parties are willing. He's so calm and sweet. I guess I was wrong to think he'd be angry with me for coming to the shelter in the first place. Maybe it could change; maybe there is hope, *give peace a chance* and all that.

I leave the shelter a little embarrassed, as I'm sure I was voted most likely to actually leave my 'situation.' Mia picks me up to protect the location. I leave in the morning, so I don't get to say good-bye to Marilyn; I'm going to miss our conversations. After kissing Sylvie and her children good-bye, the kids and I settle into the neat Subaru wagon, I love the way Mia drives, like she means it, fast and straight. Every gear change seems to bring her closer to destiny. Pulling away from the house, Zoë waves frantically at the bigger boys. I hope Marilyn will realize I meant every word I'd said. I don't want her to get too demoralized about the clientele. It's just that circumstances change and a family is something worth taking a shot at. I was planning to go out west anyway. I make a mental note to send her a post-card.

11

Together Alone

It's strange to go home; the unhinged door is only half fixed and still hangs off at the bottom, leaning in and tilting to one side. The late afternoon sun, lightish green reflects inwards at an odd angle bouncing off the small window in the door. Other than that it's the same, but our absence has made the air less used, lighter somehow. The kid's room is just as I left it, bed unmade, stuffed toys strewn. The poster of Noah's Arc with all the happy looking animals reminds me that two by two can sometimes seem like an easy concept. Judith is going to take over the house, as is, and look after my car and stuff. She's thrilled. I pack the essentials. Al seems like a new man with his new conservative haircut and shave. Not my favourite look, I'm working at getting used to his new face.

Within a couple of days we are on the plane. I'm back in the land of Al. We are waiting to change planes in Toronto. Someone says, "That's him." And without further ado the Royal Canadian Mounted Police storm toward us. One grabs Al and throws him up against the wall. The other is saying, "You'll have to come with us, sir."

"Who do you think he is?" I demand but neither officer acknowledges even my presence. "What's going on?"

"You're making a big mistake," says Al, stiffening as they lead him away. I'm certain this sounds more like a threat than intended.

Even clean cut his luck hasn't changed. I slowly, incredulously, start to think about what the kids and I should do. I haven't formulated a plan at all when Al heads back from the behind the glass doors. He is unescorted, a good sign.

"What's going on?" I say perhaps more accusatory than I intend.

"It's okay. It was a case of mistaken identity. They thought I was someone else."

"Who?"

"Obviously someone they were looking for." He is clearly pissed off.

"Did they apologize at least?"

"No, not really, what do you expect? They're assholes."

"Geez, you'd think they'd be a little nicer. That's what you get even after making all that effort to look like them." And so our adventure has begun. I guess it wasn't his hair that riled the police.

We arrive in L.A. and are picked up by the dentist, who seems very nice. He does look at us in that way that the haves look at the have-nots, like we are kind of messy and probably not all that bright. Dental hygiene and family fun do not juxtapose in his mind and neither do our hippy demeanor and the Beverly Wilshire. We spend three nights in what we are told is the nicest hotel in Beverly Hills. Our room is its own suite, with a kitchen, and view of the courtyard. He has to change our room to accommodate the kids and me. We need more beds, and so it's a downgrade. Still you can tell this wasn't his plan. We tour Venice beach, teeming with roller bladers and Wilshire Boulevard. Everything shimmers in the sun. I've never seen a lemon on a tree before; I have to touch it because the perfect shape is too perfect to be real. We've decided not to go home at the end of the dental procedures. We are going to stay in California and drive up the coast to Vancouver. This is a trip of a lifetime! I can't wait to see the giant redwoods. A plan is actually coming to fruition; there is hope for him and us after all.

On the fourth night, the free part of the trip is over and we find ourselves wandering down Santa Monica Boulevard with 15 dollars Canadian and a stroller looking for a place to sleep. We'll have to get to a bank tomorrow. We find a room for ten dollars that includes the porn magazines not so well hidden under the mattress. It will do for the night. We are on an adventure and Al and I and the kids are alone in a foreign country. There is nobody to blame and nobody else. I feel a spark of the old magic trying to ignite. In the shadow of the palm fronds and newness I'm hesitant but hopeful.

In the morning, after the bank machine, we stop at Ugly Duckling car rental. Getting a car takes some cajoling as we are from another country and have no credit cards. We eventually leave Al's birth certificate and they agree to let us have a car. True to their advertisement it is an ugly old green Valiant, but she runs. Next stop, to buy sleeping bags. This takes the better part of the afternoon as we wander around the sporting goods store just taking it all in. After a supper at Bob's Big Boy we find an out of the way park. We sleep, the four of us snuggled together under a tree and awake to the thick sweet dripping smell of eucalyptus.

We go for breakfast and Al asks around for work and finds some under the table renovation job. The guy Al is working for has a trailer we can stay in. It's a construction trailer; he says he's a Christian. Nice friendly guy. There are guard dogs at the trailer but Al has a way with animals and they don't bother us at all. We nickname them, 'The Smiling Dobermans.' As though they are a foreign acrobat troupe or something. We discover in the night, the trailer has fleas. We spend the next day de-fleaing and cleaning; we take turns and try keeping the kids outside. They want in so eventually we promise ice cream for their help, well Zoë's help. We've made it a temporary home and will save lots of money on hotel costs.

I spend my days taking the kids to the beach, which is about a twenty-minute drive from Hawthorne, where the trailer is located. J.J. loves to chase the geese on the sand, which I can't figure, because it burns my feet, but he rolls in it. I lose my balance in the surf and so does Zoë although we are only calf deep. The power of the water is unsettling and we will have to tread carefully. Al meets us after work and takes J.J. out into the crashing waves and their smiles shine all the way back to shore. I find a park near Redondo; it has a summer story telling program for kids two mornings a week. The storyteller has a tie that looks like a keyboard and he uses lots of sound effects. J.J. and most of the little one's can't get enough of the train whistle. But Zoë is unimpressed and prefers the story to go on.

We are looking for a car to fix up to drive up the coast. We find an ad in the local paper for a '57 Chevy wagon, blue and white and although it doesn't run Al thinks he can fix it. The couple that are selling the car have a little boy named Ronnie. He's a little younger than J.J. He is pasty white and stays in his crib, like a jail cell, with just a plastic sheet over the mattress. Ronnie's mother Evelyn is bigger and paler than I am and talks in whispers when she talks at all, which isn't often. She is hunched over like her shoulders can't come down far enough to hide her caved in heart. I have a fair bit of time to look at her because we are waiting for the car. She has some acne scars as well. On the third day I suggest maybe she could turn off the 'Wheel of Fortune' and we could take the kids to the park.

She says she never goes up to the park. She looks jumpy at the suggestion. Her husband seems a little gruff, like every day is a hard day. I wonder if she's afraid of him. She strikes me as what I imagine when I think of an abused woman, someone kind of meek. They have bars on the windows of their bungalow, as do all the houses in the area. Al is looking positively princely. He isn't scaring me at all. We are eating late at night and often go to the park in the dark of the evening. His time thing, it hasn't changed, so meals and life generally happen when they do. We discover that we can order a salad bar at Burger King and just keep refilling until we've all eaten, and even have Jell-O for desert. As long as I can roll with the punches, things seem pretty good.

He's actually doing it; he seems to be getting this car going. He has never fixed a car before and I am super impressed. I even help with the brakes. I decide that I will convince Evelyn to bring Ronnie to the park with the wading pool. Try to leave a place better than when you arrive. Get that child outside. "Is it a dangerous place?" I ask, trying to understand her reluctance.

"Well, we just don't go up there," she says as if this explains anything. Whatever it is, she's not telling. I try mom-to-mom, girl-to-girl. I get the impression she thinks I'm a weirdo and our presence is a disruption, because she shrugs a lot and doesn't offer me tea. I fight the rising self-judgment, that I am an intruder, and that these people are unhappy and sluggish because of that, and I persevere on common ground.

"Do you ever go to the beach?"

"No." and then surprisingly she looks wistful, "We did go once last year on a holiday week-end."

"Do you realize how lucky you are to live in this climate? The ocean is only a twenty-minute drive. Wow. If I lived here I'd be there everyday! Hey, we could just walk up to the wading pool; we won't be gone long. I'm going to take the kids anyway, and it would sure be great if you could show me exactly where it is." This is my last effort. And I know the lucky weather comment is predictably Canadian, our small talk can't get much worse. I think it could be called bippity–blank; I say inane bippity and she responds with blank.

"Okay," She says, "I'll ask Len."

I beam victoriously. I wonder what brought this on.Len says yes, looking a little alarmed himself. Off we go. My kids wade and splash and Ronnie seems to enjoy it as well. Mission accomplished. The car is now ready for a test run.

We are going camping tonight. We drive into the San Gabriel Canyon just as it's getting dark. The guy Al is working for told him it was a nice place and not too far. I've heard there's a road to nowhere as well as a bridge to nowhere in these parts. I hope we are not on that route. We are the only car on the road. We have no idea where we are and it's getting spooky. The landscape is just a mountainous silhouette. Al thinks we should sleep on this cliff. Perhaps not exactly a cliff, it's a half circle look out with a little rock barrier that is knee high. I'm afraid to sleep out there with an 18 month old. Al is very disappointed in me. I'm just a scared person I guess. I am the scared person in charge of reason.

Finally I do leave the car and manage the situation by staying awake to insure that no one toddles off the edge. It turns out to be worth it. In the early morning sun the view is the most spectacular mountain range of desert-like golden hues, and all the more so because it had been impossible to see the night before. Zoë sees fairies. Al is magic for choosing the spot. I'm never sure why I get so nervous; especially afterwards when Al puts his arm around me and says, "See, I told you there was nothing to worry about." There are no lines out here, and the merging of our instincts is a murky business because I am unable to trust. That was not exactly camping, except as defined by the use of sleeping bags.

A few days later, faith imbued from surviving the cliff, we are sitting on a picnic table in a beachside park. We are far enough from the surf that the summer sea breeze is as gentle as our lives have become. I hear myself ask how it was sleeping with Mia; Al is mildly startled by the question. "She told you?" he asks.

"Of course she told me," I lie. "She's my friend." I discover that my barely conscious instincts had been accurate. I leave the subject alone, and after all we are beginning a new life. I just wanted to clear up that loose end. It seems I may be a squirrel, and I may be a nut lover, but I am clearly not deluded. There is consolation in that.

Al thinks he saw someone come by the trailer late last night, he said they were taking photos. I haven't seen anything and I can't imagine why this concerns us. The car is running well after a month and a half or so. It is an old surfer wagon and has quite a powerful Camaro engine with a long hertz shifter. All this to say; it goes fast. The sun has already set as we pull up to the trailer. It's been yet another predictably gorgeous California day. The heat and salty air licked by the sunset and stuck to our skin. Al thinks he has seen the mysterious photo taker (who is obviously up to no good) around late at night. He thinks we should follow this person in our car. He decides this when we are all in the car. I don't know whom we are following and an explanation doesn't seem forthcoming no matter how many times I inquire. We are racing around the streets of Hawthorne at ridiculous speeds. I am begging him to slow down. I remind him that the kids are in the car. What's wrong with him? "Is this some convoluted way to test out the potential speed of the engine?" I ask as he slams it into fourth gear.

"I can't believe you think like that, Elsie," he says and doesn't slow down at all. The engine roar echoes his focus.

"I thought I saw the car turn just up ahead," he says
"What car?"

"The guy who was taking photographs of the trailer. His car." He looks at me as if he can't believe I don't know what we're doing.

"No, I mean what kind of car? I didn't see any." I catch myself holding my breath as if I can stop his reality from slipping if I just don't breathe.

"He was going pretty fast. Shit, I think I might've lost him." Al is preoccupied.

"That's because he doesn't exist." I mutter to myself. It seems this will not be over until he decides. I grip the door-handle and pray. Eventually, after a couple more quick turns and muttering mounting frustration, we give up the chase and drive back to the trailer in silence. The sunny day, like road kill, dead in the past.

What was that? I wonder. Thank God we are leaving soon for Canada. The phone at the trailer is ringing off the hook with Mexicans crying "My keeds or hoonggry". Clearly this Christian isn't paying all his laborers. I wonder if this guy will pay Al his last pay, as our money is running out. He doesn't. We have fifty or so dollars left; apparently Al invested some of his money with a friend before we left Quebec, so we don't have as much as I'd thought. I'm disappointed in myself for not being more vigilant about getting this information before the trip.

12

King of the Road

We leave the trailer around eleven in the evening so the kids can sleep en route. Heading north, we take the I Five. It's the faster route but that will mean we won't get to see San Francisco. Somewhere between Bakersfield and Fresno we pull the car over to decide the best course of action. The back of the car is huge there is room for all of us to sleep. We muse, gee when will we get a chance to see San Francisco again? With a grin we agree somehow we'll make it, and San Francisco here we come, heading towards the 101 up the coast. Al never wants to stop driving, I'm having trouble staying awake I nod in and out trying to keep an eye on our situation and pray. I have noticed that Al is influencing me to pray more. I am all too aware it's possible to fall asleep at the wheel. He surely must be tired. He is, as it turns out, and lucky for us just after sunrise he slows down and pulls over before falling asleep at the wheel. Our luck must have changed because the police are actually very nice and just give us a warning and tell us we are not allowed to sleep at this particular spot. Now I get a turn to drive. I wake Al before the Golden Gate, 'cause I'm not crazy about driving over large bodies of water and I'd rather enjoy the heightened view.

We drive into San Francisco. It's foggy. Once we get into town and park near a little corner diner with vintage chrome tables and chairs. The waitress is in her fifties and casually dressed in loose slacks and a blouse. She carries an air of proprietorship as though she is part of the family that owns the place, or has worked here forever. She brings the high chair with her as she approaches our table, J.J. starts to howl, "I want the big boy seat!" Without a flinch the highchair is whisked away and quickly replaced by a booster seat and he settles down. Zoë looks embarrassed or left out. So I distract her by pointing out the selection of little boxes of cereal neatly lined up behind the counter. The kids want cereal in the little boxes, the one with the tiger, and Al and I order toast and cheese and coffee.

"I guess we'll have to leave pretty soon, to get as far as we can before the money runs out. Too bad 'cause I'd really like to see more wouldn't you?" I fold my toast into a sandwich and break off a piece for J.J..

"Do you want some Zozo?" Al offers. Zoë shakes her mass of matted black curls. I should really braid that hair or something, I'll do it later in the car. She will enjoy that.

"Maybe we should call someone and try to borrow some money, I don't want to get stuck in the middle of nowhere with the kids," I say.

"I'm not calling anyone. It'll be fine," says Al. I am not reassured.

"Why are we getting stuck, Mummy?" pipes in Zoë looking concerned.

"We are not getting stuck, Zoë." Al says and shoots me the not in front of the kids look.

"What would we stick to?" says Zoë, the hazel flecks in her brown eyes leap at her joke.

"Cereal, I guess." I say laughing and pointing to J.J. who is wearing at least as much as he's eaten. The tension is eased except for J.J. who is only half smiling and seems vaguely uncomfortable that we are laughing at him. Then after a moment he joins in too.

"I'd say we're stuck together," says Al and looks at Zoë and then me, soft and sweet, closed mouth smile, in search of affirmation. I let out a sigh of bemused acquiescence; it's time to hit the road.

Heading up the coast is so lush. I sit in the back with the kids and untangle Zoë's hair, she whines a bit, when there's a knot but she's being pretty patient. I weave the three strands, first on the left and then she crawls over my lap for the other side.

"Then I can do J.J.'s, right Mommy?" She gently puts her recently removed, pink bow barrettes into J.J.'s still blond baby curls. I think, live it up, because I'm sure he won't be going in for barrettes indefinitely.

"Hey they match his pink shorts, Zoë," I say and J.J. smiles touching his shorts.

"They're *my* pink shorts." Zoë corrects me.

"Well, you don't need them anymore, sweetie." Avoiding what I know will be her grim face about the old favourite shorts, I climb over into the front seat and rest my bare feet on the dash in front of me. Rolling down the window, I settle in for a smoke and a moment with the passing view. There is a light blue hue that seems infused into the morning *mistical* air. This must be the air of promise. I look over at Al and he smiles sideways at me and I know, we love this moment and in doing so love each other. The car radio plays a John Prine tune,

"Move to the country, throw away the TV, have a lot of children, feed 'em on peaches, try to find Jesus, on our own." Al and I sing along, I love the connecting glance I get for the chorus and Zoë and J.J. chime in for the "feed em on peaches" line.

"Throw away the TV . . ."

Just inside Oregon, we see a hitch–hiker. He's wearing a squarish army green cap, out from under which hang two long light brown braids. I look at Al and he nods back in unspoken agreement. This is an easy one, part of our mutual belief system. Al pulls the car onto the shoulder just past the hitchhiker. As he saunters towards the car with just the right amount of gratitude in his stride I notice a medium size black and white mutt following at his heels. He assures us his dog, Astro, is a people lover as he climbs into back seat saying hi to the kids. They are both uncharacteristically quiet until Astro breaks the ice by wagging his tail, tickling J.J.'s face. J.J. giggles and reaches out for Astro without hesitation. Zoë watches her little brother's successful interaction before petting the dog herself. I watch the dog silently but carefully for character flaws. He sits up straight like royalty and allows the kids to gush over him. I relax. Rebbie introduces himself and we do the same.

"This is a great car. I got a Chevy myself. What year is this? '57?" He asks revealing a chipped front tooth.

"Yeah, original paint, but it's a Camaro engine," says Al glancing at the rear view mirror.

"57 huh, that's the year the Nomad came out isn't it? But this isn't the Nomad is it? This one's a four door."

"Nope it's not the Nomad," says Al, holding apology out of his voice.

"It used to be a surfer wagon," I add even though I'm not sure why this might be of interest. The idea that a car has a history, that people were having fun in it. I suppose that appeals to me. Gives the car meaning. Maybe it's the imaginary allure of tanned wave seekers. "What's the big deal about the Nomad?" I ask. Everyone we've run into that admires the car looks sad that it's not the Nomad.

"It's the Nomad," they both answer at the same time, bonding them in Chevy unison. They laugh. Al has become a Chevy guy somewhere along the way.

"I just went to get a part for my truck." Rebbie raises a paper bag triumphantly in the air, "and some inspiration." He pulls a bag of pot from his pocket.

"Inspiration's a good thing," says Al as though inspiration is something he's given a lot of thought to and this is the final conclusion.

"You got that right," chimes Rebbie. Is there a subtext, I wonder? Their tone is profound, but it's like I'm missing information.

"Where you all headed?" Rebbie asks.

"British Columbia," says Al.

"Wow, Canada, that's far. I'm just going up the road. It's a great spot man. There's a bunch of us camping by the river, you should come check it out. There's a swimmin' hole, we've got food. You'll like it. It's a great spot man."

We've got the windows all open and the warm wind and dust from the gravel road fill the car as we pull off the highway. We are at the grassy clearing beside the river in a matter of minutes; I'm surprised how remote it seems so close to the highway. Rebbie points to some other cars, in the middle of the grassy field. We swing the old Chevy alongside the other cars, easy as a summer day. I can see people nearer to what looks like it could be water.

Rebbie introduces us around. There are nods and smiles of welcome as we follow him, past people sitting dangling their legs off rocks protruding in the water or others on the shore tending to their campsites. Al and I exchange elated glances. I've got J.J. in my arms. He is wriggling to be put down. He's getting heavy anyway.

"Are there any kids here?" asks Zoë hopefully. I put the question to Rebbie but he doesn't hear me, so I motion for Zoë to wait a minute. J.J., once down, immediately chases Astro, squealing with delight, calling,"Astro! Astro!"

Rebbie proudly shows us his fifty something burgundy Chevy pick-up which he is in the process of repairing. He puts the paper bag on the seat of his truck. "She's a beaut, in't she?" He pats the door affectionately.

Al runs his hand along the panel of the pick-up in smooth agreement. "Back east it would be nothing but a rust bucket by now."

"Are there any other kids around?" I ask again. Rebbie looks surprised to see me, like I've just appeared. He looks around, "Hmm, I don't see any." He pauses like he thinks some could materialize, looking around with just his eyeballs and no head movement.

"Y'all wanna go for a swim?" he asks enthusiastically. I go and get the kids and myself into our swimsuits and return to the truck where Al and Reb are getting inspired.

I shake my head, "No thanks," to the offer to partake. Always nice to be offered. He is anxious to show us his treasured swimming spot. And we are pleased to be shown. The path down to the swimming hole is lined with long grasses blowing a gentle welcome as the smell of fresh water cools our nostrils in anticipation. The pond itself is a calm clear green with overhanging trees and a rock, big enough for two, protruding near the center. Rebbie seems friendly enough but directs most of his conversation to Al as though they're old friends. Old hippy Chevy pothead friends. He reassures me that there are no under currents or anything to fear. I relax and splash with the kids near the shore. Reb, Al and I take turns demonstrating our prowess at rock skipping, whilst Zoë and J.J. do their small chubby handed version of the same. I really want to swim to the rock and Al watches Zoë and J.J. as I swim out. I make it to the rock. It's not far, but there's something about swimming away. I wave back to the shore, triumphant, enjoying the momentary time alone, the rock warming my legs, fresh and goose bumpy from the water.

This couple that seems to live here. Cheyenne and Freya have built a makeshift oven out of the round river rocks. It looks like a little cave, with rocks on the bottom closed in part to support the fire. They have a big pot of rice and veg and generously insist there is enough. I like this way of thinking. My mother always said if there's rice for one there's rice for ten. I never really figured out what she meant. Rebbie adds "I tole y'all there's plenty." We decide this is a good spot to spend the night. There's a campfire; people are playing guitars, and bongos, there's a small basket of maracas and shakers as well. There are more people milling around, with more names then I can keep track of. I make a bed for the kids in the back of the car, which is parked within sight. J.J. falls asleep in my arms fighting it 'til the last lid finally wins. Zoë convinces Al to play Puff the Magic Dragon as she knows all the words, she always stands up to sing, hands seriously at her sides, her feet turned slightly out. Her newly braided hair gives her an uncharacteristic tidy air. Al plays more guitar, and Rebbie sings louder and louder as the night wears on, and the joints go round.

Zoë's choice of song provokes the predictable debate over the lyrics. I wait for it, and then Rebbie says while inhaling,

"You all know what that song's really about huh?" and the laughter rings on cue with his exhale. Ha ha. I'm relieved Zoë doesn't ask what they are talking about. It's like Rebbie has a crush on Al. "That's right huh, Al knows what I'm saying" or "Al, here, he knows what's goin' on. Chevies is where it's at brother." I feel somewhat guilty for thinking Rebbie is a bit of an idiot as he has been nothing but the nicest host, a godsend in fact. And he has a wonderful dog with a cool name. A godsend that is irritating-now is that an oxymoron or maybe an Omni moron? What is the matter with me? I will try harder not to judge. It's time for Zoë and me to snuggle in next to J.J.. and leave Al by the fire.

"That was very good singing sweet pea."

"That's because I know the very whole song," she explains. "A lot of the grown-ups don't know all the words."
Although there are several people camping down here, the only vehicles seem to be one R.V, and Rebbie's almost fixed truck, and

ours. In the morning Rebbie knocks gently on our car window, he glances by me with his familiar look of disbelief at my existence, and says to Al, "That guy with the big R.V over there can't get it started man. He needs a boost. Would you mind man? My truck's not quite fixed yet or I'd do it myself. I tole him you probably wouldn't mind helpin' him out." So we give him a boost. God is surely looking after us. This guy is grateful beyond what is warranted gives us fifty bucks American, which we wish we were in a position to not accept. Gratitude. It looks like we'll make it after all, on a whim and a proverbial prayer. Rebbie gets his truck going just in time to announce he's coming with us to Canada. "I think it'd be a good thing to go to Canada. There's not so many guns up there and cool people, What're the cops like up there? You all're cool; it'd be jus fine to go up there. It's perfect that I got my truck going! We'll have a Chevy convoy! Do you think it'd be hard to find a place to crash?"

I don't feel cool.

A lot of crazy people think Al is great. He is very sensitive to them and seems to speak their language. While I appreciate this sensitivity I do feel left out when this happens. It's like I'm not there. It's as though he's King of the crazies and I'm a Queen in exile and I'm the only one who knows I'm a Queen and I keep forgetting. It reminds me of before we left Quebec and Al had his blues band; the guitar player Phil was a genius musician who happened to be schizophrenic. Al was the only one he trusted. Apparently when Phil played he would sometimes get musically derailed and Al could bring him back with the bass line. The other band members included Rob the cokehead drummer and a real live old black blues guy from the Delta named Moose. The old guy would sometimes play "I found my Thrill on Blueberry Hill" on the kids' toy piano in our tiny living room, as he intermittently promised Al and the band *the big time*. "We all gonna be big stahs, yesirreee." Plink plink. I was constantly being accused of not really knowing what the "blues" were. I guess I didn't have time what with cleaning up the cans of corned beef our blues king so loved.

It's true, I couldn't really relate to any of them. Whenever Phil had an episode he would call Al, who seemed to be able to make sense of what seemed to me like nonsense; people who weren't visible, messages, as though Al himself had one foot in that world. Perhaps he'd missed his calling. The band disbanded when Phil tried to cook his round record albums on the round stove burners. Finally, talent or no, he returned to the hospital. I guess Phil couldn't reconcile the worlds even with musical accompaniment.

This river character, Rebbie, has a similar feel, and even though he has been gracious I find myself saying, "Y'know Rebbie, we'll be staying with family so we really can't offer you a place or anything, as much as we'd like to help you out." He doesn't seem to be able to register what I've said and again I feel like he's surprised I'm there. He heads toward his truck and I turn to Al, "You'd better talk to him, Al. He thinks he's your long lost brother or something."

"I can't stop him from going to Canada. It's a free world, Elsie."

After a couple of hours of a new family game of 'spot the Rebbie,' we pull into a gas station for some gas and snacks. Rebbie pulls in behind us. J.J. is asleep and Zoë wants to choose her drink and has gone into the store with Al. I get out to stretch my legs when he walks up and addresses me. Now I'm sure I look just like him, surprised that he is there, talking to me.

"Hey," big grin." I was wondering if you could put this paper bag under your seat for me or somethin', 'cause you're from there, it probably won't be a problem, I'll give you like half or somethin'." He actually seems to think this is reasonable.

"Gee, I'd love to help you out man, but we have the kids and it really doesn't make any difference where you're from when you cross with dope," I say more gently then I feel.

"Oh, so do you think I'd be okay then with it just under my seat? "

"It's your life. You do know you could get busted don't you?" His eyeballs roll to the left in response to the chimes on the store door. Al has come back from paying for the gas and getting the kids a drink. Zoë is jumping on the hose, her light weight failing to create the desired "ding, ding."

"What d' ya think Al? About the pot I mean d' ya think I'd be okay?"

Al is actually thinking. I am ready to grab my hair and run screaming around the gas station embodying my frustration with lunacy. Al manages to convince him that it's not the best plan and they say their good-byes. I wave as Rebbie heads back from whence he came and we continue north. It seems it only took him two hours to come up with that plan.

13

Tuesday Afternoon

I've just seen the sign for a tree so big you can drive through it. There's a painted image of a nineteen fifties family, mom and pop and little Jack and Sally waving pleasantly from their car, similar to ours, poking out one side of a tree. All American. I think they are wondering, "Good Lord, what's next, eating in our cars!" Strange thing to want to do, people seem to be obsessed with doing things without having to get out of the car, none the less I want to stop and check it out.

"We might as well, who knows when we'll be in these parts again, or how long the tree will be here," agrees Al. "You guys wanna drive through a tree?" He puts the question to the back seat.

"Yeah!" says J.J. mimicking his father's enthusiasm. "I drive!"

"Drive through a tree? How? " Zoë is suspicious, "He's teasing, right mummy?"

"No, it's real, you'll see," I add.

It costs two dollars. It's amazing how enjoyable something can be if I could just not think. So I keep it down to "I wonder how the tree feels about this?" It's a majestically huge red cedar, so tall you get dizzy looking for the top, and clearly a little more than the width of a car. The warm aroma of cedar is practically visible in the sunshine and twinkles toward your nose. It takes less than a minute to actually drive through the trunk, it's a concept thing and the kids don't even want to do it again. Closer to the tree there's a sign that explains the money goes to help preserve the forest, so I feel better. This is the martyr tree. I guess a martyr doesn't necessarily give permission. There is a picnic table nearby and it looks like a toy in relation to the tree. We decide not to stop here though; it feels too commercial. "I didn't think there was gonna to be a hole in it," says Zoë disappointed, "I thought it was gonna be magic."

       I'm spending most of the drive with my teeth clenched and dozing on and off throughout the night. Why he insists on driving well past the point of fatigue is beyond me. He gives in to sleep after some predawn cajoling so I'm finally driving. The sun is rising, everyone is sleeping, I'm listening to Cat Steven's Peace Train on the radio. We are coming up through Blaine to the Peace Arch border. It's somewhat warm and quiet on my insides when my loved ones are sleeping peacefully on the outside. I am really liking this peace theme I've got going on. I wonder if it is something like patriotism that makes me feel relief at the sight of the border. Maybe it's just the feeling of completion, we made the trip, yeah, that's more like it, crossing the finish line. The giant white Arch that straddles the borders of the U.S and Canada was erected as a monument to world peace. Kind of gives me hope, although how an imaginary line symbolizes peace isn't clear, still I feel a little sentimental. I imagine a committee of nicely dressed conformists planning a monument, and for a minute I'd like to be in that club. I must need sleep. I'm awfully far from home, but I have some friends here. It'll be nice to meet Al's brother and Al did promise we'd get counseling. I wonder if he'll remember. I doubt it'll be an easy subject to broach somehow. Al stretches and hands over his I.D. The customs official asks us if we have anything to declare and I show him the paperwork for the car and the kid's birth certificates. Satisfied, he smiles "Welcome back to Canada, have a nice day," and waves us through. I'm relieved Al isn't driving, his track record with authority being what it is.

       We arrive in Cedar Park where Al's family live. He's awake now and directs me to his brother Rick's house in one of the new developments. It's still early when we arrive, around eight or so and I'm a little nervous to wake them up, but Al is confident we'll be well received.

Very tall Tara, Rick's wife answers the door. Whenever Al mentioned her that's what he would say, "VeryTallTara." Like it was her name, and now I can see how it couldn't be helped, she's at least six foot and bony thin. Everything about her is straight up, including her short styled hair.

"Oh, my God! Al, hi, come in, come in." She ushers us all inside the large new home.

"This must be J.J..," she says to the barely awake J.J. perched on my hip. "And you are Elsie of course, and here's Zoë." She leans way down to look Zoë in the face, Zoë backs up a bit. We smile and I say,

"Well you're sure good with names." Wishing I was better with introductions. She smiles. She thinks we are vagabonds, I can tell. In lumbers Rick, just woken up. He has the same light colouring as Al, but not the poetic air. He's a little heavier which makes him seem shorter but when they stand beside each other they are practically the same height. Rick's jaw is more set and square and his hair cropped closer. They don't embrace, but move towards one another as though the intention is enough. Al introduces us. We are all standing around when I notice the absence of furniture, except for a round kitchen table and wooden armchairs. Tara notices me noticing and quickly says, "We couldn't afford furniture *and* the house." As if this is a common sacrifice. I've always found furniture or got it second hand. I'm confused.

"You are planning to get some eventually aren't you? You sure have a lot of rooms to fill!" and then I think this might be rude so I add, "Hey, if you have kids, they'll have more room to play and you won't have to worry about the new furniture." This is no better, I quickly realize. Maybe they can't have kids or don't want them or something.

"Of course that's not a great plan 'cause then you'd have to wait for them to grow up, kind of long range." Everyone is looking at me and I decide there is no undigging the hole so I stop talking, looking at Al for rescue. But it's Rick, who says,

"Do you have a place to stay? You are more than welcome here, if you have sleeping bags. As you can see we've got the space. Three bedrooms plus a basement apartment, but that's rented." He offers up the room.

"I guess it's lucky for us, you don't have furniture." I grin, still in the hole of absent social graces.

These people are DINKS, (double income no kids.) They are also dinks. They are trying to undo what they believe to be parenting mistakes by explaining to my four year old that she couldn't possibly have seen fairies.

"It's important that children distinguish between reality and fantasy." Very Tall Tara lectures down to me after Zoë excitedly told them about her special part of the trip.

I'm thinking that seeing fairies is a wondrous thing and wondering how to make that ideology explainable. Zoë pipes in, "Well, I've seen them," so matter of fact, that I realize there is no fear of conversion. She then gives me the look that has already accepted that some grown-ups are just plain limited, and I am rescued. Al stands up for Zoë as Rick starts in, "Fantasy can be dangerous…"

"Rick, shut-up. Thanks for letting us stay here, but Zoë can see whatever she sees and we're good with that." Rick looks ready to call the anti-fairy police.

At dinnertime J.J. climbs onto the chair and reaches for the pickles that are sitting in the center of the table, earlier I had snuck one myself. J.J. is severely reproached by Rick. But the criticism is for me. Haven't I taught him to wait? If I make room for your philosophy does that leave me pickleless and fairy free? My beliefs suggest I should make room, do yours? I think about voicing this, but don't. It's their house.I am slightly humiliated and make a mental note to be aware of what this feels like.

"He's not yet two," I say feigning apology. My stress level is mounting as I remove J.J. allowing time for him to get a firm grip on the pickle. I'm beginning after several days to glean that we are a bit of a project for this couple. Rick sees his brother as needing direction.

"Al, you've got to make a plan."

"Maybe I'll open my own café," says Al dreamily.

"You've tried that already and it was a dismal failure. You've got to get organized, you've got to be more realistic with your dreams."

Ooh, ouch, I'm anxious to hear Al's response.

"I'd need some financial help, Rick, you could be part owner, like a silent partner. Or better yet, have some vision. It could be a true cooperative, with artists and musicians and anyone who wants adding to the mix. And you know that I was ripped off in that restaurant. They said it was a turn key operation and then it needed all kinds of stuff, they said they'd be there and I was left high and dry." He sounds anguished. I've never heard about this restaurant attempt.

"I have other obligations, to this house and my wife." Rick is smug. "We have plans to pay everything off and then have children. We're both working really hard."

"Good thing you've got a young wife, eh?" I say trying to lighten things up. But their eyes are locked on one another. Al doesn't seem to have heard Rick.

"I was thinking I could fix the boat up and maybe have a floating co-op." He looks hopeful, leaning in as though there is an actual plan being made.

"Oh yes 'the boat.'" Rick makes quotations in the air.

"I'm planning to go back to school," I interject hoping that's practical enough to end this discussion. They don't hear me.

"You've never even seen it Rick," points out Al, somewhere between pouting and anger.

"Al, let's take the kids to the park. Tara says there's one by the water with a big whale climbing thing." Al looks somewhat relieved, but a little like he was cut off before scoring the big point or something. We have to find a place to live.

The park is right on the ocean and the salty scent of seaweed permeates the air. J.J. has found a stick and is launching large flat pieces of seaweed willy-nilly. One just misses Zoë and the new game is the seaweed toss. We can make marks in the sand to see how far it goes. "But not at each other," I insist. Al and I sit on the cement climbing whale that the kids have tired of. We are whale watching their game.

"That's just my family, they treat me like I'm the big loser. They can't even see themselves. Rick is fundamentally unhappy and hiding behind his big house, all for security." Al is on a negative track.

"He is a bit of a grump, but he's fun to debate with. I think he just doesn't like his job as a bartender, since he has a degree and everything." I try to commiserate. Sometimes I feel closer to Al when we encounter people who only seem to embrace one way of doing things. At least Al can be open.

"Nah, he's always been like that, serious and disappointed." He drags his foot in the sand, "They just don't get *it*."

Ah oh, I know this track, I don't even want to ask what 'it' is.

VeryTallTara graciously offers to watch the kids while we go house hunting. She is softer when Rick isn't home. We decide to walk and look for signs around town, or people who might know a place for rent. This is Al's method of wandering around with your antenna up and letting things come to you. I begin to understand why everything always takes him so long. The idea of getting a newspaper seems to surprise him. On the way back we get into a discussion about all the people who once again don't get it and are against Al. There's Dan his friend back east who would probably take a better deal out from under you and not admit it. There's Rick who has no faith. There's an old love interest Janna who I am dangerously like, she is too independent. And then there are those assholes at the Calliloo who don't appreciate talent. I just can't muster enough resentment toward all these people and so I'm seemingly disloyal. I am being fueled by an indignant attitude that I know can be annoying.

"You can't force me to hate Dan, or Janna. I don't want to see what you see." A small part of me hopes I'm not blind. Al pushes me, I stumble and fall hard onto the sidewalk, and my hands and knees scrape on the cement. I turn over and look up at "the face", the one I've come to fear.

"You're not listening! You can't see the truth! You're always defending everyone else!" He snarls in frustration.

"Get up Elsie," he commands as though he's had nothing to do with my sudden change in stance. I raise my bum so the weight of me rests in my arms and legs and I am now crab walking backward on the sidewalk. My eyes dart around almost hoping some suburbanite will rush from their home yelling, "Hey there, you can't do that." Failing that rescue I think I could just get up and try to make all this better, agree or something. But I just want to run. So that's what I do. But not before yelling, "I said, you can't do that!" I flip over into a start position and sprint off.

"Elsie! Ah, for Christ's sake, don't take off. You're freaking out for nothing!" He yells after me.

Adrenalin pumps through my veins propelled by an anger that dodges behind houses and weaves through sparsely treed back yards. I mustn't go too far. I don't want to get lost. I find refuge in a side yard behind a red brick chimney that climbs the side of a house. This is ridiculous. Tears well up; anger was so much more comfortable than this mix of humiliation and fear and loneliness. I get that he wants me on his team, but it is just too negative. I'm not sure where to go or what to do next. I curse the housing development for not leaving enough trees to cover my movements. I must be crazy to have gone back to him, here I am three thousand miles from home, sobbing behind a chimney hiding from the man I supposedly love. This is not the alternative lifestyle I'd had in mind. I take a deep breath, wipe my eyes on my shirt. I've got to get back to the kids.

I venture back to the sidewalk, trying to look casual, I see the house just a few doors down. I come through the door tear stained, a little out of breath and out of patience. I decide to risk confiding in Tara, sealing disloyalty as a trait. "Did Al come back?"

"No, he's not here. I thought you two were together." She looks puzzled. "What's wrong?"

"How were the kids?" How do I explain? They run into the kitchen, Zoë on J.J.'s heels.

"Are you Okay Mommy?" asks Zoë, "Are you okay Mommy?" echoes J.J..

"Yes, I'm fine, you two want to play in the backyard for a bit?"

"I didn't want to leave them out there alone. We were out earlier though…" She trails off.

"No sweat, we can see them from here." The kids go out and I explain to her what's happened, ending with, "You can't just go around pushing people, can you?"

"Well, I don't know what to tell you, being in a couple requires patience. Once in an argument Rick slapped me in the face," she confesses. "But we talked about it and it did only happen the one time."

"Weren't you afraid it would happen again?" I ask. "How hard was it?" I'm echoing Mia.

"Well, yes, I was very afraid and it was plenty hard enough thank-you very much. But thank heavens it hasn't happened again. I told him I'd leave him if it did." She glares straight at me unblinking. It's not a fun memory and I vaguely appreciate her sharing although the glare feels like a thick line daring me to cross. I do.

"I guess the real question is, have you disagreed again?" She gets up and takes a plate to the sink and then surprisingly turns, and we are on the same team for a moment. "Truthfully, I'm probably more careful how I phrase things, maybe you need to learn that. It takes two. I'm not saying it's okay what he did mind you."

"The part I don't get about it takes two, is when exactly do we get to hit them?" she looks confused, so I add, "If we weren't so aware of their potential lack of control it would be a smack for a smack, not that that's how I want to live either, I've never actually hit anyone, have you?"

"Not really" she says, we are both quiet, thinking of a sibling, I'm certain.

I break the silence, "I guess what I'm saying is; the power is in causing the fear." She nods in agreement and I change the subject as the kids come back in asking for cookies.

I've long since returned from taking the kids on another round of park hopping.I'm waiting for Al to come home from yet another round of house and or job hunting. We are expected at his Mother's for dinner. VeryTallTara and Rick aren't home. It's getting on for eight o'clock, the kids and I have been nibbling on crackers and cheese to keep our appetites at bay. Al finally arrives. I don't have the energy to verbalize the familiar frustration at being late and the kids have so far been shielded from most of it. I hope that a nice meal will calm me down. We pile into the car, Al chatting enthusiastically about his mother's cooking.

"Isn't it a bit late to arrive for dinner, Al, shouldn't we call or something?" I ask, keeping my potential humiliation barely concealed.

"Relax, Else it'll be fine." He's relaxed. "It's my mother, they'll be happy to see us." A deep sigh escapes, but I look out the window. It's only fifteen or so minutes of quelling my urge to scream. We are driving through the short windy streets of posh new development named after rivers, Fraser Street, Lawrence Street, Salmon Avenue, and then on Courtney Crescent we turn into the driveway. Al's mother greets us at the door, she is much shorter and wider than I expected.

"Ally, my big baby!" she shrills reaching up to give him a peck hello. "And *his* baby!

"Come to Gramma, J.J." she says, the fatty part under her arms jiggles with anticipation and surprisingly J.J. transfers from Al to his mother without complaint. Genetic trust?

"Come in to the den, Zoë, you too sweetie-pie. I didn't think you were coming." She says this back over her shoulder as we follow her past the Cinderella staircase, and into the den.

"Al, you remember Stan." Stan nods and mutters a deep hello that seems to come more from his beard than his mouth; he's watching T.V. from his lazy boy and pushes the leg rest back into the chair, sitting, as acknowledgement of our presence. "Your mother thought you'd decided not to come," he states.
I have no explanation for our tardiness other than it happens all the time, so I say nothing and smile uncomfortably shifting my weight. Mother to the rescue,

" I'll just heat up dinner in the microwave. Aren't they a huge convenience? We use ours all the time, you can even cook in it, it came with a cookbook y'know." The lingering smell of a roast dinner is making my mouth water and I don't offer my thoughts on radiated food.

Gramma has a Jacuzzi bathtub and so Al decides to give the little guy a bath. Zoë is chatting with Stan about whatever's on T.V, he's quite good with her, letting her change the channels. "Would you like to see the house? It's all new, we just finished building last year," Al's Mom Dorothy, leads the way out of the kitchen. "Almost ready to put it on the market."

"It looks gorgeous," I say.

"You can't imagine the work," she tells me.

"No," I agree, "probably not."
I try to stay focused, as she points out all the oak, oak cupboards,

oak stairs and even some oak floors. "It's very good value," she explains as we go upstairs. "Good for resale," she instructs.

"It's a lovely home Dorothy, why do you want to sell it?" I wonder aloud.

"Oh, we'll build another dear, that's what we do, Stan's very good at it," she nods agreeing with herself. I've never before encountered this. I always thought a home was a home; I'd never seen it as an investment. I'm not sure I like so much oak.

"I'm just going to check on Al and J.J.." I head towards the upstairs bathroom. Al doesn't normally give J.J. his bath. The jets are on and J.J. is happy to play with the button to turn them on and off. Al is being so normal that I'm thrown off. I feel out of whack, like I've walked through a looking glass. What I would've thought would be a wonderful relief is manifesting as massive confusion.

All of a sudden standing there in the bathroom watching him with his son I get it. It's like a light bulb lit atop my head. With the warm home cooked smell and a warm paternal moment I am losing my marbles. I see it so clearly, maybe it's the stress of having to be somewhere when we said we would, maybe it's the last couple of years I don't know. What I do know is, "You never wanted me at all…you just wanted the baby…that's why I don't feel loved…you never loved me…. that's why all the talk of family is so impersonal. It doesn't matter who I am. It's just a role I play." I stumble out of the bathroom. He's screaming after me that I'm crazy, I don't care, and I keep running right out the front door sobbing. I have caused a scene, what is the matter with me? Al is pretty quick because I don't even make it past the curb. He picks me up and throws me against the car door; the window shatters behind me. I don't feel much pain and I think those old nineteen fifties windows must shatter easily. "You can't leave J.J.. alone in the bath!" I scream, panicking.

"My mother is with him." Al looks shocked that I might even suggest such a thing. I am still sobbing when I notice Stan at the door. Stan orders Al back inside, his voice a full bellow bypassing the beard entirely. Al turns around saunters by Stan back through the front door. They don't acknowledge one another.

"Did you see that?" I ask straightening my shirt and myself.

"I did," he says. "It's not right. We'll walk a bit." He starts slowly down the sidewalk and I follow along.

"But I was acting a little crazy," I venture; I want to make sure his comment will hold water in the aftermath. I want to make sure he doesn't think I asked for it. Even if I was emotional.

"A man should never do that kind of thing," he says in monotone still looking straight ahead. He isn't the warmest guy in the world but right now these few words are golden and I thank him. We go back inside. The kids are playing in the den. Gramma says we are all to have a drink and everybody calm down. I'm quiet and accept the glass of Cognac, which is both warm and strong going down. The glass and the liquor itself add to the surrealism I've been swimming in since I arrived. I feel satisfied that someone, anyone has seen Al in action. I feel ashamed of myself because I am happy to have "outed" him in a sense, closet tormentor of mine. But no one mentions that he threw me at the car. I look to Stan; he stares without emotion. Al is his wife's son after all; he's not saying a word.

14

People Get Ready

I had promised myself, I wasn't going to live like this when we left Quebec. And now here I was. No councilling, no improvement. And now no home. Fall has moved through us, more yellow than red here. We need to come up with a plan. I decide to go visit a childhood friend who lives in northern B.C. to take a break after the car incident. Katrina has two kids as well. We both started young at different ends of the country. She married the father after her son Brian was born. They have a big house, she says, with plenty of room and is excited to have me come. She sends me a train ticket. We giggle at the prospect of taking the kids trick or treating as we did as children. Al doesn't argue with the idea at all. The fall is in it's late stages already. Not nearly as dramatic as back east. The threat of winter is not even a threat here. At Katrina's further north it will be getting colder. Now is probably good timing all around.

"If that's what you need to do Elsie, I'll look for a place for us while you're gone." He doesn't have much choice than to agree with me, as he knows I'm mulling over leaving him again. Somehow we are getting a place, and maybe breaking up at the same time. Just carrying on as if the timeline of life will take care of the unspoken details. We are not ready to decide much.

"It'll be much easier this way on Very Tall Tara and your brother, don't you think?" I sound decided. We are very civilized in handling this decision and it gives me some hope that he can learn.

Kat greets me at the train and we giggle like excited kids driving down the country roads to her property. "Seventeen acres," she tells me proudly as we pull up to the large green square house. We make Halloween costumes for the kids, Zoë wants to be a fairy princess and her Brian will be a skunk. The babies will be clowns; her little girl Franny is just months older then J.J.. We take the kids trick-or-treating, driving the large distance between country homes. We talk about stuff we did when we were kids, and the fun of running from house to house on our own.

"Remember, when you and Claire dared me to run down the street without my shirt and then you guys locked me out of the house." She fakes outrage but it's mostly all fake. "And then dangled my shirt behind the door!" Kat always was such a good sport, such an easy laugh.

"Oh yeah, I'm so sorry about that Kat, although you didn't seem that mad about it then, you must've been, I've apologized at least ten times over the years!" I'm laughing guiltily, remembering her banging on the door and how she was always taking her shirt off. "How old were we, eleven?"

"Around that, and what could I do, might as well laugh, but you guys were mean that day. I would do anything on a dare though, wouldn't I?"

"Yeah, you would, you'd beg for them, *Dare me! Dare me!*" I imitate her. "But only one of us could play with Claire it was either me or you, one of us was getting left out."

"True, do you think it was the only child thing?" she asks.

"Maybe, do you remember our Moms were so sick of seeing us cry at her hands that they tried to make us hang out together instead?" I add.

"I didn't find out until later that it wasn't our idea, probably a good thing," she says.

"Well, we both agreed she had better toys. And she was fun."

"I guess their plan worked because here we are, and neither of us has spoken to Claire in years." We high five.

She cans her own food, beans and salmon. She proudly shows me the cold storage in the basement.

"Wow, Kat you're a real country wife," I say smirking but she knows that I am truly impressed. "When did you learn to do all this?"

"My sister in-law taught me; the whole family does it," she announces hands on hips, straw like blond hair all attention to task. She works really hard, cleaning the house every day. I help. She laughs wholeheartedly. She scares me when she yells ferociously at her kids for which she makes no apology. Every Mother has her own way I suppose. She seems to take this domestic life very seriously, a way of earning her keep, doing her part. Maybe I don't understand it because I've never lived in a large house that required this much care. My own mother used to say, 'Play with your kids, the dust and dirt will be there long after you're gone.' She had cleaned a lot and found it didn't keep her marriage or her soul intact. Katrina's parents stayed together. Maybe she knows something I don't know. I'm soft with the kids and I don't like domestic pressure, although I've never been kept, in any way that felt like this seemed. I think I might prefer another job. "I don't want my husband to be my boss. I'm sure Al wants a woman more like you Kat. Is it love that makes you want to do all this? I feel I'm not tough enough. I just don't have enough to put out like that. People don't love us because of what we do, they love us for who we are."

"It's not like that Elsie, we're a team." Kat responds to my queries, "They can sure un-love you because of what you do though, right?"

"I don't know Kat, maybe it's me, but the undercurrent of fear, the dependency, they freak me out." I'm hoping she'll help me clarify some relationship questions about what's acceptable. "It can't really be okay for him to push me around."

"Oh, Elsie," She lets out a ferocious cackle. "Mike and I used to have humungous fights, we threw plates at each other, man they were wild!" She's rolling her afternoon joint. I guess it helps with mindless chores. I can't do it, because it seems to have the opposite effect and I don't focus at all. I might drift off into an internal discourse on the importance of using cutlery, and how distancing from our food might make us distanced from the earth. I tried to partake with her the other day and it was not at all motivating. I had to analyze the vacuum cleaner, as a concept.

"And you think that's normal? I mean, weren't you scared?"

"You know me Else, I don't back down from anyone, I just hurled dishes right back."

I remembered her as a girl, saucy, big boned and threatening to beat up a big boy with her newly acquired Karate skills. She had taken about four classes. It made me smile; it was so ridiculous.

"I'm just not like that, I guess I'm a dreamer, but I don't want to have to go to war to be loved. I'm beginning to feel like a bit of a wimp. Nobody said it would be like this."

"It's not like that for Mike and me anymore. We seem to have worked through that stage of our relationship." She says proudly, like she's received her brown belt in marriage. "If you love him, you love him," she states emphatically.

I'm somewhat disappointed, "Yeah, I love him or at least did, I love the soft side, the creative side."

"You have to accept all the sides Elsie."

"Maybe I'm just rebelling against domestication, avoiding it, it's possible?" I don't really believe my own argument.

"Anything's possible, but I'm telling you it's work, a relationship." Kat straightens up in a way that says we've exhausted this topic and there's work to be done.

Oh god! A frightening thought occurs to me. Is it possible to be too lazy for love? My answer runs in followed by her baby brother, "Mummy, come see our tower it's gargantuhuge!" Zoë tugs on my arm and I more than willingly follow her to the playroom.

We go out to a Halloween party. There is a little tension in the air, as her husband has to watch the kids. I feel guilty for disrupting their lives and without much money to boot. I ask, "When was the last time you went out anyway?" Kat dresses as a samurai and I as a hobo. We drive for twenty minutes with pine trees claiming everything but the road. The party is in a log home and cars and trucks already line the half-mile driveway when we arrive. The house is teeming with supermen, Elviras and smurfs. One guy is dressed in garbage bags; they are cut in strips, he's seaweed. I don't know anyone except Kat. It's just fun to be out with her, laughing at nothing. We have the habit of leaning over and grabbing our stomachs when we laugh. It might be her habit, but we do it together at any rate. When we come out of the party, we can't find her car; it seems to have simply disappeared. This is bizarre. We look again in the spot where we left it. It's a little Toyota Tercell, silver coloured, I remember. I scan the few feet in front of me. Barely visible in the dark of the backcountry, we see a glimmer of metal in the ditch. We lean over the ditch staring at the exposed underbelly of her little car. There is a moment of silence in which we individually check our perception to conceive of the car's position and ask ourselves how it could possibly have arrived there. It has somehow been rolled into the ditch; turned over turtle-like, helpless, as are we with no way home.

"Someone must've rolled it over, must've taken a few people I imagine. Has car tipping replaced cow tipping up here?" I ask.

"This is just great. If you weren't here, none of this would've happened!" She yells and it makes me jump. I am laughing now trying to get her to see the absurdity of the situation and the absurdity of blaming me.

"C'mon, Kat you can't seriously think this is my fault?" I'm laughing. We're a little drunk and I expect her to laugh as well. I think she is because I can't see her clearly, but as I get closer I see the clenched fists and hear,

"This is not fucking funny Elsie, Mike is going to be really pissed off."

"But Kat, you didn't do anything wrong." I say trying to make up for laughing at the wrong time.

"Just shut-up Elsie. You don't understand. Now I have to call and wake him up; we'll need a tow. I knew we shouldn't have come to this party. I just did it because you were visiting."

"Maybe we can get a lift and deal with this tomorrow, when you're not so upset?" I suggest tentatively.

"No, we can't fucking deal with it tomorrow." She sneers and I follow as we head back to the party. Kat goes off to find a phone and I ask around for anyone who might be heading back in our direction. I find a neighbour and friend of Kat's and after I explain more than once that the car has been rolled over into the ditch, he agrees to give us a ride. Kat comes back from the upstairs phone. I look to her, waiting.

"He says to try and find a ride, and we'll deal with it tomorrow."

I don't say a word all the way home.It seems it's not only Al who doesn't like my reactions. Her anger gradually subsides which is nice cause I'm leaving the next afternoon. We are parting friends as always and she gives me some of her home canned salmon and crackers for the trip. This way I can really be a visitor that smells like fish after over staying. I wish I could visit a family I could emulate. Katrina's family when we were kids was very warm and no one yelled. I loved that.

Kat drops us off at the train station; I thank her and tell her I hope my visit wasn't too much. She says it wasn't. She says she's sorry she freaked out, and of course it wasn't my fault. I'm not sure I believe her, but we hug and promise to keep in touch. The kids and I end up sitting next to a friendly bearded man who introduces himself simply as Mickey. Mickey buys Kit-Kats and Smarties from the cart. He gives them to the kids. Normally they don't get junk food but it's a long ride, and dividing the Smarties into their separate colours is challenging on the jostling tray. He does those fun tricks for them like pull a nickel from behind their ears and makes it look as though he pulls his long bony thumb apart. He's clearly had a few, but seems harmless and entertaining. It's a scenic train ride that follows the Fraser River. From the window it's a sheer steep drop to the water. It is a steep and windy track back to my partner. After a couple of hours, Mickey runs out of whatever he's got in the bag and he wanders on up to the bar car. About a half hour out of Vancouver the conductor comes over to my seat.

"Excuse me, M'am, but your husband is seriously intoxicated, and I'm afraid he's bothering the other passengers. Could you please come and get him?" It takes me a moment to realize he's talking to me; as I don't think I've been called "M'am" before. It takes another second to realize he's talking about Mickey. I then answer,

"Oh that guy who was sitting with us? No, he's not my husband, I never saw him before in my life."

The conductor looks suspicious. At just this same moment Mickey comes staggering back into the car his swagger in direct opposition to the train's sway. J.J. grins at the sight of his earlier playmate and points at Mickey. "Daddy!" he cries out enthusiastically. The conductor gives me an admonishing stare for my denial. I look at J.J.. wondering why he would think that man is his daddy. Mickey topples into the seat in front of us and promptly passes out. Zoë whispers,

"That's not your dad, J.J.."

"Really, I don't know why he said that, I don't know this guy." I try to convince the conductor and the several passengers now listening in. I look from face to face for a sign that someone, anyone believes me. No one's committing either way. With Mickey passed out the conductor decides that the situation is under control and continues on down the aisle. The train soon pulls into the station and I organize the kids to disembark. We are just going down the steps off the train when I hear the familiar tone of the conductor.

"M'am, you're not just going to leave your husband here, are you?"

I herd the kids forward, responding as I go. "Yes sir, that is exactly what I'm going to do. I told you, he's not my husband!" Just then I notice Al walking up to greet us. "Who's not your husband?" demands Al.

"Everyone, I mean, just some drunk guy on the train. I'll tell you all about it on the way out."

15

Our House

Al has found us a house. It's so nice to be going to have our own place. We pull into the driveway and I'm thrilled. It is a little white house a couple of blocks from the beach. It has a big front lawn, with a little white fence with a metal gate.

"This is great Al!" I exclaim following him to the door.

"It comes furnished too," he explains while jiggling the key and pulling on the door. We walk directly into the kitchen and while it looks clean in the florescent lighting, a waft of musty smell practically throws me off balance. I try to hide my response. "I guess it's been closed up for a bit." I look to see if Al notices the smell, he doesn't seem to and I don't want to be ungrateful because I'm really not. I can see the back of the house from the front door through the curtain to a bedroom. There's no back door. The living room carpet must be the smelly culprit as it has waves of rebellion where it refuses to settle. Easily fixed, I think. Zoë and J.J. begin to explore tentatively and in moments disappear through the other curtain directly beside the one that's open.

"Mom, come see, a bed tower!" yells J.J..

"Is this our room?" asks Zoë when I walk the ten steps to find them looking at the metal framed bunk beds. I don't see a ladder.

"Yes, isn't it cool? You can have the top bunk Zoë."

"This is mine," J.J. climbs onto the bottom bunk, "mine has a roof."

"Why doesn't the wall go up to the ceiling?" asks Zoë pointing to the gap where the wall isn't."

"Not all walls go all the way up I guess, look ours doesn't either." I show her the partition wall that divides our bedroom from the living room as well. The bathroom is clean and located off the kid's room.

"Is that bathroom for J.J. and me?" asks Zoë. "It's in our room."

"No, it's for all of us. We need a bathroom as well, Zoë." Al walks into the bathroom, closing the door to punctuate his point. The old floral couch takes up the entire side of the dark musty living room. Maybe if I can get rid of the carpet it'll take care of the smell. I'll get a couch cover. That'll make it less ugly. The small windows on either end of the living room come with dark brown thick floral patterned curtains. Maybe that's why it's so dark. I guess we'll see in the morning. In the corner of the living room behind a stuffed chair that matches the couch there is a tiny black and white television set. Al and I both notice it, and acknowledge it with covert eye contact. We silently agree that we'll tell the kids tomorrow. We don't have bedding yet so we organize our sleeping bags. Al offers to do the bedtime stories tonight. I can easily hear every word of the Paper bag Princess and every giggle. I curl up on the couch with my book. I will try to be better. It seems this mate thing begs more effort than I thought. The rent is manageable with some government assistance, and Al has a line on something, he says.

It's time for Zoë to start kindergarten, a little late but she can read a little already and we are sure she hasn't missed much. There is a tiny schoolhouse directly behind us that offers private Montessori instruction. I enroll Zoë. I'm not sure how we will pay but I'm certain it'll work out somehow. It's a perfect set-up. The lane ways that run behind the houses are lined with shrubbery and we need only walk through the lane to take Zoë to school.

There is a co-op playgroup in the neighborhood for J.J. and me to attend together. It's at what they call a neighbourhood house or community center. Al met the people that run it while I was up north. He is already volunteering to cook for events and is involved with a new band, Blind Pig. I'm really happy for him because I know he loves to perform. He's been to several practices and is getting pretty excited about an upcoming gig at the community center.

"I've got to practice, Elsie," he says when I ask if he can watch the kids. But he doesn't actually practice. He watches the little black and white T.V. for a while and then goes to talk to the guy at the community center about maybe getting a job.

"This could be a really good job if it comes through, Elsie. There are lots of possibilities at the center. Larry's a good guy to know down there and we really get along."

I'm pleased to hear him so optimistic, even if he is looking for work antenna style.

"What exactly did he say Al?" I ask quietly as though any edge in my voice might break the meniscus of optimism.

"These things are delicate, Elsie, they take time. It's the way the world works. You have to be patient. Can you do that?" He is being patient with me. I just wonder why in his world asking or answering a direct question is out of the question.

We are interrupted by the phone. Al answers. I see it's for him, so I go back to finishing last night's dinner dishes. I don't like to do dishes right away. It makes me feel like the dishes are in charge somehow. There's something about getting to them in my own time. I tortured my Mother with this attitude for years. Ah oh, Al doesn't look pleased as he hangs up the phone.

"They've kicked me out." He mumbles in disbelief. "They say my "chops" aren't up to scratch."

"What're chops?" I ask. "Was that the guy from Blind Pig?"

"Yeah, that was him, Mr. Arrogance himself. He said it wasn't just his decision but I know it was him."

"What are chops?"

"Chops are my abilities, my skills as a bassist. I was playing in bands before he even knew how to play. If they'd just given me a little time to learn the tunes. He's in too much of a rush that guy."

"Well," I ask, "Are they? Are your chops good?"

"Of course," he insists. "Y'know if you were a loving and supportive wife, you'd stick up for me, stand by me in this."

I wonder how this has anything to do with me. "How?" I ask, "I've got nothing to do with this. I can feel for you though, and I know you're a good player. Maybe you just need more practice. Did you tell them that?"

"If you really want to help me out Elsie, you call him up and tell him that. That would be being supportive." He holds out the phone receiver. I want nothing more than to work on my supportive "chops". So even though this feels completely ridiculous, I do it. Of course the bandleader doesn't change his mind when I insist that Al's chops are most certainly up to scratch. Al is disappointed but for once it is not with me. It's a blurry line in the name of love.

It's Christmas Eve although it's difficult to recognize here on the west coast, no snow, no crunch or visible breath. Just the drizzle of this temperate zone. We've survived on a little welfare and some under the table catering jobs that Al has managed to hook up through Larry. We also had a few care packages from Gramma. There are clown shows to be had at this time of year for office parties and the like, and I booked quite a few. I learned to make swords out of balloons for many a Sikh boy. That helped out with buying Christmas presents and a few decorations. It's a good thing you can make a lot out of a little for young kids. Al's holiday job is to provide the tree. The how and the where are solely up to him, the when had better be very, very soon. Zoë is beside herself.

"Mommy, we NEED a tree! It's almost Christmas Morning! Where is Al?" Zoë whines, she is practically pacing, and a pacing five year old is particularly unnerving. "I want to decorate! You said!"

"He'll be here soon, sweetie, he's bringing the tree. C'mon now, have you ever not had a tree? It's Christmas, remember magical things can happen," I assure, without revealing my own doubt. It's getting on for nine o'clock and the kids are clearly cranky and disappointed. J.J. is just plain tired.

"How about we put out the cookies and milk for Santa okay Zozo? You get the cookies." We count out enough cookies for all the reindeer, which kills some time with the naming and calculating, 9 plus 'one for the Vixen,' my mother used to say so, 10. We set them on the table near the door. Zoë is somewhat consoled, but her resigned sigh inspires me to do better.

"Wait here, watch your brother, don't answer the phone or open the door, Mummy will be back in one minute," I reach for the biggest pot in the cupboard and head for the door. I take the pot into the sand and crushed stone lane and fill it about half way, as best I can in the little light available from the surrounding houses. I rush back.

"What are you doing Mummy? It's dark out there!" Zoë yells out the door.

" I'm coming, I'm getting us a tree, Zoë! It's Christmas! There," I say placing the pot inside the door. I feel quite Christmassy, if feeling Christmassy means you notice the quick bite of fresh cool air, a moment of silent night interrupted by gravel underfoot. If feeling Christmassy means noticing a moment when you decide to embrace a possibility.

"I'll be back in a minute." I scoot out for round two. Where is Al indeed! One job to do and we can't even be certain he'll come through. Oh well, I am inspired! There is no way I'm going to gamble a little girl's trust in some act of faith. Or is it a little girl's faith in an act of trust? It's Christmas, time for faith and trust in bigger things than Al. This makes me wonder why so much in this relationship relies on a kind of nervous disbelief that Zoë may in fact be catching. I head for the nearest tree and begin to pull off the biggest branches I can. There are no leaves. There is a rubbery resistance to my efforts that makes me apologize to the tree all the while ripping with all my might. I collect what seems like enough boughs and head back to the house. A glance at the night sky, I inhale some star zest that feels festive. Other people's coloured lights are in the air.

"Mummy, those are branches," Zoë remarks flatly, as though I might not be aware. J.J. is playing in the bucket and makes no comment.

"I know sweetie, watch this. We'll just put these in the pot and make a tree," I'm arranging the branches as I speak.

"Is that really a Christmas tree?" She isn't convinced.

"It will be. What makes it special is decorating it, so you go get the decorations."

We weave one strand of tiny multi-coloured lights and hang some of the tiny shiny blue, gold, and red balls on the ends of the branches. There is the not so Christmassy smell of live green wood, although the twinkle is mystical and the kid's expectations fill in the spaces. "It's minimalist," I say. "Very trendy," I add to myself.

Zoë and J.J. hang their stockings on the back of the kitchen chairs. Since there's no chimney, I've told them Santa occasionally uses the kitchen door. Finally, amidst assurances that Santa will not come until they are asleep, I tuck them in.

I sit on the couch and admire our little masterpiece of seasonal expression. I want Al to come home. Then we can put the presents under the tree together. On second thought I remember that he should've been here hours ago and so I decide to do it alone. It's an emotional potpourri; delight at the quiet twinkle, disappointment in Al's absence, satisfaction at saving the day, anger at having to, and a whiff of loneliness. I nod off on the couch, the room dimly but magically lit. The kids will be tickled pink. I hear the door open, and am roused from half sleep as Al comes in carrying a four-foot evergreen.

"I got the tree," he whispers proudly and then noticing the lights, "What's that?"
I don't answer but get up and go get a drink of water from the kitchen tap; the clock on the wall says three a.m.

"I didn't know if you were coming." No mood is formulating, I can't seem to muster enough fury to express, 'It got so late and the kids wanted a tree Al.' So I repeat "I didn't know if you were coming."

"Elsie you have to wait 'till it's late to cut the top off of someone's pine tree!" He says it like he can't believe I wasn't privy to this information. "You have no faith. C'mon let's decorate it. When the kids wake up we'll tell them Santa brought it." He's excited.

"Are you sure? Zoë might need to know that you actually came through."

He begins to dismantle my glorified boughs that look sad and grey beside the new green. I have to admit it looks better with a tree.

"It'll be a surprise, c'mon it's Christmas," he's singing softly, "joy to the fishes in the deep blue sea, joy to you and me..." He looks over at me grinning warmly, "Everybody now... If I was the king of the world..." He doesn't even want the credit. He'd rather they believe in Santa than in him. I'm not sure; I think I'd like to believe in Santa. I'd also like to believe in him. Misplaced lack of faith on my part? Sensible? What I believe is: there is a lot of stress and pain leading up to the three a.m. moment when it all turns out just fine.

It is the squeals of Zoë and J.J. that rouse us in the morning. "Santa came!!! Even a tree!!" It is then I decide to err on the side of Santa and Christmas Magic. It is their delight that rings the truest after all.

My sacrificed tree limbs were put outside last night. They got us where we needed to go. I said a little prayer in thanks for the Christmas inspiration and my star-zest moment, which could almost pass as faith.

16

Strange Fruit

The Chevy has died; costly leaf springs were what forced it to rest for the time being, in the driveway. We take the bus to the Laundromat, grocery store and walk to the beach. Al's mother brings groceries every so often to help out and offers to pay for Al to go to school. He declines. School is not for everyone. I wish she'd offer it to me. I tell myself I've got time; these years are for the kids. Zoë takes creative dance just down the road. She is such a sweet child they agree to let her continue her Montessori kindergarten even after we can't pay. We are trying to eke out some familial life. We have dinners and bedtimes and dishes and play. On Thursdays there is a local coffee house; there's beer and wine and open mike and live music. The atmosphere is generally an adult free for all. The first week I met a single Mum, Ange, her youngest is the same age as Zoë. She and I and whoever else happens to be there, enjoy a couple of tokes and go play on the playground equipment late into the night. Since I don't smoke dope regularly, for me it's all belly laughs and nonsense. Al gets to play some music. Play is good, even if Friday's are a bit rough. We take turns with Ange getting a babysitter. The kids stay at one house or the other so we can all go out. My goal of having a family is playing itself out in the post Christmas drizzle that passes for winter. The dream version of travel, the adventure and alternative lifestyle has been eclipsed by the reality of survival. My ideas of the future are murky at best and are swept aside in the all consuming day to day.

There is some respite in the routine. Our relationship is not quite what I'd expected but I recognize that this is real life and sometimes difficult for everyone, not just Al. We can get through this. I'll make sense of it. I tell myself this, but it's as though there is a small piece of me that's still withheld. I notice Ange on her own and I don't envy that. Al is still sexy to watch and full of possibilities. Am I waiting for love or withholding it? It shouldn't be a trade should it? He is sitting on the couch, strumming dreamily,

"Elsie, I bet we could buy this place, and tear it down and build a bigger house."

J.J. is playing quietly on the floor. He seems to be calmed by the strumming. I'm reading Jitterbug Perfume at the kitchen table. "Hmm, yeah that sounds like a good idea."

"These properties are going to be worth lots of money." He's pleased with his plan.

"Well at least if we owned it, we could change the carpeting. That's the first thing I would do." I'm starting to like the idea. I take a sideways glance at the ripple in the badly installed beige wall to wall. The landlord wouldn't let us rip it out.

"Then we could winter in Mexico, like we used to talk about, remember? Can you see it, the kids on the beach learning to speak Spanish? We could live on the boat, fish. I used to think music was the most wonderful thing on earth until I swam in the sea. Then it was like the fish and the crabs and I communed in the silence. There is no peace like the quiet underwater. It's another kind of music, a language." He continues to strum dreamily. For a moment I have a vision of us setting up house under water. This is when it happens; I want to make the plan real. It bubbles up inside me like volcanic molten rock. I fear an eruption. I no longer want to continually clothe the present in future disguises that serve only to barely conceal our distance from one another. Let him dream, I tell myself, let it be. Maybe this is a required part of creating a better future.

"Yeah, that would be great." I want to stop there, but I don't, "I wonder how we can make that all happen." I manage a controlled response, because I do in fact wonder how we get from here to there. And how I got here.

"Can you watch J.J. since you're not busy? I thought I'd go for a walk by myself?" I ask, a walk to dissipate and cool the lava. I get what I'd expected.

"Oh, I can't stay, I have to go to the community center and see what's being planned, and there might be some work . . ." He trails off but doesn't move from the couch. He doesn't move from the house until an hour and half later. By now Zoë is home from playing at the neighbour's house and it's lunchtime. So much for time on my own.

Once back east I'd challenged him on why he never left when he said he was going to. He'd said that if he got more blowjobs in the morning it might give him a boost to get going. I decided then that his staying or leaving was going to remain out of my hands and or mouth. He hasn't mentioned it again. I imagine this request is a remnant from the free love era. So is the nonchalant attitude towards sleeping with your friends. I don't really remember the moment when I became so conservative. Maybe it has something to do with realizing how much energy you need to put into making one relationship work. Maybe, for me, sex and relationship have always been connected, and I was just pretending to understand that free love philosophy, which played itself out as a free sex philosophy. How this is connected to Al's unromantic demand I'm not sure.

Back when I was with Sam, everybody joked like that, and it's true the lines were not clear; it was experimental and all that, but now we have kids. There is also herpes and aids to consider. That time seems so long ago.

On one of his very important outings it seems he has come upon a mission. Missions tend to add an otherwise absent buoyancy to Al's step. I'm reminded of his dream boat/rotted hull in the garden back east. There is a nest of baby swallow-like birds that live in a nearby house slated for demolition. Al is determined to save the birds. He comes home with a cardboard box filled with open beaks. There's eight baby birds balding, peach fuzzed and squawking.

"Elsie, can you believe they were just about to tear down that little red house next to Larry's? Larry and I were talking about maybe buying it for a reduced price. We were under the eaves when we heard this faint sound. We convinced the guys to wait while we got a ladder from Larry's place, and *low* and behold there was this nest! Talk about timing, they would have been murdered! They might even be a protected type of swallow." He puts the box on the table.

"I have to go back and make sure there's no more. Anyway, we are still trying to see about that property." And with that he is gone.

Does he think I keep baby bird food on hand I wonder? I call the wildlife society to find out what to do. Apparently baby birds will eat canned dog food. I obviously have none on hand so I send Zoë across the street to the little store to get some. I have a wonderful time feeding these little orphans. Since I don't know exactly what kind of birds they are, there is some confusion as to whether or not they are worth saving. I had no idea that the wildlife society would discriminate and am somewhat surprised. They eventually agree to come the following morning to pick them up. They have to be fed every four hours, just like a human baby. I let Zoë and J.J. help me to toothpick them the mini portions of dog food. We are in it together and Al is excited when he gets home in the evening.

"How are our little demolition refugees doing?" He coos for a few minutes, clearly pleased with his rescue mission. I am pleased as well, as we discuss the best place for the box to live overnight. We decide on the kitchen table under the lamp to keep them warmish.

I am tired in the morning after getting up for feedings. I had those strange visions of emergency vehicles again; they kept me awake, shaking them off as I was falling off to sleep. They are all lined up and I can hear sirens and see flashing lights. Maybe it has to do with rescuing the birds. Still, I've got mixed feelings when they are carted away. It's such a tangible bit of good to toothpick dog food, to be a giant bird mama with my own babies standing on kitchen chairs, oohing and awing. The wild life society cannot guarantee their survival. I certainly feel that it is too much for me to take on. I learn more and more about my own resources, either by covering for Al's ineptitude or his absence. By now, I'm not surprised by either. Maybe it's the earlier west coast spring that's allowing me to roll with the punches. He does present challenges and sometimes they bring joy.

I really like it here and I have two friends with kids already. Ange from the coffee house as well as a new friend, Julia. She's the neighbour across the street, and our kids sometimes play. She's quite a bit older, around thirty-five, and on her third marriage. Her kids are roughly the same age as mine though, two boys, Ryan and Trevor. Ryan is five like Zoë and Trevor is four and so J.J. thinks he's a hero. She often has people over to play cards with her and her husband Blake. We don't go in for the card evenings though. Neither Al nor I are much for card games. Their friends are older anyway. Al is only five years younger than them but he is from a different mindset. During the day though, Julia is always welcoming and keeps coffee on the go at all times. She helps me plan out a budget; she thinks I should ask for a certain amount of money for food. It never occurred to me to ask for anything, except before going to California. I didn't follow up on the money part of it; having some financial plan together. We seem to manage on a need to spend basis, and we do eat most meals together either at home or when we are out. Our budget defies logic and Julia clucks in disapproval because she's seen us at the local restaurant far too often and she can't make sense of how we live. Aside from that, she doesn't treat me as ten years her junior.

Al wants to declare the kids and me as dependents on his tax return. I have never seen him file one and he works only for cash. I know that if he claims us then I won't be able to get my tax return. I always file because I always get something back, cause I earn so little. So far. He is suspicious of all government forms and I know he won't file. I would probably agree with his anti-establishment attitude, except I expect a cash refund. This causes a big stir.

"Elsie you are against family, you're selfish and you don't know what you are doing," he accuses.

"But Al you never file taxes. It's not going to work unless you promise to let me get your taxes done. What about all the years you didn't file. How will that work?"

"What are you talking about? Why on earth would I need you to do my taxes? That's ridiculous."

"Because Al, you say you want to do this now, but when it comes time to do the paperwork, you don't do it. And then we'll get nothing." I know that he hears this as me calling him incompetent or disorganized but I don't know how to get around it.

"Elsie, why are you trying so hard to be independent? We have to get together on all levels. You just want to think like a single person." He leans back against the counter arms crossed over his chest, shaking his head at my obstinacy.

"Okay, Al, how about you show me the papers. You get them together before the deadline if it means this much to you, and then we'll talk about it."

"There you go again, everything has to be your way. You want proof. Why can't you just agree to it up front? You are making this into a backdoor power thing, when all we need is for you to be up front with me. Have a little faith." Al speaks slowly as though I don't understand his idea and that's why I won't comply. He goes on, "I have enough to deal with without my own family demanding proof and looking out for number one. Everybody's out for number one. Goodwill doesn't even get heard let alone understood. Elsie, I didn't think you were one of those people." He continues to shake his head in disappointment.

I think about forging on in an effort to come to some sort of a resolution, but given the level of discussion I decide to let it drop. He is starting to not make sense to me again. I remind him that we agreed to get counseling when we got back to Canada, but Al says he doesn't have time or money. I suggest that maybe I could go to work and he could watch the kids. In this day and age we can surely adjust our roles to accommodate the situation. I really want to be with the kids. I remember having quite a nice set up with part time school when Zoë was little. How is it so much more difficult with two people? I thought it would be easier. He is not completely opposed to the idea so I will start to look for a job. A bookstore maybe? Some clowning around at a department store maybe. Public clown hmmm. I will get the paper tomorrow Al falls asleep on the couch a lot, staying up late at night, watching the small portable black and white T.V. until he falls asleep.

When I say he falls asleep in front of the television, it's true a lot of the time. It's not like we don't have sex from time to time. And it can be surprisingly gentle and what I'm sure would be loving if I could get there myself. Sometimes though, I find I have this weird uncomfortable reaction to his touch. I can only describe this as nausea-like, which sounds worse than I feel. It's as though my body takes a while to register it likes this. And then for some reason, in my mind, I turn into a tall black woman with a fruit basket on her head. It's like a semi-dream state. The logistics of this usually confuse me as I'm lying down and there is danger of the fruit basket falling. Somehow it stays in place, somehow I forget the nausea. I don't ever mention this to Al, it's too bizarre and plus it's not like I don't like the sex. I kind of need it. I need the possibility of what might be ignited. I wonder if Al would like the idea that occasionally he's sleeping with another woman.

So you can see that the problem might be with me. Sometimes when we are out with the kids, Al will reach over and sweetly take my hand. My heart starts to race in panic. I don't know if it's breaking in an effort to feel, or palpitating in terror that it might just give in, and then where would we be when he turns on us again. Me and my heart that is.

I hope I'm not being racist or something and I know all black women don't have fruit baskets glued to their heads, She's like a strong friend. I'm not sure exactly when she turned up. I've never experienced anything like this before. I hope I'm not developing sexual problems. I've heard desire comes and goes in long-term relationships. True, this is only a couple of years, but I've heard being busy with kids and stress can have an affect. Lots of women don't want to have much sex with their husbands when they have kids under two. I'm hoping things will improve. I'm hoping I will adjust.

Al seems to be slipping into a negative point of view again. He hasn't been noticeably upbeat since the baby birds. He came in this afternoon complaining, "Some guy at the camp has it out for me, and I can't go down there. He's got Larry's ear and I can sense Larry turning against me," Al explains, when I ask why he isn't going anywhere.

"You don't understand how cold the world can be, people just don't want to help, to believe. Elsie, I'm just going to wait it out." When he perceives my expression of resignation he adds, "Really you should open your eyes once in a while."

The myriad of questions run through my head as though on a Rolodex, what guy? The guy with the boat? How do you know he's out to get you? Just because he doesn't want to get on board with your idea of a floating co-op café in which he takes all the risk with his boat? Did you do something? Why do you think the world is negative? It's strange, I feel myself recoil with a soupçon of guilt and a pinch of self-preservation. By now I know these questions will not yield a response and so I save my energy and skip to something simpler.

"I have a couple of day's work standing on a corner!" I tease.

He stops in his tracks. "What are you talking about?"

"There was an add in the paper. They need someone to dress up as a clown, for a gas station opening. You know to jump around and wave people in. I called. They actually wanted experience, which I kind of have. It's just for the weekend. It pays well too, $8.00 an hour. Cool eh?"

"Yeah. Good for you Elsie."Al smiles.

"Maybe we can put up the swing set your mom brought?" I ask.

"The swing set, it's not a priority right now. I'll get to it. You could do it yourself y'know." He adjusts the pillow behind his head and turns his focus back to the T.V.

The job was surprisingly more and more tiring, eight hours of forced cheeriness. I dreaded the second day, but rallied. I entertained myself by getting truckers to blow their horns.I was approached by a woman who owns a costume rental store in the area. She liked my get-up. We talked and she offered me a job at her store. My job is clowning again as well as costume rental.I worked at a store in my teens, it's not where I thought I'd be now. I try to be zen about these things. Its not what you do but who you are while doing it. It's all temporary I tell myself. Grist for the mill and all that. I have a lot to be grateful for. Maybe I could go into theater and this will all be like an experience portfolio.The salary after bus fare leaves us with about 15 bucks a day. I don't mind it though, and it is the first break I've had in quite some time.It beats standing on the street corner. Al is not happy though, as all his time is taken up at home with the kids and he doesn't have time to look for another job. I am not championing the role of breadwinner, I am not winning enough bread. I can appreciate that even if I don't want to admit it. The clown shows themselves make more money than working in the store. Those elementary school films that told us we could do anything, even if we were menstruating; they were fairly lacking, as well as misleading. I have to wonder whose agenda that was. Cramps are not comedy. I secretly don't want to do everything. I am woman hear me roar, a day off would suffice, a day with no chore!

17
Trouble

What romance there was has dwindled. When I try to joke with him by being silly or tickling him, he pushes me away. He says that I'm trying too hard. I decide I'm not sexy enough. I should embrace my sexuality, and try to take more of an active role in terms of being desired. I get a hold of this teddy outfit from the costume shop. It's black and red satiny material, with snaps between the legs. I present myself to him, standing in the doorway to the bedroom. I do this in what I imagine to be a sultry pose. I do this for the utter humiliation of hearing him say, "What are you trying to do?" This is a big risk for me, way out of my usual self-expression. I consider leaning on the doorframe in a more obvious semblance of an alluring posture, but I'm afraid to become a cartoon. I'm afraid to be a rejected animated caricature of a desperate woman. And yet I just stand here, arms hanging limply at my sides. I am not sexy in the least. Tears roll down my cheeks. Who wears these things I wonder? Does it even fit properly? It didn't look bad in the mirror. I had thought I looked kind of good. I had hoped some deep-seated feminine side would emerge with just a little encouragement, with just the knowledge of those snaps. Instead I feel like a little girl who has dressed up in her mother's clothes to impress a neighborhood teenager who barely notices. To Al's credit, he does say something like, "You don't have to do that." Although I can barely hear him because the rejection is blocking my ears and I have slunk under my tears. What then do I have to do? I feel like a traitor to myself in a way I have never felt. This is the final debasement in the name of saving a family.

I've begun to read one of those self-help books about women who love men who hate women. There is a checklist on the back of the book that entices me to pick it up. I feel a bit self-conscious about it, but at this point I'm willing to look for answers anywhere. The job seemed to cause too much trouble as well as not enough money. So I'm just freelancing with clown shows. As it is we are back to the broke and not making sense lifestyle, in which I play the part of the non-knower and non-seer of what's really going on. On the back of the book there is a list of questions like, "Are you constantly walking on eggshells?" I answer yes to approximately nine out of ten of these questions. I am putting that little piece of information in my back pocket for the time being. I can't help but notice the similarity in Al's behavior to the romantic type of misogynist described in the book. I have become a detective squirrel these days, compiling tidbits to help preserve my fragile but undeniable belief that this isn't "normal." I have also been given a book about a medicine man.

Al has come into the bedroom in the middle of the night. He is waking me up, but I don't understand why. He just keeps repeating that I am not involved. "You need to get involved!" he paces in and out of the bedroom. He is uncanny; even as the secret squirrel I cannot escape his knowing that I am rebuilding my strength, subtly withdrawing. I am being very careful, staying still as I'm aware it's two in the morning and I am particularly vulnerable. It is the dark of night and he's wearing "the face". I speak calmly and try to talk him down from whatever place he is. Patience is not my forte though and some quiver of frustration must have seeped through. The next thing I know I am falling off the side of the bed, sliding towards the wall, as the mattress is upended and I land with a thump on the floor. The upended mattress is between us. My back is against the wall; the mattress slides down and is half off the bed. "Get involved," he dictates. I simply can't figure out what I am supposed to be doing while I am asleep. I'm shaking and wondering how far he could go. I gather up my strength and push aside the time and the darkness with my fear. I stay poised on the other side of the dismantled bed, eyeing the door. I am wondering if escape is even possible. At all costs I must talk him down. I promise to try to be more involved if I can please put the bed back together and go back to sleep. I promise and I promise for what seems like days but is probably less than an hour. My promises are a tactic to cover my terror; they are as much for me as for him. I am willing reassembly. Finally he is convinced, at least he stops repeating the idea that I am somehow not giving my all. He relents and returns to the couch. I rebuild and settle back in bed, but I don't sleep much.

It is morning now and I've gone to the little store across the street to get cigarettes. I call his mother on the payphone and ask for help. She says it takes two to tango. Some tango I think. "But I was asleep," I say. Does she hear the desperation in my voice? "I have no family out here, and frankly Al does not seem O.K. to me." She doesn't know how she could possibly help and suggests it is for the two of us to work out. Well that didn't go as well as I'd hoped. I feel pretty lonely, overtired and a little crazy. The world's response to me is exponentially less than what I feel.

Knowing that I'm going to leave eventually doesn't seem to be making life much easier. I have to find the right moment and I'm much less patient with everyone because I'm preoccupied with when and where. I don't want to go to a shelter again; this time I can do it on my own. I think about going back east but I think I'd like to give Al a chance to be a father. The kids deserve some kind of Dad. I'm hopeful that if we work things out properly the transition can be smooth. There is however the fact that Al knows nothing of this. I try not to think about the fact that if I'm afraid to broach the subject it says something about how it might go. Still one never knows.

It's Easter and there's a party over at the home of some people Al knows. He met them at the community center, the party is to follow the egg hunt and all are welcome. This sounds like fun and after the hunt at the center the kids are all revved up and the Easter bunny has been a big hit. We meander over to the house and Al is supposed to meet us there. He had to go home part way through the hunt to get his guitar. I think he'll be along soon. This is exactly his kind of event; music, talk of alternative societies and how to register them with the government. These are people who take themselves quite seriously. Apparently there is a community in the planning stages wherein everyone will help build these dome homes. It sounds reasonable enough, even innovative, but this one guy, Evan, is definitely in charge. Evan isn't charismatic enough to lead a small legion of builder ants let alone this motley crew. He says I don't get it. For such a peace-loving guy with such a community spirit he sure emanates disdain in large doses. I don't think anyone wants to admit that this emperor is clothed in his own rhetoric. Evan doesn't like my questions. Questions like: Where? Who owns the land? Who will pay for the materials? Does that make the landowner the landlord? Who decides who does what? How do you measure contribution? I feel I'm in over my head. A small space has erupted with only Evan and me in it, people are backing away. Al really likes Evan.

"I'm sorry," I say, "I guess I just don't understand, I mean I'm trying to understand. Everything is a little abstract. What do Jason and the Argonauts have to do with your idea?" He explains to me that it's a Greek Myth. I think this is what had been throwing everybody off. Al really likes Evan's wife. He has mentioned that I might try being more supportive, like her. I think maybe I might find some solace in the company of women and I just walk away from Evan, towards the women talking on the other side of the room. Evan is laughing at my discomfort, laughing because I didn't know about the Golden Fleece. I turn to look back as I walk away and he flips me the bird. Peace and love, I think peace and love.

The kids are running in and out with the others. Their little baskets now carefully lined up waiting for later retrieval. Every so often, one or another of the kids runs in to check that they haven't been robbed amid the games.

"Hi, you're Evan's wife aren't you?" I raise my hand in salutation, "I'm Elsie, I think you guys know Al?"

"Yes we do, he's great. He made us a wonderful meal," she smiles a warm welcome. I breathe a sigh of relief and feel my posture relax. "I'm Cassandra," she says, "Well Cassy most of the time."

Hmm, I wonder when he made them dinner. "Cassy, this may sound stupid but I'm really having trouble understanding Evan's plan and he seems so passionate and it sounds so complex. Do you get it? I mean maybe you could explain it to me?" I can really see why Al likes her. There is a gentleness that flows from her light hair right through to her tapered fingertips. A flow of acceptance that makes me feel cloaked in shards of disruption. I like her too. She leans in, "Well to be honest I certainly couldn't explain the details as well as Evan, it's really his thing y'know."

"Don't you feel a need to understand?" I ask incredulously.

"Not entirely no, Evan is really intelligent and his ideas are complicated."

"Sounds like you guys are a solid couple. Listen, if you were to get a tax return, would you consider it money to use for Evan's project, or your own money?"

"All our money goes into the common pot? Why do you ask?"

"Oh, sorry, it's really for me I'm asking. I'm getting some money back, and I'd just like to use it wisely. To be honest, Al has spoken so highly of you guys, I just wondered how you two make your relationship work?" Cassy smiles benevolently, I get the impression she does everything benevolently.

"Well," she says, "we are in it together, we support one another in everything."

"So you would use your tax return, let's say, to pay for him to register the society, even if you don't understand the plan?" We are alone in the kitchen; I pour a coffee from the pot on the counter as Cassy answers.

"Sure," she says.

And I am torn. She is lovely and fluid and loving towards the bird flipper.

"What about you?" I ask, "Don't you have dreams of your own? My check is going to be mine." She doesn't say anything. She is that kind of person whom I admire, who doesn't need to respond right away. So I add, "Thanks for your input, I really admire your commitment. You guys should come over to our place sometime. Anyway I'll probably see you at the coffee house." I head outside to get the kids ready to leave. Maybe it's having kids that influences my need for self preservation.

"Yes, see you there, and good luck with your relationship challenges," she says sincerely.

The party is winding down; I collect the kids and their baskets and head home. Al has arrived just to stay and jam. I am not happy about this. I figure if we are all going to be so supportive, then a family should arrive and leave together. Instead

I will have the over sugared, over partied kids, alone for the evening. We trudge home. I grumble to myself, that I'm not like Cassy, whether I wanted to be or not, and if Al wants someone like that or some healthy mare or whatever, he's got the wrong girl. I work myself up all the way home and as soon as I get there I phone the party house. I ask to speak to Al. Then I let loose. I can hear myself from the outside, I sound like a maniac. I'm screeching,

"What the hell do you think you are doing?"

"Hey Else what's up?" He's in his happy music place.

"What's up? I'll tell you what's not up. You lecture me about support, you say you want a family so damn bad, then why am I here alone and why are you not?"

"Elsie calm down, you're losing it. You sound hysterical." His voice is sweet soft butter greasing the gears of my outburst.

"You want fucking hysterical, that's what you'll get if that's what it takes! You talk a big game Al, but this not working; you are out to fucking lunch. I spent all afternoon over there with your so called friends, Mr. Peace and love, bird fuckin' flipper and Cassy the saccharin shoe horn. And where were you?"

"I told you I would be here, and I am here now, Elsie, calm down."

"The kid part of the day is over, Al. You want a family? You'd better get your ass home, or you just might not have one, a home I mean!" I'm surprised he's letting me yell at him this long, even in my hysterical state I'm aware that I don't want to let this safe venue for anger go. It's Easter; my anger has risen.

By now the kids are standing in the kitchen, watching me freak out. I don't want to calm down, but I suppose I should, they look a bit stricken.

"What do you want me to do Elsie, I said I'd jam. It won't be long and then I'll be home. Why don't you come back?" he invites.

One last one I think, barely aware of the little upturned faces. I turn away as if their not seeing me will make the fury less real.

"Because, I am home, with the kids!" and then, "Fuck you, get what's important to you together." I slam down the phone and turn around into a different person, "Okay, let's see what you found at the hunt!"

We have a quick supper of noodles and broccoli and then, "Okay you two; let's get you in the bath." The bath isn't going well. Both Zoë and J.J. are tired and irritable. I am chock out of patience. J.J. takes Zoë's cloth, the one she pretends is a snake. I return it and give him the rubber book. He launches the book at her and a small hard plastic figurine that isn't really a bath toy. She will not be convinced to share the snake cloth now. I give him another face cloth but it has not been endowed with the magical snake quality that only his sister can sell. I had put a squirt of dish soap in to give them bubbles. This was a delight at first, but now J.J. has soap in his eyes. I wipe his eyes and things are quieter for a moment or so. I have the little saucepan for hair rinsing perched on the side of the tub. For some reason today, leaning into the tub to wash their hair is hurting my back. After rinsing J.J., I say it's time to wash Zoë's hair. I had given him the snake cloth again, to cover his eyes. I am not paying attention to Zoë's protests that he has her cloth. They are screaming and crying and I can't make them stop to sort it out. I want to scream and cry. Instead I grab the saucepan and start banging it on the side of the bath. The idea in this moment is to make more noise than them, to take the noise level into my own hands. I start yelling, "Let's make noise, let's make noise, you wanna make noise, I can make noise too!" until this has the desired effect of shocking them into silence. I look down and see the scraped color of the little saucepan on the side of the tub. I hadn't been aware I was slamming it that hard. The two faces, red from their own tears look silently up at me. In this long second of aftershock, I recover myself from the throes of temper.

"I'm sorry, guys," I say. "I am so sorry, let's get you out of the bath." Toweled dry, cuddled and into P.J.s, I tuck them in.

"I'm so sorry I yelled, sweetie," I say to Zoë as I kiss her goodnight.

"Well, mom," she says tentatively, "he always takes my snake cloth, but you didn't have to be so mad and bang so loud."

"No, I didn't," I admit.

"You might have had too much sugar Mom," she suggests.

"I might have, yes, but I'm still very sorry."

Al gets home at two in the morning. I wake up enough to realize the hour but I'm still upset with myself; there isn't much left to say.

Several days later, early in the evening, I announce that I am going out, just like that, out for a while. I'm taking the kids. I'm only going across the street but I am no longer asking permission or seeking agreement or discussing. I only get halfway down the path before he is beside me. I have the little guy in my arms and Zoë beside me. He grabs me by the throat. "You can't just walk out like that!"

Oh Al, not with the kids here, certainly not with one in my arms, you fool. So far all of our physical wars have taken place when the kids weren't around. I guess by now things have shifted and on some level he knows he can't touch me emotionally and it's only a matter of time until I go. But tonight I am only going across the street. "Run," I scream to Zoë, "Tell them to call the police". He is still wearing "the face" but has loosened his grip. I take the moment to extricate myself and turn and run to the neighbors. He doesn't reach out to stop me and I don't look back. The police come. They see the mark on my neck. Al is still in our front yard and the officer goes to talk to him. They take him up the street to a friend's house, and tell him not to call me tonight. Fat chance I'm thinking. The phone rings all night long, but he does stay away. And I stay home with the kids, I call in to quit my job.

So now the police will automatically press charges unless I say not to. Al is agreeing to most anything and counseling is what I choose. Either it will fix Al or give me some kind of permission to give up.

18

Wear your Love like Heaven

The book about Rolling Thunder, the medicine man is really inspiring. Ange lent it to me. I think I'd like to meet a medicine man myself. After years of meditating and creative visualization, I've noticed a pattern. When I ask for help from the powers that be, I receive either someone or something to help me get stronger and give me insight. There is the unfortunate part that I did ask to fall in love in this blind and romantic way. This is obviously a clear cut case of be careful what you ask for. Did I really ask for *this?* And why did it wear off so quickly? Am I so selfish that I'm incapable of accepting someone else, flaws and all? And why am I so flipping' angry and disappointed if I'm so spiritual? Insight hasn't cleared up the outside turmoil. It has dawned on me that in his or this particular universe my needs don't exist or at least they are unrecognizable to me. Al thinks if I could just learn to put the milk back in the fridge my life would improve dramatically. Admittedly, I see the logic in this; it pares down confusion. If I could believe in one thing at a time maybe I could see a clear path. I believed I was strong enough to stay, and now I am leaning towards strong enough to leave. I will start with a walk, a stance in motion.

The way this book fell into my hands when I am in so much need. It feels like a gift. I feel as though I am on a journey of discovery, detective squirrel slash spiritual seeker. This feeling alone is helping me to pay attention to my life. It is clear that if I want to do something as simple as take a walk alone I am going to have to make it happen.

My plan is unfolding. Everyone is still asleep and the sun is just up. A little discipline, that's all I needed. I quietly leave our little house and head for the beach. The beach is only three blocks away. Well, I really have been making a big deal out of things. This is so easy. The sand is as yet not walked on and the quiet surf of the bay receives me as her earliest visitor. I feel both small and big at the same time, nature's awesome welcome and simultaneous warning of her own strength. I settle myself on a piece of driftwood and prepare my offering. I am a little self-conscious as I only just recently read about the ceremony in the book. It is as though someone is looking down laughing. "Hey there's that little white girl messing up a tobacco offering." I tell myself that as long as my intention is true all will be well. I have a little chuckle with myself at being self- conscious. I take out my pack of cigarettes and break off a piece. I offer some by sprinkling a little in each direction, north, south, east and west and some to the Great Spirit. I thank the Great Spirit for all my blessings, my beautiful children, my health, this wonderful morning, good people in my life. I then ask if its o.k. to ask for something, and provided that it is, I would like to meet a medicine man. Mission accomplished. I sit a little while longer and enjoy the quiet and the view. I am heading back to my children who are everything to me, and Al. I feel like the cat who might eat the canary. I feel whole and hopeful and hungry for breakfast.

I have finished the book on Rolling Thunder. I have made my tobacco offering and I am waiting to see if my prayers will be answered. I am at the coffee house at the neighborhood cultural center. This time I overhear a discussion about native ceremony and pipe in with my newly gained knowledge.

"Well the best time to do that is sunrise." I say. This young man whirls around and it is one of those moments where time freezes. The camera zooms in and it is only the brilliant smile that takes up my whole field of vision. I'm sure I have seen him before; sure I have dreamed him. Maybe I just wish I dreamed him, but that smile is so familiar.

"How do you know that?" He mocks and inquires simultaneously.

I think I might be in over my head. I stammer, less cocky,

"I just read this book on Rolling Thunder." And now I am actually saying, "I think I dreamed about you." What am I thinking, that he would know somehow, that he might have dreamed me back? That there is a whole other plane where we already know each other? He's a handsome guy with shoulder length auburn hair and eyes to match, not to mention that smile, oh God he probably thinks I'm hitting on him. Am I? Is this how people say those super cheesy lines because they really feel it for a second? No, I am not hitting on this man, and yes, I dreamed his face, at least I know the truth.

"Yeah, lots of people dream me." He replies matter of casually, "I lived with Rolling Thunder for a while."

This is pretty close to a medicine man I'm thinking; maybe this is the answer to my tobacco offering. He explains to me how when he was ill with malaria he actually called Rolling Thunder and went to live with him. I can't imagine a medicine man having a phone. He continues his story. His nickname was "man who little bugs like." He is fascinating. He introduces me to another man who was also healed when he was ill. This is incredible, I had no idea these things were so accessible. I feel as though God has once again found me in need and is offering me a route. This gives me the feeling of following clues to discover how to live without turmoil. There is a certain peace to feeling part of a larger meaning that actually shows itself. Just by making myself available, by absolute longing to do what is right and true I will be helped. Jake, the man who attracts mosquitos, is a painter and his friend Kim a photographer. Kim is putting together a book of photos of native elders in thanks for their impact on his life. This is powerful medicine for me. Kim tells me about an upcoming indigenous people's conference that will be held in Vancouver. I go home that night with the details, maybe I *will* actually meet a true medicine man.

Finding a counselor is turning out to be easier than I thought. Alice, a woman who works at the community center, mentions that her ex is a therapist, and is willing to barter.

This seems like a good find although I am curious as to why he is her ex. I am a little afraid, but she insists he is a fair guy and they just had different goals or something equally as vague. She tells me she really admires the way I mother, the way I am with the kids, so educational, and patient. It's nice to be recognized. I'm feeling positively upbeat, so I phone and make an appointment. He agrees to see us the following week.

I am optimistic, finally some positive action. His office is very pleasant with a soft décor and several wooden masks tastefully arranged. His name is Max Young. I wonder about how many Youngian jokes he's heard and decide not to mention it. At the first meeting it is mostly business and Al and I agree to clean his garden hour for hour. This seems like a fair, even generous exchange, someone is going to help us. I feel somewhat guilty, as I am not happily accepting my status as a laborer. On the inside that is, on the outside I'm pleasantly agreeing. Ah the small trials of the poor. I buck up on the inside and tell myself it will be worth it. I feel a sigh of resignation; I'm really kind of tired. This is going to require babysitting arrangements, as well as organizing Al. I suppose nothing comes for free. Couldn't he just tell Al that if you want a family you should love your kid's Mother, (I think I saw that written outside a church. It made me rethink organized religion.) He could explain that each of us is accountable, that the world isn't out to get Al specifically, and that intimidation isn't polite. Couldn't Dr. Young just point out that Al is bigger than me and it's not a fair fight? Also, that I am not the source of all his personal pain. Then again I could be doing something fundamentally wrong, some blind spot of my own causing me to misunderstand. Well maybe Young will be able to point it out.

I'm a little nervous that being a man our counselor will be convinced it's my entire fault. I want to be right about what's wrong but I want to be a little wrong too so that it can be fixed. If I am totally right then Al is not a balanced person and then what have I done?

We begin by filling out the forms which obligate Dr. Young to report to authorities if we are dangerous to ourselves or others. There is also a box to tick whether it is couple's or individual counseling we are seeking. I return the clipboard with the papers to his desk. So does Al. That went well.

"How do you feel?" Dr. Young starts out by asking me.

"Well" I begin haltingly, "mostly confused, is that a feeling?" He nods to continue.

"And sad and scared," I check to see if that's the appropriate response. It seems so and now it's Al's turn.

"Well, if only she would…"

"Yes, but I'm asking how do you feel?"

"I would feel fine if only she would just…"

And so it goes and keeps on going. I can't believe this, it's a simple question. At this rate we are never going to get anywhere. I guess Al just wants to skip ahead to the problem. Which of course he thinks has nothing to do with how he feels. Right now this seems to be the only problem. I can't believe we are spending the whole session and Al refuses to answer the question. I am livid because I have a new feeling around having to do yard work. I feel that in this safe environment I will express some saved up anger and frustration.

"You see," I implore, "This is the problem doctor. Al, the question is not about *me*."

"Yes I know that Elsie," comes his calm reply," But as I'm trying to explain I would feel fine if you would just let things be. Look how upset you are, you know you need to pay attention, see what's really happening…"

"Well, I think our time is just about up for today, I have a suggestion, two suggestions actually. I'd like to see each of you separately, and Elsie when was the last time you had a day off?"

"A day off?"

"Yes, from the household, the kids, and a day just to be by yourself?"

"We go to the coffee house. That's where I met Alice, who gave me your name. We go on Thursdays most weeks."

"No I mean a day?'

"Hmmm, not working or having the kids?A couple of years at least I guess, yeah, I did go to that meditation conference for a few days when we lived in Montreal."

"I think that's a great idea," pipes in Al, "We should get away for a weekend…"

"What I am suggesting, if we can work it out, is for Elsie to have a day off…"

"I know and I am saying that I believe it would be beneficial, benefit us, to spend a weekend together," suggests Al.

I am so aggravated that I am not really up for a weekend with Al. This potential day off is difficult already and that's with third party intervention. I'm surprised and a little flattered too, as I didn't know Al wanted so badly to spend time with me.

"Yes, and I agree that it would be helpful for the two of you as well, but can we agree that first Elsie could have one day on her own?" Max is neatly covering what I can only assume to be frustration.

"Sure, that's one way to go. But you'll agree that if we are here for us," He pauses as though we should know what he will say next. "That we should spend time together." Al manages to disagree and agree simultaneously.

I'm tired of listening to this. I am not saying anything because I already know that I am spending a weekend with Al even as we all agree to my day off and our next meeting.

19

Crystal Blue Persuasion

We are driving into Vancouver. The kids are at my neighbor's and we are going camping somewhere, we are not sure where. You need money for going away, and we have very little. We've borrowed a car from Al's brother, Rick. I am frustrated because we have had to make so many stops including the errand we are now on because Al wants some pot. I am at this point along for the ride; we haven't got to the *us* part of the trip. I don't really think that this is what the doctor. had in mind. That we have headed into the city in an effort to find somewhere to camp has more to do with the errand than anything else. We stop at a red light. There is a couple walking across the street in front of us, they are holding hands and looking lovingly at each other. The sun is shining, the city alight with people and traffic, the weekend buzz. Her skirt is blowing so the back hem is scooping the air from the side. The fabric is alive, fun. Inside our car is like a hole, the absence of intimacy taking up all the room. No wind. Barely enough air. We both notice the couple, I, with longing and a sigh. Al says, "He's a lucky guy." I am not stopping to consider, I don't stop for clarification, I use up all the air left to feel the pain, why aren't you a lucky guy?

"Fuck you." I hear myself bark.

We are still at the light and I jump out of the car and start to run up the street. I am not sure at first what my plan is. I expect he will circle around the block and I need to decide quickly if I am going to play the "get in the car game". I just don't feel like explaining, I don't even know if I can. I duck into the nearest

doorway, my feet making the decision. My body seems to be
calling the shots as I see him drive by and stay frozen. A bus rolls
up and it's as though I'd planned it all, perfect timing. It's the bus
back to Cedar Park. I climb on. The decision has been made. I'm a
little alarmed at the speed with which I've created a whole new
circumstance. I am a little worried about the potential fallout. I
console myself with the therapist's suggestion that I have a day
alone. So be it. I relax back for the one hour ride with the whole
afternoon stretched out before me, my own private adventure slash
escape slash solitude. All slightly uneasy. My first instinct is to go
directly to the neighbor's and pick up the kids but they aren't
expecting us until tomorrow so I wonder if it wouldn't be alright if
I just borrow a little time.

    I'm back by the sea, just off the bus and across the street. I
will walk. Walking is good. I see the point jut out and I know it's
roughly eight or so miles around that bend back From Cedar Park
to Clear Point. I think I can do this; I have to do things on my own.
I wonder if there's a path. So it is, leaving the day to my body. The
soothing sound of the tide encourages thoughts to disperse in a
rhythmic if not orderly fashion. I'm around the bend now and it
seems there's no turning back. I laugh to myself as I hope I haven't
just been given a landscape version of my state of mind. I muse
that if this sun and sea with an evergreen backdrop is madness to
be answered for later,then I might as well enjoy. I remind myself to
forbid myself to wonder what became of Al. As I climb over the
rocks along the shore, slowly I give in to the day I have given
myself. I'm about midway, I imagine and it seems like a little
swim would do quite nicely. I know I'm all by myself and I don't
know the water in the area. I am a tad frustrated with my
sensibility. It grates on me. Why must I think everything through?
Not only through but complete with the body washing up on shore
and the headline *Crazy Mother misses the obvious danger and now
children are left not only motherless but with the knowledge she
was careless.* Of course they would understand careless as not
caring enough for them, let alone me. Thus making the tragedy
open to speculation.

    Well, I'll just have a little swim. I look around to ensure
that there is really no one else about, because it's not as though I'm
miles from civilization, the coast however is clear. I peel off my

clothes and venture in, chanting a little to brace myself as the cool water comes up over my thighs. I'm out just far enough to gaze back at the shoreline. There is nothing so green as the green in B.C on a sunny day. The land and air soak up all the rain and use it as if to magnify color in its absence. This is a reminder always that sunshine is the rarer gift here. I'm lying on my tummy barely above the rocky bottom, legs stretched out behind me like a child in a wading pool. This is fun, simple fun. I have about the attention span of a small one it seems, for I tire after about five minutes. Why can't I enjoy things longer? I wonder. Stop harassing yourself I counter, you did it, that's enough. I emerge slowly, reasonably pleased with the whole experience. Scrambling up the rocks I glance down to see my legs covered in blood. What the hell is this? I go back to the edge to rinse off, the salt stings because of the many small cuts. Oh yeah, those barnacle things that grow on rocks, tiny oversight, and small price to pay.

I lie down on a rock that is about the size of my upper torso. It is so warm and welcoming. This rock is very old, as are all rocks I imagine. But this one is noticeably smoothed by age. Though its movement is imperceptibly slow I imagine it giving me the strength to feel possibly at home on earth. A funny sense of belonging to myself has come over me, and I realize that I might well be gone around the bend as I have fallen in love with a rock. No explanations, no threats, no wrong or right.My body feels the heat in between my legs; I wriggle against the hard surface and feel a tingle everywhere. I am aroused. I am also astounded. I melt into the rock and let the friction do its work. I feel like a child; it's just me, me and my body, me and the heat and me and the sensations flowing over me. Well that was interesting! I am a little shy with myself for an instant as though I didn't really know what I was doing. Of course I did, and the estranged pieces of me join each other again in a giggle of acceptance. Again I feel blessed and it is this rock that gives me opportunity to love without fear and warms my body at the same time. Joy is often fleeting in the corporeal but always touches forever, even through the slow forever of a rock. Blessed and silly are forever mine.

I'm surprised to see Clear Point not far in the distance. Just walking leisurely with no thought to time, it just went by, time that is, and by now the sun is setting. I'm a little tired and utterly pleased as I triumphantly near home. I have just rounded the corner of our little street, I see Al sitting in the front of the house. I assume he would have picked up the kids by now and that they must be inside playing. I slow my walk and hesitate at the driveway. "Where are the kids?" I venture and then before he can answer, "I walked all the way from Cedar Park!" I just can't contain my pride.

"Great, good for you" he answers. I can't get a read on him at all.

"Where is the car?" I ask.

"I had to take it back, Rick needed it, we would have had to drop it off on our way back anyway. The kids are still at Julia's, I might have to go out and I didn't know where you were. She said they could stay there."

"Have they had supper?" I accuse. He shrugs to say he doesn't know.

"Well I'll just go see how things are going over there," I say still about twenty feet away in the driveway.
"Wait," he says, "Don't go. I don't know what happened today; we were supposed to spend time together." He looks hurt and truly confused and I'm feeling guilty because I had such a lovely walk and he looks so forlorn.

"I guess I really needed a day to myself…sorry. I'll just go get the kids now." I'm pretty sure this is not going to cut it.

"I just need a hug Else." He says looking like such a lost soul. I don't trust this, is the screaming sentiment from my gut. How can I be so cold? I'm the one who took off. This is a new approach maybe he is really hurt. What if I desperately needed a hug and someone who had said they loved me turned and walked away? I would be very hurt. He's just a sad guy, I can do this, I can hug a sad desperate looking guy. I feel miles away and so separate. How can one afternoon make me such an island? I am prolonging my decision to hug or not to hug and in some small way I am relishing his begging.

"C'mon please Else, have a heart." The veins are sort of sticking out in his neck and his face is slightly contorted like a child crying. I hate being accused of being heartless. This is possibly because of the fact that it requires so much of me to make this decision. Doesn't that make it true? Have some compassion I say to myself, at the very least, compassion. So slowly I walk towards him, I gingerly put my arms around him and say, "There, I'm giving you a hug." Not the warmest spirited hug, I think, but I am here. He's not letting me go. He is tightening his grip.

"Hey, you said a hug," I say feigning lightheartedness. Ah oh, my fake heart has been rooted out and he is saying that this is not enough. I am wriggling, trying to free myself. Was it fake? I wonder, didn't I spend all that time mustering some semblance of true compassion? I am pushing onto the doorframes with the flats of my feet, legs spread in a "V".

"This is not acceptable Al," I pronounce with authority. I am aware that I might have more authority if my feet were on the ground.

"This is not enough! You are holding back!" he declares as he pushes me through the door and I hit the table with my leg. A small cut.

"You are so right about that!" I agree and it confuses the situation long enough to diffuse things.

"You made me bleed! Look!" I am pointing to my cut as if to ask him if this is his idea of the way things should be. "If you didn't believe when you threw things at me or stabbed the wall with a knife or speared the dish soap from across the room, if those were not physical proof enough for you. How do you explain this? Am I crazy again? Did I throw myself at the table? I don't think so." I am waiting. I am wondering why I would offer my being crazy as a possible version of events, just bait of a kind, I suppose.

"That was an accident Elsie. It's just that it's not enough you know, I didn't mean for you to hit the table I just want you to understand how important this is. You needed to come inside. I don't want to fight. I mean it comes down to this, we can split up or we can grind this out and make it work."

"The thing is Al, when you throw someone around, it's no longer an accident. What about the kids Al? I'd better go get them, which by the way I notice you didn't bother to do."

"They're fine."

"Of course, but it isn't you who will have to return the babysitting favor is it?" Grind this out indeed. I don't like the idea of a future based on grinding; it's too abrasive. Love, trust and understanding with the added bonus of regular grocery money is more what I have in mind. Grinding sounds like a prison sentence. I guess I'm a hardcore idealist; I'll just have to accept it. But for now,

   "I guess there is some truth in what you're saying," I muster. "Maybe we should discuss this with Max. Who knows, we've only been once together. And you are due to go alone this week." I am not completely out of hope, although I am sure that throwing me in the door is not O.K. I'm thinking once someone else tells him so he'll come to realize it. If he knew, I mean really knew, surely he wouldn't act this way.

   "Yeah, we will go see Max but I don't think you understand what's going on in here," he points to his heart. "We have to work together and I needed you to give me more than you were, I need you to see through my eyes. It's all for you, don't you see, everything is for you; you are my reason and my rhythm Elsie.

   "O.K, Al, " I say backing away, "but I *need* to go get the kids now, I'm not against you Al. You have to believe me." I wonder if that last bit is entirely true, because I wouldn't want someone who said they loved me to have to placate me like this just to get through the day. See through his eyes! What the does he think my personal hell looks like, it's a constant effort to see someone else's point of view all the time even if it is as challenging/rewarding as a poem. Seeing his point of view is like drifting off halfway through the class and spending eternity trying to make sense of what you missed. Then just when you are about to give up, some morsel of truth or beauty or understanding lets you make sense of all the absurdity. There is a case to be made for making sense of anything, even overlapping a point of view. Perhaps that is what a shadow is. It is not a safe place for me, in his eyes, and I do feel somewhat heartless, and a lot aggravated.

   We are at the coffee house as usual on Thursday, and Evan the bird flipper and Cassy are here tonight. Al has told me that my independent streak caused some problems for Evan. He and Cassy discussed my desire to use my tax return as I saw fit, and Cassy agreed with me. Evan doesn't like to be challenged it seems. He is supposed to play tonight. When I say hi, he turns away. I don't know why his attitude enrages me so much. I want to go on stage with him. I want to make a little speech about comedy.

I think it would be funny to explain how at its lowest level, slapstick, we laugh at another's discomfort. I could give the slipping on a banana peel example. Since that's how Evan made me feel, I think I would like to publicly crack an egg over his head. I am surprised at this desire. I ask Al what he thinks of this idea.

Al says, "Imagine yourself at sixty and look back, then you can decide if it's something you'd regret not doing." Al and I are having a conversation that does not seem laced with anything except genuine good advice. We are standing side by side. This spurs me on. I don't give much thought to what us agreeing says, and so I decide that I wouldn't regret publicly cracking an egg on the head of Evan. I manage to get on stage just before Evan starts to play. I walk up to the mike, "Hmm" I clear my throat to the feedback, and mutter in a voice more timid than I'd imagined, "As you know I'm a clown, and although humor has many levels, the lowest and most common is slapstick. To laugh at another's discomfort is something Evan here is familiar with."

Evan is seated, guitar in hand; he's looking over at me, smiling, his public persona in full form. I'm gripping the egg I've taken from the kitchen; it's in my hand, in my pocket. The crowd is starting to quiet down. Just quiet chat and murmurs is all I can hear. I hadn't really worked out the speech. I realize, I hadn't worked out how to get the audience caught up with my vision. The status reversal requires a back story. It dawns on me that the audience would need to see him be mean. But with the determination of a sixty-year-old cultivating absurd non-regrettable memories, I quickly forge ahead. I pull out the egg and bring it down on Evan's head. He doesn't see it coming. The audience has not been prepped and there is a little murmur of non-comprehension. The egg runs down his face and shirt and barely misses his guitar.

He doesn't move, his smile frozen in shock. Somebody gives him a cloth. I run off the stage. Okay that wasn't quite as funny as it had been in my mind. Good thing the coffee house is a zany and forgiving environment. To Evan's credit he just wipes off the egg and plays his folksy set. No one, except Al says anything about the egg incident. I am surprised I do not have any actual egg on my own face, having broken through some kind of shell. Al says, "Wow, Elsie you actually did it! So did you get what you wanted out of it?"

I answer, confused, "I feel like I may have missed the mark. I think it'll seem funnier when I'm sixty."

20

I Talk to the Wind

In order to go to the Indigenous People's Conference it seems I have to sign up as a volunteer. I take the bus downtown to The Native Friendship Center to sign up there. The woman taking names is wondering why I am doing this, as I am not native. I can't say, 'well I used to pretend for most of my childhood that I was an Indian.' I also can't say that my father used to tell a story about being drunk and going through the windshield of his car. That in that story he was lying on the side of the road near the 'Indian' reserve where the golf course is located. It was the native Indians who saved his life. They did this by putting mud on his head and thus helping the cut to heal. This is why ever after that he had a small bump on his head which he claimed still possibly had glass in it. I couldn't say that because as I thought about it, I recognized it might have been a total fabrication. It seemed disrespectful to say my father's lies taught me a profound respect for your culture. I couldn't say that all the way through school my favorite part of history was when the Mohawks beat the red coats, so please can I attend the conference? How about, I read a book written by a medicine man that feels as though it has brought a certain connection and meaning to me. Then I met two guys that had personally been healed by this man and that has led me here. Also, I'm a firm believer in following these sorts of leads/hunches, especially when they are seemingly in answer to a prayer.

So instead I say, "I think my son might be part native." I seemed to remember Al saying something about his father having some Indian blood, so it wasn't a total lie. This seemed to be an acceptable reason. I was given a pass and the itinerary and some jobs. Basically I would be cleaning up around the grounds and be present in the video room. I am thrilled, mission accomplished. My guilt is only moderate for my self-serving motivations. If in fact guilt can come in graduating measures. White Lies.

It's a few weeks later and the first day of the conference. I'm bringing the kids with me. There is a beautiful opening ceremony on the campus at U.B.C. Everyone is given a small piece of ceremonial tobacco tied with a red ribbon and the entire group weaves together in a circle which doesn't end but turns inside itself in smaller and smaller circles, like a string or a snake, like a giant group hug as the circle gets tighter and tighter. The kids are looking a bit worried, as am I. When you are small the experience of being encircled usually blocks the upward view and can feel constricting. But there are smiles all around and a feeling of nervous anticipation and warmth. That everyone wants this to work is clear. There is an eagle circling the circle, the significance of which is noticed by all. The conference is officially open.

Actually volunteering for clean-up was a great plan, the kids play and I wander around with a garbage bag. We get free smoked salmon and salads. It's like being at a giant picnic where I don't know anyone. People smile and nod but I don't actually speak to anyone. I am still on my mission, eyes peeled but I don't quite know what I'm looking for, I just know I'm looking.

Now, at the end of the day the sun is beginning to set, there will be another ceremony starting soon. Some people are already heading toward their cars. It dawns on me that I've been so busy looking I haven't given much thought to getting home and it's quite a long way with the two little ones. I decide to see if there are any buses in the parking area. I head down the grass incline to the parking lot, tuckered kids in tow. There he is! My smiling friend Jake sauntering towards me. I smile back. "Have you been here all day?" I ask.

"Yah, I've been inside at the workshops, what are you doing here?"

"Well, I wanted to meet a medicine man." I shrug and grin to myself admitting that that's what I'd been looking for all day.

"And did you?"

"Not yet."

"Well you may be in luck," he says nodding his head in the direction of three people coming towards the parking lot. There is one reasonably large man and two equally large women.

"That's Napoleon, he's from the interior. The Okanogan area," says Jake, raising his hand to wave.

"That's quite a name," I note.

"Those are his daughters," he adds.

I recognize the women from some singing they'd done earlier in the day; they were very intense as they walked into the main area singing as they came, getting louder and more powerful with each step. Their voices stretched low and high at the same time, strong and tight. I turned to Jake, "Hey, are you going back to Cedar Park area? I'm looking for a ride."

"No, I'm staying in town to come back tomorrow," he says. The three of them had by now just about reached us. Jake nods hello and they nod back in a familiar way as Napoleon and his daughters head for their car. Napoleon turns around and waves Jake over. Jake motions to me to follow. I in turn do the same to the kids, who by now are really ready to go home and dragging their feet.

"This is Elsie; she wants to meet a medicine man," Jake points at me.

"She does, does she?" They chuckle like they are having a private joke. The sisters just stare.

"Hi." I stare.

"Do you need a lift Jake?" the man lifts his chin as he questions.

"Nah, thanks, I'm staying, but I think Elsie and the kids could sure use a ride to Clear Point."

"I think we can manage that," he nods.

"That would be great, thanks a lot," I say as I usher the kids towards the car.

"Are you going to as far as Clear Point?" I say looking for reassurance that we are not imposing.

"Not far," he states.

This is all turning out so well and as long as we get somewhat close to home I can manage from there. There is one daughter in the back and one in the front. The daughter in the back is taking up half the seating. So the kids and I are squished into the other half. The silence is as large as they are. I am in a car with medicine people. I am focusing on keeping the top of my head open to receive any information that may come in the silence. I am not sure why I am doing this. It's just a feeling that I have that information comes to me in the quiet in this way. My intention is on being aware. The kids and I are squished and the car is extremely hot. They are being quiet though and polite, probably from fatigue, as we watch a bottle of sprite passed from sister to sister. Our thirst level is increasing with every pass. Finally unable to contain herself Zoë says, "Can we open the windows? It's hot."

"No," comes the firm reply.

I don't know what to think or how to feel. The place at the top of my head feels very open, I can sense something. I stay quiet and shush the kids, feeling their discomfort. The car is a foreign land and we are guests and if they want to talk to us they will. I don't recognize the road in the dark and I begin to realize that I have never met these people before. I'm not certain we are headed the right way.

"Excuse me, are you sure this is the way to Clear Point?" I say gingerly.

"Are you saying you don't think I know the way?" Napoleon replies with a faint chuckle.

"Well no," and my voice fades slowly as I finish with, "I just don't recognize this route."

"I know the route." He proclaims. It's very dark outside but somehow there is light inside the car, light enough to see the people.

I sit back chastised, put my arms around the kids, keep my head open and have a little faith. Finally, after I point to my street, we arrive at my house. Somehow the silence coupled with a long day has exhausted me. I roll out of the car and the top of my head feels as though it's strained and jumbled, it seems my seventh chakra is exhausted too. I thank them for their kindness and just as I am about to walk away, I think I will ask about tomorrow. This can't be *it* after all, I've got questions.

"Are you going to be there tomorrow?" I venture gingerly. The way I feel, they may never want to see my skinny little white personage again.

"We'll be there, but haven't you had enough?" he laughs.

"No," I say. I'm grinning away as if I have a clue about what 'enough' is referring to. "See you tomorrow, and thanks again." The fact is that all I have are clues. In my mind, 'enough' was about whatever had gone on in that car; that which left my brain feeling like happy tired scrambled eggs. I think the medicine people have done some medicine on me. Either that or they are laughing at me, or possibly both. I am optimistic on either count.

The next day Julia from across the street is watching the kids, so I can go alone. They wouldn't be happy doing it again and plus I have to work in the video room, whatever that is. The video room, it turns out, is just a classroom on the first floor; the windows are up high so there's not much view. There is nothing in the room except a T.V and V.C.R, several chairs and some tapes. VCR tapes on treaties, land issues, clear cutting, different tribal customs and other conferences. Frankly I don't know what else. I don't know because there is something incredible going on next door to my room. Right next door is the spiritual elders' gathering. I am thrilled to be so well placed, this is a big university campus and tucked way in this corner I have found the elders. I have been fortuitously placed nearby. Surely I can go. So I do. I walk the corridor trying my best to be inconspicuous. The hall is lined with chairs and filled with older native people. I am totally noticed as I traverse the one classroom distance and shyly say hi to anyone who glances in my direction. As I pass by a striking looking older guy with roundish features and thick glasses and think about where he might be from, I get a sharp quick loss of breath. I guess that this must be white paranoia. I hurry on looking straight ahead. I just attempt to make myself at home in the room with the prophets and medicine people and elders from all over the world. No one seems to mind that I'm here, and there are only 15 or so people. Ah, there's tea in Styrofoam cups and cookies being passed around on a tray. Someone must have seen my eagerness because a woman has leaned over to talk to me.

"The elders must be served first, then you can have some," she explains.

"Oops, sorry," I whisper as I put the cup back on the tray. My mother did teach me that I'm sure, how could I forget? I will pay more attention, as I feel privileged to be here. I just hope everybody doesn't think I'm rude. The guy with the glasses comes in. I look to the woman questioningly; the air is thick with serious business, but also welcoming like we are in somebody's kitchen. I'm a little nervous, and the cookie tray is moving too slow for comfort. She smiles knowingly and turns to whisper, "That's Albert." She sucks in her breath in an exact imitation of what I'd felt in the hallway, before continuing, "Lightening, from up north."

I nod relieved. "He has that effect on a lot of people," she smiles. Hmm, Albert Lightening, not white paranoia after all.

Napoleon, who drove me home yesterday is here. If he has noticed me, he shows no sign. He is proudly introducing Thomas Banyaca who will speak about the Hopi Prophesies, and about his life's mission to bring them to the United Nations. He says the Hopi call the U.N. the "House of Mica." He is a revered man who has devoted his life to sharing the wisdom of the Hopi Prophecies with the world. Everyone in the room seems to be grateful for his presence and all eyes are on him. There are silent nods of agreement when he speaks about the significance of the eagles at the sunrise ceremony. He isn't very tall and he is wearing a beautiful pink scarf as a headband. I wonder if this is some special outfit or if he has many different ones for specific occasions. I learn that he spent seven years of his life in prison because of his steadfast conscientious objection to military service.

After World War two and the atomic bombing in Hiroshima and Nagasaki the Hopi commissioned Banyaca to bring the Hopi message of peace to the world. The message seems sensible enough to me and I like the sweetness mixed with strength in his demeanor. We need to reawaken spiritually to all life forms, which of course is a readjustment in our western attachment to consumerism. It seems to me that the way things are going environmentally a little readjustment is certainly required. No one in the room is moving and the speech is slow and words carefully chosen. Ironically not unlike the way Al speaks at times. We are perched on desks and chairs that have not been laid out in any particular way. It could have been a circle but the small rectangular room doesn't seem to allow for it. I am fighting my urge to fidget. It seems that no one else is moving, that is when the urge to move is loudest. I feel propelled by all the unmoving. I am perched on top of a desk, please don't let me fall off my seat,I beg myself to stay still. It seems that the prophecies had predicted the existence of the United Nations as well as "the gourd of ashes falling on the earth two times," which they believe were the atomic bombs.

Here we are in this little classroom. I'm allowed in; this does not bode well for having the ear of the world leaders. Even so I sense the importance and sincerity in this presence. The room, the cups, the casual acceptance, all seems incongruent with what's at stake. I'm really listening to the gravity with which nature is being addressed and I can't help but wonder why these people aren't being listened to, taken more seriously. I am not being heard either. I know it's just on a personal level. However, there is something outrageous about telling a simple truth and it not being recognized. Maybe it has something to do with trying to tell the attackers that they need to take a good long look at themselves; that as it turns out, they are hurting themselves as well.

It is late afternoon when everyone files out of the smallish classroom to break for the day. I see Napoleon at the end of the hall and he turns in my direction smiling. It's one of those moments where I catch myself believing that he is waiting to talk to me, but dare not believe at the same time. I check behind me to see if there is someone else he is smiling at. There is no one there. So I walk straight up to him.

"I was hoping I could speak with you…" I trail off, the question in the tone.

"Let's just go outside, here." He motions with his hand towards the door at the end of the hall. Now that this is all unfolding I wonder what exactly I will say. What am I hoping for? Some miracle cure for my spirit? I don't even really know what's wrong. What I do know is that this is what I've asked for. I have set the wheels in motion and now I'm here. I'll just have to trust.

Napoleon points up the wide cement stair case steps that go up the outside of the building. "How about this? Chairs and everything," he smiles. I bound up the first flight heading towards the landing where there are two lawn chairs waiting for us. "Whoa, there! Don't you know you are not supposed to run ahead of your elders?" He looks at me seriously as I come back down towards him. I'm waiting for a grin or something to tell me this can't be that serious. But his face is stony with an air of fatigue at having to be disappointed. "SSorry," I mumble, "I didn't realize."

"Ahh, you're young, you're still learning," he says as I arrive by his side and turn to stay in stride with him.

"I get excited," I offer apologetically.

"So you do," his nod a vertical line, his mouth a horizontal one. We arrive at the landing and he motions for me to sit.

He settles his large frame slowly into the chair. He adjusts his weight, feet on the ground sitting back. I perch on the edge of my chair ensuring my feet will touch the ground. I still don't know what I'm going to ask. I fold one leg over the other, my ankle balanced on my knee. I'm tapping the heel of my foot nervously as I bounce it on my knee. It's odd I'm aware of my nervous movements but make no effort to stop them. He waits. I notice the vest he wears over his plaid shirt has a mariner's pattern. Ship's steering wheels and rope. It really is tacky. Geez I can't believe I just thought that, how blaringly superficial. I guess this is where one must engage in suspending disbelief, and quickly before I toss out the medicine man with the vest.

"I feel like I've been led here." I continue to tap neurotically on my foot stopping only as I look up to gauge his response. Could he know?

Napoleon clears his throat and then says, "Which foot is holding you down? That one or is it both?"

I feel a strange shift in my brain, logic fighting the obvious. I consider correcting him, saying something like 'no, I don't mean that kind of lead.' But something in his demeanor, the solidness of it, takes me to the place where literal and figurative merge. After all it was me who chose the metaphor however unconsciously. And before I know it the shift is complete and I answer in complete confidence.

"Both."

"I suppose I could do some healing for you around that," he offers leaning forward in his seat, hands out stretched towards my feet.

"Yes," I whisper nodding in agreement. He cups his hands around my already elevated foot but doesn't actually touch it. He starts to make guttural sounds reminiscent of the singing I'd heard at the opening ceremony. Except he isn't actually singing, more like chanting softly and moving his hands around my foot. He stops for a second and his barely open eyes roll slightly. He takes his hands away from my foot and motions over the side of the stairway. It's as though he's throwing something away and then flicking his fingers to be sure it's gone. He motions for me to give him the other foot with a slight nod towards it, I switch position. He does the same routine again. I sit quietly, hyper aware. I don't want to move or disturb this at all. I don't know what this is exactly. Then he stops and leans back again and his eyes return to their normal twinkly gaze.

"You know, being the woman in the family is a very important role."

I nod in agreement, except I'm not pleased. All he sees is the Mum, I think, the 'wife'. I was hoping to be seen as a human being.

"The woman is like the spiritual grease for the machine. She keeps the spirit for the family, do you understand?" He speaks slowly and deliberately. It would almost be lecturing if it didn't seem out of time. "Women are close to the creator by nature. Their job is to feed the family's spirit."

"Oh, I guess so." I answer. My disappointment is seeping through. Well what did you expect? I ask myself. He is a man and a little full of himself at that. Of course they think nothing of handing over a giant job to women without even thinking it's anything. A sales pitch for slavery. I already know more about being a mother than he ever will, and I'd never underestimate that for a second. Plus I guess he can tell I don't have the foggiest idea how to do the family job, and worse I'm not sure I even want it. In fact, I now realize I was hoping he would tell me I had a different purpose or something. I just want to be seen as a human being. Is that so difficult? I guess we are done because he gets up from his chair. I feel like I'm going to cry so I turn to look over the railing, my back to him. He comes up behind me and puts a big warm hand on my back, he's laughing.

"You are supposed to feel better." I turn around to look at him and I find myself starting to laugh as well.

"I know, thank you." I shrug in explanation of my mood.

"What I said, it's true, but it doesn't mean anyone can treat you meanly, or hurt you, you understand?"

I nod yes, but I don't understand how any of this applies. I guess this is just another step along the road. Maybe getting here was the important part.

During the bus ride home I manage to convince myself that I have been pretty fortunate to have even met a medicine man so quickly after I put it out there in the universe. Maybe I don't understand the full meaning yet. All that stuff about being a woman. It's true it wasn't an aspect of myself I had factored in when I was younger. At least not in terms of level of responsibility. It has certainly been playing a big role, the whole mother and female partner thing. Maybe that was something to think about. The strangest part is that I keep wanting to laugh at the whole deal. At Napoleon, at my life, at my tendency to take myself so seriously. I mean this guy in a tacky vest throws invisible lead out of my feet over a railing, tells me a women's role, but hey don't let anyone be mean to you. And this, I think, is life altering? They do say laughter is the best medicine.

It's dark by the time the bus arrives in Clear Point. I hope Al has picked up the kids from Angie's. Our little house has the outside light on, so I head home. The kids are there. "I picked them up just after supper," Al says cheerily. "How was your conference?"

"Actually it was pretty cool; I got to be in the room with the elders." I say between hugs of hello from Zoë and J.J..

"Did you guys have fun? Did you like your supper?" J.J. wiggles off of my knee.

"She gave me a small plate, for a baby," says J.J. incredulously.

"Apparently he had thirds," Al adds.

"I guess you liked it then. Time for P.J.s." I remind myself to call and thank her; I hope they were not eating her out of house and home. It's almost bedtime and everything seems quite taken care of.

"They're waiting for you to read the story," says Al, "I told them you'd be home in time. You go on. I'll make us some tea." Al already holds the kettle under the tap. I sit for a moment, relieved to notice I can be gone and the world doesn't fall apart. The fluorescent lights in the kitchen are off. There is only the partial light of the cloth-covered lamp that hangs over the kitchen table. Everything looks brighter somehow in the dim lighting. "Horton! Horton!" J.J.. runs from the bedroom carrying the bright orange book in both hands. I scoop him up and head back to their room. The three of us crawl into the bunk with the roof. I put a fresh diaper for the night on J.J.. "Is Horton okay with you for tonight Zoze?" She nods, I wink and we settle in to read. Their room is cozy now. Al's mother bought each of them a fleecy soft blanket; one with cars, for J.J., all dark blues and yellows, and one with lighter blues and pinks with butterflies for Zoë. I wish I could buy them stuff sometimes, but I guess it doesn't really matter where it comes from…

I'm half awake and half asleep as I hear the voices of the native singing. They are so clear that it's as though I know all the songs, every drumbeat. The particular lilts of the chant, the throaty vibrations are coming to and from me simultaneously. This is a wonderful feeling and I'm sure I have always known how to sing like this and will most surely never forget. A man appears beside me. He is not someone I've ever seen before. He's dressed in a full tan colored buckskin outfit complete with the beaded fringed jacket. I can't quite make out his face so I ask, "Who are you?" just within my mind. He ignores my question, but I can't find my voice to reiterate.

"You see the man on the couch?" He lifts his head toward the living room where Al is still asleep on the couch. He doesn't wait for my response.

"That man is spiritually ill. You cannot save him. You cannot help him." I feel the beginnings of sadness bordering on an automatic response to defend Al, and also defend my ability to help him. None of this quite makes it into full form as he says, "Come with me." The next thing I know, we are on a balcony with a wrought iron railing and he stands in the corner. "You can change your reality anytime you choose." With that he turns into a raven and flies around in a circle. He lands on the corner of the railing. Blinking, head tilted to one side. I wonder how to turn myself into a bird, and how that will make things better. Just as I begin to feel like a failed shape shifter, he changes back.

"Just like that," he says, "It's that simple." With a certain nod he returns to the form of the bird. As he flies off, in his wake the air fills once again with the soothing rhythmic chants and the distinct drumming. I find myself back in bed. The echo of the drums and the songs remain with me surrounding me. An exhilarating comfort that lulls me to sleep. I wake up and the songs are still there, like when the perfect version of a song plays in your head with all the instruments in perfect time, back-up vocals and all. I lie there before the kids wake-up. Al is still on the couch. I stretch and replay the vision. Was that a vision? It wasn't quite like a dream. Whatever it was I sure feel different. I feel like everything is going to be okay in a way I haven't felt completely for a long time. Wow! What if it was a vision? That's very reassuring. I feel like I've gotten permission to leave. I'd better not tell anyone I think I've had a vision. Maybe I gave myself one, it doesn't feel like that. And that would be a somewhat disrespectful to the forces at work, to deny them when they go to all that trouble to help me. How typically human, pray for divine intervention and then when you get it rationalize it away. Sorry. I think I'll just bask in this new feeling for a while. It's just that simple. The drumming keeps me company until the household starts to stir and J.J. runs in.

"Zoë won't let me pour my own milk."

"He'll make a big mess," Zoë yells from the kitchen. It's time to get up. I walk past Al. His back is to the room, his face hidden, turned towards the back of the couch, still asleep.

21

Put the Lime in the Coconut

It's my turn to go see Max, the therapist alone. Al went last week, on his own. Although the vision is never far from me I haven't yet formulated quite how I'm going to leave. It does seem like a bit of therapy won't do the situation any harm. I'm thinking it might even make the split a more reasonable event. Perhaps civility isn't out of the question. Al didn't tell me much about his session. He wasn't negative about it and even agreed to watch the kids for my turn. We did the yard work last week with the kids in tow. Piling dead branches, raking etc. It was fairly painless although with Zoë and J.J. running around I'm not sure it was a great deal for Max in terms of productivity. I'm curious to see what will happen today. Max ushers me in, I wonder what Al has told him but I won't ask, it seems unscrupulous somehow, and I don't want to seem unscrupulous. I want to seem like the embodiment of rationality: Rationality, and a willingness to be open. There is the nagging edge of knowing that if this guy tries to make me the villain, I will write him off in a heartbeat. Either that or I'd crumble into a million pieces. Given the choices I'd have to go with the former. Max is relaxed and the ambiance is warm, I put my defense to rest on the chair beside me, within reach for the time being.

"So how have you been?" Max asks. Harmless enough, and yet to me, it's a fully loaded question.

"Pretty good, I guess you know I managed to get a day off, although it was more like I stole it." I want his opinion on my escapade.

"Was it a good day for you?"

Hmm, no judgment it seems. "Yes, actually I had a wonderful walk; it was refreshing to be alone."

He nods. "Good, I'm glad to hear it."

Now there's a moment and I can't resist. "So how did it go with Al?" It just occurred to me that I should at least make sure he had shown up. Max seemed to perk up at my question. If he'd been a dog his ears would have stood right up.

"Did he show up?" I wonder if that's why he perked, because it didn't go at all.

"I want to talk with you about Al," he says slowly.

"I thought that was against the rules or something, I mean I don't want you to talk to him about what I say, at least not specifically. Isn't there some kind of doctor patient trust rule?"

A brief smile crosses Max's face serving only to illuminate the serious look in his small brown eyes before he speaks again. He inhales and then exhales the last of the leftover lightness. "Normally, yes, but in the cases where a patient may do harm to themselves or others that rule is suspended. Do you understand?"

I'm taken aback, "Is Al planning to kill himself or something?"

"Not exactly. He has been violent with you in the past hasn't he?" He's awfully certain. I wonder how he knows, and then I remember the reason we got here in the first place. I say yes and tell him about going to the women's shelter, the choke although I wasn't choked, the being dumped off the bed, although I didn't have any broken bones or anything. I tell him about being thrown against the car door window and explain that the 1950's glass really does shatter easily. I don't want to give the impression that I was beaten. I explain that it would be an exaggeration and not fair to the women who were really severely hurt.

"I understand," he says. But I don't think he does. I think he thinks I'm minimalizing. But I'm really not. I'm not saying Al's behavior is acceptable. I'm just clear about not saying it's something different than it was. This is important to me because the perception game that Al plays is so distorted that for my mental health I cannot veer from the facts. The facts save me. He continues, "At any rate, I met with Al and it is my feeling that he is potentially dangerous."

Now it's my turn to inhale and exhale with relief. "You can tell that after one session?" I want this nailed securely.

Max's fleeting smile is there and gone again as he says a self-assured, no bones about it (broken or otherwise), "Yes."

"There's something wrong with him isn't there? What is it? And what can you tell me about me?" Now I'm excited and a little apprehensive that some diagnosis will tear apart the thrill of hearing these words.

There's that smile again. I'm beginning to think it's a twitch. I'm doing it too; oh my God I keep doing a little nervous twitch smile too. Odd. It's kind of like we've both known this all along and are just playing it out.

"Listen, what I recommend is that you leave before you end up with a picture frame accidentally in your eye."

"A picture frame in my eye? Was that a direct threat? It sure is a strange example otherwise." I'm trying to visualize a complicated assault that requires a handy picture frame and we don't own any. If Al had made the threat it could be metaphoric. I'm still puzzling through the idea when Max says, "No. No, it wasn't a direct threat made by Al. I had a client last year who suffered that tragedy." His attention is gone for a squint of the eyes.

"Had you told her to leave? That's awful, did she lose her eye?"

"I didn't see it coming, unfortunately, but these things happen sometimes. I wouldn't want to see something like that happen to you. I'm sure you don't want your vision impaired or something equally as serious to happen either."

This last bit seems to require my agreement and so I give it. "Yes, I mean no, I obviously don't want to get hurt." I chuckle inappropriately; the picture frame still rings a bit extreme. First the vision, now this, all forces conspiring, it's a go.

"Can you help him?" I feel like I'm making the transition a little too quick, feeling a tad too much glee at being released. Part of me is still worried about Al and I have some leftover guilt about leaving someone who is spiritually sick. I wonder at which point a person changes from an asshole into a sick person. Or are all assholes just people in pain. This realization is not new but still sad.

"Let's take care of first things first and talk about finding you and the kids a safe place to live, okay?"

"Okay." It's just that simple.

We haven't used up the entire hour so I suggest I use the time left to start looking for a place around the Cedar Park area. Max offers to help me look. I was going to walk around and look for "for rent" signs but with his car we could cover more ground. I think this is above and beyond which makes me a teeny bit suspicious. I hope he doesn't hit on me cause that would really ruin this whole "What a godsend" thing I've got going on.

It's weird being out of the office with Max. He has a little blue Honda Civic and I'm glad to notice the barely visible layer of dust on the dash.

I breathe easier when cars aren't too clean; it makes the owners seem more human and the car more organic somehow. It's a standard and we clutch up and down the hills. I only manage to take down two numbers and they are both apartment buildings. When I tell Max I'm not keen on apartments and that I usually find houses of some sort I can feel his disappointment. He gives me an authoritative sideways glance and explains to me like I'm a two year old and don't understand the gravity of my situation.

"Sometimes, Elsie, it's not advisable to be too choosy. I think it would be best if you give these places a try."

I acquiesce like a small child and dutifully take down the numbers. I know he's trying to help and I do appreciate it. There is the possibility he's right, but to me it's only vague like tomorrow's weather. I have to turn to look out the passenger door to write and swallow my rage and tears. Gee of course, why would I try to find a nice place? Why wouldn't I just be reasonable and try to begin anew in a depressing environment. It's as though I deserve to not have a choice. Punishment for picking a bad man. Well I'll be polite but I'm not buying it. I have the magic, the faith, that is what's saving me, moving me, even if it's true that Dr. Young promotes some faith in humanity.

The mood in the car has shifted as I attempt to cover my sulky disappointment. Max half smiles, looks at his watch and says he has to be getting back. I ask to be dropped off at the bus stop.

"Thank you so much, this is really more than I'd expected. I'll bring some money for you very soon, thanks again," I say before closing the car door and backing onto the curb. I feel weary. It's nice to have some help but it would be nicer to have a friend right about now. Professionalism leaves me somewhat cold, but hey, at least he stayed professional, and Godsend he remains.

I see the familiar relaxed gait of my smiling friend Jake coming down the hill towards me. "Well, well, well, what have we here?" He says looking me up and down. He's carrying what appears to be a large canvas and sets it beside him. "Going somewhere?"

"Just practicing my waiting skills." I grin smirkily right back. "What's that for?" I ask by way of making conversation. The distraction is slowly lightening my load.

"Waiting is a good skill. Oh, I paint, I told you, no? I notice when he says "I" he puts his long fingered paint stained hand over his heart. Pledging allegiance to the sentence. He notices the paint on his hands. "It's a little messy. I'm just taking it down to my studio on the drive. Do you want to come and check it out? Are you finished waiting? Yes?" I see the bus at the top of the hill and make a split second decision. I shrug, "Sure," and we head off down the hill towards the drive that borders on the ocean. As we hit the main drag there is a phone booth on the corner so I say, "I just need to make a phone call, where is your studio?"

"You see the hair salon there; well we share the space, another painter and me." A couple of steps away he swings around and adds, "We'll be in the back, the other painter is Fleming."

"I'll meet you there in a minute." I nod whilst dialing. Jake saunters off. Al picks up.

"Hi, it's me; I'm still in Cedar Park waiting for the bus. I thought I might go have a coffee." I proclaim, keeping all question out of my voice. I might, in fact, go have coffee. "How are the kids?" I can hear Zoë in the background asking for me.

"They're fine, Zoë wants to talk to you, just a sec." I hear him mumble something to Zoë as he hands her the phone.

"Mum, where are you?" she sounds cheerful and doesn't wait for an answer as there are more important things on her mind. "Jessica came to play we're making a fort like the kind you and Auntie Lainey used to do. Can I use your blanket? Al said to ask you."

"Sure, Zoë. Just don't drink juice on it, okay sweetie? Where's your brother? Are you letting him play too, since the fort is on his bed?" I know she means the bunk-bed fort.

"We will. But he's sleeping in your room now." Her voice sounds so little and faraway. The kiddy afternoon-ness gives me a second thought. Maybe I should rush home, but the sound of the gulls and surf wash me ashore in the present. "Bye Mummy."

"Bye sweetie, love you, blowing you a kiss."

"Blow you a kiss too. Here's Al." There is the muffled transfer of the phone and I picture her running to get my blanket, hoping she doesn't wake her brother.

"So I'll see you in a couple of hours," again, no question in my voice.

"No problem. Else, take your time." Al sounds like a friend. "We'll see you later."

"Okay I won't be too long, see ya." I hang up. Now this is confusing. For someone who is usually paranoid he doesn't seem worried at all at what Max might have said. I feel like a double agent, there is a certain part of me that likes the feeling. Secret Agent Elsie, dapper dresser fighting known demon. There is another part of me that feels like scum. Sleazy Nark, fake friend, betrayer of the weak.

The hairdressing salon is still open. It's a black and white checkered motif. Checkered tiles with black barber shop chairs running the length of the room facing mirrors. It smells of peroxide. I stand in the doorway and then Jake pokes his head out through a curtain in the back and waves me in. I tiptoe by the beauty people. Fleming is nowhere around.

"Wow, that's a big head!" I say pointing to a large painting; five feet maybe, it's all one face, done in various yellows except for the scarlet red lips.

"Sure is," Jake agrees. "What about those lips?"

I don't understand if this is a question so I just agree "Yeah, what about them."

In response to this, Jake laughs and then admits that this one is not his work. He pulls out some smaller canvases and asks what I think. The lines are scrambled and unclear, the colors mixing at will. I can make out that one is of a man. Somehow I sense he's a workingman, a farmer or something. The blues and grays are warm but not sad and I say that he seems like a guy who accepts his life. Not a dramatic character I'd say. I'm having fun and the more I say the more seems to come to me. Jake is egging me on. He is absolutely passion filled, oozing like filling from a cream puff pastry.

"What else do you see?" Finally after three or so of these sojourns into what I think is my imagination, Jake asks what I think is up with the girl with the big lips. I tell him I think he has a crush on her. I say I have to go and that I was thinking of getting a little snack and a coffee at Kelley's Korner. I leave the door open and Jake saunters through.

"Okie-dokie, let's go then." He grabs his leather satchel. And with that we take the back door into the alley so as not to disturb the beautification.

Kelley's Korner is just one block down and as you'd guess, on the corner. It's a joint, with regular fare, hamburgers and fries. I order a coffee and fries. Jake gets a chamomile tea. He reaches into his satchel and pulls out a black leather bound book and a brown crayon. I see when he opens it that it's a sketchbook, as the pages have no lines. It's no bigger than a paperback. He opens it randomly and starts drawing circular heads. He had been unabashedly staring at one of the other patrons.

"What do you think?" he asks, "is going on with him?" He continues to draw, peering up from under his falling hair to encourage my response.

"Well," I feel the blood rush to my head, "I don't know, it's not my place to say, I don't know him…" I trail off … a failure.

"You could read the paintings, and they were people."

"I didn't know them; I don't know. It didn't seem so personal, so judgmental." It was fun at the studio. This seems like a test, plus it was really the colors and energy of the paintings that had spurred my playfulness. These are live people who can respond.

"What's that?" Jake demands pointing to a tree just outside the window.

"It's a tree." At least I thought it was a tree, until he asked.

"And that?" he points again, to the small stones around the nearby plant.

"A rock," I answer with a mixture of pride and hesitancy.

"It's that simple, a rock is a rock, a tree is a tree, now, what about him, happy or sad?"

"Oh, he's a little sad because he misses his kids," I blurt, leaning in so as not to be heard. I don't know where the info came from but it feels like such a release. "I think there's three of them" I add, "they're little, he started late." The man was slightly balding and from his demeanor didn't seem like a bad sort. "This feels like spying, looking at someone else's cards, it feels weird Jake."

Without answering, or making any effort to assuage my guilt, Jake turns to the man who is about three tables away. He continues to draw, more like scribble really, and then lifts his head and says, "Do you have boys or girls, your kids I mean?"

The man looks confused for only a second then gently puts down his mug; Jake's smile seems to reassure him. I'm thinking don't bother the guy; boy you're a real showman aren't you. Because the other six people in the place are looking now as well.

"Two girls and a boy, why do you have kids?" He asks.

"No, no, not me but my friend here has a couple." Jake says inviting conversation.

I smile demurely adding, "Do they go to school here? Maybe I've seen you there." I'm searching for a rational explanation for knowing anything.

"Not here, no." He stops right there and looks away; clearly I'm not as compelling a conversationalist as my companion.

Something is clicking, formulating in my brain. I mean I have impressions all the time. I try to make them go away because I don't want to judge. Maybe what I observe isn't the same as judging; to know is not to judge. Jake begins to sketch other patrons.

Somehow the drawing helps him key into people. He can tell whether their relationships were good or not. He does a quick drawing of their heads down to their shoulder area. Sometimes he adds in other faces around them. He announces how many brothers and sisters they have. Everyone is enthralled. Most people are hungrier for information about themselves than they are for food. Of course aren't I, quite satiated with the knowledge that I could possibly do this too? This reminds me of that *knowing* feeling I got when my cat died, or when Al slept with Mia. Maybe some of my problem with Al has come from not trusting what I know; a rock is a rock, you don't make sense. All those times I've tried to understand, I think I was possibly trying to turn a rock into a tree or something to that effect.

22

Holding Back the Years

Luckily there isn't much to pack. My plan is to be gone before Al gets back from his day. I'm only taking what we'll need; it isn't like a move just yet. I'll call him and explain from a reasonably safe distance. I have some hope that we can work out some kind of agreement so the kids don't completely lose their male role model. I'm vaguely aware that fleeing from the person you refer to as a role model is incongruous somehow. Angie who has been following my story on Thursday installments at the coffee house has offered us her home. At least until I can find a place. When I mentioned the "face" of aggression to her she confided her own experience. It turns out her status as single mother and landed immigrant is largely based on a similar face she left behind in Seattle.

I quickly organize what few toys there are along with the kids' new blankets and clothes.

"Zoë, we're going to stay at Jessica's for a little while. It'll be like a sleepover. My friend Ange, your friend Jessica."

"And J.J and Gus" she interjects. "

Could you please collect your books?" I immediately regret phrasing this as a question. Zoë is eyeing the packing process suspiciously. I'm stuffing things into garbage bags. I'm trying to stay lighthearted, self-contained, but the flurry of stress must be seeping through. I'm like a confused sieve not knowing what to strain, cold metal stress clangs like an alarm. I notice too late as it rings in Zoë's heart.

"But Mummy, what about Al? Won't he be sad?" She hasn't budged from my side and I'm stepping around her trying to figure out the appropriate answer. In the parenting books everyone always has time for a nice sit down discussion. People have time to think. What I'm not saying is probably more valuable. What I'm not screaming at her is *why on earth are you looking out for him? Do you have any idea what small thread I'm hanging onto right now?* I go into my room to stop the seepage from pouring onto her. I remember the other evening when Al called me a big zero right in front of Zoë. It was then that I knew in a place more certain than I could ever be just for myself. I knew I couldn't allow her to grow up thinking it was okay to talk to a woman like that.

"You're not being nice," she charges, already learning whom to critique.

"What?" I answer vaguely as though I don't understand the question, buying time. I need to remember that Zoë is saving my life. Seeing her see me as a zero is possibly saving us all. But right now she seems like a five-year-old traitor.

"I said, you're being mean to Al," she's holding her ground. She's picked a fine time to let me know she's no coward. The 'poor Al' signature does seem to have made its mark on her already though. I want to cry, but the survivor sieve is holding out and the sound of gritting teeth is the only thing getting through.

"Don't you worry about Al; he's a grown-up. It's not your job to worry about him. Now please get the stuff that you want to bring."

Thank goodness J.J. is napping.

Once settled at Ange's, Jessica and Zoë are spending the afternoon flying makeshift kites in the lane way. The little boys are playing cars on Gus's side of the bedroom, making them fly off the bed and crash dramatically onto the floor in a never ending fascination with gravity and sound effects. We smoke, and Ange tells me about the perils of single life. It doesn't sound too appealing. Her last love interest lasted a weekend and it wasn't exactly what she'd had in mind. Ange is graphic and the details of their lovemaking positions (she was lying on her back but her legs were practically over her head, like this…) take on an animated, cartoon flavor in the telling. She reminds me of a west coast version of Mia in a way. She is more out-doorsy and without the east coast cynicism. She is down to earth but raucous. Ange is a devoted mother; her kids are her world. I see her as a real gutsy single Mom. I also hear her loneliness in every rowdy joke.

From time to time we notice the white plastic grocery bags tied to a string are floating past the window beside the couch. The girls run back and forth and they catch some air. Jessica is running much quicker and seems to be more enthralled with the game. I can tell out of the corner of my eye that Zoë is paying bag service to the whole thing. She really likes Jessica.

After a supper of cheese omelet and the kids off to sleep, I decide to make the call. Al is soft. "Okay Elsie, maybe this is for the best."

"I was hoping we could work out some kind of schedule. You know so we can both be with the kids. Work together, I mean just because we are apart they shouldn't have to suffer." I'm not sure I totally believe what I'm saying but I still wish this could happen. On some level I still wish he were all right.

"I miss you guys already." He is speaking super gently. "We'll work something out." Terrifyingly tender.

"Okay," I say, "I'll call you later on in the week and we'll discuss the details."

"Else, could you call tomorrow?" he is pleading, gently kneading the unstable ground.

"Sure Al, I want this to go well, talk to you soon." I hang up, my raised eyebrow hanging there still waiting for the other shoe to drop. I turn from the wall phone towards Ange. She is still sitting at the dinner table, protectively staying in the same room during my call. She lights her smoke and extends the match to me.

"Y'know sister," the smoke blows like jet stream out of the corner of her mouth. "You're going to need a lawyer, if Al is anything like my ex."

"Do you really think so?" My two fingers slide down the tube and catch on the burning ember. "You're probably right." I say changing hands to remove the cigarette and shake the singed fingers. "Ouch, I have a suspicion this isn't going to be as easy as it seems. Did you see that?" Ange shakes her head in a way that suggests I have failed smoking 101 and possibly the handling of objects on fire.

The legal aid lawyer I manage to contact is a woman named Constance Devereau. The appointment is set for next week. In the meantime I've got to find a place to live.

The first weekend I've agreed to let Al have the kids. I have some misgivings, I mean I'd just like to say he was a big mistake and get on with my life. I imagine that's how all break-ups must feel. He's never been aggressive with them. I want to be reasonable, fair. There must, there would be, a lack of trust. I will force myself to work through it; I will force myself to share. Once I agree, it turns out he's got some work this weekend and will just take them on Saturday for the day. This suits me fine. I'll look for a place during the day then.

I'm walking up hill in Cedar Park looking for signs in windows. I think the little town will be a good place to start over. It's about a ten-minute drive from where Al lives. I'm only one street up from the ocean, the hills are quite steep, and I find myself leaning into the hill in order to walk. The day is hot but with the ocean breeze and absence of mosquitoes it doesn't feel quite like summer yet. Despite the hill and the heat I'm not even sweating.

On my right hand side, the ocean side, I see an open door. There is a man frantically moving stuff around in a drawer. I can see right up his steps and into his house from where I am on the sidewalk. I try not to look like I'm staring. Admittedly this seems in direct contrast to what I want and a bit ridiculous. I'm stopped on the sidewalk and looking directly at the man willing him to notice me. After a minute or so that seems much longer he finally lifts his head from the task at hand and turns in my direction. I nod. He nods.

I shift apologetically," Your door was open." I say this as though we all must stare in if the door is open and he must've known this and indeed wanted someone to do just that.

"Yes, yes it was, and it still is." His voice is soft and made softer juxtaposed with his rifled appearance. He's a large man hunched over the counter. He doesn't smile. "I'm clearing stuff out," he adds. He barely turns to speak, "You're new around here aren't you?" He removes the drawer from its socket and puts it on the counter. "There, it should be easier like this." He looks over awaiting reply. I get the impression I can take a little extra time answering this guy. Like the spaces between his seconds are longer than most people's.

"I'm hoping to be new around here; you aren't moving by any chance are you?" It's worth a shot; he is *clearing out* after all. He tilts his gray bearded head to one side; his hair is cut just below his ears and flops out straight edged looking wiggish.

"As a matter of fact I might just need someone to take over here. Do you want to look around?" He motions for me to come up the two steps. "C'mon in." I walk directly into small the kitchen, just inside the still open door. "Seriously, you're moving?" He nods and mutters "Mhmm as I said."

"When would that be? I don't want to seem pushy; I just need to find a place as soon as possible." I follow him from the kitchen into the living room, which contains a bed and a kitchen table.

"I'd like to leave the stuff here 'til I get to where I'll need it. How does that sound to you?" This sounds absolutely grand to me. The entire front and sidewall are glass from midway up the wall, and the view is of the pier. It seems this is the upper suite in the house. Because of the hill the top floor seemed even with the street so I don't notice there's a suite underneath until I look out the window. The windows run the entire upper half of the living room and realize I'm quite high up from the lawn below. I can see the pier jutting out to sea.

"What about the back yard?" I ask gesturing out the window.

He looks as though he's never considered it. He's distracted; he may live there, in perpetual distraction. "Well I suppose you could use it. What did you want to use it for?"

"I have kids."

"You can work that out with the neighbor downstairs. I'm leaving tomorrow." He opens the door to a little back bedroom. Perfect for J.J.. We head back through the living room to another big bedroom. That'll be for Zoë. She'll be thrilled, her own room. I'm going to stay in the living room. I won't need privacy. Each bedroom has a bed.

I want to ask him all kinds of questions. Why is he moving? How much is the electricity bill? How much is the rent? When will he want his stuff? But I don't want to break the spell of fortuitous findings for the faithful. I wonder why I think good fortune is so fragile that it might break under the weight of a few questions.

"So, umm I should come back tomorrow to talk to the landlord or would you give me the number or something?"

"Come back before noon and I'll give you the key. The landlord will show up sooner or later to get the rent and you can talk to him then. By then you'll be the new tenant."

"Okay, what's the rent approximately?" I don't know why I only want an approximation except that if it is out of range then I can convince myself it's possible to negotiate later.

"I'm paying four fifty now. I don't know if he'll try to raise it on you or not." It is already out of his hands.

"Thanks," I reach out to shake his hand, "By the way what's your name?"

"Fleming, I have a studio on Marine drive. I am going to stay down there for a while, save some dough. You must be Elsie, Jake pointed you out once when you walked by." Now, he grins. He knew who I was all along.

"So you're Fleming." I don't know much about him so I nod up and down to leave some mystery. "Nice to meet you, I guess I'll be back to see you tomorrow."

Ange is no doubt relieved that I've managed to find a place so quickly but mostly the enthusiasm of a good friend is what shows. We pile all six of us into her blue beetle. The stereo blasts her Paul Simon tape. The kids sing along to "Diamonds on the Soles of her Shoes" as we take the coastal road that links her town with my new one. The trunk of the car is full of what little I'd brought with me. The morning sun is shining, reflecting our excitement. It's a short road trip, but with full road trip feeling. Possibility. We pull up outside the new place and Ange pulls on the parking brake.

"Everybody, the hell out!" She says as though it's a common celebratory way to disembark. Her kids are nonplussed; mine are a little startled but take their cue from hers. They've learned that she can bark but almost always with a smile. She'd sometimes say things like, "My kids know I hate them, don't you kids?" She'd be hugging them and smooching their cheeks all the while. You could practically see her heart pained with mother-love. Zoë might stand back at first and shoot me a worried look.

Ange's big heart out shone her roughness almost immediately. Although when she'd wield the big cutting knife and say stuff like "…or I'll cut your arm off," I couldn't help but cringe a bit myself.

Like Mia, she loves shock value. Also similarly they both enjoy talking about their healthy sexual appetites making sure to let you know they'd been told they had some talents in that arena. Ange is loyal and always tells it straight. She is less devious and less privileged then Mia. I guess I find them both at once fearless and reckless and strangely vulnerable in the way they pretend not to need. Characters. Ange has lived through this same undoing as I'm going through. Her ability to relate is invaluable. I think that Mia is understandably more interested in her own ability to avoid this particular kind of mess. Of course, she did sleep with Al and so wasn't repulsed enough to stay away completely. I shudder to remember that, and her commiserating with me at the shelter. It almost hurts more than Al disappointing me. I feel her betrayal was in not believing me about Al. She didn't try to see what I was experiencing; she didn't trust my point of view. This is the same thing that Al was always accusing me of. Are we all afraid of each other's experience, if we can't relate? Before I go too far down the road of my own betrayal of Al, I tell myself to focus on the facts. He hit me. She slept with him.

It's a strange expectation we have of those we love to see from our point of view, to back our reality, so we don't feel so separate from one another. Sometimes I think if we just thought the love place was bigger than the details it would cover everything. But in life, the details of how we live affect each other.

I wonder if I'll start to talk about sex the way Ange does when it's not available anytime. It's become a subject best avoided except to acknowledge another thing that wasn't working out. Once you're afraid of someone, their touch is tainted, plus it didn't seem like I had talent, at least not the kind that elicits the sorts of compliments Mia and Ange rave about. It strikes me as bizarre that these big fans of theirs often desert them, and I can't get rid of someone who doesn't even compliment me. Fleming answers the door and I introduce Ange and all the kids.

"Good timing, I was just leaving." He scans the room, turning away as he's speaking, leaving Ange to shrug at me. Then he adds, "The key is on the table. I may want the place back in a few months, but that's all up in the air for now." He nods little nods while he is speaking. I think he's nodding to himself but I'm not certain so I nod little nods right along with him. I'm wondering where the key would've been had we not arrived just then. "I was going to leave the key in the mail box for you."

"Sure, thanks." How would I have known?

"Bye now, enjoy the place." And with that he leaves, with that, it is my place. Anything can happen in a few months. A place with a view can happen within a few months. I sigh as Ange and I take in the scenery. People work a whole lifetime to retire with an ocean view. Gratitude.

I ended up doing my taxes as a single parent. Al never did show up with the paperwork. My springtime refund was going to come in handy, as there were no dishes or pots and pans. After lugging in our lovely luggage, vintage Glad™ and dumping them we head to the thrift shop uptown. Two dollars worth of second hand (slightly fearful) aluminum (one pot, one frying pan) and a bowl, a plate, and knives and forks each and we are set with the added bonus of very few dishes to wash. We stop by the grocery store and pick up some essentials; milk, tea, granola, veggies, rice and bread and peanut butter. We drop them off. It's early afternoon so we all head to the beach for a celebration of fish and chips and juice. We make trails of French fries for the seagulls to follow, to tempt them to come as close as possible. We top it all off with frozen yogurt. The child size is only fifty cents, and although the cone is doll size the kids are all happy with them. We are about two feet from the store when J.J.'s yogurt does a nosedive onto the hot pavement leaving his quivering lip peering into an empty miniscule cone. I pick him up and run back for a quick refill. The lady behind the counter doesn't charge us, and smiles cheerily at J.J.. who is still deciding whether or not to be upset. Squeals and delight stuck to juicy sand stuck to happy hands. Easily rinsed when it's time to go. We are walking up from the beach, up the stairs from the main drag to home, the kids are up ahead, J.J. and Gus hanging off the railing at intervals. Ange and I walk slowly and let the kids wear themselves out. We know that's what we're doing, without having to speak it. I realize that this is the end of our six-some and soon it will be me and mine again. I'll miss the company and the support. Someone to decide dinner with.

Part II

Pictures and Stories

23

First There is a Mountain

When I walk into Carol Devereaux's office I'm thinking that this is just good common sense. I fill out the forms that make it clear that I'm poor enough to warrant her legal-aid service. I wait for my name to be called. There's no one else in the room. Empty chairs line three out of the four walls. It's a central waiting room for several legal aid lawyers' offices with pamphlets of available government services filed in wall racks. Lawyers doing their mandated time and getting paid by the government. I flip through the pamphlets without registering the content, preoccupied with the designs. I notice there's information about how many people in a family and their corresponding income. There is also a little drawing of one or two androgynous grownups, big silhouettes, and little silhouettes for the amount of children connected to maximum allowable income by a dotted line. I don't have to check if I qualify. It reminds me of grade two mathematics. I am both insulted and grateful for the simplicity. That's an actual job, I think to myself, designing simplicity. The central secretary calls my name.

"Ms. Devereux will see you now." She motions to the doorway where a medium sized woman with shoulder length blond hair stands like a signpost, smiling absently. She is reminiscent of one of the silhouette drawings. Her grey dress pants have a pleat down the front. Somehow it's the pleat that makes me feel scruffy in my loose cotton sweater and jeans. I wonder how someone finds the time to go to law school and master ironing, and I am tired just thinking about it. I'm impressed and think that it's a good thing to have a woman lawyer; surely she will understand and want to champion my cause.

"I don't want to have a fight," I say once inside her office with the door closed. "I just want to be sure that he can't take J.J. away or pull any stunts. He's violent and somewhat unstable." I add hesitantly. I feel guilty for saying this as though it's somehow my fault. It's as though once you've hooked up with someone like that it's kinda your own fault and it's really bad form to use their behavior against them so you can get away. All this distorted rationalizing doesn't matter, as Carol doesn't react one bit to my allegations of his near insanity.

"Okay, Elsie, we just need to send him notification that you are seeking custody and then we'll see what comes from that." She closes the folder and straightens up in clear indication that our meeting is over. I don't feel quite ready to move, I'm under water and I'm scared. I don't feel reassured or even seen.

"I'm not a vindictive ex," I explain. "I'll let him see them; I mean I want to work something out. If he's violent, I can't possibly leave the kids with him, not that I'd want to. But I mean it's not possible that being violent to their mother doesn't count at all in relation to his relationship to them does it?"

"Has he ever been violent to the children?" She asks it as though asking if you've ever had the measles. I try not to react too much, I need to trust my lawyer, if that's possible, it would help if she exuded some human warmth, but instead her desk is like a line between species. I'm torn between trying to imitate her officious style or be extra human for the both of us.

"No, he hasn't. But he has called me a big zero in front of them, and grabbed me by the throat, amongst other things."

"Do you have hospital records, for yourself?" she asks without looking up from the yellow paper she's taking notes on. I get the impression that she knows I don't have hospital records by the tone in her voice, daring me to prove the allegations.

"Well, no I didn't actually have to go to the hospital," I feel like an imposter, "but I did call the police." I say this like it's a good thing, as conflicted as hopeful can be. She closes the folder and stands up.

"Did you press charges?" Carol now looks vaguely interested, and I am loath to disappoint but, "No, he promised to get counseling." We are playing legal go fish and I don't have any of the right cards. It feels as though she's not even in the game, just going through the motions and coming up empty. She's still standing and the folder is still closed. She comes out from behind the desk to usher me to the door. "I'll send the papers; we'll talk in a week or so."

Halfway out the door I turn, "So I'll call you then?"

"Yes," she nods.

And that's it. I feel a sense of foreboding loneliness.

I take the bus out from the city, meditating on the bus trying to imagine that it'll all work out. I'm not sure how to proceed. I want to be fair; he is J.J.'s dad. I will put my flight instincts on hold and try to set up some weekend visiting. This thin blond fellow about my age recognizes that I'm meditating and makes friendly conversation with me. He seems harmless and is going to the same stop. You'd think if you knew someone was meditating that would be the exact time you wouldn't strike up a conversation. Even so, I welcome the diversion as he prattles on about the practice of meditation; transcendental vs. creative visualization.

"Transcendental, that's where you focus on your teeth isn't it?" I say slyly.

He pauses for only a second before responding, "Yes, where in creative visualization you would focus on your palette." He cocks his head raising his shoulder, and it looks like a curtsy. The bus ride flies by hastened by mild flirtation.

I settle into my new digs and am much relieved to discover that I enjoy our new place. Jake stops by often and as I am not in the habit of locking doors. It is quite pleasant to occasionally arrive home and find him lounging. We set up easels in the living room where I sleep, and I begin to paint my way out of emotional turmoil. I am becoming a tad obsessed with painting. It feels somehow medicinal. Rolling into summer with an ocean view and an art form seems like freedom to me, in keeping with yet another cliché social stigma "the welfare artist." Although the artist part is a bit of a stretch. Money is still scarce and I've had to go to the food bank on several occasions to get through. It rankles me. I don't know how to feel about it. I want to just roll with it but somehow feeding yourself is a the bottom of the barrel requirement. So here I sit at the table, my own room so to speak; writing, sorting it out. The kids are sleeping, and here is the story of me, or at least someone like me, going to the food bank. Hoping it will stay in the past, reassuring the present.

The Food Bank
by
Elsie Shaw

I'd only been down to the food bank on one other occasion. It was a basket of mixed reactions; Gratitude and humiliation dominated; disappointment and frustration layered themselves thinly behind necessity. Not to mention guilt, yes the guilt based on the belief that the truly, truly desperate wouldn't have those other emotions. It was in a small wooden annex to some city building. I stood in line, the late morning sun warming my sense of displacement. The lady behind the desk asked my name and if I'd ever been there before. I practically whispered my name "Elsa Shaw" and muttered a muted "Yes." I showed her my I.D.

They take down your name so as to prevent people going through more than once. The fellow behind me, also in his mid-twenties was clearly a regular. He was bursting with cheer; "Hey ladies," he said through my back, "Anything special this week? Any of those fresh apples left?" his lightness bounced around the room finding cracks to shine through. I thought I was portraying a decent mood until I found myself an impenetrable shadow slinking to the first counter. "Meat or fish, hamburger or canned tuna?" asked the portly woman with no expression. "Meat, please." I answered. She handed me a cellophane wrapped blob of ground beef, which I plopped into the plastic bag I'd been given. I'd have preferred tuna but knew the kids would like the hamburger. I knew I couldn't have both because last time I'd been a real pain by asking for half and half. "We leave the tuna for those who are real vegetarians," she'd said. Today, she turned towards the light and her voice took on a sing–song quality, "Odey, now you know if you want the good stuff, you've got to come early."

"I thought you'd save me some." He opened his arms palms up in expectation.

"First come, first serve sweetie!" came her contralto reply.

I stood looking around, where to next? The breadbox or the vegetable bin? The vegetable bin had a mix of potatoes and carrots, few enough to see the bottom of the box. There was a self-serve plastic bag at the side, but I knew I was being watched. The rumble of rooting around echoed my own discomfort. I grabbed four of the giant horse carrots and four potatoes, leaving about the same in the box. I glanced behind me self consciously as I felt someone near. I saw now what I hadn't noticed before; sunshine Odey was in fact Odey Durns who had grown up two streets over from me in our middle class suburb back east.

I straightened and looked harder, his face melting in and out of the teenage mould that had been set in my memory. He looked back, head cocked to one side.

We both said at the same time, "Are you..." and then stopped to let the other continue. I went first "Aren't you Odey Durns who used to live on Bellevue?"

"And you're little Elsie Shaw aren't you?" We both paused for a moment smiling. For me it was a long moment of recognizing where we were. A moment of wanting to say, "What the hell happened to you?" Here we were in the club of those incapable of feeding themselves (temporarily at least, I told myself).

"How's your sister, Eleanor, wasn't it?" I faked a bit of bad memory. I knew full well it was Eleanor. Ella whore, duh! She was jeered at. The kind of girl, older than us who held her nose jumping off the low board at the pool and entered the water knees bent and flatfooted. The kind that didn't fit, that served as a warning to us younger ones as to the potential social torment that might await if you weren't paying attention. Oh God did he think I was one of those jeering and am now getting my just deserts foraging in dim lighting for roots?

"She's good, married, living in Ontario."

I nodded, "Good, good, any kids?"

"Yeah, two boys."

Right, of course people don't stay trapped in an awkward mid-air stance for life; they move on and become accepted into gentler circumstances. Some people anyway. Odey was always a certain kind of cool; he was so in he seemed to think the food bank was where it was at these days. I was frozen in between torture and envy. "What about you, do you have kids?" Throughout this exchange the question as to why he was here hung in my mind and I thought he must have been wondering the same about me. This was not exactly the trip to Europe or University Education our neighbourhood had promised. But if it even occurred to him there was no sign.

"Yup, I have three," he beamed.

"Me too, I mean I have two," I added. I then became very interested in what was in the bags, seemingly assessing my take for the week, feeling a little shy.

"Listen," continued Odey, "There are other food banks around you know. Unhuh, they are open on different days. If you make the rounds you can actually get some good stuff. That's why I'm late here; I had the days mixed up. You really do have to come early to get the good stuff."

"I don't want to sound ungrateful, but what is the "good stuff"?" I croaked through a half smile.

"Oh some fresher bread and more choice in the canned soups, more fruit and veg. The veg don't keep so they don't get much y'know."

I was transported out of embarrassment and into the present. Odey's knowledge of these survival techniques had unhumiliated me as I made mental note of potential food sources. He smiled, he laughed, the old neighbourhood vanished like a veneer and we were the real unvarnished wood underneath. I might as well be here if I'm here, I thought, but being raw wood left me somewhat vulnerable.

We never mentioned the circumstances that led either of us to meet and when we parted it was in a light-hearted, "see you around" kind of way. I wanted to run away from Odey and the charity schedule. I wanted to buy albacore tuna without a fiscal dilemma. I refused to be comfortable.

When I came back the following week I looked for him, the smattering of familiar the doorway to acceptance. I began to emulate his demeanor. The shackles of pride that had been so heavy were unlocked for me. Unlocked by Eleanor Durn's brother, Ellawhore whom I'd once felt sorry for. Here was food for the taking, yeah so beggars can't be choosers, but the misery is optional. This isn't Africa after all.

"Hey Lorna, any fresh fruit left?" I practically hummed. I was met with a blank stare; I clearly didn't have Odey's charm. I couldn't even pull off the food bank without looking like a misfit.

Then, there she was, right there with me, the ghost of pre-splash Eleanor Durn, hovering over the water, after springing off the board, with a little dribble of added spittle for dramatic effect, staring blankly as she always seemed to. Not even alarmed at her condition. I took her aside mid-air and said, "It might go better if you point your toes, straighten your legs and back and don't pull your bikini up to your armpits." But no, that wasn't quite right. Maybe I'll just say hi and try not to be afraid it's catching. No, "hi" seemed glib. Finally I did my own mid-air rendition of the funky chicken with complete abandon, as gangly and joyful as I could manage. Amid the sound of the water blasting open I heard a faint voice, when I surfaced, alone again and gradually focused, the Lorna food bank lady was speaking. "You know what dear; we just might have some nice crisp apples." I think I saw a wink. I wiped the water from my eyes and came up for air.

"That would be great! It's a perfect day for apples."

The End

I still don't have a phone but I use my next-door neighbour Alex's to call Caroline Devereaux. Once connected she says, "Hello, Elsie, it doesn't look good, it appears he's contesting."

"What does that mean, exactly, that we'll share?" I ask expectantly.

"No, the document his lawyer, his expensive lawyer, has sent me, says that he wants full custody of both the children," she pauses.

"That's crazy, how? Both? Zoë isn't even his real daughter! Can he do this? I mean I'm not exaggerating he's not stable."

"Well, he is claiming that you are unstable, Elsie, and he is entitled to do so in court, in fact it's one of the only conditions that custody would be removed from the mother."

"But he can't possibly win, right? I mean he's violent and doesn't make any sense? Surely someone will notice."

"His allegations are serious ones; we'll just have to see what happens. You'll need to see the court appointed social worker to start with. I'll give you his address."

"What allegations? I haven't done anything!" I am now on the verge of some very unstable behavior.

She interrupts, "Make the appointment with Mr. Hartley as soon as you can, and we'll see from there, call me after you've seen him, and just be honest." She gives his number, and then says good-bye.

I hang up the receiver. The kids are playing on the balcony having a Popsicle, Alex is a Popsicle addict; he always has a box on hand which the kids discovered very quickly. He works the night shift paving roads so he's home during the day and usually up until early afternoon. This, I'm afraid is where I turn into the neurotic needy problem ridden neighbor who one might regret opening their door to. But Alex shows no sign of repulsion just yet. I sit there staring, tears welling up, hands shaking. I know I said everything was great in my new home but I guess I'm still recovering. I don't want a fight. I don't know if I have any fight left. There is too much at stake. I think I may be actually growling and muttering when I notice Alex beside me,

"Are you okay? I couldn't help overhearing, you sounded pretty upset." He asks, offering me half a raspberry Popsicle.

"Thanks," the icy flavor cools me down. I explain the situation to Alex. "Do I seem nuts to you? Do I seem like a bad Mother?" He answers, "no," predictably, to both questions, but I feel a little better anyway. "Thanks for letting me use your phone, see ya later," I say, "C'mon guys," and they dutifully come through the house to follow me home. They follow their pie-in-the sky-eyed-protector; still carrying the red stained stick.

O.K. so there are now some official documented accusations that I am a crazy person. I'm fairly certain that this is not the case. The continued question; what would a normal person do? Clearly a very sane person wouldn't be in this situation. This perspective seems little help in defining my next course of action and yet I find myself clinging to it like a life rope. When I feel like I'm hanging on to the world, to myself, by a blade of grass I assume that the metaphor itself renders me sane. A real whacko wouldn't be constantly assessing.

Things are becoming more complicated than I had anticipated. I can't help but wonder if I didn't provoke Al by getting a lawyer involved. He's picked up the kids a couple of times for a day or two and it wasn't too bad after the initial 'should've been predictable' unreliability. That is to say, I bought them little pack sacks and got them pumped up to spend some time with him, 'a sleepover' I called it. I didn't really want to send them; I was told that co-operating would be the best course. I don't get this logic, but I couldn't bear to lose them, especially knowing as I do what I'd be losing them to. We sat on the porch for a while as the six o'clock pick up time came and went. They took off their packs, (they'd been wearing them around). We let the packs wait on the porch alone, and went in to eat leftover stir-fry. The sun went down, the retracting light and hope keeping pace, and we/they gradually gave up. He finally showed the next day around two p.m. So I had to retell myself to be fair and give this a chance. I don't want to be one of those ex's, always trying to control everything. Anyway, I remembered whom I was dealing with. Probably we needed time to adjust, still, those packs waited out there all alone in the dark all night.

24

Fashion

I receive copies of the affidavits in the mail; they are ridiculous and very scary. He has letters from people I've never met saying what a wonderful father he is and how he misses his kids. Someone called Chloe, oh wait; I did meet her once, she moved in down the road the week I left. I mean what is this, can anyone have an opinion on my life now, and it gets read in court? Where were they all when he had me by the throat?

I read some of the accusations and they are true. I did write the violent and sexy story, and *someone* did find it. I was experimenting with a new style, because I thought I had always been a bit of a starchy writer. And so here I am trying to be all innocent and motherly whilst the courts will read something about blood trickling down legs while orgasms are being painted, I think the artist was the one getting off, but I really can't remember. (There may even have been some explicit reference to oral sex; I was really trying to be graphic.) Worst of all, it wasn't even beautiful prose and it was on a scrap of paper I'd left lying around. It was an experiment for God's sake, not a testimony to my state of mind or my writing skill. Well, I'm not even sure where I left it, and that might be the best indicator of the state of my ego if nothing else. I wasn't proud enough to leave it out, none of my writing is lying around. It's usually tucked away in a drawer. I hesitate to say I suspect it was stolen, as I'm somewhat paranoid of seeming paranoid. My first public forum; my worst piece of crap. So this is what it must feel like to be Al, all misunderstood and paranoid. His paranoia is different, but I'm not certain the importance of paranoia is in the details. Overall alienation and trying to get people to see a point of view is crazy making. The truth is somewhere in the middle they say. I say the truth is in the details, like the hole in the wall where he rammed the scissors, intent to frighten. Isn't that truth enough?

Then there was the part in the affidavit about me having gone out of the house in my five year old's doll's clothes. All true. That is all they will say, the one word answer, yes or no. Well …yes. As it was I took her doll's skirt and used it for a social experiment. It was made of a mesh type fabric, like tulle and the waistband was just the right size to fit around my forehead. I put it on like a headband and I found it was very veil like. The world looks a little different through a veil; sort of like sunglasses but more risqué. I wore it out to the local coffee house, which was a publicly proclaimed 'anything goes' environment. It was actually quite interesting. It was surprising how many people have veil fantasies. I only got to wear it for the first few minutes because people kept wanting to play with it. I suppose its toyish origins still clung to it even in this new arena. New voices found themselves in the safety of a thin disguise. It was worn as an armband as well as a veil, people were shaded, men became women, and everybody's a widow. By the end of the evening the director of the event was in his underwear, on stage, the veil neatly around his thigh like a garter. Lucky for him, his actions aren't under scrutiny. I considered this a success. It could have been an installation piece if I'd documented it, but instead it has documented me.

It is also true I wore my daughter's little patchwork skirt over a pair of leggings as a mini skirt. This was a direct imitation of Judy from back home, who always seemed so fashionable. She had actually used the same skirt once back east. There is a fine line between fashion and fool and the crossing can be subtle. This seems quite damaging to those nearby. I try to write sexy stories and get accused not of crimes of passion, but yes, crimes of fashion.

My lawyer also includes notice of 'their' intent to check me out, a home visit, to assess what? I wasn't sure, the home itself? How I act in the home? The décor? Perhaps the question should be more like; what do I need to do to seem like I'm normal? When I waited for Fleming to leave and then simply moved in hoping the landlord wouldn't mind, things had all worked out. Things working out and seeming normal, I knew, were not necessarily the same thing. I'm just not certain which one is more important to the people who decide if you are normal enough. The lives of little live humans are at stake; the word normal is starting to seem glib to me.

At any rate they are coming, it's only one man but he brings with him the 'they' in terms of criteria of which I am not fully aware. They should send out a list. Normal mothers will have the following in their homes . . . acceptable people will say. . . . At least that way I could be prepared. I am a little discouraged that the intention to prepare, as a demonstration of commitment isn't more encouraged. I'm vaguely aware that they are not checking Al out, in the tiny rental the documents refer to as "the marital home." This strikes me as odd because we're not married and we only lived there for 6 months or so. Ms. Devereaux says that's because I'm the one going for custody. I guess the idea is that he could win by default. I think it's only me being investigated because I'm the one with the legal aid lawyer; his mother is paying for his. Wealth can normalize eccentricity, whilst poverty delivers dysfunction.

I visit Mr. Hartley, the social worker, at his downtown office. I bring the children. I see that girl; she's one who wrote about Al being a loving father. She gets in the elevator with us in the lobby. She presses the number five, so I press nothing. Since we had only met briefly once and I was surprised to see her, I try to be friendly.

"Hey, isn't this funny," I say referring to us being in the same spot at the same time, far away from the old neighbourhood.

"Ya, what a coincidence," she seems to move into the corner, literally taken aback. I knew she had been tricked by Al's very real pain, so I add nicely so she'll know I don't blame her, "You don't know whom you are defending, in fact you don't know us at all."

"As a matter of fact," she says, smelling of smug, "I know Al and I know Zoë and J.J. don't I guys? We put the swing set up together."

Zoë collaborates, "Yeah Mum, Chloe is Al's friend, she's new. She lives in the house with the rope swing."

"Oh, I see," I mutter.

"I think it's important to defend good parents," she says, smirky, smarmy, smug.

"I would think it would be difficult to assess so quickly." I put on what I like to think of as my real estate voice, factual yet perhaps there are hidden defects. "You don't even know me." I try really hard not to sound pleady or to care.

"I believe I know enough," she stares. And that's that. The doors open and I usher the kids out, head held as high as one can when ushering short people, it is not the fifth floor where I need to go. In fact there is a big metallic number three facing us. It comes into focus just as the door closes behind us. While I was talking J.J. must've pushed number three. It was just within his reach. Zoë gives me her knowing glare. The clarity of her little voice, "Mum, mum, mum . . ." Is there like an echo, it is now on replay since my own emotions have subsided. I had barely heard her as we were leaving the elevator.

"Sorry Zoë," I say, "I got distracted." Once I realize this is what's happened I don't mind having escaped that woman. I do cringe momentarily though, at the thought that both she and Zoë watched me blow my bluff. So much for my real estate voice. We'll just wait and take the next ride up. " Zoë, would you please push the up arrow sweetie."

The waiting room is surprisingly right outside the elevator doors, the secretary's desk, blocking the adjacent office entrance. I scan for reading materials or toys. There isn't much. Just as we are seated the office door opens and Ms. Neighbourhood Watch from the elevator, strolls out and right past us to the elevator. In the instant that it takes for me to fully realize her presence is related to my situation, she is gone. Ouch.

Mr. Hartley would like to see me, and then the kids. The secretary offers to watch them for a few minutes in the waiting room; clearly she has done this before and proffers crayons and paper. The office is predominantly brown and Hartley's silver hair contrasts, making him like a silver fox, not enough camouflage to protect him. I think this is a good thing, maybe.

"Elsie, hello. Come in," he gestures to the chair in front of his desk. I lean over and shake his hand as I'm sitting. "Nice to meet you," I say.

"We are here to try to understand the custody issue between yourself and Al, the children's father. I've looked over the file and I have a few questions for you and then I'd like to speak to the kids."

"Mhmm, yes, okay." I nod. I'm cooperating.

"So, what are your plans for the future? Do you have any? I mean have you given any thought to this? It is quite important as you might imagine, to let us know where you stand in terms of the future care of the children."

"Ah, to go back to school." I think that this is a good stable concrete answer and most likely what I will do eventually within a year or two. But nonetheless what I really want to say is ' *What kind of ridiculous question is that, my life has just done a 180, my plan is to live through this horrendous court induced hell, hang out with my kids and paint pictures to keep me if not sane then working steadily towards that end.* '

"How are you going to manage?"

"Well sir, I haven't quite worked out all the details. I'm sure I qualify for some student loans. The children are still quite young and we need to readjust. Y'know, change dreams for the future from that of a two parent family to that of a single mum. But I'd definitely like to finish my education so I can provide for myself as well as them." I pause, "I was wondering how long this is all going to go on. Are you aware it's been months now and he's been through two lawyers who have fired him. Doesn't that tell you something?" I try not to sound accusatory, just simply stunned at the absurdity. Meanwhile, I want to scream!

Manage! I have just extrapolated myself from the grips of a sick individual, it has taken remarkable strength, I am in the process of being crucified by the people in the neighbourhood who all think they have your qualifications. And by the way I saw the one, new in the neighbourhood, in the elevator who doesn't know me at all, by the way. I didn't figure it out right away and so was a tad over friendly and excited about the seeming coincidence of being in the same downtown elevator. But I am not so blind. I did perceive in her uncomfortable recoiling demeanor that she was just here telling you that Mr. Sicko is a wonderful man, his pain is so very real, and I'm a nut. I've read the other affidavits.

But I don't scream. I probably look pathetic because his tone turns sympathetic as he responds, "Elsie, this is the way the system works; it takes time and everyone has the right to be heard. That is the only way it can really work best for everyone. We need to be thorough for the children's sake." Hartley did in fact seem kind-hearted. He is not clearly on my side though, as he is supposed to be impartial and assess what's best for the kids. I like him better than my lawyer.

I take a deep breath, "Yes, I do understand that everybody has a right to be heard and these things take time. What I don't quite get is how someone can just decide to call someone else crazy and then this regular person must undergo scrutiny, just because she made a bad choice." I point to myself when I say bad choice. And they wonder why women don't leave these nut jobs. "I do hope you can recognize that his accusations are out of context. He's being vindictive, and I'm not saying that in a name-calling kind of way. I'm saying it in a diagnostic kind of way if you know what I mean." I am hoping he says yes he can totally see what I mean, but he doesn't comment either way.

"These sorts of documents usually are a quagmire, I guess that's why they call it mud slinging." he smiles, "they require sifting through. It's a *he says, she says* sort of game, that's where I come in. I talk to all parties and try to help. The court takes my recommendations very seriously. So I advise you to cooperate fully and hopefully that will speed things along. You understand that I'm going to need to talk to the children alone for a few minutes."

But I haven't slung any mud. I would like to sling mud, I could see how it could be very gratifying but I'm too preoccupied with wanting to be seen as sane. I chuckle, "Of course, I intend to cooperate fully; you just tell me what I need to do. May I ask what you are going to ask the children?"

"I think it's better, if they answer me spontaneously." He stands and is waiting for me to get the kids.

"No of course, you wouldn't want me to coach them, I understand. I'll bring them in." I say as I stand and turn towards the door.

Right, why would their mother be allowed in the room? After all they are 5 and 2 and are fully capable of taking care of themselves and impossible to coerce. You are undoubtedly a completely unbiased individual who never had human contact in your life to disturb what I am expected to believe is a clear perspective. I'm certainly glad your name is Hartley I can only have faith that this has impacted on your being.

"It'll just be a few minutes," he reassures me.

I tell the kids, "So just tell the truth, I'll be right outside." The little one thought he had eight brothers and sisters last week. I have a quick flash of the guy on the train he thought was his Dad. Other than that he pretty much says whatever comes to mind. I sit outside the office smiling awkwardly at the secretary. "Were they well behaved?" I ask.

"Oh, yes, they were fine." She looks onto her desk. I think against asking for crayons, just in case she has pull, secretaries often do, I think. It's less than five minutes when the door opens and the kids emerge nonplussed.

"Ahem, Mr. Hartley, I know that you are coming to do the house visit at the end of the week, but I was wondering is it really necessary for me to go to that meeting with the psychiatrist that their lawyer recommends. I don't want to seem paranoid but doesn't that make him on their side in a way?" By "their side" I'm referring to Al and his mother who has rallied for Al as the self-described woman of means in his documents.

"It's best you cooperate all around, that would be my honest advice to you. Remember he's a mental health care professional so he's not really on anyone's side per se. Try not to worry. I'll see you at the end of the week."

"Oh I see, well I hope you're right about that. It seems we are putting a lot of stock in professionalism. I'll do whatever it takes; see you in a few days." I shake his hand and he shakes mine and then Zoë and J.J.'s, which is really pretty cute. My mind is still in a paranoid whirl though wondering if he ever gives dishonest advice. *Worry, who me? Did I mention I think my lawyer isn't taking me seriously; also one has to wonder how someone can be dangerous to adults but perfectly O.K to be around children. He told them I don't love them because I don't make them use the burning mint toothpaste. When Zoë told me, "Al says you don't love us, that's not true is it Mom?" I reassured her, but my fury was deafening to my own insides. It'll be in a document somewhere. What kind of cruel soul would tell any child they were*

unloved? I want to scream I do! I do! I make them brush! Water's
good isn't it? Did I mention that the other day I gave very serious
thought to toothpaste and won't be making any more mistakes like
that? Is it on the list of my abnormalities? Is cruelty to children on
his? Just sounds like mud slinging to objective ears. Too bad the
kids aren't objective.

"Of course I love you; I would love you if you brushed your
teeth with mud! I loved you before you had teeth! I will always love
you; now go brush your teeth!" Just in case I overlooked some
fundamental link about teeth and love I will be less malleable on
issues like toothpaste for the time being. When one has fled and
basically commandeered housing it is not surprising to me that
everything isn't quite worked out.

Hartley has come and gone, I think it went well. It turned out to be
an amusing visit all in all. I am confused by so much riding on
such a limited exchange. Amusement was not exactly the aim. I
think it went alright, so I will write it into a little story, maybe the
story will serve me and I will be twice served today. As a child I
made up the stories now they are making me up in a way. I see I
may not have said or done the perfect thing when I write it down.
It wouldn't be a story if I had. When I paint I can see feelings
coloured by perception. When I write what has happened I can
actually see how I behaved, and even a little of what I thought.

Neighbours
By
Elsie Shaw

Mr. Hartley, the court appointed social worker was due to
Arrive later on this morning. I hadn't expected it to come to this.
The kids were watching the morning T.V shows, so I tidied up.
There wasn't much to tidy in the sparsely pre furnished place, but I
made the beds and wiped down the table and the counters. The
walls were covered in a recent series of paintings, a mixture, some
of mine and some of my friend Jake's. I couldn't imagine the
artwork being a problem, it was art after all; subjective taste
couldn't work against me could it? I tried to imagine what he was
expecting to discover. Apparently my craziness would belie itself in
the décor. I paced, out, onto the veranda and back inside.

I looked over at the porch within several arm lengths of my own and there was my relatively new neighbour Alex, we'd had a cup of coffee or two and he was aware of my situation; the custody battle.

"What are you pacing around about? Is today the day?" He leaned over his porch railing and was only about a foot away. Alex worked nights on the road crew, paving and what not, so he was having his usual evening in the morning.

"Yeah he'll be here later on this morning. I don't know, do you think only having a bed in the living room is weird?" I motioned for him to come over and added, "I mean I made it look like a couch," I muttered as we stood in the center of my makeshift gallery/bedroom /living room.

Once inside we attempted to look at the room through the eyes of a government employee. Do you think the art work is too wild, Alex?" I gestured towards the wall. Almost every available space was covered with canvases full of bold abstractly composed colors. "Maybe there's too much red, maybe he'll think it scares the children."

Even as these words escaped my mouth I felt censured, judged. Alex shrugged, "There is a lot of it," he said. "It might be an unnecessary distraction, I don't know, it's your call. I have a plant you can borrow."

"Really, a plant would really spruce things up, that would be great! Kids, I'm just going over to Alex's for a minute." I followed Alex out the door and down two steps and up the two into his house. I stood there eyeing his interior for clues as to what might be appropriate. He had only one picture in his living room; a metal framed sketch of mountains. The image started off in dark blue and faded to a lighter and lighter grey hue, as though the mountains were disappearing into the distant mist, or the viewer's eyesight was failing. It was impact free, a decoration, perhaps normal. It sure made me think that my decorative expression of late was amongst other things, less then subtle.

I guess Alex must've noticed me coveting his normalcy; he put down the three-foot fern near the door and sauntered back to me I the living room. He had a sectional couch, brown, some kind of upholstery material as well as several other spider plants and a large fig tree. Across from the oval coffee table and under the front window there was a beige canvas cotton love seat and matching chair. The fern I was borrowing barely made a dent in the room; it had been kind of squished between the wall and a big old antique wooden fridge that covered the entire wall adjacent to the couches. It seemed to serve as a mantle without the fireplace. The room was a perfect blend of cluttered and cozy, the kind of clutter that doesn't move when the person lives alone.

"That thing is gargantuan," I said pointing to the fridge, "What do you use it for?" I wandered closer to inspect; the kids wandered in the still open door.

"Hi guys," smiled Alex, "You want a popsicle?" He said it to them but quickly looked to me for the nod of approval, which I readily gave. "You'll have to eat them on the deck, though."

We all followed him through to the kitchen, "Do you have purple?" Zoë was into purple of late, Alex searched through the box, all the while trying to explain that purple isn't really a flavor. His explanation fell on the most determined of deaf ears. J.J. oddly grasped something and demanded orange like he was getting a two for one. We went out onto the back deck for stress free melting. The sun was shining in a friendly sort of way, not bearing down oppressively as it sometimes can, but just there in the sky like in a child's drawing. There was a breeze off the ocean but not enough to rob the popsicles of their cooling treat. It was pleasant all round except for my nervousness at the prospect of my guest arriving within the hour. I thought it best to keep this mood, surely this mood alone would float into Mr. Hartley's soul and all potential criticism would dissipate. This could explain how it's the simple things we enjoy with our children...Oh my God I thought, I've got to take down all the art, I've got to make the room simple.

As though reading my mind, Alex whispered, "Elsie, do you want to borrow the couch?"

I didn't even hesitate, "That would work, yes, I think that would really work and I've decided to take down the paintings as well. I want it to be simple. This was the stuff of speed decorating. I hadn't thought of this possibility, borrowing furniture, I hoped it wasn't unethical. And frankly, if they were going to decide what kind of mother I was based on the furniture then I had to be resourceful. "It'll just be until tomorrow, I really appreciate it."

We moved over the three pieces of the couch, the plant and on the last trip, Alex threw in the non-threatening mountain-scape, frame and all, which we hung directly above the couch, a very balanced approach. You'd think I'd get extra points for being a creative person, painting my own stuff, but they hadn't given me a checklist of what to be. Being in this position at all was so shocking that to err on the side of simple might be most prudent.

The kids had no problem with trying out Alex's stuff in our place, just to see how it looked, to see if we might want stuff like his one day. I hoped they wouldn't mention anything to Mr. Hartley, but I wasn't going to instruct them not to.

He arrives just ten or so minutes after our newly contrived living room is installed. He is wearing a suit. The kids are a little shy and barely acknowledge having met him at his office the week before. Once reminded that he was the man who asked them what they would wish for if they could wish for anything Zoë perked right up and shook his hand. As she very professionally stepped forward her tiny hand outstretched, I felt a burst of pride.

"Nice to see you again, are we going to Disneyland?" Zoë asked expectantly.

Mr. Hartley smiled the gentle guilt ridden smile of a misunderstood grown-up and looked to me for help. A good start, I thought, before explaining to Zoë that his question about wishes that day had just been out of curiosity.

"Then why are you here?" she asked. J.J. was still wrapped behind my knees, my own nervousness clearly transferred onto him as we squirmed in concert.

"Oh, I'm just here to talk to your Mother, do you like it here? Which is your room?"

"I have the big room with the big bed and the T.V. and sometimes I eat dinner in my closet!" Zoë explained as she showed him her new digs.

"Why do you eat in your closet?" There was an element of concern in his voice. I was tempted to jump in and whisk him nearer to the non-threatening mountain-scape designed to soothe, but I decided to just smile and await her response.

"It's my fort and I can decide if J.J. can come or not. Sometimes I let him, don't I Mum?" It seemed Zoë's desire to be perceived as a nice sister overshadowed the possible weirdness. I

suppressed a sigh of relief with an offer of coffee motioning to the kitchen.

"Yes, yes, that would be great." He answered looking around the kitchen. It was then that it occurred to me that I had no coffee. Surely a good mother/ host of a government assessor should have thought of this. Thinking on my feet I did the next best thing, improvised. "I'll just be a minute." I said walking out of the kitchen and towards the side of the house facing Alex. I leaned out the window, "Alex," I yelled, "Two coffees please," and then turning back towards Mr. Hartley I asked in a softer tone as though this was a daily occurrence, " What do you take in your coffee?"

"One cream, one sugar please." He replied un-phased. I smiled somehow proud that I could conjure coffee with ease, thinking that somehow this would show him that I was a person prepared to handle whatever might arise. He smiled back, and I like to think he got it, or at the very least he liked me. I issued the specifics out the window.

"Two coffees one and one, coming up," chided Alex. While we waited for Alex to deliver the coffee we chatted and I explained that I let Zoë eat in her closet because after careful deliberation I couldn't see the harm in it. "Not everyday, mind you," I was sure to add, as though frequency was the issue. "That would be weird." I felt sure he would understand that the deliberating was the important part, the caring about the long-term effects of parental decisions.

Alex came in, I couldn't believe he actually put the coffees on a tray; two clear glass mugs. "Thank you, hey, you didn't bring one for yourself," I said quickly wanting Alex to seem and feel less like a waiter. I handed one to Mr. Hartley and took the other for myself.

"This is my neighbour, Alex, Alex this is Mr. Hartley." Mr. Hartley raised his mug to Alex, "Thanks," he said.

"No problem," he nodded, "I've got to get going Elsie, just drop off the mugs later okay, see ya," he headed out the door and I called, "thanks again," after him. Turning towards Mr. Hartley I added, "Alex is a nice guy to have for a neighbour, I seem to be getting luckier and luckier these days." From this I hoped he would glean that my life was on the upswing, I was

resourceful and attracted good people and things, after all we'd just had a perfectly normal interaction with the community. He seemed like a nice man but his position assessing me rendered him very difficult to read and the fact that I was being assessed rendered me continually paranoid.

The End

25

Clouds

      My life has become a painting in which the wrong colours are in the foreground so the depth and story and the image are out of whack. At the very time when the pressure is on to be planning and forward looking, I am unable to move from the present. I reread my story and wonder if I made the impression I was hoping I would. Did I make sure my values and value were loud enough? Did I convey the person I wanted to convey to Mr. Hartley. Well in the end it is difficult to be somebody other than myself, so I just pray that that will do. Alex is in no rush to have his furniture back. All I want to do is take walks, enjoy the kids and the view, write little anecdotes, and paint. Jake has left his paints here and I am free to use them as well as the canvas in an unspoken exchange for his access to my place. I paint everyone in bold abstract impressions of what I think or feel about them, strangers, acquaintances, exchanges between people at the diner. Beauty is not my aim; a color representation of what I see seems to serve me. The colors sometimes arrange themselves in a way that could pass for composition. It's like I'm painting out of a need to find out what I perceive. Painting myself from one life into the next. It's reassuring to find out that even if I see a red streak of anger straight down someone's middle, once I've painted it I feel some kind of compassion for the subject. It's a sense of release for me. Zoë's not thrilled about my new focus. She sometimes stands in front of the canvas, and screams "Muum!" It aggravates me to have to stop. I absently get to her needs, jolted back into motherhood. After several of these unpleasant exchanges I have decided to paint mostly when the kids are asleep or watching T.V. or with Al.

So now it's just a matter of waiting to see what his report says. In the meantime I will have to go to see a Dr. McGuffy, the psychiatrist. Instead of these appointments smattering our lives, it feels to me like my life is smattered between these appointments. I just want things settled. Everything is riding on their outcome. Ms. Devereaux says that we have to wait for all the reports before the courts will decide what to do. I wonder what would've happened if I'd painted Al before we got together.

Al and I aren't talking much except to arrange pick up and drop offs. He picks the kids up from time to time and keeps them for a few days and then brings them back. It makes me nervous to leave them alone with him. Ms. Devereaux insists that I cooperate.

Sometimes it's midweek, sometimes the weekend. Since it's summer and there is really no schedule to speak of, this seems to work, within a forty-eight hour give or take kind of arrangement. I don't want to push things. Al hasn't been around for a couple of weeks so it was no big surprise when he showed up at the beginning of this weekend. And so off they went for the weekend. It turned out that the timing was good, so when Jake had asked me to accompany him to the island I was able to say yes. The trip to the island had more to do with Jake than me. It was a nice little adventure. I'm waiting yet again for my babies to return. I wonder who was I, the single girl, the painter, the childless mother, the trusted friend this weekend? Why was she in their story? Jake has gone down to sleep at the beach as the kids are due back this afternoon.

Benny
By
Elsie Shaw

Jake got Lois pregnant the first time they had sex. I thought it was the most romantic manifestation of destiny I'd ever heard. No words were spoken. They exchanged some flirtatious glances at a restaurant. She probably blushed; Lois is a fair skinned blusher. He followed her down the railroad tracks that run parallel to the beach, and they made love in the grass. I know the spot because I've been there with Jake but not like that.

A month or so later, after she found him again and told him, he came to me. He paced back and forth, each step a petal torn from a daisy; marry her? Marry her not? I counseled they shouldn't marry just because they're having a baby. They're separate relationships. I hoped my view wasn't skewed by not wanting to lose Jake myself.

When he told me how it happened I could picture her long legged gait just ahead of him and then him coming up on her, motioning her to follow. I'm sure she blushed again. I'm sure he flashed his cocky grin. She went home. Back to her live-in boyfriend of 11 years. Jake and I carried on our usual colleague type relationship. We'd paint together and he'd crash at my place pretty much whenever. Sometimes in my bed, sometimes not.

She had yet to tell Benny, the guy she lived with. She started to come to town more often. This meant they came to my place. Occasionally Lois would arrive looking for Jake and just hang out with me. She said she really didn't want to be with Jake. I didn't say much, whatever.

"What about Benny?" I asked.

"I haven't told him yet, it's hard y'know." She looked down, reddening.

I walked in on them more than once, and I didn't like it much. Jake didn't have any other place except the beach, where he lived most of the time. He wore a Ski-Doo suit if it got too cold. Once when they were in the bed, I painted in the other room, to sort out the mixed emotions. An image of myself holding my own energy up, a yellow ball, the face almost the size of the canvas in bright oranges and purples. The nose looked like a sailboat and the huge full lips more like hers than mine. I painted a dark blue dog over my heart. Guard dog, I thought.

Weeks went by; mid-day Lois turned up. "Hey do you want to come out to my place and meet Benny? Maybe you can give me some pointers on how to break the news. It's getting kind of tense." Her soft voice didn't convey tense very effectively.

"Sure." Curiosity and a drive to farmland being primary motivators. I really didn't see how I could help her tell him.

Frankly, I felt somewhat bad for Benny. During the drive it occurred to me that my presence might be required in case Benny reacted badly. I hoped not.

"Are you planning to tell him today, with me there?" I asked in the car, too far into the trip to back out at any rate.

"I dunno, I guess I'll see how it goes," was her noncommittal reply. She was like a blond mystery. I could see what compelled Jake. Like a glass of water with cellophane pulled tight over the top to avoid spillage. Untouchable Transparancy. She turned the white Duster into the drive of a white clapboard bungalow. In we went.

"Hey Benny, this is the girl I've been telling you about, Elsie." Lois motioned to me on the way through the living room where Benny was sitting.

"So you're the mystery friend from the beach." His warmth seemed muted, preoccupied. Or maybe it was just my guilt.

"Hi," I nodded following Lois through to the kitchen.

She rolled her eyes in the direction of Benny and suppressed a giggle. I started to giggle a bit, too. Then I realized I was somehow involved in a distasteful conspiracy.

"Lois, did you pay the electricity bill? 'Cause they sent another notice. We should get everything up to date before we move," Benny spoke from the living room.

"Yeah, I just paid it, they probably sent it before. Do you want tea?"

"Okay," he answered but made no move to join us.

"You're moving? Where to?" I asked, wondering why she never mentioned it and again what I was doing there. It didn't feel like a soured relationship. It felt comfy.

"We decided to move to the island about a month ago. I found a little place there." She spoke casually, the "situation" absent in her tone. "I'm on U.I.C. anyway so I can look for work there." She served his tea, rolled her eyes again, and took it into him. She came back mouthing the word b-o-r-i-n-g.

She and Benny moved. A couple of weeks later amidst our usual routine of painting and napping and walking, Jake asked if I'd go to the island with him. She'd sent a message through a friend to invite him. I agreed, flattered when he admitted he needed my emotional support.

It was dark when we arrived. Once off the ferry, we bummed a ride to somewhere near where we were headed. I'd no idea where I was; Jake had the directions. We knocked on the door; Lois opened it, looking back over her shoulder. She said it's too late, not good tonight. I heard Benny ask, "Who is it?"

She answered, "No one."

We found a grassy spot near the house and curled up together. "I guess she hasn't told him yet," I said.

"I guess not," agreed Jake, "Hey, do you have any more of those cigarettes?" He asked. I gave him one. We each smoked, we didn't talk, no need. Huddled together for warmth I felt a blue light encircling us both. "Feel that?" whispered Jake. "MMhmm," I murmured back.

The next morning Benny went to work, we went out for coffee. Lois and Jake flirted and played footsie whenever they were near enough to touch. I imagined what their baby would look like. He was dark, which would probably win out in the gene selection. They were both tallish. Lois said she knew a beach where we could picnic. So after getting some food together, we loaded our paint supplies and headed out in her car.

It was a long stretch of beach, dark blue water with a fringe of white froth curling in on the shore. Coolish. Eventually they became so focused on each other that I thought I should leave them alone. They were getting more carried away and I was starting to feel like a voyeur. I walked up the hill to the car and hauled out some canvas and paints. I painted their entangled bodies, stripes of color, layers of each body lying prone and clearly merging. A different kind of voyeurism as it turned out. Sweeping broad brushstrokes captured their movement. I was just finishing as they came up from the water.

"You've been busy," laughed Jake.

"So have you," I said turning the painting for their approval.

"Kind of a ménage a trois," he added. I would've blushed, but as it was, I smirked instead. I saw Lois blush out of the corner of my eye.

We all chuckled a transitional chuckle, and the mood slid away as we slid into the car. I perched the still wet painting on the back windowsill. I'd had enough, and after spending the night on the couch, I asked for a ride to the ferry. Jake was staying on and getting a ride with Lois later in the week. He borrowed Lois's car to take me.

"Good luck," I said, we had a quick hug.

"It made a difference, you coming with me." Warmth.

"I'm leaving that painting, can you bring it? It's still wet."

"No problem, see you later."

I arrived home that evening. I took a deep breath of the familiarity and comfort that are home. The next evening, I was reading when Jake burst in the door, "Happy to see me?!"

I intentionally didn't look overly glad, "You're back so soon. I'm surprised."

"I kind of had to get out of there quickly." He breathed excitedly. "After you left, Lois said she was definitely going to tell him. She told him she was pregnant but not who the father was. I'm sleeping on the couch if you can imagine, thinking how's this guy going to react?"

"Oh God, did he figure it out?"

"No, not then, that's just it; remember when I told you you'd made a difference?" I nod.

"Well, this morning I went for coffee alone. He found your painting in the car, put who and blue together, if you know what I mean. Lois ran to find me at the café, there was talk of guns, and she said I should leave; it was only me he was after. Cuckolded, humiliated."

"At least now he knows." I offered.

"That's some powerful painting," Jake grinned. "He destroyed it. He sure doesn't like the art much." Jake shrugged. "Sorry about your painting."

"That's one way to kill the messenger," I mused. "Still at least now he knows."

The End

Lois, by the way, is the girl with the scarlet lips in the painting that I saw the first time I went to the salon/studio with Jake. I was me in the story, except outside, looking in. And I wonder about my motives as I accept I couldn't have known. I hear the thud-thud of little feet bounding up the wooden stairs around threeish. Threeish it seems is a good time for Al. If I'd thought about it, I should've remembered how long it takes him to get organized to leave the house. The kids both have new brightly colored caps on. They seem happy, even excited.

"We went to Burger King!" bursts J.J. and pulls a cardboard crown out of his little pack.

"Lucky you!" I say but not without being able to hide my *I thought we were against fast food* look. The look does not get past Zoë, and I immediately regret having an opinion.

"Remember California?" smiles Al by way of explanation.

I shrug, "Yeah. Okay." He doesn't moan or cajole or talk about getting back together. It slowly dawns on me that perhaps my prayers of being replaced are being answered. That I wouldn't wish his confusion, depression and violence on my worst enemy is a fact I don't focus on when I pray. It's more about getting Al what he wants and thus releasing me. There is the smidgen of belief that maybe he'll be different with someone else, maybe she could handle what I could not. I don't seem to be getting rousing support for my own reality. This waiting for some objective decision is causing me some doubt, but making me a more obstinate case for being allowed to be me, whoever that turns out to be.

My appointment with the psychiatrist is today, downtown. I had to ask Jake if he can watch J.J. for the afternoon and Zoë is with Angie, playing with Jessica. I am really nervous and I can't find anything to wear. I have one nice sweater, white, lightly knitted cotton with a v shaped low back. I can't seem to figure it out. How do you wear a bra? I don't think I should go braless, and I really want to wear my nicest sweater. I guess I'll wear a t-shirt underneath. It'll be a tad hot but better to err on the side of underwear. That kind of cancels out the nice open back but it does mean I can wear a bra without the strap showing. I really hate these kinds of dilemmas. What if this choice makes me seem sub normal? I suppose whether I agree with *his* fashion selection will have no bearing. I will be clean and neat and with the appropriate undergarments. Oh well, off to be judged by someone paid by the opposition. I just can't get past that.

The office is pinkish, a dusty rose I guess you'd call it. There are some floral landscapes very neatly framed, in the waiting room. There are no windows as the inner office is the part facing the street. The trim is white as are the doors; there is one to the office and one I assume is a washroom although there is no insignia. I suppose it's supposed to be all very calming. I try to let the environment do its work and tell myself I'm going to be open because I have nothing to hide. I'm a good and devoted mother and a bright young capable woman. The secretary's desk is just to the side of the office door like a gatekeeper at a parking lot. I smile intermittently at her whilst giving myself the little pep talk. She smiles back when she looks up from time to time. She's middle aged with a short ash blond haircut and wearing a neat summer blouse with short pouffy sleeves drawn tight around the bicep. She could almost be one of the floral landscapes; arms as stems, desk as ground, she contrasts pleasantly against the wall. Only her brown glasses thrust her forward into more of a relief. If I painted her I would call it "Intermittent Smile." I bet she would've known the answer to my earlier fashion dilemma. It's a long ten minutes or so before he opens his door.

Dr. McGuffy is portly, stocky with a reddish beard and short messy hair the same colour. I am optimistic, as this seems a friendly sort of stature. His freckled little hand ushers me in, past him, to a chair against the wall. His desk is adjacent which means he turns his chair to face me without the desk between us. The window is behind him as he faces me. I guess this means he can look out the window when he has no client. For the time being it is me who can see the city spreading out behind him from the tenth floor vantage point.

He sighs, his belly spilling over his belt as directed. "So, there is an issue between yourself and Mr. . . ." He is not really looking at me. He looks at his shoes and then glances at me on his way to his desk. He's not even the least bit jovial; he's like jovial inverted into a small balloon. Only once the air is gone and the little piece of rubber is flying around is it funny. He continues, "Let me tell you a little story about couples and society . . ."

I nod. I think, he's going to outline what's expected.

"You see, couples who have children are part of a larger group, that is; our culture or society. They by nature, need to be included. In order to be included they must adhere to the rules and customs of the larger group." He pauses and glares, small blue eyes open wide to punctuate, and then retract as he continues. "Do you realize that in some cultures if a couple could not get along the villagers would send them away? They would send them away and take their children from them?"

"Really?" I don't know what else to say. Why is he telling me this? I see the city spread out behind him and try to imagine some vague village in an entirely different climate zone. I envision earth pathways and tropical plants.

"Yes, yes, in fact they would take people like you, and feed them to the crocodiles!" I don't know whether to laugh or defend myself from being fed to the crocodiles. The fate of my kids is dependent on this guy, this is frightening. I can't begin to digest the idea.

"Well, I wouldn't say that we are simply refusing to get along," I offer. "He's abusive and something is not quite right about him." I hope he hears this as an understatement.

"I've met Al. He says you refuse to take the children to church, is that so?"

This question takes me by surprise. I'm quickly trying to make the link between church and crocodiles. My being normal could rely on links like these.

"I don't recall it ever coming up, but Al can take them to church if he really wants to. I've never actually seen him go to any church himself."

"So you would have no problem if he were to take them to church?" Is this a dare?

"Well, I suppose that would depend on which church, I don't agree with indoctrination, but no I don't have a problem with him taking them if it's that important to him." This is an easy one, as I know it is only designed to make me look like a fringe person.

"Hmm. Al is very worried about the children. He feels he has no say and he also says that you refused to get them vaccinated. He provided me with a doctor's note to that effect." Ah oh, this is tricky. I have made a conscious decision after reading up on this matter. I know it's not the accepted stance. I begin to babble.

"Well J.J. has a runny nose quite a lot, and once in a while a kid dies and although the statistics may be one in a thousand I don't suppose it's much consolation if your kid turns out to be the one." I look to him for any sign of understanding but his face is like a cement wall, so I add, "I guess if it's a really big deal when his nose stops running we could do it."

"Mmm," his chin moves almost imperceptibly. I really have to leap at this to consider it a response, make it into a full nod all by myself. I think he is about to continue when he abruptly turns his head to the other side of the room and appears to be staring at a painting of a boat on the wall. I don't know what to do. I steal a peripheral glance at the painting but don't turn my head. I'm deciding whether or not people normally just stop and follow another's conversational agenda or lack thereof. I feel I am being manipulated and something in me refuses to turn my head to look at the damn painting. I stare stubbornly at his profile waiting for him to return. This probably isn't taking as long as it seems. It reminds me of the way Al slows down his talking until it's practically painful for me to pay attention. I wait. Is this a nutty thing to be participating in? Is this a test? Is this guy for real? Finally he's turning back to face me. I smile knowingly as if we both know what just happened. But the truth is; I don't. I don't like this. He leans forward on his chair.

"Do you know what I, as well as many in my position, believe?"

"No," I shrug.

"That people like you and Al don't deserve your children at all. They should be taken and given to people who will put the needs of the children first. Children are a privilege, not a right."

"I, I love my kids," I stutter, "I'm just trying to protect them as well as myself."

I feel a lump rising in my throat causing my reasoning to choke and sputter. "When people get divorced, the children are not generally removed from both of them, in our culture." I nod towards the window; vaguely aware I feel no real at oneness with that particular cement land that somehow holds my values.

"You don't seem to have done a very good job so far." He is accusatory. I crumble. Tears streaming I blubber, "I have my rights as a human being, I have a right not to be abused or frightened and so do the kids . . ." I sniffle looking up, praying silently that I do indeed have some rights because I need something right about now. He leans back in his chair looking satisfied which strikes me as oddly cruel. He hands me a Kleenex, "Well, I think we are done here." I wipe my nose, "I hope you will notice I came here in the spirit," I blow my nose, "of cooperation." He gets up and gestures to the door with that same pudgy hand I'd mistaken for friendly. Something doesn't seem quite copasetic. I look into his face as I head for the door.

"Wait a minute, what was all that about? Were you playing some kind of identifying game with me to see how I'd react? Was that a test? Because that didn't feel helpful at all." He smirks as I walk by, nodding, but not in agreement, more like he's nodding me out of the room. I leave still sniffing in the aftershock of his brutal treatment. Geez, cooperating may not have been the best game plan. My only consolation is that perhaps he treated me like that to see somehow if I'd been abused by how I'd react. Then he would've seen how difficult a time I'm having defending simply ridiculous assertions. Fed to the crocodiles indeed.

26

Free Spirits

The furniture I'd borrowed and the wild paintings have gradually returned to their proper premises as I wait for the paperwork to arrive. It's taken several weeks, as it has to be sent to my lawyer first. Alex gave me the plant, for housewarming and good luck, he said. I told myself the coffee thing with Mr. Hartley really didn't matter because kids don't drink coffee anyway. I know that Alex really saved the day and it didn't really say much about my resourcefulness or any of that stuff. I had several moments in which I saw his whole visit a pretty funny scene. I could only hope Mr. Hartley had movie moments himself or at the very least a sense of humor. The visit with McGuffy was another story, one I don't see as accessible anecdotally as it has left me more wobbly than I would've guessed. I just can't make sense of it. It's unsettling to think that it's not just Al that could rattle me enough to make me wonder if I completely missed something. I can't even fully formulate the idea that there might be something wrong with McGuffy, that would be too much like saying everyone else is nuts except me. That pathway is predictably a dead end. How is it that I worked so hard to keep my head above water during that visit and still ended up like melting jell-o inside someone else's mouth? I can only hope I was gritty.

It says in the official social worker document from Hartley that I am a free spirit. I am about to take this as a compliment when I realize the exact phrasing is "*Although* Ms. Elsie Shaw appears to be a free spirit . . ." I'm afraid to read on. I do so slowly, only to happily discover my disembodiment does not seem to impede my ability to be a nurturing and loving parent. And clearly it hasn't precluded my nervousness. His final recommendation is that I be granted custody. The document also says that Mr. Hartley sensed that I have hostility toward conventional societal norms but he did not see this as a threat to the children. I'm not certain I'd really felt hostile; terrified maybe. Funny that, the faces of fear being somewhat difficult to distinguish, even by a professional. All in all I was very grateful to Alex for helping to normalize my home. Sometimes, it seems to me, there's more to the décor of one's life than we'd expect, and a plant given in good faith can go a long way. I'm walking along the main drag on my way to buy some cigarettes. I'm just past Kelley's Korner when Fleming pops his head out. "Hey Elsie, I think you'd better come in here." There is something in his tone, something worn, like used sandpaper. I feel a sinking ominous feeling that is incongruent with our convivial if distant relationship. "I'm just going to buy some smokes, I'll be back in a minute," I gesture towards the corner store. On the way back I notice I'm shaky and hurry reluctantly towards what I'm sure is the news that someone has died.

The Bus People

When I first saw her, she was sitting directly behind me during a short bus ride. We were on our way from the beaches to uptown. We exchanged pseudo smiles of acknowledgment. I wondered why she looked so over-cast. Did we all reflect the weather after a while? I certainly couldn't feel the sun.

I had met him, as in before her, on a somewhat longer bus trip out from the city. I'd been trying to meditate on the bus. I thought I looked like I was asleep except for my poised and alert fingertips.

"So, you do that on the bus too," he announced. I smiled the smile I give when I've already assessed myself superior. It's a smile that welcomes, because let's face it: my status is secured by the other person's lack of it. It turned out he'd recognized me from the local coffeehouse. He seemed congenial enough, having the nerve to talk to me while I was clearly relaxing. Odd enough, in his khaki pants rolled up to reveal high top sneakers and no socks. Safe enough, not overly smooth or too good-looking. We walked

together until we reached my road and then bade farewell. Well actually it was something like:

"See ya later."

"Ya, bye."

Then I got that familiar feeling I get when I haven't seen the last of someone. Friend or fool is usually the next question, not that the answer does much in the way of moving me to discriminate. I kept bumping into him at the seaside restaurants, walking down Coastal Drive, in that funny way people appear as though out of the fog. We had been walking those streets in parallel worlds that had somehow recently converged. By now we had this mutual 'the key to the universe is meditating on the bus' thing going on. He was a very creative fellow and painted entire landscapes using the word 'if' as his brush stroke. This had the interesting effect of looking like an image from afar but up close one could discern hundreds if not thousands of tiny little "ifs". Acquaintance bordering on friend, I decided. Attraction out of the question. He indulged my sense of humor, laughing eagerly when I tripped and curtsied. I could tell he thought I was cute. He began to hang around; he began to lean on me, waiting for me to introduce a topic of conversation, waiting to return a smile. As though he was a reactionary being.

She, however, was a different case altogether. During our bus ride she informed me she had just left a violent relationship and was on her way to a counselor. Her confiding manner was as raw as her pain. I wanted to distance myself from her palpable vulnerability.

She had strong features and a deliberate tone as she pinpointed the injustices that lurk in the alligator ridden waters of certain relationships. She said she was a feminist. I thought she was a bit scary. I try to stay away from "ists" of any sort, except artists of course. I thought she must have 'isted' her lover into a violent frenzy. Exactly how violent, I wanted to know. She didn't appear to be broken.(I hoped I didn't appear to be broken.) With her being twelve years his senior, I felt the poor puppy didn't stand a chance. The bus struggled uphill; the drizzle of our coastal town dulled the scene, the wipers kept time, the bus noises like a sound track for the sludge this conversation had become. For a minute I thought I glimpsed nervous panic in her eyes as she began to extol

the qualities of her therapist. I assumed the panic was related to
my drifting attention. After all I knew all about the therapist as I
was seeing him myself. I had just left my own violent relationship
and my perceptions were now enhanced from not having to look
through my partner's eyes, or so I thought. Still I longed for
details, for distraction.

"Did he hit you? Did he get that face? (The face that
reflects you're less than human status) That's really scary." I even
added the conspiratorial, "I know..." followed by a small sigh and
a nod. I was so suspicious of her. She's too confident, too pushy,
too right. The challenge is to understand the beast, not try to kill it.
Anyway she should have just left. What's the big deal, I left.

"He threatens, he breaks things, and he has some
problems..." There was something here that irked. She was
delusional I decided. She was clearly too wrapped up in a boy she
should never have been involved with in the first place. Playing the
victim, a dangerous game that leaves the rest of us scrutinized
when there is a real danger. If she tried to force her feminism on
him of course he wouldn't get it. Doesn't she realize they hate that
they can't cope and then they explode? It's that simple. The air
gushing through the breaks signaled the end of the conversation,
the doors parted, as did we.

"Well, I hope it all works out." I hope we are not the same.
I made no excuses for her. She would be the me I could not forgive.
I trusted I would never see her again.

I continued to run into him on the main drag from time to
time. The main drag is between the storefronts and the beach. The
restaurants offer an ocean view, windows facing the sea. You can
actually perch on a windowsill and chat with someone, and so he
did. I was inside with nothing particular to do, sipping chamomile,
my life on pause and my point of view under reconstruction. My
kids wouldn't be back for a couple of days. Newfound freedom,
empty space, two free hands, room to breathe. Smoke lots of
cigarettes, gaze at the water, watch the sun begin to sink, mark the
day.

"Going uptown today?" asked my birdlike visitor.

"Sure, I've just got to make a quick stop at my place on the
way," I answered. Why not?

I picked up a couple of dollars and a pink top hat. I had dress up clothes around and decided in the spontaneity that only a second round of adolescence can provide, that only this hat would do. It was just getting dark as we walked along the beach before climbing the steep stairs to the roads uptown. We slid on handrails and I was feeling generally goofy. I was intoxicated by the confidence that all my quips and stories were being well received. Uphill we went. He put on the top hat. The streetlights cast magnified shadows onto the wooden construction panels that lined the road. He was projected as an image of a man dancing in a top hat. A larger than life-size shadow musical, the movements were at once eerie and amusing. In the presence of shadow I instinctively searched to find the source of light. This particular combination made me pause and look around for people to share with so I wouldn't be alone with the shadow. There was no one around so I ignored eerie and decided to err on the side of silly and festive. There wasn't much to do uptown, especially for the financially restricted, so we bought a treat at the health food store and strode back downhill pausing at the green areas to exchange points of view on this or that.

"What if the alphabet was outlawed and people had to rush around trying to save individual letters?"

"You could be hung on a hook for harboring the letter A in your pocket!"

"What if wars were fought with water instead of guns, and the idea of being wet was so horrific it became the unknown?"

"Ya the waterproof gear companies would put the arms people out of business."

"Super soakers wouldn't seem so harmless would they?"

"Ya, but no one would have to die."

"Better even, dying wouldn't be the worst thing would it?"

"What is that anyway, rules of war?"

"Hey, what would a wet willy look like on a global scale?"

We goofed. Maybe being on my own wasn't so bad, just a pleasant walk, pass the time. I went home. After that he came round more often and it wasn't goofy at all. At that time I didn't know you could tell someone to go home or it wasn't a good time to visit. So he mooned around my house, watching me too long at a glance, standing a tad too near, but never too, too near. He even watched me read.

"For God's sake I'm trying to read!"

"Sorry." Feebled, humbled, no glimmer of goof.

What does this guy want? I asked myself. He began rambling incoherently about not being perfect. He said he couldn't stand who he was, the kind of person he was. He said he was violent and extra not perfect not just the everyday flawed human. The strange thing was he wasn't acting that way at all, he was acting like a beaten dog in search of comfort. He was obscuring my new point of view. He mentioned that his true father in heaven was perfect and once he was in heaven he too would be without the burden of his flaws. I was getting somewhat impatient with all this self- loathing. It looked like grandstanding. I was just trying to read. Is he trying to be vulnerable, I wondered? Are all the potentially violent this vulnerable? I couldn't possibly stand another desperate soul desperating at me. It made me feel so cold hearted that I tightened my grip on the pages, not actually reading a word.

"Well," I mused barely looking up from my novel, "You might as well kill yourself then, although it seems a bit silly since it's the only thing we know we've all got coming. I chuckled to myself determined not to be drawn in to his mood. He sulked and I ignored him.

Finally, "Go home." And he did, for a while.

In the meantime, I ran into her again. She said she had moved to the city to live.

"Oh" I said. I didn't like people moving unless it was to a warmer climate. When they move to the city, it forces me to defend my own choices to myself as though I could conceivably make all choices at once, theirs and mine. The city was, well, probably all right if you were into self-help and workshops spending money, and being trendy. I could never understand why people would visit me from the city and wear fancy footwear that prevented any sort of walking except on a sidewalk. It was just this type of behavior, this fashion-centri-city that made me suspicious. She did seem less abrasive however, and even quite friendly. I gradually I began to thaw and found her warmer as well. She said things were better and that she and her lover (God how I hated that word) had been

keeping in touch, trying to work things out. Y'know maybe I was wrong about her. It might do me some good to spend some time with women. After all I am one. It only seems right to like one's own kind. Although he couldn't have been that bad if she is still in touch. I mean, why?

"So, what brings you to this neck of the woods?" I venture. I had just been to the grocery store and the plastic bags were wearing into my hands. I had gotten off at the bus stop nearest to home but it would still be a difficult walk.

"I was just here to visit my ex, which way are you headed?"

"Home, down that way" I nodded in the direction down hill.

"You look like you could use some help."

I put the bags down and surveyed the damage to my palms.

"Sure, that would be great."

And so we started off. I didn't ask right away if she'd already seen her ex and was just hanging around. I didn't ask if she was going later and was killing time. I didn't ask her if she would like to stay for supper since I was alone. I was practicing not caring one way or another if she wanted to be my friend. What I did wonder though, was if everyone thought about being a lot nicer than they could afford to be, depending on whatever they were practicing? We brought the bags in just as the sunset lit my tiny kitchen from the corner window.

"Tea?"

She nodded and she put the kettle on as I put the groceries in the fridge. I didn't want to get into the whole ex thing. So I thought I'd bring up some strictly female topic. I told her about this guy friend of mine who left home every time his wife got her period. He actually left. He said that women shouldn't cook for men during that time.

"It's not such a bad plan." I said "It would give everyone a break from each other, although it would be nice to have someone cook for me especially at that time."

"Speaking of which, it would be right about that time now," she said.

*"Do you mean supper time or moon time?" I smiled
knowingly. "Hey maybe we could cook something up, kind of girl's
only?" I suggested.*

*And so began our little impromptu moon-supper-evening. It
seemed things had been going well for her in the city, she was sure
she was finished with her ex, although not as sure as I. It was
funny she was so hard and fast about what was healthy in a
relationship but still visiting this man/ boy who was violent,
ostensibly to help him. I, on the other hand, didn't want to give up
on love, and so wouldn't go near my ex with a ten-foot pole lest I
see myself reflected in his ruthless self- centeredness. I had walked
the coastal hills every day since I'd left looking for his flaws in me.
Someone had once left a poem at my house that read 'What's
wrong with you there, is wrong with me here.' I took it to heart and
figured that if I could find, even in miniscule quantities, those
qualities I disdained and face them I would be free of that
particular mirror. My own internal landscape of 'ifs' as it turned
out.*

*When I mentioned this (which I thought was quite witty) she
went very quiet and then asked me where I had seen these pieces of
art made of 'Ifs'*

*"Oh just this guy, he's a little odd, very creative, he's been
kind of hanging around a bit lately."*

"Is he fair haired?"

*I nodded. "Ya, kinda thinnish." We stared at one another
for a moment, trapped in the realization that we were talking about
the same man, hers. I hurriedly added that it wasn't like that or
anything. She nodded.*

*"I just met him on the bus. We just happened to be going to
the same stop."*

*This is weird, I thought, she was me and I had disliked her
so. And he was another of them. I congratulated myself on sending
him home. O.K. she wasn't me, but I felt like her afterbirth or
something. I was yet again a soft distorted reflection; of course
they weaken when you leave.*

*"He seems to feel quite badly about it all; he seems to miss
having someone in his life; he seems remorseful."*

"Hmm," was all she said nodding, but not in agreement.

The next time he dropped by he seemed more relaxed and I had more or less forgotten our uncomfortable exchange. He wasn't quite as chipper as in our first encounter but not quite a nuisance either. Still, barely acquaintance I decided firmly, given my newly acquired information about him. We hung out and I listened with interest to his new art ideas. He offered to lend me a ring of his that I had admired and I took it without ceremony or any thought to its meaning. I was like a magpie drawn to the shiny object without regard to attachment. For some reason I didn't mention her at all.

A couple of days passed and I missed having anyone drop by; his absence was somehow conspicuous. On the morning of the third day as I lay in bed, just having woken up I noticed myself admiring the ring as it caught the morning sun. All of a sudden I became obsessed with returning it to its owner. I took it off and laid it on the table. My plan was to carry it in my pocket. I'd go into town and find out where he lived so I could give it back, why on earth had I borrowed a ring? Why on earth had he offered it? I walked all over town hoping to bump into him to give it back. No luck, but I did succeed in finding some other friends to have a little lunch with. They were a cheerful crew and my earlier mission sunk into the background as we chatted and laughed. Just as we were nearing the end of our meal I caught a glimpse of him strolling by. I jumped from the table and invited him in to join us. He was very quiet and distant and his unfriendliness was beginning to make me regret I'd brought him over. When there was a break in the conversation I leaned over and said,

"I'd almost forgotten, I am so relieved you came by, I wanted to give you your ring back, I'm afraid I might lose it, so here." I held it out to him, "Are you alright?" He took the ring silently and nodded. He sure is a moody guy I thought. He left shortly thereafter. Oh well I guess I've been removed from that pedestal, probably a good thing.

*

He arranges all his belongings neatly on the bathroom counter: comb, toothbrush. Toothbrush for teeth, hmm best not to linger he thinks, it won't be needed. Now prize possessions, paintings piled neatly, no, he will only leave his favourite. He starts a small fire in the back yard and burns the rest one by one. It

*doesn't take very long. He sits down to write: To whom it may
concern and you know who you are. I am greatly flawed. I need to
be with my father in heaven in whose eyes I am perfect. I will be
forgiven, even if I can't forgive myself, I don't expect you to
forgive me.*

*Then he did the unthinkable and wrote to her: I wish you
had come back. Oh, how he still wanted her to feel the utter and
total devotion he would take to his grave. Then he went back to the
yard where the embers were still red and burned this note. He went
back inside to dress. He dressed in tails (an old grad suit) his
blond hair slicked back and carefully combed; he highlighted the
contours of his greenish eyes with the eyeliner she had left behind.
He glanced in the mirror and barely recognized himself. He was
playing a part. He grabbed the kitchen chair and rope and went
out again to the tree not far from the small fire.*

*At least that's how I imagined the scene when the details of
his attire and the small careful fire were described to me. What
kind of qualities, I wondered when I heard, would my new friend
have to plumb in herself, to be free of this. We had a small wake
like gathering a couple of days later; a few of us who'd made his
acquaintance.*

"Well whose life is it anyway?" I heard someone say.

*"It's everyone's life, isn't it?" someone else added
gingerly, I think that was me.*

*When she walked in, everyone went quiet; condolences
were muttered in muted tones, eyes darted in every direction afraid
to see where death would land.*

*"He called me," she said, "that night, I wouldn't speak to
him, I hung up."*

*"That's what you do when you're breaking up." I offered. I
took her hand for a moment. I was so relieved I'd given back his
ring. I did mention that he'd said he'd be happier dead. I didn't
mention that I'd suggested suicide. That I hadn't really meant it
seemed so small and dependent on tone and context that I feared it
might open up a chasm in the cliff of ifs where we were currently
perched. We needed to keep it together.*

The End

So I'm home now from the so-called wake and I guess you've figured out it was that guy from the bus. I think I'll take a walk to the beach; the kids aren't due back til tomorrow. It wasn't much of a celebration of his life. A week has passed since Fleming called me into Kelley's that morning. Too bad my now dead friend had never asked Fleming for help. Once down at Kelley's when I was sitting alone, I must have looked dejected. I was blaming myself for ending up in a silly melodrama. Guilty for the trauma my kids would have to live. Guilty for not being able to love Al enough to help him. Feeling powerless in having to leave them with him when I knew he was messing with their minds. Berating myself for not being in a position to hire a tycoon lawyer that would listen to me. And second-guessing everything I was berating myself for. In moments like these reality pulses and I become a jellyfish expanding and contracting in my own salt-water world of illusions. Pity and Pride, tyrant or victim.

Fleming came and sat down. He picked up one of my fries, chewed it thoughtfully and said, "Y'know you gotta be your own best friend." It wasn't the first time I'd heard this but it was the first time I'd gotten it. I guess timing is everything. "Thanks for the fry," he'd nodded and went back to his sketching at another table. All of a sudden I started to imagine how easy it is to forgive your best friend almost anything. I thought about how I try to be compassionate and see the best in their intentions. It made me think of Mia and how I would forgive her and try to understand where she was coming from even when it was difficult. When she ditched her kid, I didn't like it, when she acted out in sexually inappropriate ways, one of which included sleeping with my partner, when she felt the world owed her something. These were things I couldn't approve of. But I'd try to understand and then forgive if not forget. I could love her in spite of herself; cause I knew who she really is, isn't defined by any of those things. Who she is, is just someone I love. What if I treated myself like that? Perhaps with myself I could actually try to do better. I think I can apologize to myself for my errors in judgment, for my youthful haste for romantic love, my inability to read the signs, my part in the cycle of abuse, for not knowing better. When I left Kelley's I'd felt much better and considered Fleming's little cliché as a godsend. People think there's nothing in those little sentences like

"Be yourself" "Be your own best friend" "Remember who You are." I think they are whispers from heaven, portals to peace; Charity begins at home after all, in the heart.

I've arrived down on the beach now, sitting on my favourite piece of driftwood. It's a little off the main drag so there is seldom anybody here. I'm feeling a bit pissed off at Jake for his assertion that suicide is an individual choice, "Whose life is it anyway?" he'd said at the wake.

My gut just won't give in and yet I have to accept. What if *he* had been his own best friend? Maybe he'd still be alive. I remember *him* saying he wanted to die because he was so flawed. I didn't fully perceive his hopelessness. It occurs to me that if I believe the Great Spirit or universal energy helps me see the way through whatever happens to me, then it's probably great enough to help even Al without me. Maybe our capacity to be our own best friend and forgive ourselves gives us our best shot. If you can't be that to yourself how then can you do it for anyone. I tried so hard to see myself as different from *her* in that story. I had wanted to give myself a strong voice. When I reread it, it looked an awful lot like judging and distancing myself from myself. Al had even written his own suicide letter. I didn't want to be in her shoes even less then I want to be in mine right now.

No offense to the universe, but it seems that the people that need the most help would have the hardest time. No wonder I've been trying to help in my own way, trying not to judge, and failing, trying to forgive and failing. I guess each person has to do it for him or herself. I just wanted to be able to love effortlessly. It's so easy to love my kids unconditionally; it's so difficult to love myself when I see this mess. Finally tears are rolling down my face, unclenching angers hold. I don't try to wipe them away. They are soothing, they are a saltwater bath of release, for *Him*, my bus bound friend and for me. For loss and being lost and for a millisecond I feel forgiven and possibly even loved. It's getting late; I brush the sand off my butt and head home.

27

Suspicious Minds

I've had the kids back from Al for a few weeks now and I haven't heard from Al at all. We are due to go back to court again next week, with all the documents and assessments. I'm concerned about Zoë. She seems to go with the flow pretty well but she has developed the habit of clearing her throat continually, not only when she speaks but just when sitting quietly as well. It's like a nervous tick or something. It feels like such a betrayal to put her through this. My big sister, Elaine is coming out to visit for a week, so I borrow Alex's car to go pick her up at the airport. Since he's sleeping most of the afternoon it's not too much of an inconvenience for him and works out great for me. I manage to negotiate the drive and parking and we are now waiting at the gate. J.J. doesn't remember her, but Zoë does and is excited. Elaine usually fawns over her in a girly girl kind of way and plays with her hair. I think it will do Zoë some good. I'm hoping it does me some good as well, to have someone around who knows me. I just hope Elaine doesn't think I deserve this mess.

She walks out of the gate, her long thin legs giving her a model's strut, she waves shyly and her neat bob haircut and shoulders jiggle side to side in quick gestures with the wave. I'm surprised at the flood of warmth that rushes over me, the flood of relief that someone has come. Zoë runs headlong amidst the other passengers,

"Auntie Lainey!" Zoë clears her throat and then shrieks excitedly, "Auntie Lainey!" Elaine puts down her carry on and scoops up Zoë. Holding J.J.'s hand I walk a little towards them as they approach the waiting area.

"Hey, where's Aaron? " I can hear Zoë ask, glancing around, expecting him to appear. I was just wondering the same thing.

"Oh, Aaron is with his Nana and Poppa this week at their cottage," explains Elaine, as much to me as to Zoë. She gives me the "explanation to follow" look while lowering Zoë down and retrieving her bag.

"Are you hungry?" I ask. This seems as good a question as any.

"I will be soon. How far is your place from here?"

"About forty minutes. Can you hang on 'til then and we can either go out near the beach or make something at home?"

"Sounds good," says Elaine. Once her baggage arrives we head for the doors.

"Auntie Lainey, can Aaron do this? We all stop and watch as Zoë holds out her arm and snaps her fingers sticking out her tongue in concentration.

"Y'know Zoë I don't think he can, I've never seen him do that. You'll have to show him how," encourages Elaine. Zoë looks pleased and we start to walk again when J.J. runs back in the circular door, luckily there is no one in there and we can let him go around twice yelling "Can you do this?" before I have to jump in and retrieve him, it's a slight struggle to get him away from the doors as he tries to wiggle out of my arms but I hold on forcefully as we cross the road and he gets the message. "It seems you've got your hands full," Elaine smiles,

"Of late," I say, "that is an understatement."

We arrive home, drop off Elaine's bag and return Alex's car. She loves my little place and I tell her to wait until she sees the perfect lighting later on, as the sun set reflects in the kitchen. We head down to Kelley's for some food. Elaine tells the kids to order whatever they want. They both want burgers and fries and because it's a special occasion, milkshakes. We order the Mussels, because Elaine says it's fitting by the seaside. It does seem fitting so I don't mention that they are fresh water mussels. I fill her in on the latest court battles, the social worker's visit and the crazy psychiatrist whose opinion will carry a lot of weight according to my lawyer.

In the midst of our serious conversation, I notice out of the corner of my eye that J.J. is edging his milkshake closer and closer to the edge of the table. He is highly focused as it sits there and then suddenly as if he has reached some important decision he gives it the final light touch that topples it over and sends it crashing to the ground. I snap.

"Jesus Murphy J.J.! What do you think you're doing?" I'm yelling at him in that repressed public yelling that is so intense it's scary, sneering, accusingly villainous. "You don't just push things off the table on purpose! Now, you just sit there and don't move! I can't believe you do these things!" I look to Elaine embarrassed, first at J.J.'s behavior then gradually as I register her own retreat from me, my behavior. She consoles J.J. who is by now crying for another milkshake. I don't want her to get him one. I'm sure he did it on purpose. But maybe if he gets one both our mistakes will be erased. He gets his milkshake and Zoë gets another one as well for being a good girl. (As she wastes no time in pointing out). We silently agree to pay attention to the kids for the duration of the outing. I feel like I've been sent to my room and worse I feel like I deserve it.

Once we are back at the house and after numerous bedtime stories, the kids are finally both asleep in Zoë's double bed. We make a nice cup of tea.

"Well, that shrinky guy doesn't sound very professional. I thought they were supposed to help people," says Elaine.

"I guess when it's for a court case it's different." I shudder to remember him.

"Is there a way to discredit him or have someone on your side? Isn't that what they do on television?"

I look into my tea and wonder if it's even possible to explain how far from fair this seems and how far from a TV lawyer mine seems. Elaine continues, "Has anybody spoken about what a good mother you are? Remember when you made all those Montessori toys by hand? And how you made sure the kids always had all kinds of educational stuff to do, what were those things you made out of sand paper? Remember? How you studied all that child development stuff?"

"Oh yeah, the sand paper letters for texture. I don't think they carry much weight. That kind of stuff just gets lost in the shuffle."

"You know Mom used to brag about how you didn't worry yourself with the household and external impressions. She used to say that you had your priorities straight, spending your time playing with your kids. It used to upset me."

"It upset you?" I couldn't imagine perfect Elaine being affected by my choices.

"Well you know how I like a perfect house. I do think she had a point though. Even though you didn't have money and I couldn't understand how you managed, somehow the kids were always the focus. Although, it drove me crazy that you never had a washcloth on hand for their dirty faces." She gives me the look that says she sees more than Mom. "It just seems ridiculous to me that they'd even consider giving them to him at all. No offense, but I never thought he was all there if you know what I mean, he was always so vague and unreliable."

I shrug I guess that's a given at this point. She goes on, "Okay, so I admit you always did like to do things your own way, and not follow the normal trend, you always were a little airy fairy. That didn't take away from your smarts though and frankly Else, I was a little jealous that you got away with doing it your way."

"What do you mean by *got away with it?*" I get up to put the kettle on again. "More tea? And for the record, a little dirt never hurt anyone."

She glances into her cup, "Yeah sure." And continues, "What I mean is, having Zoë without planning, and it all turning out so well, no one thinking badly of you."

"Lots of people have babies, Lainey. Anyway, I wasn't thinking about what people thought. I thought I knew what I was doing," I say walking back into the room. "Anyway, the babies aren't the issue. The issue is that I didn't pick the dad very well. Shit happens, you're in love and then you're pregnant and then keeping the whole thing together takes over your whole life. Tell me your family isn't the big deal in your world?" I challenge as I get up again. The kettle is near boiling.

"Of course it is." Lainey sighs. "Hey what about that shelter you went to, could somebody write you a letter, y'know something official, to say you're a good mother?"

"I called," I say from the kitchen, "and asked, but the social worker that I spoke to most often isn't there anymore. They sent a letter stating that from what they saw I had positive interactions with the kids. I don't know what else they could say, really. I gave a copy to my lawyer." The weight of the paper war is wearing me down. Paper war, makes me think of that day with my now dead friend, our game of war with water guns. Conflict as a drippy business, *inner sog outer bogg,* he might like that one.

" Lainey, I know I was a good mother and I probably still am. It's just, well it's just, I'm losing my patience more often." I set the cups down.

"C'mon, Else that's to be expected with what's going on."

"I know that in my head, Elaine, it's just this is so bizarre, it took me so long to see that Al was unstable and finally make a move. And now to have all these accusations that I'm crazy. People think it's just bitter break-up nonsense. And of course the more emotional you get, the more unbalanced you seem. Elaine, I'm scared. Could I really lose my kids?" My eyes start to well up.

"Elsie, please don't cry . . . you know how useless I am with tears," she pleads with a strained smile.

I hold it back, gulp and take a deep breath, " Lainey, I even thought about just leaving J.J. with him. Just taking off back home, can you imagine? I thought about giving him up. It was just for a few minutes until I recognized I'd be leaving him with someone who once wrote a suicide note that was intended for both of them." I look at her imploring empathy for what is a horrible confession for me. "I don't think I could, y'know, leave him, but I thought it." I light my kazillionth cigarette. Elaine motions to give her one. She's one of those people who can have an occasional smoke. She lights up and takes the long first drag, "Whoa, dizzy, I don't know how you smoke so much." I don't comment.

"Elsie, listen to me, I know you wouldn't leave J.J.. This is just a really difficult time. You are bound to think some weird things. You're going to have to be strong, remember who you are, and get through it." She says this as though there is actual content in her statement. I can't help but smile, "What, did you record Mom's backbone speech?"

"Well, it's become internalized by now," she raises her eyebrows with satisfaction as the mood is lightened.

"I thought he was spiritual." I offer as explanation for the whole mess.

"You do mean spatial, don't you?" At this we both snicker.

"Speaking of Mom, has she read my tea leaves lately?" This is code for Mom giving advice on any topic. Although she does in fact read tea leaves, but 'just for a lark' she says.

"I haven't told her anything more than you said I could, if that's what you're asking." Elaine cuts to the chase. "I said you'd left Al but were sorting things out and you have a lovely ocean view."

"Good, I don't want to ruin her image of me as the one who lands on her feet." This is a tiny shot at Elaine who for some reason requires more encouragement and more sympathy from Mom. I don't really know why this is, since she succeeds at everything she touches. Perhaps it's the hours of council and debate it takes for her to make a decision. Perhaps it's that she includes Mom in every detail of these decisions. Perhaps the family phrase, " Oh, we don't worry about our Elsie, she always lands on her feet," became something I took to heart.

"When I last visited, she did literally read the tea leaves though," Lainey enthuses. "She said I'd be going on a boat, she saw it 'as clear as day,' she said. And also that you'd be going on a train. You know, and then she shows you in the cup, the splotches."

"So do you have a boat trip planned? Did you see anything in the splotches?"

"No. She said it was a cruise, like that's going to happen! And you, any train rides planned?" Elaine says facetiously.

"Nope. But you can't say Mom's not an optimist."

The kids wake up Auntie Lainey by running into J.J.'s room and jumping on the bed. I am of course awake to hear it all. My bed is in the middle of the living room. I'm happy to stay there for any extra time. After breakfast and some morning T.V shows, we head down to the beach. Lainey wants to look at the little shops. By lunchtime we head over to the mall, as there is an inexpensive taco place there. Lainey wants to look at some clothes so I agree to go order and she'll meet us there. Zoë wants to look at clothes as well. I explain that there are no clothes for little girls in that store and maybe we can go to a children's store after lunch. Elaine looks somewhat relieved. I mean she is on vacation, I reason to myself. We are all hungry. I'm carrying J.J.. I gave up on the umbrella stroller ages ago; it became too difficult to carry both him and the stroller when he refused its confines. We are about three stores down from Elaine and two away from a pleasant lunch, or at least somewhere to sit and have a smoke. I see a lumbering figure materialize before me. It's Al. My heart starts to race. Be calm; be friendly, I tell myself. "Oh hi, I didn't expect to see you here." I say in the nearest to friendly voice I can muster.

"Oh no?" his voice betrays no mood I can peg. So against my jitters I try to be civil. I put J.J.. down. "Hey Zoë," he beams ruffling her hair, "are you shopping?" Al gets down on one knee with open arms, "Hiya Jye-James, come and see your dad."

J.J. runs over and Al scoops him up as Zoë says, "We're getting tacos."

"Hmm," says Al nodding absently down to Zoë. He raises his head to glower at me.

"What do you think you are doing? It's my turn to have them."

"Al, what are you talking about? We're at the mall, this isn't how it works. We go to court at the end of the week, it'll get worked out." J.J. is in his arms. How am I going to get him back I wonder. I think of that story where the real mother refuses to have the baby chopped in half as I consider ripping J.J. out of his arms. Probably not the best plan, possibly traumatic at worst and a failed attempt at best. I turn to Zoë, "Do you remember where Auntie Lainey is?" She nods yes, "Go and see how her shopping is going." Zoë looks at me quizzically, so I command, "Go on, you go ahead, I'll be there in a minute, it's okay." Zoë takes a second and then runs off in the direction of the shop. I turn to Al. "Well, I've got to meet up with my sister, so say see ya later to J.J. and we'll see ya later." I hold out my arms in expectation. Al hugs J.J. closer.

"You say see ya to J.J.. He's staying with me. You can't control everything Elsie. It's my turn. He's my son." I keep my arms up. J.J. is surprisingly quiet and still. I know he loves his father. This just isn't the way it's supposed to go.

"Let's try to do this properly, come get him at the house or wait 'til after the court decision. You don't just take the kid at the mall, for Christ's sake! He doesn't even have his stuff. It doesn't have to be like this, c'mon," I plead.

"Well this is how it is, Elsie. He's staying with me; this is where he should be. The mall is irrelevant. You are going down, little girl. You think it hurts? Damn straight. We gotta go. He'll be with me when we go to court, and that's where he'll stay. He's mine."

Al starts to walk away, and again I think of the mother not chopping the child in two. I quell my desire to run after him and rip J.J. out of his arms. Al turns at the doors, "Say, bye bye to Mommy," he instructs J.J. who doesn't say anything. He is just looking; he doesn't seem to mind going for a walk with his dad. This tears me apart even more; two year olds are known for finding their dads exciting.

They disappear out the doors. My fury is blocked by shock. Elaine and Zoë appear.

"What's happened?" asks Elaine looking around, "Zoë said you ran into Al." The registering absence of J.J. makes the scene self-explanatory.

"Why did you give him J.J.?" she asks.

"I didn't give him J.J., he took him and he wouldn't give him back," I snap.

"Did you tell him to give him back?" She is having trouble it seems, in understanding what transpired. "He just took him? Can he do that?"

"What do you think Elaine? He just did." I let out an exasperated sigh, "I guess I'll go call my lawyer."

"What about tacos?" pipes in Zoë. "I'm hungry. J.J. is going to miss his tacos. He really likes them you know Mum. I think they're his favorite." This sounds like an accusation, as though I have somehow allowed his taco deprivation to occur.

"I'm not sure he likes them all that much." I say, as though in my own defense.

"They are his very favorite, Mom," Zoë insists.

"I don't think he'd know the difference between a taco and a bean tree if he was hungry, Zoë," I insist back with a building anger. My existence, my status as a parent, as a person with any clout depends on knowing that missing the taco lunch, is the least of the traumas I've put my son through. I know they're his damn favorite.

"A bean tree?!!" squeals Zoë, "Nobody eats bean trees, Mom." Clearly I require educating. Zoë gives an exaggerated eye roll.

Elaine jumps in to the rescue, "Okay then, Zoë let's go get some Tacos! You show me the way." Elaine takes Zoë's hand and we start to walk in the direction of the Taco place. Zoë glances over her shoulder at me as if to point out that at least her Aunt Elaine is on the ball. I amble up behind and grab Zoë's other hand, she almost smiles, forgiveness is on the tip of her lips.

"Let's go," I say, "one two three wheee! " and with that we whisk Zoë into the air. Once we are sitting down to eat Zoë says through a mouthful, "He does like them you know."

I answer, "Yes, Zoë, he really does. I guess I forgot." With that her full food mouth expands into the 'all is forgiven grin' and some mushed up food spills out. In a show of support I open my mouth and show her my already chewed food. Together we have successfully grossed out Auntie Lainey who makes a big show of her disapproval. Just get through lunch and then call the lawyer.

Caroline Devereaux is not as upset as I am. Not even outraged. I guess it must be part of their lawyer training. It doesn't make me feel very supported. It's odd that one's advocate can be so distanced. I don't know where I got the idea if someone is on your team, they should rally behind you. I imagine I'd feel better if she shook a fist and said "We'll get 'em in the next round kiddo," or something to that effect. What she does say is; "Well Elsie, since we will be in court on Friday, it's probably best to leave things as they are. Al's behavior more than likely won't look very good to the judge. Elsie, have you got a phone now?"

"The phone company are coming Monday, I'm calling from my neighbor's, the same number I gave you." How did that become a priority of this conversation?

"Oh, good, I'm glad to hear that. Give me your new number." She sounds so incredibly far from what I'm dealing with its almost possible to imagine her in a parallel universe where nothing matters except her phone list.

"It's at my place. I'll give it to you at court. Aren't I sending the message that it's alright with me for Al to just up and take J.J? If I don't respond to this nonsense, it could go on and on like this." I so want to have some recourse. Elaine is standing beside me in Alex's kitchen where we are using the phone. She is nodding her approval. I move the receiver to between our heads so Elaine can hear as well.

"I think it would be best to show some patience and a willingness to work within the framework of the court system. The judge will recognize that Al has not done so himself, and this will be more evident if you yourself behave in accordance with the agreement. That is my advice." She sounds certain of herself. Elaine and I exchange confused looks, digesting the certain logic in this advice.

"But don't I have the right to call the police?" I ask. Elaine gives me the thumbs up.

"Well, possibly, but in the strictest terms, no," answers Ms. Devereaux

"Why not?" I don't get it. Elaine gives me the thumbs down, and we smile inappropriately like we did at Dad's funeral. Stress I guess.

"This hearing is for interim custody, so there is no firm ruling yet on anything. You run the risk of being perceived as a troublemaker or too controlling. Again I'd advise you to let things be as they are until Friday. I'll see you then." There is a pause of dead air while I'm processing and then she adds, "Try not to worry." I don't get how both Al and my lawyer agree that expecting reasonable behavior is perceived as controlling. Elaine seems at a loss and is shrugging with her faced all screwed up.

"Okay, I guess, I'll see you Friday. You do think it'll go well don't you?" I'm begging for a scrap of reassurance, anything to get me through the next few days. Both Caroline and Al don't seem to want me to be perceived as in control.

"I hope so, I can't see why it shouldn't, but a lot of attention will be paid to Dr. McDuffy's report, which I'll have early Friday. See you then. We'll talk before court."

"Okay, see you then." I hang up.

"Wow," says Elaine, plunking herself down on the kitchen chair. Her backbone is visibly malleable. Alex and Zoë return from his front room.

I turn and fill him in. "Well J.J. will be staying with his dad until Friday when we go to court." I'm incredulous. He looks to Elaine and they both look at me, me in synchronized pity.

"Popsicles, anyone? Purple, Zoë?" Alex asks. Although grateful, I'm not paying any attention to the cool treat exchange. I turn to Elaine, "I've got to go home." Before anyone can respond I'm halfway out the door, I yell back, "Thanks for letting me use the phone Alex." I'm sure I don't sound very thankful. Elaine will handle Zoë.

Surely it'll get sorted out on Friday. I just have to hang on; it's only a few days.

I received the letter from Mia stating that she thinks I am a good mother and also that she had been present when Al was aggressive and also aware that he hit me. It came in a package with some others she'd collected. Judy's came with a personal letter in a separate envelope. I planned to open that later. There was even one from Zoë's paternal grandparents written in good faith praising the capable girl they had known. I felt a wave of gratitude flow through me, especially for Sam's parents, because we hadn't kept in touch. I hope I'm still that girl in here somewhere. I asked Alex if I could use his phone to call Mia to thank her whilst he was at work tonight. He left the key in his mailbox. Lainey agreed to stay with Zoë.

"Mama Mia's fetish line," she sings, "What do ya think of my new job?"

I pause, thinking, this person is my reference?

She cackles, "I knew it was you, sucker. Hi, how goes it in hell?" I explain the latest; that Al now has J.J., stole him at the mall, and that I'm optimistic that it'll be sorted out on Friday. Especially since lawyers seem very rule oriented.

"I can't even imagine, who'd a thunk it would come to all this?" she sighs.

"Thanks a lot for the package Mia, every bit helps at this stage of the game. It's all pretty humiliating. I know, it's pretty crazy making. What've you been up to?" I don't want to be all self involved, I am shocked at the amount of energy it seems to take just to listen. Have I that little left to give? It's good though, to hear the voice of an old friend.

"Well, things are actually on the move for me these days. I'm still doing dance classes and my dad has this building that the lease is up on, it's kind of like a storage space, but the tenant no longer wants it, so I'm going to convert it into a dance school. It will be mostly for kids, I think. The parents will pay of course. The parents finally figured out that I'm not going to go into law or even secretarial school so they might as well get behind me. As I've always said to them; you're either fer me or agin me. I'm planning to put a pole in, you know for special spicy dances!" She chuckles. "On the romance front, well there are plenty of takers, so…"

I don't know if it's because things seem to be on the up for her, or something in her philosophy just tweaked a nerve but I hear myself say, "Wow that's spectacular Mia. Were you fer me or agin me when you slept with Al?"

"Oh, you know about that." There is a silence, me like an animal waiting for the moment of release, her ascertaining the best tactic.

"That was neither fer you or agin you, it was between me and him." Naturally her reply would go so far as to erase me from the equation. I guess I've been feeling erased enough lately.

"Really," I say to buy time. "Do you think that was being a good friend, it was tantamount to saying you didn't believe me. Like you didn't believe what I was going through. You didn't even tell me."

"Elsie, you know how it is with me and guys; it's chemistry, you know Al, he always had a thing for me. I could tell. When did you get so uptight?"

"Well frankly, at the moment I can't figure out what you were drawn to, so I'm hardly jealous. You can fly here and fuck his brains out." I'm seething.

"I thought you were broken up at the time…"

"I WAS IN A SHELTER, YOU FOOL! I guess I got so uptight when I had a family. Anyway, you talked to me at the shelter, you agreed with me that he's not in his right mind."

"Look Elsie, I think you're a little irrational, I wasn't looking for love, just one night, or maybe two and if it's any consolation it wasn't that great. He was sad." This is in fact no consolation.

"Well as you can see now, we were not done at the time." My voice softens, I don't now how to get her to understand the feeling of betrayal.

"More is the pity as it turns out." She sounds like ice freezing, more solid and cold with every word. How did I get here when I just wanted to thank her for the letters? I decide to change tactics.

"Look Mia it's not just me you do this to, are you still dating Ronaldo, the married Ronaldo?"

"You mean Dominick? No." She's still frosty.

"Did you have an attack of conscience, a realization?"

"His wife got pregnant if you must know, and it pissed me off cause he said they never had sex. I mean they only did it once, but still it turned me off." Her voice completely changes as she tells me about her hurt and I get that she honestly doesn't get it. I'm in it now. Might as well try.

"And you believed him? Come on Mia, just like you believed Al was somehow crazy with me but okay for a good time with you? You had a special connection? Whilst I, your supposed friend, cried, over the break-up of my family. Do you really believe that just because you're so sexually loose that you're not like the rest of us, you really think you're so special that men are honest with you whilst they are lying and cheating on someone else?" I'm talking really fast and my heart is pounding. "It's really kind of sad Mia, you need to accept you are a female not in some better league of your own. What do you fancy yourself a Venetian Courtesan? Well right now you're more like a Venetian blind!"

"Elsie, you are obviously freaked out by what you're going through, I get that. Who cares about Al anyway, it's him that's putting you through this, not me. I just sent the papers, remember." She says in a consoling voice. "I had to go to the notary and everything, you think that's not friendship? If I were you, I'd be pretty grateful. I mean of course I was happy to do it. But I do think you should know it took quite a bit of my time and energy." She is clipped and self-righteous.

I am grateful, but I wonder if I'm supposed to feel guilty for even asking for help, because that is what I feel. Guilty and pissed off about having to feel guilty. And also pissed off for having to always be grateful in a guilty way. I want to be grateful in a graceful way.

"Okay, again thanks for the papers. I'd just like to believe that there is world where your best friend wouldn't go near your insane partner out of some sort of principle, y'know." I'm tired, expressed out. " It's all too much lately, Mia, listen I gotta go, I'll be in touch. Thanks again I do appreciate it."

"Just so you know, I'm not exaggerating. My car was in the shop and I had to take the bus because of your Friday deadline, that's how there for you I am okay?"

"Okay, thanks again. I didn't realize."

"And Elsie, dear Elsie, I imagine you fancy yourself so special that only you can understand the likes of Jesus H Al. Perhaps you'd like to rethink those principles you hold so dear. Because at least one of us is having a good time, so don't preach to me. I gotta go. Good luck."

I am frozen trying to process. I force myself to speak into the dense silence, "Okay, thanks again, bye." I hang up.

Lainey looks up from her book as I plop myself into the chair with an accompanying exasperated sigh. "Zoë in her room?"

She nods, "What happened? You look upset. I thought you were going to have a chat with Mia?"

"I did, then it turned into something else. I attacked her, for sleeping with Al. Then she made me feel bad for her having to get the papers together, and take the bus."

"Well, seems like you covered a lot of ground little sister." Her little bob tilts gently, as she turns her head to the side anticipating more of an explanation. I don't respond. Somewhere in what Mia said there is some truth that I don't want Lainey to confirm. Something about us both thinking we are special, but I'm not cheating or lying. I feel hit, like with a bullet so sleek that it only penetrates if it finds its mark.

"She's an odd duck that friend of yours. I never quite got what you liked so much about her." She turns back to her book.

I take a deep breath, "She's just a friend, we hung out a lot when the kids were babies. We had a lot of laughs, she's quick and witty, and smart." I say this to answer the same question to myself. I realize I didn't even ask about Kiefer, more guilt.

Lainey doesn't look up but says dryly, "Oh yes, that particularly stupid kind of smart, all flash and no pan." I find this funny, I laugh and Lainey half smiles, pleased with the effect of her comment.

"What does that actually mean, 'no pan'?" I ask.

"I think an explanation would ruin it don't you?" She grins still pretending to read.

"You're probably right," I say, relieved to be with my sister. And then, "You don't know what it means do you?"

Lainey closes her book, looks at me in all seriousness and says, "I have no fucking idea." We burst out laughing. Lainey both swore and didn't know the answer. She did this for me.

28

Painted Lady

The week is passing super slow as it counts down to court. I miss J.J.. but I confess a small break from the constant care of the little guy isn't all bad. Then again all the stress comes from not having the little guy with me. Plus, I'm sure the judge will deliver him back to me come Friday. How could he not? I miss tucking him in at night. I've tucked him in almost every night of his little life. I hope he's all right. Elaine is leaving Friday. It just happened to coincide with court, so hopefully she'll be here to go with me. Just one more sleep until court and my baby comes home. I am nervous. I smoke; I pace, I take out my paints. Zoë and Elaine are involved in an elaborate game of "house" in Zoë's closet; I am the grandmother and so live in another room. They visit every so often, they have to go outside and around the house and come back in to get to me. I figure grandma will be painting during their next visit.

I decide to paint Lainey. The way I see her now… She is straight edged, her bob like a helmet. Somehow in the painting her hair extends out from under the bob, until it has gone from brown to golden sand that descends and covers her feet. Her original hair has become a sunhat of sorts; it covers one eye. The background is in blues and descends from dark blue to azure where it meets the shore of her hair. Her arms hang down, periwinkle at the shoulder, fading to white; her not so well defined hands form a triangle at her pubic bone. It's more like the left is covering the right, the supposed thumbs interlocked. Inside the triangle is white except for a larger than life sapphire blue stone on her wedding ring.

Since there is so much flowing hair she really doesn't have much definition in her upper body. I think about attempting some hint of breasts when there is a knock at the door. I realize that I didn't even notice Zoë and Elaine leave the house. From the look of the painting at least an hour must have passed. The smell of paint thinner mixed with the oils is pervasive, and my fingers are covered in paint from swirling the colours by hand. It may have been the smell that drove them out a while ago.

I open the door remembering to pretend I'm Grandma, by formally addressing Zoë, "Hello Granddaughter, you look very grown up these days." I say in my croakiest voice.

"I am a grown-up; you are baby Seana's Gramma. I am the mommy, Jane." Zoë is a little frustrated, but since she has an ice cream cone in hand she continues formally. "Seana, say hello to Gramma and ask her if we can visit."

Lainey dutifully replies, "Mom said it was a nice afternoon for a little walk and to get some ice-cream, can we come in for a visit Gramma?"

"Of course," I croak, opening the door for entry. "Did you bring Gramma some?" Some cream for the croak.

"It might have melted; you can have a lick of mine.It's bubble gum flavor. Your hands are very messy," says Zoë her cone outstretched.

"Gramma," says Lainey, "we saw that Jake guy. He said he's coming over for a visit too. It'll be a tea party at Gramma's." Her sarcastic excitement is lost on Zoë, who hands me her cone and says, "I'll put the kettle on then," in a tentative imitation of me.

"I'll help you *Jane*, dear," I croak.

"I think my baby Seana can drink grown–up tea for the special casino of visiting Gramma, don't you, Jane's, I mean, my, mum?" Zoë says as she drags the chair to the kitchen sink and proficiently fills the kettle. We trade kettle for cone, so I can put it on the stove.

"You mean 'occasion,' *Jane* . . ." I was going to play with this a bit, but I see Jake coming in and flirtatiously tipping his invisible hat to Lainey.

"Gramma!! Someone is at your house," squeals Lainey in her Seana voice.

"Welcome, welcome," I croak, "will you have a spot of tea young man?" Zoë nods encouragingly at Jake, who after a moment of confusion plays along.

"Yes, please, *Gramma*," he replies. "What have we here?" He saunters towards the painting.

"Gramma's painting, it's a little messy because she's old now," explains Zoë clearly wanting this game to go on all day.

"Just a little messy dear," I mutter croakingly. I feel the need for a floppy sunhat.

"That woman is afraid to have a baby?" Jake queries while gesturing towards the painting.

"Hmm, ya think?" I say looking at the painting anew.

"Why on earth would someone be afraid to have a baby?" asks Lainey with keen interest, "Why would you say that?" Lainey doesn't know the painting is of her. As far as I know, it's not obvious.

"Sometimes," begins Jake, "people aren't actually afraid of what they think they are afraid of. Like you can see, that lady is a real romantic. You see, she has it in her, but she doesn't see it, so she tries to pull it out of her husband. She tries to pull out the thing he already loves in her. She's afraid to appear needy, so she protects herself, with convention."

I'm thinking, cool. "You can get all that from that?" I croak at the painting. Jake shrugs.

Lainey is not buying it, "I'd have to argue that it's the artist that has those attributes."

"That's possible," I add just happy to have been called an artist. Forgetting to croak.

"Gramma," says Zoë, "I mean Mom," I hear her but am unable to change channels in my mind.

Jake says, "I don't think so, I think she's going to have a baby anyway. It'll be a boy and it actually brings the love out of her. She's on edge this one, a bit tight."

"Just because someone wants to take some time to plan important decisions in one's life doesn't necessarily make one afraid y'know, Jake." Lainey challenges. Jake wheels around; he walks closer to her, sits, and stares at her intensely. Lainey shifts uncomfortably. I've seen him do this before. Silence.

"Muuum!!" yells Zoë.

I am jarred, and snap "What?"

"Can I go watch T.V since *no one* wants to play anymore?" she sulks.

"Sure, go on." I nod. Zoë heads for her room. Lainey sits straight-backed. Jake bursts out laughing, throwing his head back, "You gotta take what you need. I like that you take your space," he does his signature grab at the air. "Sometimes you are afraid that you might have what you need already and someone else can take it away!"

Lainey looks to me, puzzled, irritated but refusing to let go. It reminds me of Zoë saying to me once, 'Mum, I just want something to want.' I say as much, hoping to interrupt the intensity.

"Oh that Zoë, where does she come up with those things!" says Lainey, relieved to shift the focus. I take the hint.

"So, Jake, speaking of babies and romance, what's happening with Lois?" I ask. Jake tries to take a last swig of tea, letting the silence nibble at the question, but there is nothing left in his cup so he takes one of my cigarettes instead.

"I called her, she wants it. She'll be a good mother. I think, yes; she'll be a good mother. She's leaving Benny," he reports.

Before I can push for more details, Jake continues, "I saw your fellow there, the one you left. Seems he has a new girl, they were y'know spooning down on the boardwalk. How do you feel about that? Thought I'd give you the heads up. Maybe it will help you in the court case or something."

"Was J.J. with him?" is the first thing that pops into my mind. Followed by *'spooning'* really? Who says that?

"I think the little guy was running around, yeah." Lainey looks to me. I don't know what to think. I grab for a smoke; they watch. I light it quickly. They watch. I stub it out angrily. Lainey looks to Jake, "How does this help?"

Jake gets up and puts a hand on my shoulder, "Your little sister here, she prefers to know." I am silent, stewing, sorting. Jake heads for the door, "It's between painters, isn't that right Elsie? He winks me into his club and I like it, even though I'm still trapped under the ice. "I like that one," he gestures at the canvas. I know he's complementing both Lainey and me at the same time. He tips his invisible hat to Lainey on his way out.

"I bet you do." I call after him. A couple of seconds pass and I run out onto the porch, "Do you know who she is?" I yell trying to whisper, cause Jake is already at the end of the walkway. Jake nods, "Deirdre, the jewelry girl from the boardwalk." He turns and keeps walking.

After omelets for dinner, there is a bedtime story for Zoë, the one I made up about the dragon who sends sandmen to earth to collect dreams. Lainey and I settle in for her last night of the visit, and my night before court. It feels like a beautiful sunset on the verge of a thunderstorm. I'm borrowing Alex's car for the big day and Lainey will watch Zoë. I'm also pleased that Lainey is lending me a very conventional blouse, which I'm hoping will keep my spirit embodied for the occasion.

"What do you make of all that stuff Jake said?" Lainey asks, as we install ourselves at the table with more tea.

"Deirdre you mean?"

"Actually, I meant about that painting, it's me isn't it? She sounds uncharacteristically hesitant. I realize she must have been waiting all day to get to this. I hope the whole image isn't a slight, cause she's been so great to have with me.

"Well, it's kinda based on you, but then I just go off on the colours and textures. At least it's pretty colours don't you think?" I offer.

"No, no, I like it; it's one of your less intense ones. But it's just that well y'know, I don't quite understand how he got all that information about a future baby and fear. Okay, so it's true that I sometimes feel like my Aaron kind of replaces me with his father. They are so two peas in a pod and Paul's family has their own agenda, and sometimes I feel a bit left out, like I'm just the reproducer. I do usually manage to take my space as your friend put it." She pauses but only for a breath, "It's a bit like walking a tightrope, everything is great. Paul's wonderful, as long as I stay here, on the rope. It's not as though anyone is telling me to. I don't mean that I see greener pastures either. There isn't anything else, no other pasture; I mean nothing else except the rope that I can see, being where I am, and its terror. Total happiness, that feels so reliant on random weather, which we all know is unreliable. It's a balancing act. This probably doesn't even make sense." She raises two fingers in request of a puff of my smoke. I comply, and she continues, " I think I'm afraid of fear. The kind of fear that comes from wanting to hold on too tightly, oh my God, that Jake even used the word tight didn't he? He's so strange, provoking this in me. I guess watching you go through all this has affected me a little, sorry. You didn't even give me boobs," she says pointing to the canvas."I don't know how he could've known it was me, I mean I'm not stacked but c'mon." She points to her chest and it's true she has a noticeable bosom. Which I wasn't sure I could do justice.

"It's not finished. Don't worry about it; Jake has a way of honing in on soft spots and everybody has them." I say reassuringly. "It's probably not a great idea to worry about being too happy. I don't know, maybe you want to get rid of that tight rope image? Maybe you should talk to Paul or maybe not. I mean it's been three years, and he didn't even cheat, he actually confessed beforehand. I mean I'm no expert but I think that may be the sign of an actual good person." She doesn't answer and I don't think I'm in the best place to be giving relationship advice, unless its 'run for your life.' "I think he's kind of sexy though, don't you?" I say trying to lighten things up.

"Who? Paul? Of course I think he's sexy."

"No, not Paul, Jake."

"You would." Lainey is clearly a tad disturbed by Jake. This amuses me, but I see we are not going to distract ourselves with the allure of *yet another strange guy*.

"It seems to me, Paul just wanted some of your attention. Y'know you were in mummy-la-la land with Aaron for a while." Lainey seems to be listening but all she says is, "Maybe. Do you know that jewelry girl? Have you met her?"

"Well no, not really. I met her once, but I've seen her selling her stuff. It's very nice. It's the round loopy kind of jewelry with some largish stones. It kind of matches her in a way. She wears those big peasant skirts and she's got big hips and big hair."

It seems my instincts were accurate about Al having found a new love interest. So, her name is Deirdre, and she seems to have her act together. She runs her own handmade jewelry business, and no kids (she mentioned it to me the one time we spoke). I hadn't been in the market for jewelry at the time, but I thought she was cool. Figures that Al would have to pick someone that I could like.

She has that together kind of cheery hippy demeanor, complete with a perfectly tied batik kerchief. The kind of full figure that can sport a peasant skirt without looking either like a sack of potatoes or a stick. Her own design dangling spiral earrings look so good on her. You find yourself wanting to buy her whole head, complete with gold waves. I remember the earrings because they were so pretty. But when I held them up to my ear I looked like a Charlie Brown Christmas tree, sporting bobbles bigger than my eyes. So that's his new gal. I sure don't want her head anymore, or the tangled mash her mind and heart will eventually become.

I couldn't help but think how impressed Al would be with her "can do" practical approach to life. Even though part of me entirely believes that he is mentally ill, there is a small bit that thinks perhaps with a different person he could be all right. I know this is tantamount to saying the problems are mine. This doesn't sit right either. Wouldn't it be great though if everyone could just find a new circumstance and be alright, that our war was a misunderstanding, an innocent ideological mismatch that could be righted when each was seen in a new light? At any rate, I had prayed for a replacement, and she had arrived. I'm torn between being happy that a certain pressure is off and feeling responsible for letting someone else take that place. Ah well, if she's gaga in love with him for the moment she wouldn't listen to me anyway.

"Should I try to warn her, Lainey, what do you think?"

"I guess you should, but I doubt she'll hear you." Lainey offers.

"Yeah, well if opportunity arises, I'll do it anyway. What time is your flight again?"

"Two-thirty p.m. don't you remember? Alex is going to take me on his way to work. We are dropping Zoë off at Angie's on the way." Lainey says this in her *get with the program* voice.

"Right, Right, sorry, I *so* don't want you to go, I keep forgetting. Do you think he'll bring her to court?" The thought gives me the willies, although I'm not sure why. Being out numbered, I guess. For some reason I kept imagining that Lainey would still be here when I got home. God, I had constructed a whole scenario complete with me not having to take the bus. Alex was going to lend me his car before we realized Lainey needed a lift, and Zoë needed to be dropped off. I don't recognize myself, I know that for what seems like a long time, I've been the plugger of holes to appease Al. Could it be that without him I'm as flakey as he is? I hope this is only temporary.

"I sure wouldn't bring her if I was him," Lainey reassures, "But that doesn't say much. I doubt it though. Hey, cheer up, once you get J.J. back we'll organize a visit, you guys can come see us okay? Zoë will be so happy to see Aaron. Everything is going to work out; Al is so obviously unable to function; things will be settled." Lainey gathers up the teacups and takes them to the kitchen. The picture of normal.

"I'd better try to get some sleep. Thanks Lainey, I'm off to bed." I walk the five feet to where my bed is and peel off my clothes. Once under the covers I look up to see Lainey heading into J.J.'s room. "Hey, don't forget to set your alarm please, for 7:00 so we'll have time for breakfast," I remind her, Zoë will probably be up by then, but I don't want to take any chances. "Lainey" I whisper loud enough to be heard in J.J.'s room.

"Yeah?"

"Can I keep the blouse?" I add sneakily in my little sister voice.

"Yes, you can keep the blouse Elsie. See you in the morning. Night."

"Night," I whisper.

29

Shadows in the Rain

After a restrained but sad good-bye, amidst Elaine's reassurances, I take the bus to the courthouse. I couldn't afford to let any emotion even near me. I still can't as I walk into the building. It's just a building. In and of itself, not intimidating in the least. And there she is, Lady Justice, the goddess Themis herself, as if to bolster my faith. She, who presided over proper relations between men and women, she, who was also a prophet; bring on the divine justice. I don't know what I expected; robed deciders of fate to greet me at the door and me humbled, to fall to my knees pleading for the quality of mercy not to be strained. Better yet to see myself flanked by justice incarnate and Al shackled, his head bowed as they drag him out, then I could say, 'leave him be,' graciously followed by, 'his nature has been exposed, let him not waste more of our time, go with God.' At which point he would dissipate into the sky. Which is not the same as wishing someone dead I tell myself. I wish she wasn't blindfolded.

I am pulled out of my daydream as I go through the foyer into the big hallway. There are a couple of vending machines; I purchase a two pack of chocolate chip cookies for procrastination and fortification purposes. Munching, I spot Caroline Devereaux down the hall. I put the second cookie back in the wrapper and in my pocket and head towards her. She smiles a perfunctory greeting and motions to a seat along the wall.

"You look nice," she says, vaguely surprised and pleased with her own observation.

"Thanks."

As we are sitting she gets a file out of her brief case.

"So, what did the psychiatrist say?" I ask hopefully.

"It's not great. Which is going to make things a little more difficult," she delivers in a business-like tone

"How, not great? Do you have his report? Can I see it? I really think we should've gotten one of our own," I add as though she will finally see the wisdom of my suggestion. She hands me the file. I scan it in quickly. It says that I am too intelligent to benefit from therapy; that I would play with it. I wonder if that's because I didn't acquiesce to the idea of being fed to the crocodiles. I try to explain this to Caroline but it seems a moot point. It also says that Al feels victimized by me. To which I respond by saying to Caroline that before Al had me as a foe, he felt victimized by the entire world. I've become a funnel to pour the fuel that was once the world.

"Perhaps, we could line up all the people he has thought are out to get him, then I wouldn't seem like the only villain," I suggest. I feel set up. Like a victim myself and round and round it seems to go, outrage the driving force. Tears barely kept at bay. She looks at me with a face that suggests she doesn't necessarily disagree with the report. She seems to read my reaction, and she says, "Look Elsie, it doesn't matter what I think." Reassurance is not her strong suit.

"I get that, but you should remember that you don't even know Al. And you weren't too impressed when his lawyers fired him for being unreasonable."

"That's true, but it's also beside the point Elsie. We are dealing with today. Now listen, before we go into court, the two of you will meet with a mediator to try to come to some sort of agreement." Again reading my expression of prescient futility, she says, "It's standard procedure in custody cases."

I'm vaguely aware of people going about their business in the hallway. There are a couple of other people meeting with their lawyers on similar benches, talking in lowered voices, sitting on leather seats with no backs. This prods me to lower my own voice as I mutter, "He told my children that I didn't love them; he's hit me, strangled me, I don't understand how all this can be glossed over, so much cruelty." I feel like I am under water with barely enough air. It's so lonely in my perspective; nothing anybody is saying is making sense. If I wasn't so busy trying to stay alive in the moment I might just run, if I wasn't certain of one thing: That J.J. needs his mother, that someone who would tell a child that they are not loved does not have that child's best interests at heart. Despite Caroline's neutral emotional state I know that love most certainly must trump. I have to believe that love holds no place for violence. It's seems a stretch to hope that her neutrality is on my side. I have misunderstood the meaning of advocate, I think.

"I haven't even seen Al," I mention, "maybe he won't even show up? Then what happens?" I ask hoping I can win by default. The last time he didn't show they said he couldn't do that again.

"Oh he's here, I saw him earlier. He's with his new lawyer; they are just down around the corner," says Caroline pointing down the hall.

"Oh. But I mean they have to order J.J. back, don't they? You can't just take a kid at the mall and keep him, right?"

" Let's hope the court takes that into consideration. This is a preliminary hearing for interim custody, we'll just have to wait and see what the judge decides."

She looks at her watch. It's eleven twenty-five am. There are two large ornate clocks hanging perpendicular to the walls at different ends of the hall. I guess she looks at her own out of force of habit. Or perhaps to give a cue, because then she says, "Time to go. I'll show you to the mediation room upstairs." She gets up and I dutifully follow. We arrive outside the door.

"I'll meet you back downstairs when you're done." I look at her imploringly, and for once she seems to get it, "I know this isn't easy Elsie, it's just procedure. Stay open minded. Something good may come of it. I've seen it happen."

Caroline strides off down the hall, and turns back, miming a knocking motion to encourage me. I nod. I need a minute; I need a lifetime to figure out how it'll feel to be mediating with someone I believe to be manipulative due to mental illness. I'm kind of scared. I can't figure out where he'll be at, which Al will turn up. Co-operating hasn't been working so well. I take a deep breath of the seemingly limited oxygen available, and knock. Maybe this *can* turn things around.

I certainly don't expect a young man to open the door. Uh-oh, a guy, he'll probably totally see Al's point of view, Al's oh so very exposed pain. Fuck.

The slightly built, pony-tailed social worker type extends his hand, "Hi, I'm Marcus Tully. Come on in and have a seat." He motions to the empty couch and I notice Al isn't here. Perhaps, I dare to dream, procedure isn't on his agenda. It's a sunny room. The relief that washes over me comes to an abrupt halt in unison with the soft rap,rap, rapping at the door. Relief is immediately replaced by rancor, as Al is ushered in. I don't like the smell or taste of my own state, or is it his? I move perceptibly to the other end of the couch, as Al smiles. "Hey there, Elsie," he says softly, but I can still smell it, and now I know it's him. Maybe Marcus being a guy isn't such a bad thing after all. I've heard some men actually deplore violence against women. But then again, this isn't about that; we are here about the kids. It's difficult to keep these issues separate.

"So Elsie," Marcus pauses, then looks at Al. "Al," he nods, "we're here to try to come to some sort of agreement that you can both live with, that will be best for your children."

I think there is going to be a lot of him looking from one of us to the other and us nodding. But Al doesn't let him get to even a suggestion of what the 'best' might look like. Al gets right to it, his voice suggesting that he and Marcus understand each other. Al leans towards Marcus, "She is crazy, and that's why I have been forced by circumstance to do what is best for my son. This whole thing is her idea. I just want peace. I mean kids deserve a home."

I look first to Marcus who is deciding how to proceed. The tears that have now found their way to the edge of my eyes surprise me. That does sound reasonable enough. It's just not that simple. I lower my head instinctively; to try to blink them back in. I succeed for the most part. I hear Marcus ask me if there is anything I'd like to say.

"Well, it's difficult to come to an agreement because there is a lot of anger between us. I don't trust him to be responsible and he keeps trying to take my daughter, who isn't even his, away from me just because he knows they probably wouldn't split up the kids. It's like revenge or something. It's been such a fight that I don't know…" I lose my trend of thought. Damn. The tears rise up again. I want anger back. It's easier not to blubber through. "It's all been a big mistake. I don't think you're well." I say, turning towards Al, but I'm not sure it's discernable. I see Al looking at Marcus out of the corner of my eye; his demeanor suggests that my tears are par for the course. I want to jump up and yell: *this isn't me; I wasn't like this before! I swear, help me get me back.*

Marcus hands me a tissue and compassionately waits for me to get it together. Quite different from that shrink, I can't help but notice. Just when I think I might be all right to continue, Al begins, "Look Marcus, she had the kids young. She's just incapable."

"Incapable?" I snap back, "You were hardly ever there, and you always deny you're violent." This is awful. I can see us through Marcus Tulley's eyes: pathetic, bickering. Al shrugs off my accusations as though they are the ramblings of an ineffectual person.

He shakes his head pityingly, and then says, "She leaves vegetables in the bottom of the fridge. She just lets them rot there, unused." He declares, as though anyone in their right mind could see the inherent incompetence.

This is true. The trueness of his accusation tears gaping holes in what little strength I have left. Al made sense. I would let things go bad sometimes. I didn't do it on purpose, but it wasn't a priority. This is very bad. I have no defense; the horrible awful possibility that I could lose my children over an impetuous oversight (I'd rather go out than use up all the old veggies.) is like a knife in the gut. I sob, " I didn't know, I didn't know it would end up being so important." Everything is so confused again. Surely an on the ball person wouldn't ignore food. I feel like I'm inside a rain cloud, it's wet and soggy and grey, I'm beginning to feel all hope slipping away when I hear Marcus say,

"A fridge and its contents are usually considered mutual property, wouldn't you agree Al?"

The spirit of Themis has come through in young Marcus Tulley with the ponytail, cutting fact from fiction. There is a pocket of clear sky. I lift my head, sniffle once as though beckoning myself back with the inhale of sweet sensibility. Now why hadn't I thought of that, it's so obviously true. I love Marcus Tulley. It isn't my entire fault; no Judge would make me solely responsible for those drawers at the bottom of the fridge. They are not that important. Now is not the time to assess what just happened to me, except to be grateful for this opportunity to say to Al, who is now hemming and hawing,

"Yeah Al, I think a fridge would be considered mutual property. You are clearly grasping at straws." I turn to Marcus, whilst I subtly wipe the last tears from the corners of my eyes,

"So how do you think we should proceed?"

Marcus outlines that his function is normally to help people with custody schedules and sometimes property issues as far as sharing the kid's belongings or school or activities. He explains that from our little meeting he thinks our case is one of those that need go before the judge. He says he's sorry he can't be of more help as he ushers us out. I find myself standing in the empty hallway, outside the closed door, alone with Al. His hair has grown back, shoulder length. It's quiet as we face each other and the situation we're in. I turn to walk away, trying to walk as straight backed as I can. I hear Al coming up behind me, my stomach feels all tangled.

"Elsie, wait up a second," he implores. I keep going, slowing my pace just a tad, turn the corner and head towards the stairs. I'm looking around furtively for another human being. It's not like I'm afraid that he'll physically harm me, but I seem to be afraid somehow. Nervous that the tangled knot is entangled up with him. Oh good, here's what looks to be a security type guy in a uniform at the end of the hall. Al catches up.

"So," he says, "You are going to take it all the way then?"

I don't know how to respond. He continues softly, in the voice I'd once heard as poetry, just the sound of it. "We shouldn't be here. Not us. Not in the courts. You know that. You have to think of the kids Elsie. You don't need to push it this far."

"I was just trying to get some kind of sensible arrangement organized Al. I didn't intend for it to be like this. How's J.J.?" Why am I even talking to him?

"J.J.'s fine. Listen, you know Elsie, you've never done anything you wanted to do. You could travel, finish your school. All you've ever done is be a mother. Why don't you just leave them with me?" He suggests quietly and sincerely. I can't even believe this is happening. Is he asking me to abandon the kids? To go on a trip? Is this supposed to tempt me? What does he mean all I've ever done is be a mother? Is he saying that's nothing? I stare at him attempting to make sense of this ludicrous entreaty.

"That's right Al, I am their mother. You can't just erase me."

He leans in abruptly; the attempt to intimidate clear. *The face* is back, eclipsing my vision of the guard. Gone the sweet voice, just like that, and it all floods back; the insanity, the confusion, the fear.

"You know I'm going to take you down one way or another," he points his index finger scathingly and pokes me in the chest, "You still don't know what's going on. You can't see the big picture, and you will be left alone with your delusions. I have an excellent lawyer and this will be the end for you. You just don't know it yet."

The quick change in his demeanor takes me by surprise and I back up a little, reaching for the cookie in my pocket. I feel like a sleeker version of myself, the knots unraveling into strings that can be cut. Something about now knowing that the vegetables were not my fault has bolstered my confidence. It's slow motion as the thoughts register, I break off a piece of cookie, chewing it slowly. Al is waiting, presumably to see if I've reconsidered. I break off another piece of cookie, eyeing the guard in my peripheral vision. My arm cocks back and I launch, directly into Al's face, what remains of my chocolate chip fortification. As it hits him I snarl, "I may not have known enough then Al, but I sure know enough now!" I storm off defiant, but in the direction of the guard just to be on the safe side.

Leaving the courthouse is all a blur. I think I must have stumbled to the bus stop. Because this was a preliminary hearing the judge just asked where the kids were living. Al's paper work said he still resided in the marital home. Although we weren't married, it came furnished and we hadn't been there all that long. I think the terminology inferred some kind of imaginary stability. All of my assertions of his instability were cancelled out by his assertions that I was crazy. Mr. Hartley's recommendations would not be considered until the actual hearing. He (the judge) said to leave the children where they were so as not to disrupt them. Then he set a date a couple of months away for the actual hearing. When

I looked to Caroline Devereaux to object or something, she did nothing. It turns out that a few months is no big deal to them. I tried to point out to Caroline that it's a huge part of J.J.'s life, but she just said it was not the end. Some facts began to dawn on me. I'd heard the expression that possession was nine tenths of the law, but I didn't think that would include children. If the judge would leave J.J. with Al now, certainly it would be no better in a couple of months. At any rate, I managed to get myself back to the beach by late afternoon.

I fumble around Alex's back door looking for the key hidden under the potted palm on the back veranda. I dial Ange. I want Zoë near to me. But I also want no one near to me. I am numb to the extent of no one and everyone seeming like pretty much the same thing; I'm cocooned in trauma and marooned by emotion. When my explanation of the outcome at court comes out as sobbing sprinkled with outrage and peppered with pauses of disbelief, Ange suggests Zoë spend the night. I just agree.

"Get some rest," she says. "I'll come over in the morning and we'll get some breakfast and figure this out."

I hang up. On the counter there are several bottles of homemade plum wine. Alex had offered me one once. But I'd declined. Now seems like a good time to take him up on his offer. I think, "Why thank you, Alex," I whisper to his absent self, "I don't see what harm it could do at this point." I spy some actual wine glasses, and to his imagined suggestion that they are more fun than recycled jars, I nod, "yes, I think you've got a point." I grab the bottle and two glasses. I replace one glass. Heading home I think a little guiltily that this may not be the rest Ange was referring to. Once inside I put the bottle on the table and deliberate my plan. Perhaps I'll run a bath and do one of those scenes in which a glass of red, and bubbles will pass for cleansing the soul. Sitting here alone with a semi stolen bottle of booze in an incomprehensible circumstance that is called my life, I realize two things: One, I have achieved an ocean view, this is good, and two, I do not have a wine opener, not so good. Somehow I'm giddy. I will have to go back to Alex's again, small mission, doable.

I'm in and out and home with the opener in hand in no time at all. Mind you, time is an eerie companion today. It's like each minute sits beside me before passing. Every thought introducing itself to the minutes. Pour wine, hello time, grasps glass, hello time, take sip, hello time. By the time I finish the first glass it seems like an eternity has passed. My thinking has begun to liquify and the earlier strain only occurs as thoughts slosh to the edge and realize there is nowhere to go. I pour another, and the thoughts smarten up and stay away from the edge.

The sun is setting, the orange glow illuminating the tiny kitchen. I watch the light for a moment before I'm drawn in. If I keep the bathroom door open maybe that will make for a lovely sunset bath. I'll use dish soap for bubbles. I turn around to see Jake come through the door.

"What have we here? Are we having a party? I wouldn't mind a little alcohol," he says, filling the glass from the bottle on the table. "A little drink can be medicinal at times, don't you think Elsie?" He raises the glass to me, I air toast back cause he has the only glass.

"By all means, have some." There is a pause and I return to sit at the table putting the bath idea on hold temporarily. I just sit in silence, hands on the table, and Jake sits in silence sipping. We have done this silence thing before. It has the effect of making me hyper aware of every nerve, every twitch. It also slows everything down. It's as though in the focused quiet is created more space, the interaction is in the sharing of that space. To think of moving, lighting a cigarette would shrink the space. It's kind of a test to see how long I can sustain this, especially under the influence. I'm aware I just thought about lighting a cigarette, that thought can be absorbed into the space. I breathe myself back to the moment. But it is Jake who breaks the seal, the extra air escapes, and we are back.

"Wasn't today your court thing?" he asks, putting down the now empty glass and refilling with what's left in the bottle.

"Yup." I say, taking a swig for myself, I put the glass between us.

More silence. I'm hogging it, the silence. I notice, like Al or sometimes Jake. If you want to know then ask, lay down your cards, show you care a little. I guess he might care a little, as he did remember it was today. But still, whatever. I can barely report the glorious out-come, that the wisdom of the law would leave my baby where he is, supposedly for his convenience.

"Are we celebrating or drowning? Is there more vino?" he asks hopefully, "I'm up for either occasion, medicinal, like I said."

It's gotten almost dark by now. "I guess drowning." I mumble. "More like plumbing," I say referring to the plum wine in a lame attempt at humour. It occurs to me that there is more wine at Alex's. I don't decide right away. How much can I help myself to? Well these are sort of special circumstances and I can replace it or something if it comes to that.

"I have to take these back," I say picking up the opener and the glass, "wanna come?"

Jake nods and we head for the door. I feel pretty good now, lighter. I stop on Alex's porch; the stars are now out and making that twinkling sound that only my eyes can hear.

I fumble with the key, I can't seem to find the right angle, so I hand it off to Jake; he does no better so I grab it back giggling. I try pulling on the door, it works, and we're in. With a conspiratorial glance, I put down the glass. We just grab a couple more bottles, keep the opener and turn to leave. Jake's phrase "take what you need" rattles around in my head but doesn't find any sound.

I point off the deck to the neighbor's hot tub, they live underneath Alex, and their deck protrudes out further. The lights are all out down there and it doesn't seem like anybody's home. The lid is off the tub, and the water is barely visible, just catching the moonlight.

"Let's go," whispers Jake.

I shrug, grinning. And we make our way down the rock pathway that joins the upper and lower deck. It's sketchy walking on the uneven sloped stones and I focus really hard to not trip with precious cargo. I stand and look at the tub; it's recessed into the deck with just the lip to climb over.

Jake whips off his clothes and in what seems like one movement slips into the quiet water as though it's a different sort of clothing. I sit on the edge, dangling my feet, trying not to notice his bare chest and the pull I feel, something's amiss, it's too calm.

"Isn't it supposed to bubble?" I ask whilst trying to uncork the wine.

"We have to turn it on," says Jake. I take a swig, of course, I think, scanning for the buttons.

"One sec," I say, handing Jake the bottle, "I've got an idea, hold this," I jump up and head for my place. "I'll be right back," I say over my shoulder whilst navigating the rocks. I get back to see Jake glistening peacefully, he's been submerged while I was gone. His hair is all wetted back like it does when you come out from under water. The bottle is perched on the side of the tub.

"Ta Da," I say holding out the dish soap. "How much should I put?" I ask squeezing a good amount into the tub.

" Whoah there, cleanzella, that oughta do it." He manages to say in a way that makes me feel warm. I exchange dish soap for wine as he pushes the button.

"Are you getting in? Or is this a science experiment?" Jake motions to the already starting bubbles and I laugh.

"Is it hot?" I ask to cover my nervousness as I peel off my clothes and toss them to the corner, the wine bottle at the edge. I attempt to quickly ease in, well I think I'm easing in, but my foot catches on the lip and I topple into the center, the white foam is rising quick. My splash just makes the bubbles rise seem like laughter, from a widened smile.

"What have we got here," teases Jake as he scoops me up from the middle, he doesn't let go right away, our bodies have slid together it's just that one second too long and I panic.

"I'm okay," I say as I splash to the seat at the side catching my breath. Breathing in the denial that I need, the denial about what may happen, uncertainty. 'Just have fun,' says what sounds like a very reasonable part of my mind. I have another swig and hand the bottle through bubbles to Jake. I really must have put a lot of soap. The purr of the hot tub engine pushes the wet whipped foam up and up til it's flowing over the sides. We have foam on our heads, we have Santa Claus beards, each submergence finds different parts of each other to tentatively explore. The wider and wider grins until finally, we have to stand up to see one another above the bubbles. The laughter stops, the play stops, our breathing slows. I don't move towards him. I know I don't move because I can't, but there he is and his lips are on mine, our bodies are still warm from the water and there is the smell of dish soap, when I peek I can see steam. I can still hear the stars, even with my eyes closed. We slowly slide back down into the water, still kissing, still delicious.

The car door sounds distant, probably drowned out by the tub noise. But we both hear it, instincts I guess. We stop and stare at each other realizing that the owners of our luxury must be home. Jake hits the button to turn off the jets, barely suppressing our laughter, I manage to say, "Run for it?" to which Jake nods.

We jump out the tub, at either side; I can't remember where I threw my clothes, crouching I scan, oh yeah, the corner. I grab them; Jake is waiting at the path, with the last bottle in hand. We skulk nakedly up the precarious path between the houses and collapse onto my bed laughing. After discussing whether or not we'd be caught we realized we'd left the empty. After getting re-warmed up in each other's arms under the covers, Jake says, "Now where were we, fellow painter?" It seems we both remember exactly where we were.

I think it's the socks on my teeth that actually wake me up. Either that or some echo of Jake leaving. I haul my heavy head over to the window in time to see him heading down towards town. He looks up as I look down. We wave at the same time, grinning. It feels all right. I check myself for residual guilt feelings, or desires and everything seems surprisingly acceptable. I allow myself to fall back into bed for just one more minute of distraction, one more minute of a sunny morning after the night before. But of course the moment you ask is the moment yesterday's reality usurps a leisurely yawn. It might have been almost too much except for Ange's, "Wakey! Wakey!" And then, Zoë's running to jump on the bed. She gives me a quick kiss and then, followed by Ange's two Jessica and Gus, they run off to her room. Like a whirlwind.

"Could you put the kettle on Ange? And then we'll go." I'll just splash some water on my face and brush my teeth." I say, hauling on a T-shirt as I drag myself towards the bathroom.

Breakfast is pancakes at Kelley's for the kids and not a lot of talk from me. Intermittent reassurances from Ange. Coffee flavoured with little creamer size containers of guilt wash down the sweet memory of a lighthearted good time. Ange assumes my distraction is because of J.J.. Which of course it is, for the most part. Who commits a break and enter when they are trying to prove they are reliable? I can't even bear to ask Ange, and that tells me that I'm reluctantly ashamed.

I explain to Ange about possession being nine tenths of the law, she is predictably as astounded as me. She also doesn't know why the law is divided into tenths. Neither do I. I have to get J.J. back. Since there seem to be no repercussions for just taking him we sit in silence each coming up with a potential plan. Then, "How about just taking him?"

"We'd never get him out of the house, plus that might traumatize him."

"Yeah, its gotta be trauma free. Do you still get weekends?"

"Hmm, maybe. I'll check I couldn't stay here though."

"Oh no, I guess you'd have to run..."

"I don't want to be an outlaw," I whine as though the costume is too small. "Hey Ange, thanks for everything, thanks for being with me."

"It's not like I've got a lot of other stuff on the go," she smiles.

30
Ordinary Love

The days crawl by. I try to paint and play with Zoë as the shock of J.J. being gone weighs as only absence can, heavier than prescence. Zoë is asleep. I smoked one too many cigarettes. I don't feel like writing. While stubbing out what I tell myself will be the last one tonight, I'm absently playing with the manila envelope that contains the court documentation in it. Open. Close.open. Close. I'm distracted. It's as though J.J. has disappeared into the abyss of paperwork, maybe I can get him out. Here's something; a letter, it's handwritten, it's from Judith. Oh geez; the letter from Judith, I'd just taken the reference letter, and forgotten all about the accompanying personal letter. I open it.

Dear Elsie,

I hope the reference letter contained what you needed. The long and short of it is that of course I have always thought you were a wonderful mother. I hope your situation improves quickly. It must be so awful. But you'll get through. I just know you will.

Now, onto some headline news from home: Some fantastic! Some Bizarre! Some Heartbreak! You heard it here first! There have been a few changes lately. Shocking changes, at least from my point of view. You'll see why. As you know Lukas has been the love of my life. (Don't worry he is alive, although I've had moments- you'll see why.) My one and only since we were in our early teens. You remember the stories of him rapping at my window in the night? You know how much I loved those stories. I was looking forward to telling them to our children one day. How I would climb out to greet him in my nightie, in the garden. Such a storybook romance we had. Lukas with his glorious curls! Wasn't he just out of a novel? Such a sense of theater he has! It turns out to be an understatement. This will all make sense in a minute.(hold your breath)

   Well as it is... I will indeed be telling the stories to our baby!!!(and release your breath.) In about six months time.

   Lukas' reaction was a bit different than I had expected. I expected wedding bells as you would have guessed. He does want to be a father, rather always wanted to be, but not so soon. He professed his undying love for me. He wanted to pick the dress. He just didn't want to be the groom! He expressed great appreciation for our time together (he had needed me, my acceptance, which turned out to be incomplete. Incomplete because I didn't know who he really is??)was invaluable to him. then (before I even had a chance to spread the joyous news) he professed (confessed) his undying love for Simon. You remember Simon?(Simon was MY FRIEND that I had over here, when you were at that meditation course.) He is the poet/potter/actor, or so he calls himself. Whose creative nature then impressed me, and now makes me want to gag. If you notice a lot of this is in brackets, I guess it's symptomatic of the duality in Lukas' life. I just didn't know to look, let alone where. (Sigh) (I guess Lukas and I have similar taste)

   Allow a moment to let that info sink in. Yes, Simon is a guy. I am aware that you and Lukas have a close connection. In your case this probably doesn't change much, and I am not asking you to pick sides or anything. (I am who I am, who I always said I was, just saying.) But I am hoping you'll see from my perspective what this might be like. It's been going on a year, A YEAR. He wanted to tell me but blah blah blah. I know, ewwww. He was my best friend, my love. I had no doubts he was the one for me. Elsie, maybe we will be friends again, eventually. I don't know. I am not talking to him at the moment.

   I am planning to move in with my parents to regroup and have the baby. My parents are being stoic- sparing me the 'I told you sos.' They didn't know about Lukas of course, but they had been worried about my being on my own, foot loose and fancy-free as they put it. Lukas says he could be involved, but I don't want to make a half-life with him. Especially since he is moving to Toronto to Church and Wellesley, in with Simon. In for a penny in for a pound I suppose. I will need my parents' support, so I can't stay here. They will help me with the baby while I finish my degree. (Incidentally, I changed programs, I got into engineering) What would you like me to do with all your stuff? Please let me know soon k? And don't misunderstand, you know how I am about babies so I am VERY happy about the baby. Possibly the same way you were with Zoë. The circumstances not ideal, but somehow it still feels right. Zoë turned out great, so that bodes well. Are you getting a phone?

I almost forgot, the landlord sold the place, so, new landlord as well.

Lots of Love,
Judith
P.S.

Sorry I didn't let you know about this sooner, but I was waiting for the AIDS tests to come back negative. Thankfully they did. Of course Lukas assured me it wasn't necessary. But you know me. That was a very long wait as you might imagine. Also Elsie, things are all so much more real, once you write them down. I wasn't in so much of a hurry to write this.

P.P.S.

It's not that I don't like Simon. Afterall he was my friend too. Did you know he was in fine arts? With a minor in theatre? Arggh. Such an obvious choice for Lukas. I'm still very angry but am trying to get past it so as to not pass on angry vibes to the baby.

XX00
P.P.P s

Am still hoping to be as good as mom as you. Hugs.

Almost forgot- the car died. Nothing can be done. I will leave it in the driveway. You are still primary driver so you need to be the one who scraps it.

Wow. It seems there are lives going on outside of my little world. Of course I know who Simon is, I guess she forgot. Nice of Judith to say Zoë turned out great. I'm not sure if age five can be considered turned out, but it's a lovely thought. That's for sure. Lukas is gay, just when you think you found a guy you can talk to. It does make me want to go back over every interaction to see what

I missed. I wonder whose side he was really on when he brought
Al to the shelter. I mean did Lukas effectively deliver me to Al? I
shudder to imagine that I gave him that much influence. But it's a
little bit true, and he came and left with Al that day. Ah well, I'll
take that up with Lukas if I ever see him again that's for sure. Back
to Judith, yikes, a baby, wow. Judith is going to love being a mom.
She loves all kids so much. I think Judith herself sounds stoic.

My old place comes alive in my mind's eye. The lake, the
tiny wood stove, the porch, the sunset that even rivals the one here
through the kitchen window. I hadn't noticed that similarity before.
I don't know if it's the vision of having my little place back or the
wish for this nightmare to end. But I am beginning to feel as
though going back to where things last made sense is the best
advice Al ever gave. Everything would be different without Judith
and Lukas and who knows about Mia. I guess you can go home but
you can't really go back. Yikes. Somehow because it's Al's advice
it seems less like breaking the law. Am I actually becoming Al? I
can't think about it that way. I will check to see if Ange can help.
Alex isn't home so I let myself in to call.

Hello sweet plan! Ange is on her way; I will give her the
details (mine and Judith's), while the kids play at the beach. This is
a day for mini frozen yogurt if there ever was one.

The kids are piling smaller rocks onto bigger rocks.

"Holy Crap!" barks Ange. "That whole AIDS thing is
freaky, the worst thing used to be herpes. Good-bye free love, hello
possible death sentence. Did you hear about the hooker who left
the guy a note on the mirror written in red lipstick, 'NOW YOU
HAVE AIDS!'?" asks Ange.

"That's awful," my mind swings around to Jake, and I
really don't know him that well. I take a deep intake of breath, "I
thought it was the guy, not the hooker, who left the note, because
he hated hookers or something. Like a modern day Jack the
Ripper," I say, imagining a Dracula cape, although I don't know
why. Ange shrugs.

I add, "I also heard it takes a long time to show up on a
test. So what are people going to do, start making out, and then ask
each other to draw blood? Like, will they invent little pocket
pretests?"

"Yeah, I heard it takes about six months I think. So when you think about it, your friend Judith sure is lucky!"

"I suppose, but not only gay people have AIDS."

"No, that's true but mostly, so far from what I hear."

"How can a person not know who they are, Ange? Like how can someone be attracted to boys and not know? Or how can love turn to hate?"

"Maybe life is more like an avocado, than we think. Maybe most things are acquired tastes along the way…" says Ange optimistically.

"Avocados don't even really know what they are, fruit or vegetable, so you might be onto something there." I say.

"Sure, they do, they're a fruit." says Ange innocently.

It is decided that I will take the train back east. It's too far for me to drive alone. When I hemmed and hawed about whether to do the drive and called myself a chicken, Ange said, "Hey, don't be an avocado! Do you want to drive or not?" and I admitted no, and I felt much better.

I'll buy the tickets, set the whole plan in motion and get J.J.. at the last minute. That way there will be no chance of it not working out. Al will be distracted with beautiful buxom Deirdre, and not thinking. I will ask to bring J.J.. to the SeaFest Celebration; they are supposed to have those air bouncy things that he loves. I will promise to return him at the end of the weekend. Ange will go with me to pick him up in her car. I will be packed.

"Isn't Zoë going to wonder why you are packing?" asks Ange.

"Good point, I don't want to lie to her. So we will have to wait to pack until just before I leave, after SeaFest."

"Okay, so you're sure the train leaves on the Monday?"

"Y'know Ange, I am really going to miss you. When I am settled I'm going to try and have a nice life with my kids, like you've got. No more of this insanity. No more men for now. Honestly I think I'm starting to lose it a little."

"Then you can focus on important stuff like trying to find some good sex for a start! Get your life back!" She nudges me teasingly, and then adds, "Remember this is just what you've got to get through.You didn't feel so weak when I first met you. You're worn out is all. You'll rally you'll see."

"How did you not get caught, when you left? How long did it take to feel like yourself again?" I ask.

"I dunno, partly luck, partly he was a moron, and partly because he was in the U.S. I hate to say it, that my kids' father is a moron. Really I do, but what choice do I have?" Ange pauses changing the topic, "Just curious Elsie, did you ever, you know, 'do it' with Alex?"

"Alex? No." I answer absently. She is looking at me, so I offer," Alex is well, Alex is, a good guy though, he's been a great neighbour to me."

" Yeah, Yeah, he seems alright. Have you ever heard him play the fiddle?" asks Ange. "He's really very good, no pun intended."

"I don't get it." I say. I am vaguely aware of him entertaining the kids, once. That would've been something I would've paid attention to before, and it's literally like background noise now. I shake my head trying to dissipate the fog.

"Really, like jigs and reels..." she raises her elbows up at the sides cheerfully.

"Oh," I nod, "right." I half smile apologetically.

"It takes a while to feel like yourself again, but you will... Just keep going," offers Ange.

It does feel like my life got hijacked, and I'm getting it back. Yeah that's right, I'm getting my son, and I'm taking my life back from all this bull!! We high five. I feel split-second fake brave and super lonely.

I call Judith from Alex's to discover that she will have left by the time I arrive back east. Which is a shame because I'd like to see her, to have a friend. Her parents moved to Kingston so that's where she'll continue her schooling, at Queen's University. This is probably a solid plan. The plan makes her sound so knocked-up to me and it's sad, or maybe that's just how I perceive her parents to be reacting. I really didn't expect so much of adult life to be focused around whether a woman gets pregnant or not. It's true there was a lot of talk around the topic what with sex-education and stuff. I didn't really take it all that seriously. Tell not show, that's for sure. She will only be about five days gone before I arrive so the place won't be empty for long. She said she'd leave the landlord's phone number on the table and let him know I'd be returning. It was just in the nick of time cause her friend Sarah, whom I don't know, was going to take it over, such cheap rent. Judith was supposed to confirm with her this week; she'd been waiting to hear from me because she didn't want to leave my stuff. Someone is surely on my team here; darn good thing I'd found that letter when I did. Darn good thing Judith is so reliable. It makes my escape plan seem preordained. I am vaguely aware that the letter was here all along, but still it's the timing that counts.

I leave Alex a couple of bucks to go towards the phone bill. It's probably not enough, I feel like a charity case. He says he is happy to help. I will let the giver give, in hopes that one day soon, I will be the giver. I thank him and whomever put him on my path. On my way back from Alex's I notice a brown paper bag on the porch. My first thought is a ring and run, a bag full of dog pooh that kids used to leave on doorsteps. They'd light them on fire, ring and then run away. The person who answers the door gets dog pooh on their shoes by stomping out the flames. Of course this bag was not on fire. Nevertheless, I approach with caution, nudge the bag with my toe. It doesn't move much, so I bend over and give a little sniff before picking it up. I open the bag to discover four red beets. I glance around furtively as you do, holding a mysterious brown paper bag of nothing but beets. There is no note, no accompanying vegetables. In the novel Jitterbug Perfume, beets arrive un-beckoned. Is somebody toying with me? Now? Really? While I'm reading the book? I bring the bag of beets inside. Zoë is still in her room watching the tiny T.V. "Did anyone come by?" I ask.

"Nope," she answers without taking her eyes off the set.

When life gives you a few beets you make a little borscht. As I wash the beets I muse about the bizarreness of their arrival. I think it has to be someone who knows the novel, and then it comes to me: Deirdre. She had the book at her jewelry stand. Oh no. She might have been here to spy. Zoë was alone whilst I made the phone call. Why the calling card? Is it possible that someone with a sense of humour like this could be spying? I don't think so. I don't remember if I told her I was reading Jitterbug Perfume, it seems I must've. Tom Robbins says about the beet:

"The beet is the melancholy vegetable, the one most willing to suffer. You can't squeeze blood out of a turnip . . ."

Suffering is something Deirdre must be up for. It feels like a backwards torch passing of some sort, I think as I wash my stained hands. I'm not sure how to go about wishing her all the best. She's taken on the beet. I think of beets as the vegetable that knows the blues, bleeds. She could've been spying on me for him, and still be the heart of the beet. It makes sense that I would like her, similar to Judith liking Simon. Except in my case, I have to thank her.

The plan is set. The lies are formulated. The guilt is repressed. Zoë, Jessica and Angus are with Alex. We pull up in the most innocent of vehicles, the VW bug. No matter what happens I will grab J.J. while Ange distracts Al with cordial small talk. He will have to hear her out.

"This feels like espionage," I say.

"Yeah, but this is undercover work. I always preferred the robber's little black hat and gloves, as far as criminal outfits go." Ange adds. "Or cat-woman."

I smile at her appreciatively as we are pulling up to the street. My heart is homeless, leaping between my chest and throat. We park in front of the "marital home." I think about that slander, and fuel my own intent to deceive out of necessity. I am saving my kid. From deception and violence. Stop thinking. Deep breath.

It is Grama, not Dierdre who saunters out the front door. Ange and I look at each other, Crap.
Without speaking we nod to one another in acknowledgement that the plan must carry on. Ange is going to be extra nice and I will be accepting of my position as the part time parent who has been 'taken down'.

"Hi Grama, so nice to see that you have been visiting with J.J. I know he loves his Grama so much! This is my friend Ange." I gesture in Ange's general direction.
Gramma looks slightly askance and then in a neutral tone says,

"Hello Ange," before turning to going back inside.

"Are you all planning to go to the Seafest today?" Ange asks after her. "It sure is a perfect day for it!" she adds enthusiastically, exactly as we had planned. "My kids are waiting for us, but we just couldn't leave J.J. out." She continues, "We were hoping you'd allow him to come with us."

At this moment Al emerges with J.J. running in front.

"Hi Mom," says, J.J. very casually. "Where's Zoë?" He is so fine. I can't help a flash of doubt that races across my vision. I wave it away. I am doing what I need to do, what I believe in my heart is not only best, but necessary.

"She at Alex's," I say. " Mom and Zoë and Gus and Jessica are going with Ange to the Seafest today. They have the bouncy things you love to jump on, so I came to get you!" I scoop him up. This is bad parenting 101. Telling the kid it's a go before it's for sure. He squirms out of my arms. "If your dad says yes that is?" I add humbly.

"I am going to the bouncy thing! The bouncy thing! I'm gonna do flips." J.J. is still wriggling with his face scrunched, his eyes closed, doing flips in his mind. We will have to stop at the festival for sure now. Al looks so nonplussed at J.J's excitement that I can't get a read on him.

"That's why I drove, so we wouldn't waste precious time on the bus. The kids wouldn't have to wait so long," reassures Ange. "I hope *we* are okay, Al, I mean I don't take sides. I am just trying to help out. Y'know cause Elsie doesn't have a car."
I cringe, but the idea here was for her and Al to agree on me as someone who needs help.

"Because it's the weekend, I figured it was my turn. Isn't that what the court decided?" I say, hoping to highlight him as the winner.

And because I can't help piping in. Al glances at me briefly but he doesn't say anything.

Ange pushes on,"I mean we are going anyways, and Gus would really love it if J.J. was there as well. We didn't want J.J. to miss out, just because of the new arrangement." Ange has now moved into *doing a favour for Al modality.*

Wow, Ange is a natural. I am deathly afraid that if I open my mouth, snakes will slither out. I feel a mildly motivating nausea. I detest lying, and yet it is surprisingly easy to stand here, knowing full well that I am carrying out what I would think unforgiveable if it were done to me. Maybe *easy* is an exaggeration. I am standing here, musing about how accessible it is to be dishonest.

Al seems to be taking a muted pleasure in being the decision maker. He is smiling genially at Ange. "Oh I forgot about Seafest. I think some musicians I know are going to play later. You remember Blind Pig, don't you Ange?" He is practically flirting, taking a little jab at her for a thing she had for the drummer.

"Vaguely," laughs Ange good naturedly. This probably means he wants to go to Seafest now. I can't tell. We shouldn't have made the outing sound fun. Will we have to grab J.J. at the event? What if we can't find him? This is weirdly still a pleasant exchange, so that's promising. I decide to take a chance. Make it seem like it's no big deal now.

"Oh do you want to take J.J with you then?" I offer. Al doesn't say anything. There is a protracted silence. Al's specialty.

Gramma now joins us from just inside. "What's going on? " she asks.

I am sure she can see though what must be so transparent. I take a small step back, planning how to get J.J. into the car. Making a run for it isn't looking at all a plausible plan. What was I thinking?

"We would bring him back tomorrow afternoon or evening, whatever works." I say obligingly.

Gramma looks at Al. I am sure she is about to protest, to expose us. But she says to Al,

"Then you could help me move the ladders up at the house. I don't want that husband of mine trying to do it on his own! He is always climbing around trying to fix stuff and his knees are not to be trusted."

"Okay." Replies Al, "That could work. Maybe I'll catch up with you guys later, when the music gets going." Al winks at Ange, who then winks back, all in good fun.

I am in a fun house. This was too easy. J.J. kisses Gramma and hugs his dad. I want to run, before they are onto us. But I walk slowly towards the car, J.J. is right beside me. Almost there. I try to keep cool, the smell of fear is odious, and could set off an alarm. Gramma calls out, "Wait a second!"

I freeze. Time is jerking. until I notice her run after J.J. carrying something in her hand and quickly search my mind for what it could be. Gradually I perceive a cloth, a washcloth, freshly wetted. I force the tension to fall out of my shoulders as she secures and wipes J.J.'s squirming face, muttering, "there, you can't go off with a dirty face!" She plants a kiss on his securely squished cheek, and then releases him.

We climb cleanly into the vehicle of innocence and wave. Good-bye *marital home*, I think to myself.

We are off to the bouncy thing otherwise known as the future.

31

Into The Mystic

I've never taken an overnight train ride; this will be two nights. I got the sleeper so the kids will be comfy. The ticket took almost my whole month's cash. Fleming is going to move back in, it's as though I was never there, at my ocean view launching pad. It's somewhat risky, but I'll figure it out when I get back east. We ended up in Alex's car, because it fit me, and my two kids plus Ange's two. Alex had decided to come along to say good-bye. Quite the send off really, considering the clandestine operation of the trip. I hug both my west coast buddies and the little ones. No tears, today we are on a mission. There is however, a persistent lump in my throat.

The conductor shows us to our seat that will be bunk beds and I load our stuff into the storage compartment. The kids will share a bunk or J.J. will sleep with me. They take right to playing up there. There is time to get settled in before the train pulls out. I can still see Alex and Ange; I wave hoping they still see me. They do, and wave back, both at the same time. Alex waves at a faster pace of enthusiasm, and Ange a slower wave of encouragement. The kids doing the double arm, stop the presses, kind of gesticulating and jumping up and down. Altogether a lot of action down there on the platform; it's making me sort of homesick for this place and these people. They look familiar. I assumed the link was me, but it dawns on me slowly; they are standing just that close, that maybe they get along with each other. I think I should suggest them getting together when I talk to Ange next time. The moment of Ange complimenting Alex's fiddling does a quick replay in my mind, only there is a nuance that I didn't get the other day. Something, just a smidge vulnerable. I wonder when exactly had Ange heard Alex play his fiddle. I think of breathing onto the window and drawing a heart to let them know I've cottoned on. But I don't. I imagine Ange can read it on my face. I think that's what I see in her smile. But instead I blow kisses and mouth thank-you's, and part of me likes to think I brought them together. We just don't know what anything is for. Alex puts Gus up on his shoulders and Gus grins fists pumping into the air, as the train starts to lurch along romantically.

We decided to hang in the dome car after supper. It's quiet. The scenery of night isn't quite as compelling for as many passengers as it is during the day. Somehow the starry night is soothing. The kids have wound down. Zoë was 'reading' "Where the Wild Things Are," to J.J.. He nodded off in the seat next to her. There is a woman on her own, across the aisle. She looks to be in her late 50's or so. Woah, more of her life gone than left to live at any rate. She has been staring at me and not even trying to be discreet about it. Earlier when the kids were running up and down the aisle, I smiled in a friendly, *I hope the kids aren't a problem, too bad if they are, can I compel you to understand,* look. She nodded and smiled back, and just continued to stare at me. She made me feel slightly uneasy like she was looking through me. I think this is post Al paranoia. I always think people know I messed up somehow, like it oozes out of my pores. Dream tally four for zero. No education, no relationship, no home, no nuclear family. Sorry it all went nuclear! What does it all mean anyway? No money, no love, no security, no fitting in. For a society that prizes individuality so much it certainly doesn't pan out, out here on the fringe. *Depanned.*

I notice when she isn't smiling her wrinkles reveal white lines that haven't tanned. Are those the smile lines I've heard about? I can tell she has been outside a lot. Her hair is thick with white streaks and is brought up in the back and held by a silver etched barrette. I notice it when she leans down to get something out of the woven bag at her feet. She nods at me, I nod back. The car is quiet, except for the now *churring* sound of the train hauling its way east. She points to the kids asleep across from me, and puts her finger to her lips. Shhhh. She purrs, and then beckons me over to her seat with the same finger. She had been sitting in the aisle and the seat beside her window is empty. As I approach she shifts into the vacant spot and motions for me to sit. With a quick glance back to the slumbering kids I do as suggested. She lifts up the rectangular block in her left hand, whatever is there, is wrapped in a silk scarf.

"Can you guess?" her accent is slightly Italian, I think. She speaks very softly. I have to lean in a little just to hear her.

Can I guess what? I wonder for a moment as she unveils the cards. She obviously sees my confusion, as she answers her own question.

"Cards," she announces, as if that says it all. "Special."

"Yes, are those tarot cards?" I am excited thinking I've lucked out, she will read them for me.

"Like, that yes, but very old.... my grandmotha, she gift them to me. You like?" With that she hands them to me. I start to politely admire the cards but am surprised to discover that they are almost blank. Whatever images used to be there have been rubbed off by years of use. The outer edges are a golden colour but where the suits or discerning features might be is worn to a grayish gold smear. Their age is somehow tangible in their weight, which even though they are worn, is still substantial.

She pulls out the tray in front of her. "My grandmotha, very special Italian lady. She say to me, 'If they don't want you, they don't deserve you.'"

I nod still holding the cards.

"You shuffle." She dictates. I obey mulling over the implications of not being deserved, the good as well as the bad. I wonder why the bad popped into my head first, yikes.

"My grandmotha, she is leaving her husband, very fast. Along time ago, like you, she knows, it s a woman's world, she will no live in a cage. Later on, she was blind, a man in the village came to take her chickens," she pauses, "its true. She call him to her door, she say, 'I see you take my chicken!' and she kick him in his leg, like so." She mimes kicking someone in the shins and then starts to laugh to herself, "She saw, even if she was blind, she kick him, hehehe," she does another swift kick, and turns and looks out the window. I busy myself with the cards.

"Okay, now cut the cards in three piles with your left hand," she instructs. I do as told. She turns the piles image side up and lines up them up on her tray in front of her.

"The father of your daughter, he is not the father of your son. The father of your daughter protects her. Why you did not love him?" I don't have a chance to answer. I am considering the question when she continues, "Ahh, he was a baby, you were a baby. He died too young, this guy. Always laughing this guy, not a serious boy. This other guy that you left, he has some problems, it's not his fault."

I am about to interject that this is not quite fair, to give Al a free pass like that. When she says, "It is never his fault, this guy. He is persecuted, poor guy."

Now I am feeling that I have finally made the right move, and this old lady is defending Al. "Really?" I ask. She moves another card off the pile, pushing the last one to one side. There is nothing on them, let alone anything to tell her all of which she has said.

"Some people have this…it's like a disease, this persecution. He is not a happy guy, this guy."

"Yeah, I know, but he has made my life hell," I say under my breath.

"You don't want to hold a grudge," she says. "It's a woman's world, you pick them, then you put them in the garbage! You are like my grandmotha, who teach me the cards, she left my grandfather, she was young. He was not nice with the women."

This seems like a real understatement to me. "My family is all torn apart now." I surprise myself by confessing my sadness and disappointment.

"Torn? No," she shrugs and takes a deep breath,"My grandmotha was like a witch in the village," she adds in reference to what seems like nothing to me. "She say," she leans in, 'they don't want you, they don't deserve you.' One day the water stopped running in the village. The villagers thought it was because of the witch. But it was the tap. When my grandmother fixed it, they still thought it had stopped because of the witch. They didn't know how the tap worked. Oh, they were afraid of my grandmotha." Hehehe.

"Your sister is very polite," she says after regaining her composure and moving another card into the center. I nod in agreement, yes, tidy, organized and polite, Lainey. "Remember, politeness is a sign of intelligence. She is very sincere with you, you help her. Because you are a detective and you love to help, she listens to you. She thinks you are crazy, and she still listens to you, ha! When you were a small girl you wore a cap for bathing. You wore it everywhere, even not to swim. Your mother she didn't say nothing, and your sister called you a name. Yes?

Oh my God how did she know that! Lainey had called me 'the ponderer,' cause once I thought pondering was what you called swimming in a pond. I liked to wear my 'thinking' cap cause it blocked out the noisy world in a similar way to if you covered your ears. I decorated it with an indelible marker. I copied the symbols from the typewriter like @$#% and just put them all over it. It was a short make-believe phase. But the name stuck for quite a while afterwards. They would always preface it with 'the', as in tell 'the Ponderer' it's time for supper. This was a big deal, because it began to get out of hand when Lainey would tease: *Earth to pondy, maybe when you grow up you will be a Pond girl instead of a Bond girl. Then she would make hideous faces pulling at the sides of her mouth, and endeavoring to say 'swamp rat' with this ugly self- imposed lisp.*

I don't know why this was the trigger, me representing cold cream instead of a sex symbol, but that's what happened. It was probably one of the only times I have had to stand up to Lainey, who is generally a pretty nice older sister. This looked mostly like a tantrum, where I ran around screaming and tossing clothes and screaming… "No more, Pondy!!! No more!!" And finally burst into tears. Lainey backed down with a calm but final request; to kill the cap. I insisted that I hadn't worn it in ages. I had worn it only once or twice to do homework. She said it was the only way to prove I was no longer 'the Ponderer.' She got out the big scissors from the tin box we called the sewing kit. She waited whilst I went to get my cap from my drawer. Strangely I knew exactly where it was. I felt brave as I carefully deconstructed the cap cutting around each symbol. I had in mind to glue them to something later, but at the time I piled them neatly, asterisk upon exclamation point upon number sign upon dollar sign upon percentage and so on. Little flat circular rubber symbols which I carried back to my room in open palms like a wounded bird. Them or me? I left Lainey to cut up the cap itself, she seemed so satisfied, silently slicing through the rubber until it was in bits. And that was that, we never really mentioned it again. Mom asked about it once, and I deflected as though it was a discarded toy and she let it go.

"She will have another baby boy, bigger than his brother." The card reader doesn't miss a beat, moving another card, she adds, "She doesn't like her mother in law? She doesn't talk to her. Tell her to talk to her. Her husband is a good man, a hard worker. This is good." After regaining her composure and moving another card into the center she says, "Your sister is very polite." I nod in agreement, yes-tidy Lainey. "Remember, politeness is a sign of intelligence. She is very sincere with you; you help her. She will have another baby boy, bigger than his brother," she repeats. "Your sister is the boss who doesn't know she is the boss! She looks and looks for the boss!"

"Once there was a lady who was sick in her bed all the time. I can't get up I can't get up she would say…then I said to this lady, look under your bed. She did. And then she jumped out of her bed! Why? Because I had put a plastic rat under her bed! I got it at the K-mart." She begins to laugh all out and repeats gasping for air, "K-Mart, it was plastic!" I laugh too, hesitatingly though cause this seems like a break with the conversation and I am trying to understand the metaphor, if there is one. "She thought there was a problem, but there was no problem," she says as though this is obvious. "You should get some rats, to put under some people's beds. They are more afraid of having a problem than actually to have one. It's not good to make yourself sick by being afraid to be wrong."

That talk of hard work being the be all and end all is making me tired. Who would put a rat under my bed if they suspected me of being too tired? I am always afraid that I am too tired.

"What you think you are lazy?" says my 'card' reader.

"You are not lazy, you work all the time. It's true, no, you don't think so?"

" Okay, I guess." I answer, not at all sure what work is anymore, but know that whatever I do tuckers me out.

"You are a good writer. You will have success. You will write for young people."

"Well, I used to write it's true, but I've changed to painting. Now painting is like a medicine, to see. Do you understand?"

"Oh yes, you see. You will write. And you will read the cards like me. You always want to help. Paint or don't paint, doesn't matter. Just remember just because you see something is going to happen does not mean you will make it happen."

I want to argue that it does in fact matter if I paint. I have found a way to express what I see. Something stops me from speaking. I want to hear whatever she has to offer. I feel extra still, straining my perception of each moment in hopes of a glimpse at mattering. I am thirsty. I'll get some water later I tell myself, swallowing the dryness. She moves another card, "A blond woman will be very sincere with you." That must be Mia. I guess we will patch things up; that's promising.

"It is time to stand up for yourself, time to know who you are," she says in a monotone. "You have the psychic force. When you are happy, everyone is happy in the room. You have the psychic force. You have answers already."

Oh crap, I don't want to be responsible for everyone else's happiness. Isn't that the mistake I've been making already? I keep running into to these spiritual people. They aren't really giving me any answers by saying I already know stuff.

I decide to switch it up. "How about the kids? Will they be okay?"

She places another card in front of her, "You must remember, brainwash them, tell them they are good, then they are good. Your daughter can sing like her father, yes? She loves to sing and dance." She pauses, "Better than you, you think to stand on a chair is to sing high notes!" Hehehe. She laughs at me. I laugh along; the picture she sees in her blank cards is so true. I used to stand on my tiptoes in an attempt to sing higher notes. "Your son is like you, even more like your sister, he loves the math's. You are good mother; you will not poison your kids against their father. You can make people happy by being happy yourself, not by becoming them."

"How was I becoming other people? Was I becoming crazy, like Al?" I ask gingerly pulling golden morsels of counsel.

"When you have the psychic force you will feel what everyone around you needs. When you don't know this is what's happening, and selfish people let you, you will put their reality first, because they are selfish! Hehehe, and you won't believe yourself anymore. Your life stops to make sense of what you have seen. And when you do believe yourself first, it causes trouble with the selfish people. They only want you to see through their eyes.

Oh my God, that's what Al used to say! He said that he just wanted me to see through his eyes. And I thought it was a compliment that he thought I could do that. When he was really just asking me not to be me. How could I not have known that?

"I don't know what you mean exactly, but how do I stop? Won't I be selfish if I don't try to see their point of view?"

"Yes so selfish you would be crazy like your ex so he won't be alone? Hehehe. No you are not so selfish, to be a good mother, so loving for your kids, this is not selfish. See the point of view, yes, but from your own eyes, much better."

"That's why I messed it all up!" I laugh nervously.

"Don't worry," she pats my shoulder slightly, as she glances around dramatically, "You won't go to jail, and you won't lose your beautiful children. Now, go, put them in the beds," she orders. I carry J.J. in one arm and Zoë drowsily trails holding my other hand. We snuggle into our bunk. I feel strangely renewed, like everything is going to be okay. I don't know what exactly the woman said to make me feel so good. Maybe it was the acknowledgement that I am a good mother; maybe it was just being seen, being made to feel as though I matter. Whatever little magic she worked with those blank cards, I am cozy inside, snug and sleepy. Maybe it was as simple as 'you won't go to jail', I look for her after breakfast in the morning, but I can't find her. She must have gotten off earlier, in Alberta.

32

Parallel Lines

The new landlord shows up not an hour after I've gotten home. My old room is the same baby blue that I left it, my furniture still there. Jude painted the kids' room a kind of leaf green on one wall and the paneling that was gray is covered with an off white paint now. The quarter-round, which passes for molding, is also white all around. That's Jude for you; she sure has the patience for details. She put the kids' poster of Noah's Ark back up; it looks so fresh and clean. There's the crib. When we left J.J. was still in a crib. That situation will have to be remedied. He can sleep with me, tonight. I am just looking around remembering what I like about this place. The bathtub - without the dirt clog memory that is threatening to erase pleasure. I like the ceiling height kitchen cabinets with doors made of grid glass, like mini French doors. The old piano is still there. Jude painted the keys in some kind of colour code to the scale, which I have yet to figure out. Hopefully it can be fixed and maybe Zoë and J.J. will learn to play. This is so strange; it's like recreating the future and the past at the same time. I can't erase Al, and I have J.J. of course, but I am kind of where I was when I met Al, except I am so different. I am, weaker and stronger, more vulnerable and more resilient, jaded and optimistic. Hey, I am a double-edged sword, a sleeker and hopefully sharper version of myself. I look forward to getting the piano in working order.

His name is Finn McCabe, the new landlord; he shook my hand respectfully when I answered the door. Seems like a nice guy, at least he didn't raise the rent. He said he was going to renovate the upstairs so he would leave the rent low, if I could live with the noise for now. The only issue is the wood-burning stove, which he says is not up to code. I guess my pittance rent is contributing to the renovations. He doesn't look very old, but he acts like a father type person. All matter of fact: "Are you aware that there are regulations and codes that govern safety around woodstoves?" He might as well have added, "young lady." Of course I wasn't aware. I just got home. Well I wasn't aware before either, just put it on the list. I am feeling so optimistic, and am so grateful to Jude for having left the place in such a good state. I feel a bit guilty about how I left my place out west, not exactly pristine. McCabe said hello to both of the kids as well. I really appreciate when people treat children like they are people too.

Zoë is going to do the last month of school and she's excited. There might even be some kids from her old playschool. I had to get her a special paper from the school board showing her inherited right to an English education. The school starts French immersion right away in grade one for half the day. I think it's great, more language more brain I say. She can go in English because I went in English. It's like a grandfather clause or something. The French Canadian people have no option. I think that the French people are paying for an idea, because many languages seems optimal to me. Eventually all the new people will have to go to school in French. So there will be a bunch of Chinese and other ethnicities preserving the Quebec culture. I guess that's the long-term vision. How do we measure what's worth it? Saving I mean. Or is it just the people with the most oppressive rules that will save themselves in the end? We will see if you can legislate culture. I asked them at enrollment why the STOP signs in the area have 101 spray-painted across them.

"Oh that's about bill 101, just vandals," the secretary said. 'Stop' is not a French word as it turns out. It didn't seem like the time to ask for details so that's all I know for now. Political, traffic vandals, hmm that's new. There has always been something going on here, I'd forgotten that. I remember when I was a kid there was a Halloween that was almost cancelled by the October Crisis. The FLQ killed Pierre Laporte; he was strangled and found in the trunk of a car. They kidnapped an English guy as well, but they didn't kill him. Bill 22 was enacted when I was a kid. Everyone all up in arms about having to go to French school or something, that there would be tests for the English. The English; a minority but not ethnic. Adults were calling the Premier, Bourassa, Brass Ass. I don't know why. It didn't have any impact on me, not that I noticed. The next Premier, chain-smoking René Levèsque was perfect for satirical cartoons.

Adults in general were satirical cartoons to me. My adults were like apostrophes which don't exist in French. They were illegal on public signs, then that was overturned. I haven't kept up with the legal status of public punctuation. Some people moved away. Not as many mind you as left later. I don't know if it was the Quebec referendum to become its own country, or declaring French the language for business that did it. Lucky for the French Quebecers, that the Huron or Mohawk didn't declare themselves the language of business. Either way many families got transferred. That's when Sam's family left for Mississauga and my mum shortly after. So I guess when I think about it, it did affect me. Even if we didn't talk politics, even if we laughed it off. I wonder what kind of 'English' decides to stay? Is it the stubborn, the rich and the poor, while the middle makes a run? Is it the sort of person that doesn't mind being called 'an English'? Doesn't everyone learn 'Sur le Pont d'Avignon on y danse tous en rond,' when they are a kid? All in a circle. It's funny what you notice when you return from being away. This is still home. I hope. I seem to be swimming against the tide. Even if I missed the French.

It turns out that the front porch might be a really good place for an easel. I don't have one yet but I can imagine where I will put it. Mia is coming over this afternoon after Zoë gets home. When she said she was coming I had a picture of her in my mind holding a little vial, I hope she brings that Royal Jelly stuff we used to get in the city.

I am pacing, tidying, the kettle is on. It's going to be great to see Mia. She's bringing Keifer as well. I hear the car pull into the long driveway. Her hair is dyed black and way shorter than I remember, kind of spiky and styled, I wonder what makes it stay like that. She's got these tall boots that come up over her knee. She looks very lean and urban. But it's still Mia, "Hey, Friend," she calls, "Open up!"

I practically race to the door, the kids and I arriving at about the same time. They scoot out, Keifer and Zoë circling each other like little dogs. J.J.. is watching. Not giving away his youngness by talking just yet.

"Tea?"

"You need to ask?"

We exchange hugs, woahs, oh my gods and look how the kids have grown. It's been too long's and I've missed you's, before we settle in to talk.

The nasty phone conversation we had isn't far from my memory, but I am not sure if I should bring it up. I don't know where it will lead, and it's so nice to have my friend here. Whilst the kettle is boiling, Mia says, "Look what I brought from downtown." She pulls a rectangular box out of her bag. "It's RenShenFengWangJiang."

"Oh yeah, try to say that ten times," I chime like we used to do. She used to always bring the two inch size vials of classical ginseng and royal jelly over. I loved the tiny straws. They take like ten seconds to empty, but the cuteness factor combined with the name make them so fun.

"So cool, I thought you might bring these. So what happened with your dance studio?" I ask, sipping.

"My father wanted me to take a bunch of jazz ballet classes at some dance academy before he would lease me the space. He didn't think I was professional enough. He said my previous dance experience wasn't art; he referred to it as pagan Maypole shenanigans. I told him he didn't know anything about art and even less about Goddesses. Than my mother piped in, in my defense for a change, she said art was subjective and that the Sumerian Goddess of Love used to pole dance. 'And love is what it's all about dear,' she says to my dad. Can't you just see her, her ice cubes swirling in her drink?" She mimics swirling a glass, it's comical with the vial.

She continues,"I just wanted to scream, "don't try to help me, Mother!" because she ultimately backs his every decision. Then my father digs in with, 'money is not namby pamby subjective,' and 'people are not going to pay good money to have their little girls taught to pole dance by an ex-stripper.' And then it was silent. We stared each other down. I didn't flinch that's for sure! You should've seen me Elsie. He didn't even try to intimidate me. I don't get why he just can't support me, it's not like he doesn't have the money."

"What if you took the classes?"

"That's not really the point Elsie. The point is to be supported by your family. For them to believe in you."

"Did you really stare him down? Would he pay for the classes?"

"Well, not so much stared, no, but in my mind. There are better ways to handle him. I mean he is a successful businessman you know." I hear the muted adoration as I head to the kitchen to get the tea.

It sounds to me like they do believe in her. I don't say anything because I don't want to fight. People's family dynamics are their own business.

"Well I feel different. After everything." I offer, to change it up, "It's good to be back, weird, same house, it really is like starting over. New landlord, same cheap rent though." I am standing by the door checking on the kids, having a smoke, sipping my tea.

"Let's go out into the sun porch, God we had fun out there didn't we! Remember those crazy vignettes we'd make up? Who were you again? Mireille the French tramp and I was Lovisa the damsel turned warrior. You made me piggy back you in a brave rescue…"

"I didn't make you, you offered, you thought you were good at piggy backing, like it was a skill or something…" she teases.

"That's true I am good at it. And driving cars backwards," I say, "And anyway, I saved you from evil Pierre the rocker with that piggy backing!"

"Until you tripped on that sandbox that Al built and nearly killed us both, not to mention the kids who I missed by an inch."

"More like a mile," I said, "and Pierre was not only evil, he was fictitious!"

"The worst always are," she declares, smiling. The mention of Al hangs in the air, an unsupported dish of betrayal spaghetti. I want to keep playing.

"That was a really nice sandbox, though wasn't it?" I ask.

"As far as sandboxes go," says Mia.

"I suppose, ultimately, not that far." I say

"No, they sure aren't the be all and end all..." says Mia, "plus they may be a health hazard."

"You got that right!" I add, now certain we are not talking about sandboxes anymore. I would defend a sandbox. I am not sure which relationship we are talking about, mine and Al's or mine and Mia's Relationship: a place to learn and play, but full of germs.

Mia whips out a tiny vial and pours some white powder onto my cigarette pack. Then she takes out a gold credit card and divides up the lines.... I am not sure which is more shocking, the credit card or the coke.

"Where did you get the gold card?" I ask

After sniffing one, she offers me the other, " My dad," then reassuringly, "c'mon we're celebrating, it's not addictive," Mia swipes her nose with her forefinger and swallows.

"I don't know..." I hesitate, "This can't be good. Where are the kids?"

"Here, I'll turn my back and block, so they won't see. They are actually in the sandbox."

"Okay, only live once right?" I am not convinced as I snort the little white line. I don't really feel much. Just kind of like everything is okay. "I mean in this body anyway."

Mia starts talking about how she is going to do her dance class business in spite of her father not financing her. She is pumped about what a natural business mind she has, easily as good as his. For some reason I believe her every word and rally behind the idea, talking about the potential franchising of pole dancing schools. We agree that we have always thought too small and been hemmed in by conventional thinking. "Wait," I say catching our breath, I don't do dance.

She jumps up and starts dancing singing Blondie's one way or another except inserting the word vial, so it goes;

One vial or another I'm gonna find ya I'm gonna getya-getya-getya,

One way or another I'm gonna find ya...

I am laughing and sort of singing along as she gyrates holding up the coke vial and the little RenShenFengWangJiang.

"We could have art as well," she says.

"I couldn't teach art. I do it for the medicinal aspect of seeing how I feel and to read others. I saw you coming with the vial," I add. I remembered what the train lady said; just because you see it doesn't mean you cause it. Does that mean if I don't see myself involved I didn't cause that not to happen?

"Okay, then we will incorporate that," she says enthusiastically. We talk on and on, about what a marvelous future we two marvelously creative people will create. I compliment her; she compliments me and so on. We deliver snacks to playing children, tidy the place and even rearrange some furniture. Then I start to feel slightly on edge. The unsaid stuff, "Like how can I trust you?" or, "How could you" or "Why aren't you sorry?"

But before I get a chance Mia says, "Sometimes after people have been abused they make the best partners. I never knew an abused woman before, not that went to the shelter and all that. But it's like you are more careful about what you might say now, like you really consider the other person's point of view. Like you hear me, and believe in me, not like my family. Like all that learning to keep your mouth shut actually had a merit." She smiles. This is not a taunt. And it's true I didn't stop the dream building because I knew I didn't want to do that.

"Yeah maybe, there's some truth to that. Except I don't think abuse is the key to learning how to listen. I don't really see myself as someone who keeps her mouth shut, like some wimp. And it's not like you are asking me to bankroll you either." I feel defensive.

"Of course not, you have no money. But if you had some you'd surely back me, I know you would," she offers confidently. "We are like that, you and I."

"Well, hypothetically, maybe." I say. She offers up a better, but less true version of myself.

"If it's hypothetical than why is it 'maybe'?" She resembles a feline huntress; I never really noticed those eyeteeth before.

"Because, I might just back myself, hypothetically! Art therapy or something." I feel like a kid who is refusing to play by the rules. "At least university is affordable here." I say.

"Ooh, tough talk, hypothetically," she sneers. She holds her nose, and speaks in a nasally voice, "Art therapy, sounds dull, are you afraid of real art?" Mia laughs as if dullness is most humorous.

The happy vibe is abruptly gone, the raw unspoken stuff has somehow bubbled to the surface. I am not laughing. Not on purpose, I just don't feel it, and that makes me unhappy.

"Are we in a hypothetical fight?" I force a laugh. I want out. Now. The torn sheet metal feeling in my brain coupled with the fear in my gut can't cope with a fight, even a pretend one. "Cause people who do coke are notoriously bad with money," I say, might as well get a shot in while I have the chance.

"Well, I guess you'd know all about that."

"What, I did one line?!" I shriek in my defense.

"Which you aren't even very grateful for, I always share with you and you won't even hypothetically support my dream!"

I'm beginning to think that Mia has been doing more Coke than I am aware of. I rerun the afternoon and wonder about a couple of well-timed trips to the bathroom when I was in the other room.

"How much Coke have you been doing Mia?"

"It's not addictive, like I said, I don't do it every day. Anyway its not as though I like smoking it that much, and that's the addictive way to do it," she says expertly.

Hmm… casual cocaine, the new normal, I don't know. I begin to taste the contents of my decision making process. I am chewing on the dismal chemical taste my new life would have if I partake any further.

"Okay, you caught me. Maybe I didn't share it all with you, but it's because you don't need as much," she confesses. "Anyway Elsie, you don't have to get so high and mighty!" Mia shows her trademark smirk as she realizes the pun. I smirk back and nod in acknowledgement.

"I don't want any more. Why are you doing so much?" I don't know where to go from here.

"See, I know you," she says. "It's okay, I know how unnerved you get about getting high. Just don't try to impose that neurosis on me and we will be all good. Trust me, I still think you're fun, just a wee bit of a wet noodle." She elbows me in an intimate friendly teammate way. I don't know where my friend went. I don't want to be a noodle. Even if I think she plays to close to the edge.

"Can I trust you, really Mia?" I ask hoping she will catch on.

"What do you mean? Sure," she answers.

"Well, what about sleeping with Al behind my back? And now you are into this coke thing, what's happened to you?"

"Ah c'mon you are not going to blame me for that. I can't believe you are still there, I mean it was pretty clear you wanted us to. You made jokes about it all the time. Anyway don't forget you slept with my Jimmy." After she sees my shocked face she adds, "So you did forget. That's right missy, you are not so innocent after all." This is followed by a friendly finger wag.

Woah, it's true I am not so innocent after all. The circumstances were a little different, I think. I ferret around through the globby fog of guilt; I really don't think I snuck around. That's it; I dig down and retrieve the circumstance. "It's not the same." I say, "We were trading, remember? You went with Sam also. I mean we were all there at the cottage; we were teenagers!" No wonder I buried that memory; it was all kind of weird.

"You practically pushed me into sleeping with Al. I think you actually said you didn't mind." Mia implores.

"Yeah maybe, but I didn't think you would really do it, I mean we had a family."

"What's that got to do with a little sex? You were always like, 'hey why don't you guys just get it on?' You had all the power."

"Power? What power? I thought as my best friend you would know I didn't want that. You were so sexually overt prancing around topless. I saw what might happen so I made jokes. I had to abide by my own law which was to accept you as you are."

"Yeah, your pretend law, not mine. You probably judged me all the time. Anyway you two had broken up. You were in the shelter anyway for crying out loud!" explains Mia.

"Doesn't that say ANYTHING TO YOU?" I plead.

"It says that you are twisted, first you tell me to sleep with Al then when I do, I am not to be trusted? How does that work?" She questions, then adds, "Besides you shouldn't test people if you are not prepared for them to fail. People fail Elsie."

"What? Well I certainly didn't tell you to do it then, behind my back! I don't think I ever actually asked for this. I was hoping that somehow by seeing the attraction in advance and remarking on it, I could somehow keep myself in the mix. Or make you guys aware I was seeing it."

"Jesus, Elsie you want every ounce of power don't you? I can't even pick the timing?"

"What power? It was my boyfriend, my family." I say. "Your position is that I caused my own pain using you as a pawn?"

"Well, I didn't do anything to you, that's for sure. Anyway it wasn't love or anything, and it was only that one time. Everyone was sleeping with everyone back then. It had nothing to do with you personally," she says calmly.

"Oh, that's very Buddhist of you." I say. Somehow the betrayal feels worse because of a lack of meaning to her.

"So now, you think I'm a druggie, just because I do a little coke. I sure wasn't too much of a druggie to babysit Zoë for you when you were in the hospital having J.J." She's pointing at herself.

"I didn't think you were a druggie until five minutes ago, frankly this coke thing is a little unsettling."

"You judged me for leaving Keifer with my parents--"

"That's not fair. I tried to understand, which was difficult when I had to look after my own kids and wouldn't dream of leaving them, as recent events show. Maybe I couldn't totally get it, but I tried to understand. Doesn't that mean anything to you?"

"Not really. '*I tried*,'" she mimics. "I know you were jealous of those trips I took. Did you ever consider that leaving your kids is better than dragging them through custody battles?" she proffers. "Why don't you just say what you really think for once!"

"No. I don't think abandoning your kids is better." I wonder if this was a trick question. To take a stance, my own, seems to go against Mia's choices and therefore Mia. "Neither is ideal. You did what you needed to do I guess, what you thought was best." Was she right was I just jealous of her freedom? I mean who says they can't handle their children and then goes on holiday? The rich I suppose. Can't they just want a holiday, without precluding it with a nervous breakdown? It occurs to me we haven't sorted out how to have a difference of opinion and accept it. I notice that Mia isn't confident, lucky or rich by her own description. She is broken and desperate and 'not' doing drugs. She is defending someone I don't know. A shadow. "Were you abused?" I ask, it just pops out of my mouth the same way her sleeping with Al had popped into my mind. I cover my mouth with my hand as if to stuff the question back.

Mia glares accusingly, "You say you accept me but you don't. I struggle to make things work. I'm a sensitive creative person. I've told you a bunch of times how hard it is for me. A person just doesn't wake up, and recover from being raped. I was just a kid. He's my cousin for fuck's sake; that golden boy. I have real pain Elsie, and you judge me, so who is it really, who can't trust who?"

I feel like I am in an emotional blender. "Rape? That thing with your cousin?" I gape. More like assault or abuse? Why do these distinctions bother me so much? I distinguish between being beaten and pushed around. It's so those whose experience falls clearly under these definitions are heard. And those being accused are accused of an accurate crime. I don't think it's fair to say all experiences are equal. Being raped isn't the same as being coerced, even if both are painful. I mean we have different names for things for a reason don't we? Are there degrees of pain and brokenness? Are these just the semantics of healing? Broken and fixed. Can one dip their toe in the waters of trauma without it rippling throughout their entire being and life? A ripple is not like an immersion.

"You said that you and your cousin had a weird kid thing. That it was nothing." I say coldy, dismissively, preferring to defend the other actual rape victims whom I've never even met. "You said you guys were kids, rape is a strong word to bandy about." I add, whislt oddly wondering where the word *bandy* comes from. "You can't blame everything you choose on him."

She glares. "Not literally raped! It's like you don't want to hear me! How can I possibily trust you."

I don't understand, is Mia saying I am not to be trusted? Is she saying that I haven't been a good friend to her? She is asking me to see her as at once being a disenfranchised victim as well as entitled. I am confused. I really do love her. Not this part, this shadow dance, maybe not this day, but I did, I know that much. Is it judgmental to see the truth, the facts? And is the truth in the facts?

Zoë comes barreling though the door in a very dramatic way, "Muuuhm!" Tears streaked in dirt all down her face.

"First, we splashed the sand on our legs!" gasp, gasp, and then Keifer said that the truck was stupid and J.J.. drove the small one, the yellow metal one, the one..."gasp, sniffle "onto Keifer's pile, going beep beep beep. But it wasn't right cause he was going front ways and the truck only makes that noise when it goes reversing and then Keifer grabbed it and then I just went to get it and and then Keifer threw sand at me!!" Wail.

This jars us out of our discourse.

"Okay Zoë, calm down." Her breathing begins to slow, as Keifer comes in behind her.

"I didn't do anything, Zoë threw sand at me and J.J. wrecked my castle," he explains still holding the little yellow metal bulldozer, "with this!" He holds up the evidence triumphantly.

I run to the window to see J.J. obliviously still playing with the bigger dump truck, the whole sand box to himself. I wave, he waves back, beep beep beep.

"I didn't throw sand! Mom, I didn't!" says Zoë still sniffling.

Throwing sand is akin to a violent crime. Consequences could range from mild to quite severe, depending on the proximity to the eyes. The defense teams are in full rally and it would take a well-run trial to determine what actually went down in that sandbox. Not to mention deciphering intent.

"Zoë kicked it at me when she got out! You kicked it at me!"

"Okay, okay, you two," says Mia, "Keifer do you want to hurt Zoë? Why?"

"Yes, she kicked sand at me," pouts Keifer hopefully.

"I didn't," insists Zoë.

"He has sand in his hair," says Mia.

I shrug, inconclusive.

"Did you want to kick sand at Keifer, Zoë?"

"Yes," answers Zoë. "For taking J.J.'s truck. But I didn't cause I knew I would get in trouble."

"Ah, did you mistakenly kick sand in his direction when you got out?" I venture.

"Maybe," she confesses.

"How is it a mistake, Zoë, if you wanted to do it, and you told your feet to do it?" asks Mia.

"Because it could go in his eyes." Zoë's lip starts to quiver. "And he could go blind," full out guilt wailing.

"Some mistake," mutters Mia.

"Do you want to hurt your friend, Zoë?" I ask

"No."

"Do you, Keifer?"

"No, I just want the other truck, my dump truck. Not this too small stupid one! That is all that I want."

"Go wash your face, Zoë. Let's go outside and get everyone their right truck."

"It's not stupid," mutters Zoë on her way to the bathroom. I light a cigarette.

"Well we should get going anyway," says Mia. "I think the kids have had enough."

"Yup," I agree stiffly, "seems like it." We organize Keifer's toys and see the two of them off in the driveway.

I am so very tired. Can you say RenShenfengWangJiang ten times very fast? I try it, grinding out my cigarette butt.

If I can be so wrong in the way I see Mia, I guess it's possible that Mia sees me in a different way as well. The house of mirrors that my life has become is confusing. Even being back home, everything looks the same but feels different. The mirror here is so strange; when I stand up for myself, I am accused of being all-powerful. She was only frustrated that I am not empathetic enough to her pain. Wow. I guess when we stop believing in each other's versions or experiences then the relationships fall apart. I stopped believing Al, and now Mia, and I don't particularly like either of their versions or expectations of me. At one time I loved them both. And they said they loved me. I push away the thought of Al and failed relationships. Fear aside, I hope this doesn't mean I will be alone forever. There must be a better way.

33
Hanging on the Telephone

I've been on the phone getting information on possibly going back to school. I finally got a hold of Marilyn from the shelter. She's not working there anymore, and they wouldn't give her number out, so I had to leave mine and wait for her to call. I am trying to get organized while Zoë is in school and J.J. is playing quietly in the sun-porch. I thought maybe Marilyn could give me a recommendation to babysit at the shelter or something along those lines. I'm just not in a clowning headspace. And I am not up to dealing with Mia's exuberant nature. The initial rush of being back home has worn off quickly, and I am feeling a little overwhelmed. Pacing between the sun-porch and the phone, smoking, looking at the old black dial phone (everyone else has push button now, not to mention an answering machine), willing it to ring. The phone finally complies and I leap from the sun-porch in little more than a single bound to answer. It's Marilyn.

We chat a little. I catch her up on my circumstances, and she is just as friendly as I remember. She is not with Jeffrey anymore and she does have a recent new beau as well as a new job, and promises to fill me in. She's helping in the organizing of a camp for single parent families. She has this sort of liaison type of position, still in social work but not the hours she had at the shelter. She does go by the shelter from time to time. Her job now seems to mean she helps organizations find people and vice versa. It's government funded. And I might be able to not only go to the camp, but to work there. She remembers how good I was with the other little kids at the shelter! I suggest that I could do art workshops and or babysit/be a counselor. Does she think she can get me in? And what about the kids? I am over the moon with this possibility. I am literally jumping up and down and realize I have to pee. The phone doesn't reach the bathroom, so I ask her to hang on. It is uplifting to have Marilyn call back and remember me fondly. I didn't know I was so worried about it, until I felt the relief wash over me.

The Mother Meets the Medic
By Elsie Shaw

The mother flushed the toilet, and headed back to the phone. She'd left her friend to hang-on, for the quick trip to pee. On the way back the Mother glanced onto the sun-porch to check on her young son who was playing quietly. A little too quietly she mused, half expecting him to have gotten a hold of something he knew he shouldn't. She peeked around the corner, smile on its way, and his name on her lips.

No boy.

Empty space. Oh boy. Down the garden path to the lake she ran. Calling his name. Left to right, right to left, scan, she scanned for clues. "Where are you?" the mother demanded, and then listened, she willed her eyes to see him.

Nothing, the water lapped the shore. No hint; a common lap, water-slapping rocks, indifferent. She ran back up the path, into the house. The phone cord dangling, she pressed to hang up to get a dial tone and dialed 911. He wouldn't have, I have drilled it in she thought. Or would he? His push scooter, the road?

"My son has gone missing! He's just two and a half. Petit, petit! He was just here! If he went to the road anyone could have taken him! Please help! Thank-you." They were on their way.

She ran to the front of the house, the road-side, frantically looking up and down the street. There was no car in the long driveway; the landlord was not there to ask. She saw one neighbor. He had not seen anything, just one brown car. The police pulled up. The mother explained to one policeman that he hadn't been missing for more than 10 to 15 minutes. She was too frantic to feel guilt. The Mother was too frantic to question the veracity of the time frame. The policeman wrote it down. The boy was wearing dark blue sweat pants and a white and light blue striped shirt. The neighbor told the police about the brown car. One policeman phoned it in; the son's description as well as the car's. The car, a brown sedan, they called it a sedan, took on a sinister potential. The neighbor, a veritable stranger, was a comforting presence; the concern. Should she get a photo? the mother asked.

It was quiet, windless thoughts ,an eerie pause in cognition. The Mother could not process this moment.

And then, a man walked down the driveway. He came from the direction of the house, and there was the son walking alongside, pointing at the police car. "Is that your son?" asked the police, but the mother was down the driveway in one step scooping up the boy. "Do you know this man?" asked the policeman to no one in particular. His partner was already talking with the man. The partner said yes he knew this man. The mother thought he was a 'known to police' type of man until she saw one police and the man laughing together. Slowly the vaguely familiar countenance emerged into the mother's consciousness. Ah yes, she knew who this man was.

The man was smiling reassuringly at everyone. Everything was just fine was it not? His policeman pal needn't be concerned. The boy had merely wandered up the outdoor staircase and into his upstairs apartment, where they had a little chat and the boy had admired his dinky toy collection. There was one still in the grips of the boy's pudgy hands. And all the men and the boy admired the small fire truck, the police offered to let the boy sit in the police car. "Am I in trouble?" asked the boy.

" No, no." said the men. The policeman said to the Mother, "It's okay mademoiselle, we know this man, he's a paramedic."

"Maybe," said the Mother to the little boy.

"Oh yes, you listen to your Mother," said the men.

The little boy squirmed out of his Mother's arms and climbed into the back of the police car with the policeman. The mother was yelling without yelling, at the medic. The veins in her neck were pulsating.

Why didn't he tell her that her son was up there? Where is your car? I don't care if you have a million toys, didn't you hear me yelling? I find that difficult to believe! Well it sure seemed like a long time to me! I called the police for Christ's sake!

The relief was trumping the Mother's anger, which was slowly being fueled by embarrassment instead of fear. The man medic seemed to understand and did not defend himself. Except to insist that he did not hear her, and say he was truly sorry. The Mother was shaking. She kept saying that this was unacceptable!!

"A person cannot harbour a child!" She couldn't seem to stop and even added; "I think we all know who should be in the back of that car! A grown-up with kid's toys! C-R double E-P-Y!"

The police said they had to go. They all looked rebuked, because they all liked the toy. They said that everything seemed to be under control here now. The medic said that it was. The mother thought she should be the judge of that. They looked at the medic with some pity. The boy waved to them, but looked sheepishly towards his mother. The man walked back to the house. The boy ran towards the man, he squatted down and told the boy; he could not be his friend until the mother said so. The mother liked that, and managed to take a breath and even smile a bit. The medic said the boy could borrow the fire-truck for today. The mother liked that as well.

"I called downstairs," he said getting to his feet, "the line was busy."

"I left it off the hook." she explained. "I didn't see your car."

"It's at the garage until tomorrow. I just installed my air conditioner today, its kind of loud," he offered, can't hear much outside."

"Just another reason to hate air conditioners," she said, "they prevent you from knowing what's going on in the world!" She wondered if this was exactly true, so added, "and they are horribly noisy, also they damage the planet!" she then whispered to herself, "In a way I can't quite remember." Exploding at last with the found word, "Fre-on!" which she realized sounded more like she wanted somebody named On released from prison on political grounds than it did an environmental comment.

"My point exactly." He shrugged calmly, and then added, "I am sorry for your worry. That must've been an awful scare. I would prefer the boy not to think I am a C-R-double E-P-Y kind of person if that can be helped. I will look into the perils of the air conditioners, I promise".

"You do seem somewhat less C-R-double E-P-Y, now. I guess we shall see," said the mother definitively.

The end

I had to write this after the fact in order to simmer down. I think that defining everyone by his or her roles is an interesting limitation. It's as though the emotions just seep out of the cracks then. What a terrifying few moments. I can use my fear as an excuse for my anger, which is even louder when I read it. Finn handled himself reasonably well I thought. Perhaps he's alright. He invited us all up for supper tonight, to make amends.

I am pleased not to have to cook, so sure. He made one rule, no smoking in his place. He said it was bad for the environment. I suggest that I can go outside on the landing, anyway. He says fair enough. He's put a couple of chairs out there so it's a bit of a tiny porch now. It occurs to me that I still don't have Marilyn's number. I do hope she calls back. I was going to ask her for it before all the excitement, before I left her hanging. It feels like an eternity waiting for the phone to rings again. I leap on it, hoping it's her. Nope, it's Lainey; she wants to know if I've settled in okay.

"Yup, listen can I call you back and fill you in, I am waiting for an important call." I am a little short with her I know, but there is a certain pleasure in having an important call on the horizon.

"Oh, of course," says Lainey. "I was just checking on you," she sounds a little disappointed.

"Right, call you later." I hate feeling like I owe her; I can't hang up fast enough. Of course the phone doesn't ring.

The place upstairs is very similar to ours. Just one bedroom instead of two, other than that the layout is the same but with the ceiling slanted, following the roof line and a tiny deck on the landing over the sun-porch. He's already put in a gorgeous skylight in the kitchen. The bathroom is directly over the one downstairs. I ask Finn not to put on his air conditioner because A) I hate them; B) They make a lot of noise; C) Given the events of this afternoon, I feel I can ask this. After all the air conditioner caused all the trouble. I want to be able to hear the phone should Marilyn call.

"Let me call your place, and we will find out," he suggests.

This seems such an obvious solution, that I am slightly peeved I didn't come up with it. He just stands there holding the receiver and staring at me. Oh right the number; I tell him the number and shush the kids, and wait. The resounding Briingggg is extremely audible. "Stay here," I order the kids, and bolt for the door, "Count the rings," I yell back over my shoulder as I head down the stairs.

"So how many?" I say breathless into the receiver.

"Six," he answers, "Are you coming back up?"

"Do you think six is too many?" I ask.

"Not for someone calling someone they know has kids. Someone who really wants to get a hold of you," he offers.

"Wow, you might want to consider insulating that ceiling, I really heard the phone ring up there."

"Are you coming back up to eat, now?" he sounds either bemused or confused I can't tell which.

"Oh right," I say, "I guess it would be pretty hard to eat through the phone." I laugh; I know this is not funny. Yikes, I am a social moron sometimes, "So ya, I'm coming back up."

I am just going to the bathroom and then I'll be right up. I brush my teeth and hair. I dawdle. I go back to the phone to make sure the receiver is on the phone correctly, just in case Marilyn might call right now. I really want the camp job. I want to feel like I am doing something; not just hiding from Al. How did Finn know my number earlier, when he said he'd phoned, when J.J. was up there at his place?

With one long backward glance at the very mute phone, I trundle back up stairs, where the kids seem indifferent to my absence. Finn has set up what seems to be a card table at the far end. Despite it being only about a dozen feet away I hadn't noticed earlier.

Zoë is happily setting the table. They have an assembly line going from Finn to J.J. to Zoë who is placing things. They are almost done so I just watch the chain of events. Finn brings the serving bowls of which there are two, one full of spaghetti noodles, and the other one full of sauce, with a ladle in it, also a container of Kraft Parmesan cheese.

"It's my Mom's sauce," he says, "after I invited you I took it out of the freezer. It's not too spicy so it should be fine for the kids. It's really good."

"I can eat spicy," says Zoë defiantly, sticking her chest out.

"Everyone likes their own mother's spaghetti sauce," I say taking a bite. "This is actually really really good. I see she puts a lot of vegetables in." I add in an obvious attempt to cover my pleasant surprise.

Somehow J.J. gets the Parmesan container. He turns the largest aperture to wide open and pours. A mound of grated cheese has falls onto his plate. So, we, Finn that is, gets another bowl and scoops the bulk of it into the bowl and we use a spoon to sprinkle it on our spaghetti.

Zoë asks if she can inhale her noodles, like we do at home. She knows this is not visiting behavior. Before I can answer, Finn sucks up a noodle and the game is on.

"Seems like you're used to being around kids," I say as we clear the plates. You didn't miss a beat on the close encounters with the Parmesan," I chide.

" Ya, well my older brother has kids, so I am a practicing uncle," he explains.

"Nice skylight," I say. The rest of the kitchen has no walls, in fact there are no actual walls anywhere. The roof rafters are showing in the living room, but somehow it still feels livable. The kitchen just has shelves, no cabinetry, but I kind of like that look.

"I might put a balcony out the side here, eventually. It would be a nice view."

This is directly above my kitchen window, where I have the beautiful sunsets. For a moment I don't want to share the sunset, that particular perspective of it. Then I realize how absurd that is. Plus it wouldn't be exactly the same view.

"Great for the sunsets," I hear myself say.

He has a small television and the kids have asked if they can watch Perfect Strangers and Full House. In colour. Zoë always seems to know T.V schedules; the kids must discuss these things at school. I don't have a television downstairs so I agree.

Once the kids are settled on the couch, I go out onto the landing/deck for a smoke. Finn brings me a jam jar lid to use as an ashtray, and asks what I take in my tea, then disappears back inside. Then he reappears, blue grey speckled ceramic mugs in hand.

"Finn," I say gingerly. I don't want to sound accusatory. "How did you know the phone number earlier and not just now?" I wrap my free hand around the warm but not too hot mug.

He smirks, clearly aware of the accusation. "It's in the bedroom, in my phonebook, under Tennant—Judith. Actually, I just thought it would be faster than if you told me. I haven't got it memorized just yet, Elsie," he says, sitting himself down.

As if that is what I was asking!

"Hey, Finn, do you mind my asking, why do you have a bird tattoo? I mean why did you choose a bird?" The small black bird is on his forearm, like Popeye's anchor, but there is a touch of red on the wings.

"I always liked that Beatle's song 'Blackbird'." He says simply.

"I like lots of songs, but I don't get a tattoo of them." I add waiting for a more extended version.

"I'm a big Redwings fan, will that do?" he offers.

"Frankly I don't get it, if you are going to have something permanently on your arm, I mean, people are going to ask why, aren't they?" I ask expectantly.

"Okay fair enough I suppose. It's just most people don't ask, they say 'nice bird' or something like that. I got it to mark a turning point in my life." He pauses. My silence encourages him.

"I was in kind of a drug scene, partying quite a lot when I was younger. And there were no limits with these guys. They would sell anything and they would do any drug. I started off with the usual, than some blow, and then some of the guys started getting pinned, that's using heroin. They were just chipping at first but then it got a hold of them." He's looking into the past, staring straight ahead.

"What's chipping?" I interrupt.

"Oh, 'chipping' is only doing it on the weekends."

"Weird, I wouldn't have thought that the workaday week was that clearly delineated for heroin addicts. Brings a whole new meaning to the word 'chipper' when it becomes a noun," I quip.

"Sure does," He pauses, looking at me quizzically. "Nobody is an addict at the very first y'know, at least these guys weren't, and they still had jobs. My friend the one who died, Marc Loiselle, he worked for the airlines, doing some highly skilled maintenance on parts. He was no dummy. When he had to learn new stuff he said he had to study high and then write the exam high. It seemed like a rationale, but he did pass his tests.

Apparently they have a whole rehabilitation aspect in their contracts; it didn't help him though. He did try one round. He made an attempt; I'll say that. I was there, the night of the first overdose. He was just lying there, not breathing at all; He was like, not breathing, he seemed dead. There was some girl named Ellie running around asking nervously, "Should we call 911?" Everyone else was standing around. Everyone had dope of one sort or another, or was so out of it that calling for help took a second thought. I guess everyone was a little in shock as well, looking back. Something clicked in me. I don't know if it was because I wasn't doing heroin, or because I had just arrived after work, and I was fresh from the outside world, or what it was. But I just started giving orders, yes call 911, help me turn him over. I started doing the life saving techniques I'd learned at the pool when I was a kid. He started to breathe. Turned out that Ellie had called 911 before asking if she should. I don't know what that was all about, but the paramedics were there almost immediately. They put him on oxygen and put him on a stretcher and wheeled him out."

"Did you mean, you weren't on heroin that day, or you were never on heroin?" I ask.

" Oh, shit. It's weird telling the story. I can't believe that I left that out, no I never did junk. I hate needles. Plus I had the benefit of being out of town when they all tried it the first few times. Did you know that you puke? I'm quite certain I wouldn't have gone down that road anyway, but there you have it. No, I saw 'Panic in Needle Park' when I was a kid and it gave me nightmares. Well that and vaccinations," he adds smiling.

"I know, me too, I saw that movie when I was little. Did you see the needle in the eyeball part? If that's not enough to turn you off needles I don't know what is. The whole tourniquet thing makes me a bit queasy. Come to think of it nobody really monitored what we watched when we were kids. Like us now." I stood up to get a peek at the kids glued to the show *Strangers,* harmless enough I thought, and I sat back down. "So, you saved his life then?"

He nods. "That was the best feeling in the world, to me, better than anything I had felt to that point in my life, maybe even so far in my life. I also noticed that I immediately wanted to distance myself from the people that were there. I wanted to be one of the paramedics; I wanted to be one right then and there. I looked around the room at some of the people I'd known since I was a kid, and I felt like I didn't fit. I couldn't recognize myself in the picture; do you know what I mean? Like I wanted to pop out of my own life."

"Yeah I know that feeling. That is so cool! How long did it take you, to change everything?"

"It took about three years, seemed much longer at the beginning. It was a little lonely..." He trails off. " Anyway, I've been a paramedic for about a year and half now. It's good. And now I have the house to renovate. So things is lookin' up!" He makes a clicking sound, like you would use to encourage a horse, and grins at his own success.

"What about the tattoo?" I am hesitant, "Was this all true? We got very far from the tattoo," I ask.

"No, none of what I just told you is true," he says straight-faced. "The tale of the tattoo is a more sordid story of drugs and intrigue. He's smiling, "My friend Marc who died..."

"But, he didn't die!" I exclaim.

"Yeah, he did die, sadly. It just took another month before he did the same thing and didn't wake up. And here's how that links to me, and my tattoo. We called him Birdie, because his name in English meant something to do with birds. Little bird or something close to that. And also because of the blackbird song, cause I think it was practically the only song he knew how to play on the guitar," he laughs. "Some girls sure liked it anyway." We played it at his wake; it just stuck with me, and I wanted a reminder of him, because in a roundabout kind of way, he saved me." He looks somewhere between pride and apology. He seems to acknowledge the very tidy ending. I know he has said this before he knows I know and we both know that it is best put that way. It's interesting to me that when we tell new people in our lives parts of our stories we often like to use the same words. He shrugs.

"I like the red and yellow bit on the wings." I say, "I always like a bit of colour."

We are quiet.

"It's pretty nice up here," I say breaking the silence. I am glad not to be talking about my saga for a change. Obviously, Judith has filled him in on some of my story.

34

A little Help

I don't recognize the silver coloured Volvo wagon, as it crunches quietly down the gravel driveway. My heart starts to race. My first thought is that Deirdre and Al have driven across the country. I hadn't actually told everyone I was back yet. The constant state of apprehension has become such elevator music to my moods, that I barely notice it. That is until something like an unknown vehicle reminds me that I'm sort of an outlaw. Then my mouth goes all dry and I try to formulate a plan. So far no plan has been needed, which is good cause I really don't have one. I mean this is as far as I've gotten. I guess I will tell someone soon, like Al's mom or something, that her grandson is fine.

It turns out to be Marilyn, in the Volvo. She looks slightly bohemian, but there is something about her leather saddlebag purse and brown sandals that seem too well thought out to be an accident. The wire encased amber stone necklace hung long and loosely, somehow the perfect length as well as a match for the chunky rings. I always notice these little things and yet I can never manage them for myself. I am not sure why that is. I think she got a perm.

Marilyn was a little concerned when I left her hanging on the phone. She sits down on the futon couch. (Thanks Judith.) We do a little catching up. I explain how Al had seemed to get stranger and in Los Angeles had really freaked me out, when we were driving around. I didn't know what mission he was on. I felt like the 'Mother' in Mosquito Coast, "You know," I said, "like there could be no dissension in the ranks. It was so weird in that story.

Although, we were in America not the jungle. And we weren't trying to create a utopia, just a family."

"So instead of dystopia you get dysfunctional," she notes.

"Exactly. Oh here," I hand her a copy of my story to read, the one about the Mother and the Medic. " I just liked the idea of people only being referred to by their role as a restriction." I say over my shoulder as I head off to make the tea. "That's why I wrote it that way. Mother is not the worst title, as far as titles go." I add.

Only a moment after I return tea in hand, Marilyn looks up from the page. "Sounds like you had a scary circumstance, no matter what you are called," she says. "It's good. You got your point across."

She brought some actual paper work for this camp job; officially I'll be a counselor. I'd been to brownie and guide camp when I was a kid. That is a prerequisite, some kind of camp experience. You also have to be either on welfare or unemployment to qualify for this job. I qualify on the first count. They really just pay twenty-five dollars extra a week on top of your check. But the great part will be being housed and fed for the better part of the summer, not to mention by a lake, the kids with other kids. Now, usually you are either a counselor or a single parent family, not both. So that could be the glitch. Marilyn says she has known the people who are running it for years; I fill out the papers, while Marilyn reads another story, the one about the shelter. She likes the way I described her. And when she reads the part about Juliette, she sighs, and says, "ah sweet Juliette, they left shortly after you. I never saw them again." She says she forgives me for not staying in touch. I ask her if we were friends or if she is just being a social worker. I have to ask. I mean I really like her but relationships have been so wonky lately. I also ask her if she thought I would've gone back to Al, when I left the shelter. She says she had hoped not. I pressed her, yeah, but did she think I was going to? Marilyn admired her sandals, and then looked up out from under her own eyes. "Kind of," she says, "Elsie, we got along and I like you, but you were kind of in shock most of that time. Very sensible shock, and at times very funny shock, but it usually takes a little longer if someone is going to leave the abusive situation for good. I wanted to be wrong about that. So I'm really happy that you've left now. I like to help, and I want to help you, so in that way, I don't know if I ever stop being a social worker in a way. This however is a purely social call. So would you like to hear about my new beau?"

"Yes please!" I nod eagerly.

"He's a teacher. He also works with delinquents. That's how we met; I did a stint in the youth protection sector. There's a lot of overlap with kids that don't have anyone and kids that commit crimes. It's quite ridiculous, they end up in the same institutions. Anyway that's another story, don't get me started on that!" She takes a deep breath and exhales the frustration of a flawed system. "Steve and I are talking about buying a farm together… in the townships. He's a red head, and sings in a choir if you can imagine. It's so sweet, my sweet baritone. He's been doing it for years!"

"Do you sing?" I ask.

"Me? No, not really, in the car to myself, I might try it. I am still doing my yoga and I've got these Tibetan singing bowls, so now we, Steve and I, do some chanting together. You would love it. I'll bring them next time."

"That sounds very fun." I say, and it surely does. "I do believe you are in love!"

"I do believe I am!" She grins.

It all sounds so lovely, normalcy with a hint of the spiritual, perhaps I could add a soupcon of suffering to the mix, by my presence alone. No, I suppose that their clients provide that. I had tried so hard to run from normal when I was younger. It all just makes me want to smoke, and wish I didn't. What had looked too easy, too predictable! Too safe! Wow I probably deserve this predicament just based on the arrogance of that thought. I believed I wouldn't have anything to write about if I didn't just sail on a wing and a prayer. I didn't give real imagination a chance. Am I still in shock? I wonder; vaguely aware of the persisting elevator music that is my tension and fear.

I ask about whether they were going to get livestock? Marilyn had said she always wanted horses. "Didn't you say you weren't the digging type. She looks at me quizzically. "You don't remember? You said that when I started that garden at the shelter. Whatever happened to that anyway?" I want to know.

"Funny about that, after you left some stuff started to grow, weeds mostly, but also tomatoes and the yellow string beans went crazy. I tended it a little, weeding turned out to be a nice way to talk. This woman Cynthia who came in mid-summer had a real green thumb. She knew to thin the beets and spent a lot of time at it. It was very light garden work for me, but I discovered I don't mind digging in at all; in fact I enjoy it. So thanks for starting that."

I ask whether she thinks I could get into trouble for just leaving B.C., and coming home, breaking the law. She says that I could.

I ask her if she would stay while I called out west to let them know where we were. The dreaded call. She said sure. So I call my old house where I'd lived with Al. I guess it could be called the marital phone to go with the 'marital home': what Al had called it in the court documents. I'll show you *family home* I thought, while it was ringing. I am now back at my home, so there, and then Deirdre answers. Al wasn't home.

She says I deserve to go to prison; that I have caused Al considerable pain. I try to warn her that Al's pain, while I am sure is only worsening, was always there. I tell her he is not okay. From one beet lover to another, I tell her, please be careful. She says the beets she had left on my doorstep were a peace offering; she had not been spying. She says I am nuts and hangs up.

"I like to think under different circumstances, we might've been friends," I say turning to Marilyn.

"Well at least you tried," offers Marilyn. "You should get a lawyer here."

"Yeah you're probably right, but let's go to camp first, k?" I say.

"Sounds good," she agrees. "Are you planning to do anything with those stories you wrote?"

"I wanted to write when I was younger. But I am waiting until I have more to write about, until all this crap is settled. Painting is much more medicinal, for me. I think I need to travel, and learn more about the world before anyone will want to read anything I have to say. English and waspy, doesn't seem too popular these days. The world is getting smaller and stories from other countries or the immigrant perspective are much more enthralling. Really, do I want to cry about being a middleclass let down, when people are starving or refugees? Or worse yet, starving whilst traversing some perilous mountains somewhere to arrive here. Please, my stories are too easy, too cliché.

"Juliette is not a cliché. And just because you get through difficult times doesn't make them too easy. What, will you have a better story to tell if your hero dies tragically? In the story about the shelter she goes back to the abusive guy. That's kind of tragic, don't you think? "

"I suppose it is. I'd like a joke or two. Can you have a comedic tragedy? I have some people who die in some of my stories. You know, now that you mention it, they're not the heroes or the villains."

"How about a tramedic dramedgy?" Marilyn suggests.

"Ooh sounds fringe, ledgy even," I add thinking of suicidal anecdotes.

"Did you ever notice that genre and gender are only one letter apart?" asks Marilyn as though this is profound.

"No, but it is weird that it doesn't apply to vegetables, as in 'what genre of vegetables do you prefer?'

"The root, definitely the root."

This brings to mind the haunting guilt of letting the vegetables rot in the bottom of the fridge. (More interesting stories have less fortunate people whom the middle class should be sending their unwanted peas to, one by one, to belabour the guilt, ingratitude and insolence that comes from the privilege to dislike.) The taunt of the fridge drawer; it's the humiliation and anger about being in that circumstance. Just for a split second, just long enough to know I am not completely healed.

When can I live in peace I wonder? Will it ever go away or will I pay the price for those decisions for the rest of my life? Not the veg, all the stuff around the veg. I sure hope leaving wasn't another one of those questionable choices. Right now it seems like it was the right thing to do. I imagine the threads from my solar plexus that connect me to Al. It's the threads, I think, that trigger the hurt in my gut when I remember him. The connection to it, our relationship. I imagine myself cutting them; they are silky white and transparent. I do this every time I feel myself reacting to a memory. I didn't realize that cutting ties had such a literal application. When I cut them they don't just go limp, they have strong vibrant ends, like an energy haircut, to grow, revitalized.

Before she leaves I take down her numbers, so I won't be in that position again. She had come on a Friday so it was unlikely I'd hear anything before Tuesday about camp, but the mere possibility has put a spring in my step. I haven't heard from Al at all. This makes me wary. I doubt that Deirdre would not tell him that I called. Does that mean he's just going to come after me?

I am a little jumpy. Distraction seems the best idea. Camp starts the first weeks in July. We are having a summer breeze of a June. The lavender I'd planted four years ago along the fence, in the most sunny spot, is all purple and just starting to give off its spicy warm smell. The water is not too low this year, they must have gotten plenty of snow last winter. There is clear passage for canoeing to the island, rock free. Of course we know the rocks are there, but we won't run aground. Even though there are places that are shallow at the best of times, navigating that is part of the fun.

Never underestimate the depth of shallowness someone once said to me. I think it might've been Mia, sounds like her. On the island there are plenty of purple shimmering mussel shells strewn about near the rocks where we park the canoe. These shells can be small magical boats for wee folk as well as beds. There is an old foundation and stone fireplace, the perfect spot for picnic and pretend, where Zoë, J.J. and I can be characters from the olden days. We take a day off from school to go back in time. There is a tiny bridge that connects another very small island to the shore. This island is just large enough for the one old brick house. It's as though we are travelling through an ancient canal. The canoe, the idea of it, carries with it every story of the courieur de bois, the French fur traders, whom I learned about as a child. The adventure of discovery is always there, even if I always go along the same shoreline, or under the same little bridge. I may be getting back my imagination, thanks to the still water ripple of a paddle and children. The traders may have been all about commerce, but there is something about trying to imagine them here, everything unspoiled, that makes it feel so un-commercial. It's not long before I wish I could identify with the original people more, but I only know a French song about paddling, and no native songs at all. I want to both apologize and be apologized to for this fact. I actually only know one line of the French song anyway, *C'est l'aviron qui nous mène en haut.* Which I'd imagined meant that the paddles deliver us to a higher place. The song is not about that at all, but about a guy who gets a pretty girl. I don't know the words to the verses which tell that tale, only the chorus, which was added by the *Voyageurs* themselves. We were shown the Norman McLaren film in school, for French class, I like the tune. The canoe being paddled through a black sky with white clouds was both haunting and promising. I sing la la la la to the tune and add the chorus "to a higher place." There will be canoes at camp I hope.

I've called Mia several times over the last couple of weeks. She hasn't been answering her phone. I want to catch up with her at least once more before heading off to camp. I've only spoken to her once on the phone, since she came over. I told her about the camp job and we spoke about our mutual love of brownie and Girl Guide camps. I told her how I'd had to get a letter of recommendation from old Mrs. Walbridge, who had been in charge of the counselors in training. Mia remembered her well.

Mrs. Walbridge was a very Christian woman and well meaning. She made the mistake of praying for us, well that wasn't the actual mistake, really the error was in telling us after any minor transgression that she would pray for us. Imitating her sincerity became a game. It could be something as innocent as taking the last piece of toast. When we got caught smoking Mrs. Walbridge gave us a lecture on the health problems associated with smoking, as well as explaining the blasphemy that it was to dirty ourselves with addiction. Addiction is a replacement for the Lord she said. She assured us that she would pray for us. While she prayed we blew smoke rings behind the tuck shop, and called them halos, to at least make a gesture.

I reported to Mia that Mrs. Walbridge was actually not as old as we'd imagined and very sweet and gave me tea as well as generously wrote me the recommendation; I think the prayer was implied. At least I hope so. Mia told me about the downtown scene, and her new job at a trendy spot called Bar Mix where the tips are great and her boss even greater in the sack. He is a bit older, and has his own kids but they don't live with him. She sounded a bit distant, like we are not quite on the same page anymore. She is working mostly weekends, which suits cause her parents can watch Keifer and her dance classes during the week are very demanding. She talked really fast about running from one thing to the other, but was excited to finally be following her dream.

I guess she is very busy that's why I haven't heard from her. I miss that fun friend and spend a little time wondering if it's me that has changed or her, or both of us.

I hang up after trying to reach Mia for the umpteenth time. I hope she didn't change her number or move or something. There is a light knock at the door. It's the landlord, "Oh, hi Finn, come on in." I say replacing the receiver. "What's up?"

"I was wondering if you heard about that job you were so excited about?" he asks looking around furtively.

"Might I ask why?" I say trying to walk the line between defensive and respectful. Wondering if he thinks it's a mess in here or something. He is still the landlord.

"I was just wondering, because I have some work to do upstairs and it, uh, could get a little loud," he explains.

"Really, and what loud work would that be?" I feel as though I have him slightly off balance and I like it. "And what's that got to do with my job?"

"Oh nothing, I just thought I might try to accommodate your not being here, I thought it would be a good time to get it done is all. Did you get the job?"

"Yesirree! I got it!" I say nodding, not concealing the excitement at all. "Actually, I'll be gone most of July and half of August, so I am sure it would be a good time to get your noisy work done."

"Are you planning to sublet while you are gone?" he asks suspiciously, "because I might have someone."

"I really hadn't thought about it. I mean I have my stuff, what's left of it, and it's still my place, and I don't know, and I still need an address and well I suppose it's up to you really since I don't have a lease. But I could come back right? I mean you wouldn't do that would you? I'm a good tenant; I won't just leave if that's what you're worried about. I'll still pay while I'm gone, obviously I can't pay in advance." I stop to assess his reaction. It hadn't even occurred to me that I could sublet or that he might. I mean it's mine as long as I pay, I think. He is just standing there, all serious.

"Are you okay? Take a breath! I was thinking that I might stay down here, while I was doing the drywall. If you won't be here, then it will save me going all the way home, and we can arrange a discount in your rent while I stay. It's up to you, it was just an idea so I don't have to sleep in the dust. And you can save a bit of money. Why pay for something you aren't using? There may be some plumbing work as well, so water service could be interrupted anyway."

"Oh." I say visibly relieved. "Like what kind of discount?"

"Like no rent while you are away. I'm on my way now, gotta fly, so just think about it, and we'll talk later. See ya." He smiles and then turns and waves over his shoulder on his way out.

"What's to think about?!" I yell after him. I will not question this good fortune. I will pack.

Camp was great. Since it was designed for single parents in a certain income bracket, everything is provided or subsidized by donations, even the sleeping bags could be purchased at a discount.

I still had to hide from my charges to smoke, and I wasn't the only one. It felt safe there. Other single Mums, loads of kids, and songs, campfires and walks, arts and crafts; basically a Utopia. Even with different parenting styles the set up seemed to work. Somehow in this environment there is an understanding that an hour or two to oneself every few days is a basic need. There was a rotation of chores and responsibilities that made it seem so easy. J.J. was a bit clingy but he got quite independent after meeting a little friend Drake, who was a bit older, but they romped like brothers, and J.J. copied his bathroom habits, which made my life much simpler. Summer is so precious here. No one wants to waste it by being nit picky. The extended light makes summer an innately forgiving season. Plus, we unified against a common enemy: the mosquito. Quite the service that little bug offers if you look at it that way. This kind of experience makes me want to give back, one day, when I can donate.

    I can't believe it's already fall again. September is well under way. It's still warm during the day but the nights are cool. I like to leave the windows wide open and wrap myself in my covers in the morning. It should be New Years in September, new school year, people are always excited to start new projects and get back to work. Sweet and crisp shiny purposeful apples, and school.

    Resolutions are taken seriously in September. This is the year my notebooks will be neat. Or this is the year I will do all my homework. And just like resolutions in the winter they only last a month or so. Of course Zoë is very happy to be in school and too young for re-solutions, she is all about solutions. My September resolution is to start my new life, no more boys and no more babies. And to plan, to try to plan; I want to choose my actions, not just my reactions.

    1)   Volunteer teaching art at the shelter to develop portfolio or experience and help out.
    2)   Quit smoking
    3)   Paint
    4)   Keep painting what I see.
    5)   Meditate
    6)   Have more patience.
    I light a smoke to finalize the list that has now become boring. First I need a car. I have asked Finn and Marilyn if they know anybody getting rid of one. I could look in the paper I suppose. I have very little cash, just what I saved on rent, so it will be more of a shit-box that I am looking for. That's the thing if you live out of town you can get cheaper rent, but it costs more to get anywhere. I will meditate on that conundrum, like the sound of one hand clapping.

And if I don't have cheap rent I'm not sure how I would make ends meet. It will take too long without a car to get to the shelter where I want to volunteer and I won't be able to get home in time for Zoë. I will ask the universe to get me a car. Meditating has caused the universe to reinforce itself, and me I hope. I think this is a strange way to operate, but somehow it works. You'd think if the universe saw fit to take care of all my needs then I would have a car already, I wouldn't have to ask. Perhaps the whole thing is working the other way around and I am asking for one because in the future I already have one and I need to get to the future. And so the 'universe' has put it to me to ask for one. I will keep an eye out then for my car to pop up.

This is like Al's antenna way of operating. Some of his ideas are worthwhile, I don't want to throw all good stuff out with the crazies. It just proves that you can still be reliable and there for the kids as well as walk in faith.

35

Love is The Seventh Wave

I tell them I would really like to volunteer at the shelter. I just don't have a way to get there. I didn't exactly tell the director this over the phone. She said I could bring J.J.. I hope the stress in the environment doesn't affect him. We will balance it out with playcare or something like Zoë had. This is day one and I had to take the train for half an hour to the bus for half an hour and then another bus. Living out of town has its drawbacks. At least there's a train. I am wondering if I will make it home in time for Zoë getting off the bus. I am arriving at around quarter to three just ahead of Zoë. So it's doable. J.J. is cranky from being in transit. I am also cranky; I was up at 6:45 left at 8:00 this morning to volunteer for two hours. How is it almost time to get it together for supper? Am I planning correctly? Because I am pooped. Thank God I only said I would do this three days a week. I am nowhere near ready for item number two on my list, I think as I light a cigarette.

I hear Zoë coming down the path preceded by her insistent nature kicking the gravel. Sounds like a good day. It's overcast with a warmish breeze, good for dawdling but not too hot. Only the tips of some of the leaves know that it's autumn. Zoë runs in and hugs me. She drops her school bag, takes out her new French story books and offers to read one to J.J.. Well actually he grabs it out of her bag while she is saying hello. I suggest she read it to him. She says she doesn't know French yet, I say J.J. won't mind. J.J. runs off with it. She implores me to get it back as it belongs to the school. We coax him back with the promise of being read a story.

There are sighs and eye-rolls from Zoë, pleading looks from me until finally Zoë reads and J.J. is entranced by his sister in a way I cannot broach.

I have all day tomorrow to recover and plan. I'll give Elaine a call and see if she wants to come and have Thanksgiving with us. It falls in the second weekend in October. Being back east makes it a great time of year to celebrate all the colours. I'm anxious for the leaves to complete their transition; I've missed that.

"Elsie, you should come to us," Elaine suggests. "It's expensive to feed the whole gang." It irks but I know she is right.

"I know Lainey, but how? On the bus? I don't have a car yet. And frankly the bus is also expensive. It would be great though to get the kids together. And see you two. I can't wait to tell you about the shelter job."

"Sounds great. It's more like volunteer work though isn't it?"

"If you are referring to the exact pay then yeah I guess, but I look at my combined income of welfare plus the job pay, as all being for the job." I explain.

"But it isn't." she adds factually.

"It's all about perspective," I explain.

"So about Thanksgiving. You know we do Steve's family on the Sunday, so how about Monday?" she suggests.

"Well, I still don't have transportation." There is a silence as we both try to figure it out.

"How about this, how about I come to you on the Monday, just us girls.The kids and I will drive down, can you get a turkey, if I bring the rest?" rescues Elaine

"Well sure! And I will stuff that turkey as well. Can you make that grated potato scallop thingy, it's my favourite?"

"Yeah I can do that," she says.

"Thanks Lainey, see ya." I don't ask why Steve can't come; the answer will just be bullshit anyway. He's a good guy, but I will be happy to have my sister all to myself.

Lainey arrives mid-afternoon, the potato scallopy thing in hand, and some cranberry jelly made from scratch as well as some turnip pureed with a smidge of brown sugar and butter, she explains as she hands me the items. I have the turkey stuffed in the oven, and we will steam some green beans. It's actually a lot for three little kids and us. "Leftovers," she explains as she unveils a bowl of various roasted potatoes, carrots, Brussels' sprouts and parsnips, they look a little worse for the wear but the lingering aroma of rosemary preserves edibility.

"Just need a little warming up," she reassures. Cheers to my mother –in- law!

"Fantastic! And look what I've got," I pull the pumpkin pie off the top of the fridge to show her. I walked over and got it this morning; they go on special today, because most people have done their family gathering yesterday.

"You couldn't bake a pie this inexpensive," I chime. She nods.

"Let's take the kids to the beach, they can throw rocks for a bit. Tucker them out, " she suggests. The tiny sand beach is a couple of lots over, it seems like it should have a different name from the ocean beaches of the west. This is really a 'beachette.' It's so cute, with the one picnic table provided by the town. After a small foray into rock skipping, we sit as the kids run around. Aaron has grown, he's taller than Zoë now. He is tentative and sweet and Zoë looks like a wild child beside him, especially that hair. Not unlike comparing Lainey and me except the hair is Sam's.

"How are you planning to get a car?" asks Lainey motioning to mooch that occasional butt as she does with me.

I don't like her tone, all inferring that I don't have it together.

"It's coming." I say confidently, "I have my eye out for one. I hope it's soon though because the bus is making my part time venture into a full time commitment."

"Keeping your eye out? Elsie that is not going to cut it. Cars don't just fall from the sky." She is oddly amused chastising me.

"Well you find one then!" I defend, "How's that for proactive?" I don't like being managed by her. "I am afraid to make a mistake with the limited funds, okay." I confess, "If I get a lemon I won't be able to fix it, so it has to be the right one, a really good deal, a special one. You wouldn't understand." I am pouting a little. Feeling sorry for myself on Thanksgiving, yikes.

"No you're right," she consoles generously. "It needs to be the right one."

Sometimes I think she just pisses me off so she can make me feel better, to look after me like a little sister, I think ungenerously.

"Did I tell you the psychic on the train said you would have another baby?" I add.

"Yes Elsie, every time we speak, you mention it. Everything in its right time as you say," she concedes to my logic, I feel a little better.

We have to walk by her car on the way back to the house. I have car envy.

"Do you like this car?" she taunts.

"Yeah, it's okay for a station wagon," I say. "I do, I like the colour." It's navy blue.

"Hmm," she muses, "I like the colour as well." As we walk by, she pats the roof affectionately. Rub it in why don't you.

Once inside she starts acting all strangely excited. Digging in her purse and mumbling, "I've got a surprise for you," in a high pitched tone, over, and over.

She finally locates what she is after, and in a grand gesture pulls out a small earring size box. She hands it to me wearing this restrained but cockeyed grin. I am wondering what the heck this is about; we don't give presents at Thanksgiving. I open it, slowly, self-consciously. A mixture of the guilt of not having something to give back, and the childlike pleasure of receiving are fighting for emotional priority. Pleasure wins. The box makes a click as the lid reaches its maximum open.

There are keys in there, her keys, her car keys. Complete with a new circular key-chain, with a yin yang symbol.

I don't dare think it. So instead I question, "You're giving me your car keys? Is this a symbolic gesture? Like, have a keychain, and the car will come?"

She gives me a look that says we both know she doesn't do symbolism. Lainey then explains that they were going to scrap it anyway. She wants to get a better car, and so the timing is perfect. The station wagon is now mine. Her hubby will arrive later to pick them up; she has filled out the proxy forms so I can do the registration changeover. She has thought of everything!

"Don't worry, it's road worthy, its just old so we wouldn't get any cash for it," she reassures me when I unwittingly flinch at the word 'scrap.'

I am thanksgiving all over the place, thanks Lainey, thanks the lord, thanks the turkey, the kids, the sun, the leaves, the feast, the car, thanks the life, things are going to get easier. Thanks for the support. In the spirit of thanking, the kids all get on board and we are grateful for bugs, and rocks, and cats and dogs and cheetahs and noodles and air and love and family.

I am also quietly guiltily thankful to Dierdre for being the new woman in Al's life, for relief. As we raise our teacups in a toast like manner, Lainey and I exchange a glance and a nod that lets me know she gets it.

36

The Needle and
the Damage Done

The workshop yesterday morning went really well; in fact they have all been increaingly fun. I was so nervous at first. I was honest about having been there as a client and that seemed to put everyone at ease. The car has made everything so much easier. I am looking forward to tomorrow because there will be painting, today was babysitting. Tomorrow I get to encourage everyone to see, to see shadows as well as light, to really look at the lines of what they want to depict. I find there is a release of stress when people are being creative, even if they are expressing a lot of anguish. The vibe in art rooms is not unlike the feeling of healing to me. Then again maybe that's just because I like it. I basically started out with a book about drawing from the right side of the brain; it's a step-by-step approach that helps everyone feel like they can draw. That along with some free expression and colour theory, and everyone seems happy. I suppose to be fair it is a little time off from the day-to-day reality of being in the shelter that helps a lot. The program doesn't have to be long. It has to work so that people can join along the way because the stays are always different in length. It's still a work in progress.

I approached the five main skills in drawing by tying them into the shelter situation, to help remember. Are you feeling a little on *edge* about your circumstances? Is your head-*space* swinging between *negative* and *positive* because of your relationship *perspective* that is out of *proportion*? Does it feel like a game of *light* and *shadows* that is affecting your whole *life*? If you can answer *yes* to any of the above then you are a candidate for creating your way out of here.

I do the mornings two hours, three days actual babysitting and art with the kids and then two mornings with the moms. Marilyn looks after the shelter kids on the days I do the Moms. It's not really her job but she enjoys it and no one is complaining about having art 'classes' available. The women are generous not to notice that I am just winging it. And I in turn have come to see that it may be more difficult than I had originally thought to leave an abusive relationship after many many years. I am so happy to not have that experience.

The shelter association was pretty generous with the supplies I was allowed to buy. I've got everything from crayons and plasticine for the kids, to acrylic paints and easels for Moms.

Marilyn and I came up with the plan after camp went so well. I am actually hired as a babysitter, so I still get to keep my welfare check as long as I don't make too much. It's a little extra money; twenty-five dollars a week, as well as gaining experience. I think I want to study art therapy once J.J.. is in preschool. I haven't heard boo from Al or Deirdre. I still worry though that he could turn up at any time. I wonder how long that fear will last. It's a lot better than the daily fear I see at the shelter. Geez measuring fear in increments, that's not how I imagined being an adult.

Mia's mother Audrey answers the phone on the third ring. I often see people in my mind's eye just staring at a ringing phone deciding whether to pick it up, curiosity finally getting the better of them.

"Hello Mrs. Cliff, this is Elsie Shaw, Mia's friend. I have been trying to get a hold of her for a couple of months now. I was wondering if she changed her number or something. Could you tell me how to reach her? I hope everything is okay."

"Well, as a matter of fact dear, everything is not what I would call okay. But that's neither here nor there. Mia has had some troubles as I am sure you are aware," she says slowly, as though the difficult subject of Mia makes the act of speaking equally difficult. "Everyone seems to know."

"No, I don't think I am, don't think I do know, not exactly, is she all right?" I interrupt. "I've been out of town, at a camp." I explain.

"Yes. Well, we'll soon see," she says definitively.

"Do you have a number for her?" I ask. She is not giving much up.

"Oh yes, just a minute," she shuffles some paper and clears her throat before dictating the number. "You can reach her there. Young Keifer is here with us for the moment. Don't he and your little daughter play together?"

"Yes, yes they do."

"Could you please call again, and perhaps we shall organize something for the children." I think she is just going to hang up when she says, "When you do speak to Mia, tell her I am thinking of her would you?"

"Yes of course I will. Take care,"

Click. She's gone. I still don't know where *there* is.

So I dial the number.

"Sojourn Lodge, White Birch Lake, how can I help you?" This perky, gravelly voice welcomes me.

"Hi," I say, trying to get the phone cord to stretch as far as the kettle, which I know it can, if the angle is just right. "I'm looking for Mia Cliff, please." I am just about to turn on the tap. I have the phone receiver wedged between my ear and shoulder. I am preparing to hang on.

"Mia is in a meeting right now, I can take your name and number and have her call you back this evening." I don't turn on the tap. *A meeting?*

"Where is this that I've called?" I ask.

"This is Sojourn House Rehab, do you want to leave your name and number?" She says in a tone that has heard it all before.

"Oh, okay, sure," I say. After I leave my name and number, I remember that Mia knows both my name and my number. She doesn't necessarily know I am back from camp. Given the state of things she may not even have my number.

When she did call me back, we arranged for me to visit. So I am driving up north to the Sojourn Lodge. Apparently it's a lovely setting on a lake. So many thoughts are running through my mind. I suppose it's my turn to be a friend to her in need. I am glad she trusts me enough to want me to visit. She said she hadn't been ready until now; she'd been too raw. She mentioned that she needed to discuss her feelings with me. I hope she is not going to emotionally blame everyone else. She sounded a little strange. She said it was part of her 'learning'. I said I thought learning was a verb. She didn't react. I hope it's not like a psych ward where they dope people up to keep them mellow.

She was right that I judged her, but it was because I saw her as more capable of taking responsibility. I wanted to write the script where she says, 'Geez Elsie, upon reflection I can see how sleeping with your partner might have hurt you, especially with you being in the women's shelter, it was like saying I didn't believe your experience. I guess I just really needed some attention and didn't think that it would impact you the way it has. I thought that the violence was limited to *your* relationship with Al, like a lover's quarrel. I am sorry, that was shortsighted of me, and will not be that kind of friend now, because we've both grown up since then.'

Then I could say, 'I am sorry too Mia, because even if he didn't rape you in the conventional literal sense. It was figurative in the sense that your innocence was raped. Clearly you are still in a lot of pain, from that and subsequent choices, and I should be more sensitive to your experience. Just because you are privileged doesn't mean you are immune to emotional problems or protected from life. Also I suppose it is a stretch to expect you to be grateful to your family, when to you they are part of a problem. I will try to be more compassionate, because I truly don't want you to suffer.

The whole thing, even in my mind, is like people speaking a different language around sex, and betrayal, expectations, and not believing each other's experience. In a way we had seen each other as better and stronger, perhaps our friendship was just a fictionalized version, or a projection like a movie where there are time lapses and suspension of disbelief. Is that blinded by love, or love being blind?

I don't like the feeling that thought brings. So I turn up the radio, enjoy the harsh vulnerable beauty of bare trees before the snow. It's just before lunch and I am hungry as well as nervous.

I've been invited for lunch. I light another cigarette. I wish they had rehab for smokers. I wonder if she will get out before the holidays. I wonder if she was this nervous coming to the women's shelter to see me.

There is a long gravel circular driveway, like you might see at a hotel main entrance. The parking lot is off to the side. When I pull up to the front door I am directed to the parking lot. I have the feeling of being watched. The radio, the tires on gravel, the noise in my head are abruptly turned off and met with the silence and sweet smell of pine. The oxygen of the north is almost liquid, I take a deep drink to displace my nervousness. From the side of the building I can see that it backs onto the lake. It really is a gorgeous setting. There are a lot of evergreen trees, which warm up the view. The small slope towards the lake has some picnic tables dappled around. One looks to be on a slant, probably to catch the sun or something, I think. There are a couple of other buildings off to the side, probably for sleeping. I walk towards the reception area. There is a woman at the desk. She asks me who I have come to see, checks her book, and then nods. She directs me to sit in one of the four chairs set against the wall. There is a pamphlet about the lodge and its philosophy with a very pretty sunrise on the cover, and the caption New Day, New Hour, New Minute, New Second, getting progressively smaller into the sun.

So I sit. Lunch isn't scheduled until one and it's about five minutes to. I feed the minutes to the pamphlet, one letter at a time. And then there she is. She pops her head around the corner. One eyebrow raised, she looks me over. I stand up. Her hair is predictably longer, although I hadn't thought about it. The black has grown out and the dirty blond roots are like a skunk stripe. She has no make-up on and looks more like her old self. Even her body language is less abrasive. I hadn't realized how much I missed this version, or a similar one; the erosion had been low and slow. I have been away. Her erosion had been on my back burner.

"I'm really glad you came, Elsie." She opens her arms, and I walk into her, throwing my arms around her.

"Of course," I answer stepping back, taking in the lobby once again. "I brought you a treat," I say. I go to reach into my bag, and she looks all worried.

"What?! It's only renfenjengwengshen," I say reaching into my canvas satchel to retrieve the little vials. She is not laughing. I stop fishing for them when I hear her say,

"Not now," through a gritted smile.

"Oh, Okay." Vials, right, they would be suspicious. "Sorry, I didn't think it through..." I whisper.

"Let's go for lunch. You'll notice that this is less a home setting like the shelter, and more like camp in a way." She motions for me to follow.

"Yeah, I can see that," I say, as we turn the corner into a mess hall type room with eight or so large tables set for lunch. It's a cafeteria type arrangement and people start to pour in and sit. Each table is asked if all the people at the table are accounted for then called table by table to come and line up for lunch.

"Table four, is everyone accounted for?" The woman who is serving bellows cheerfully.

'Yes, Brenda," table four sings in unison.

"Come on up then." Brenda waves them up.

"Thank you Brenda." The people at our table chime, over the sound of chairs being pushed out, to get quickly to the food.

I follow Mia. We pick up our trays. We are handed a plate each, complete with a piece of salmon, veggies, and rice. Despite the regimented nature there are smiles and Brenda is bossy but friendly. There are salads and condiments and tartar sauce and the end of the line, set out on another table.

"Addicts tend to like to eat, if there isn't another substance available. Watch the salt usage, it's wild," she adds. "Lots of people gain weight in here. For some it's much needed, for others, not so much." She smiles grabbing a very small roll around her middle. She actually looks really healthy, in a way I haven't seen since we were teens.

Everyone is engaged in what appear to be serious conversations, sitting across from each other.

"Is it always so serious?" I ask,"even at meals?"

"Oh yeah, well people are always doing therapy, all day, even when they are working or cleaning, they are always talking about feelings and cravings and family and whatever their story is," she explains.

"That must be tiring, plus, like how do you trust someone else who is also in here for similar reasons, to help you?" I wonder aloud.

"There are case workers as well."

I glance around but I am having a hard time distinguishing workers from residents. All of a sudden some blond guy gets up and starts yelling that he's ashamed of the family for the mess the dorms were in this morning and they are all likely to die in the streets if they can't even keep their cubbies clean, and they are a bunch of frauds, pretending they want to change and not changing at all. "You are all just playing a good-looking game. The cubbies are the first line of defense, the first place to fall! Relapse is around the corner!"

"Thank you, Hank," everybody responds, and goes back to eating and talking amongst themselves. I am a little shaken. But no one seems flustered. "Caseworker," mouths Mia.

"Why do you say thank you?" I whisper to Mia.

"Because he's been there. He knows, he cares, and he is here to help," she answers. I see a guy crying, not touching his lunch sitting by himself, not looking around, just sobbing.

"What about him?" I ask. "Why is he alone?" The emotions in this place are flying around the room like teenage hormones, sticky smelly palpable. I must look a little unsettled.

"Don't worry Elsie. Oh, he just came in; he's probably going through withdrawal. Don't worry, his caseworker and 'shadow' are not far." Just as she says that someone sits with him. He doesn't look up.

After lunch Mia has gotten a special dispensation to skip clean up, so she can talk with me. The person who would've been her partner in clean up is assigned to come along. This doesn't seem to bother Mia a bit. They are like sisters she says, and even though she introduces me as her best friend, I feel their bond. They are in and I am out. I don't want to be in, but there it is.

We walk over to the picnic table, the one in the sun. It's still cool but we have coffees and can smoke. They smoke in the dining room also, but it's too much for me. Mia hands me some bread she's brought from lunch. A couple of Whiskey Jacks, seem to have been almost waiting. They swoop in and eat right out of our hands, calling their little tunes until the bread is gone. They are like a party bird. The lake is flat today. It's delicately holding the balance to the emotional turmoil in me, and in this place. I know it's not flat everyday, but I am not here everyday, so for today, the lake works with me as a balance. The lake is becalming me.

Allison and Mia use jargon I am unfamiliar with such as, *personal inventory, taking care of feelings, act as if, no feedback, hold it up.* Granted most of them are self explanatory, but it's not like I can jump in.

Allison gives her some kind of nod of encouragement and Mia turns to me in earnest and says, "So Elsie, can I take care of feelings with you?"

"I don't know," I stutter, "what do I have to do?" They smile.

"You don't have to do anything," explains Allison, her red hair is tied back in a ponytail. She is wearing a Montreal Canadians sweater but even under the sports jersey you can tell she's very well endowed. If I didn't know Mia better I would suspect her of being Mia's bodyguard. She has a big toothy smile and the kind of soothing voice that puts me at ease. "You just listen."

Nonetheless I look to Mia. "I guess so."

Mia starts, "Towards you I feel gratitude for all the fun we had as kids, all the good memories. I feel happy that our kids are friends, I feel frustrated that you would take my parents' side, and not hear my point of view. I felt abandoned when you went to California. I also felt angry and unappreciated when I got you the letters and you didn't seem that grateful."

"Wait a second-" I try to interject.

"No feedback," says Allison holding up her hand. To which I say, "Are you 'holding it up'?"

"No," she says, "that's what you do when you take criticism, and you just take it."

"Phew, that would be tough," I say.

"No feedback," she says again.

"So I am not allowed to respond?" I ask. She shakes her head no and nods for Mia to continue.

"I feel sad that you didn't believe me that I was raped, sad and lonely."

They look at each other. This is not easy for Mia.

"Finally I am thrilled that you would drive up here, and I think you might be open hearted."

I nod taking it all in. "You know Elsie," she adds, "I may have been self abusive, and I might surely be an addict. But it seems to me like you might be the same as I am, and you just got someone else to do the dirty work for you."

"Am I allowed to respond now?" I ask. Allison nods, yes.

"Wow, how do I begin?" I ask, relieved that the structure gives me a moment to digest.

"Oh, you just say 'can I take care of feelings with you?'" directs Allison.

"Okay, can I take care of feelings with you Mia?" I ask sincerely.

"No, I am closed." she says.

I look to Allison, "Can she do that?"

"I am afraid so," says Allison. She looks like she is about to burst into laughter.

But it is Mia who laughs first and then Allison lets loose, "Of course you can respond," she says while laughing. "Mia said you would totally play by the rules," and then I join in the laughter, and the tension is lifted.

"Yeah, Mia you still can do the dirty work for me, that's for sure! I mean c'mon!! Consider this though; at least I can walk away, right? If I don't like the way someone else treats me, I can get away.But I will mull over your point of view, alright?" she nods, I continue, "And now, here are my feelings. I am happy for you, is happy a feeling? Isn't it more like a state? Y'know the state of happiness that you want to get clean? Anyway, I am optimistic that you can do this. Which seems like more like an attitude, don't you think? This is not as easy as it sounds, is it?" I grin, "I am touched that you trust me to come here to talk with you. But I don't trust you yet, possibly, because I don't trust myself, but I am working on that. "

"That was a good start Elsie, thank you," says Mia with not a trace of sarcasm. "I gotta tell ya though that rehab is for people who were very precisely trying to *get away*." We are all quiet mirroring the lake. It is preparing itself for a frozen surface, or perhaps it is whispering, 'maybe if I am quiet, winter won't notice me.' Then a cheeky otter swims *sleakily* by, and the ripples fan out, like time on the move.

As I am leaving I remember her Mom's message, "Your Mom says to tell you she's thinking of you." I say this, knowing I'm walking the line to near to her parent's point of view, and hoping she doesn't recoil. She doesn't, instead she nods, "Thanks," she says warmly. We hug good-bye.

"See ya later," I say waving out the car window, "Stay brave." I don't know why I add that; I just think it takes courage. And I've often thought that of her. Even most of her outlandishness was on the brave side.

37
Our House

It's early December but the dark of evening is lit by Christmas lights. Ooh, I like that song, I turn up the radio just in time to catch the end of 'Our House' by Crosby Stills and Nash, I am just thinking about getting another cat when the song is cut short. There is a special news report of a shooting that has taken place at some school I've never heard of, it has a French name, poly something or other. I don't get it; someone shot people while they were at school? I suppose the guy went to school there and had some kind of beef. How the hell do people get a hold of guns? How horrifying, not here, in Canada?

By the time I pull into the driveway they are sure that many people have been shot and that he may have killed himself. All I can think of is that school should just be about ready to let out for Christmas holidays. Oh those families! They will want just one more minute to turn back time, and change it. I've just popped out to the store before supper, such a simple act, to drive home, to where the kids are watching the Littlest Hobo at Finn's. Everyone safe. It's probably on T.V. by now. They are saying he shot nineteen people, 14 are dead and he's killed himself. The people are all women. Finn has the kids in the other room, colouring. "Hey," I say. I switch on the T.V. The newscasters are discussing whether he shot only women on purpose or not. I think to myself that this is not possible. Even as they say he yelled, "I want only the women!" Even as they say he sent the men outside, we are sure, the newscasters and I, that there is a misunderstanding. How can this be? They were studying to be engineers, they were girls who were strong and had direction. Dear God, Judith could've been one of these girls had she studied here. And why can't I get my head around it? I feel such a resistance. Even though I know what it is to be yelled at and mistreated as a woman. Maybe I never actually believed it was that, even though I accused Al of misogyny. As I stand in the little living room in Finn's part of the house, I see an array of emergency vehicles lined up, lights flashing against the night sky; the sound of sirens in the visible cold December breath. I turn from the T.V. in disbelief. The reflection in the window catches my eye, and I see them. I see the emergency vehicles from my dreams. They are not the blue and white police cars on the television. They are the toys, Finn's; the emergency vehicles are lined up on the windowsill, complete with black and white police cars. "When did you put the dinky toys all along the windowsill?" I ask to Finn in the other room.

"J.J. likes to line them up," answers Finn walking into the room. He looks at the T.V. and neither one of us says a word. I am sure he is thinking of his co-workers at the scene. I notice that there is an order to the toys on the windowsill, not found in the real life tragedy playing out on the television. I recognize the order from my dreams. It's difficult to imagine how frightening they had been, without a context.

My personal nightmare has come to an end. I am certain I won't dream those vehicles again now that I see them as toys in real life. I understand that this is the end of something, the end of a certain point of view. I listen to the news, the incomprehensible news, that these students were killed for being female, I am gradually coming to understand that being a girl has been a big deal. It has been a defining deal, despite what those elementary school movies told me. In spite of all the messages of free love, and feminism. 'You can do it all girls.' Read: You should be able to do it all. In spite of the nuanced bias, boys can spit, and swear and be funny. Where are your tunics and manners girls? In spite of these easily surmountable prejudices; it is still possible to be killed for being a woman, in an impersonal way.

Intimacy is not required. Domestic context is not a pretext.

Hate, murder and violence are somehow, always, and never, impersonal. It was a good idea to run. Even if Al wouldn't have killed me. It was still a good idea to run. It turns out I not only *am* a female, it turns out, I also represent women. I may not even have been mentioned in Al's 'suicide' note, the one, those years ago, the one which he said was 'taken out of context.'
But for now, we, J.J., Zoë and I, are in the context of the living, the context of healing

www.ingramcontent.com/pod-product-compliance
Lightning Source LLC
Chambersburg PA
CBHW051230260626
47162CB00002B/360